THE ALAMO

MARK DAWSON

PART I

SUNDAY

1

Tramon Howard looked around in disgust. There were a dozen men and women in a room that was big enough for half that many, and they lounged around in a squalor that he found difficult to stomach. There were piles of soiled clothes that had been removed and dumped in the corner next to soiled diapers from the unfortunate babies who were brought here by mothers focused on getting their next hit rather than on the well-being of their children. There were dirty mattresses with addicts sprawled across them, none of them moving even as cockroaches scuttled over them in search of the uneaten food that had been left where it fell. T-Bird bottles full of piss stood along the wall; some of them had toppled over to spill their contents across the naked floorboards.

Tramon looked over at his number two, a white kid called Styles with a dirty face and hair that had been forced into ugly braids, and told him that he was going home.

"A'ight," Styles said. "You here tomorrow?"

Tramon said he was, stepped over the arms and legs of his regular clientele, and followed the corridor to the front door. He opened it. It was freezing, and his breath clouded in front of his face. December in Brooklyn could get cold, and the weatherman on WCBS had warned that they were due a major snowfall before the week was out. That had set Tramon to thinking. The cats who bought his heroin might find it difficult to get to him if the streets were buried under snow. He spoke to Acosta about it, and they were going to empty out the rooms at the back of the house and put in more mattresses. That way, his customers could buy their gear and more of them could stick around to use it. They'd be a captive audience, too. Provided they had the cash, Tramon figured he'd be able to push more than he usually did. He had applauded himself for thinking of the idea. Acosta encouraged his dealers to think like entrepreneurs, and the Dominican had told Tramon that he was impressed. He used the word *ingenuity*. Tramon Googled it and found the definition flattering.

The house was on the corner of Danforth and Crescent, just south of Cypress Hills station. It was a poor and down-at-heel part of Brooklyn that had been ignored by the tide of gentrification that had swept south out of Manhattan. Danforth Street was a two-block alley that ran east between Autumn Avenue and Crescent Street. The house was at the end of a row of attached brick buildings with bowed fronts that were typical to the streets in the area; some of them had ugly additions built, replacing what would once have been grassy front gardens. The house was shadowed by the elevated section of track that carried the J Train above Broadway, Fulton Street and Jamaica Avenue to the terminal at Parsons Boulevard.

Tramon crossed the sidewalk and opened the door of his 1976 Ford Gran Torino. It was the two-door hardtop, and he had picked it up from a customer in Woodhaven in exchange for him wiping out the debt that the man had run up. He put the car into drive and pulled away.

He didn't notice the glare from the headlamp of the motorcycle that had been parked at the other end of the block. He didn't notice as it, too, pulled away.

He didn't notice as its rider settled in behind him, following at a safe distance on the quiet streets.

2

Tramon never felt like eating while he was inside the house. The atmosphere was so unpleasant, and he found that the smell of the addicts—the sweat and the filth—robbed him of his appetite. He wound down the window to breathe in the fresh, cold air and found that he was hungry. He diverted to the 7-Eleven in Ridgewood, parked the Torino in front and went in. He bought a sandwich and a six-pack and took them back to the car. He pulled away again, found his way to Broadway and settled in for the short drive to his place in McCarren Park.

He hit the lights on Union Avenue and glanced up into the rear-view mirror. The street behind him was empty. It was after midnight now, and there were only a few cars around. A police cruiser turned out of Heywood and rolled up alongside him. Tramon knew he was good: he wasn't carrying his piece, he only had a few hundred dollars on him, and the car was registered to him, just as it should be. The knowledge gave him the confidence to glance across the cabin and out of the window, eyefucking the cop, who glared back at him sourly.

The light changed. Tramon let the cop pull out first, then tailed along behind him.

Tramon's place faced the Williamsburg waterfront on the East River and had a view of the city from Lower Manhattan all the way up to the Queensboro Bridge. He parked the Torino in the garage and went up to the fourth floor.

His place was the corner apartment in a block and had big floor-to-ceiling windows that he left uncovered so that he could enjoy the spectacular view. It had rich, wide-plank American walnut floors, a custom-designed kitchen with a Sub-Zero fridge, Viking ovens, chrome hardware, and marble countertops with a pure crystal white backsplash. The bath was offset with custom tiling, and he had dropped a small fortune on contemporary chrome fixtures and a frameless glass-enclosed shower with rain head and separate soaking tub.

He went into the living room. He reached for the light switch and then paused, changed his mind and went to the window instead. He stared out at the view. It was the reason he had bought the place. The Empire State Building and the Chrysler Building were right in front of him, slender daggers that glowed in the darkness. His business was in Brooklyn, and it made no sense for him to go and live on the island, but he found it reassuring to know that he would have been able to afford it if he so chose. To have the vista laid out for him here, his own private show, was a reminder of what his hard work had made possible.

He saw the ghostlike reflection of the man behind him, but he didn't have enough time to react; he felt strong hands on his shoulders before he was shoved, hard, across the room. He crashed into the sideboard and bounced back, turning around and walking into a straight right jab that connected flush on his jaw. It was a stiff blow, hard enough to tremble his knees. He was halfway through blinking the blackness out of his eyes when he was struck again, on the jaw once more, and he crashed back into the sideboard and slid down to land on his backside.

He was woozy, but remembered enough to reach up for the knife on the kitchen countertop. It was an instinctive reaction that was, perhaps, one that he might have been better to ignore. His face was at the same level as the attacker's knee and, before he had even managed to slide his fingers across the smooth marble to the block, the man had kneed him in the side of the head.

A curtain of darkness fell over everything. He was aware of the side of his head bouncing against the floor before he blacked out completely.

3

_____

Tramon was aware of a light shining directly at his face. His eyes were closed, the lids glowing so that he could see the lattice of veins that were spread across them. He opened his eyes and immediately closed them again. The standard lamp with the adjustable bulbs had been moved across the room so that it was in front of him, and the light had been adjusted so that it shone into his face.

He had seen the silhouette of a man sitting behind the lamp.

"Hello."

Tramon tried to speak, but the words wouldn't come.

"How's the head?"

He tried to move, but found that he could not. His arms were straight against his torso and his hands were in his lap. He opened his eyes and looked down: he had been trussed up with duct tape. He could see loops of it around his torso and arms; another loop kept his wrists together, and another secured his ankles.

"What the fuck?"

"I'm sorry about that. We wouldn't have been able to have this chat otherwise."

Tramon squinted through the harsh glare. He was sitting in his armchair. The light had been moved away from the wall so that it was directly in front of him. The man was sitting behind the lamp on one of his wooden dining chairs. The rest of the room was still dark, with the sparkle of Manhattan still visible out of the windows beyond.

"You've got a nice place here," the man said. "How much would an apartment like this cost? A million?"

Tramon tried to focus on him. The lamp in his face made it difficult, but, as his eyes adjusted, he could make out a few details. The man was dressed in black. He was wearing gloves and, as he looked up at his face, he saw that he was wearing a balaclava.

"That's all right," the man said. "You don't need to answer. I just need you to listen."

"Who are you?"

"I'm a concerned citizen. That's all you need to know."

"Yeah? That right? And you know who I am?"

"I know everything about you, Tramon. And you're very boring. Small-time. So don't waste your time thinking that you can frighten me."

"What do you want?"

"You have a place on Danforth Street. Somewhere you do business."

"What's it got to do with you, man?"

"You're going to close it."

"Say *what?*"

"You heard me." The man reached up and adjusted the lamp so that the bulb shone directly into Tramon's eyes. "I don't want to see any more business being done there or anywhere near there. Understand?"

"Who the fuck are you to tell me what to do?"

"Like I said—I'm just a concerned citizen."

"You can take that and shove it up your—"

The man leaned forward and, before Tramon could react, he punched him, hard, in the nose.

"What the—"

He hit him again.

"Finished?"

Tramon nodded.

"Good. This is me asking you politely. I'd rather we could leave it at that. If I have to come and find you again, I won't be so pleasant."

Tramon felt the blood running across his top lip. "You know who I represent?" he mumbled.

"Of course. Carlos Acosta. And I don't care. I'm talking to you, not your boss. Find somewhere else. Don't make me come around again. You won't enjoy it."

The man got up. He went behind Tramon and, when he returned into view again, he was holding up a bundle of bills and the Beretta that Tramon carried in his jacket.

"You gonna rob me, too?"

"This is for making me come all the way over here."

The man opened his jacket and shoved the bills inside. Tramon had hidden the money inside one of the kitchen cupboards. He couldn't remember exactly how much was in the bundle—at least five grand. The man put the pistol into the waistband of his jeans and closed the jacket.

"What about this?" Tramon said, jerking his chin down to point at the duct tape.

"I'm going to leave you like that tonight so you can think about what I've said."

The man went into the kitchen and came back with the roll of tape. He unrolled it around Tramon's head, covering his mouth but leaving his nose clear. He cut the tape with a knife and patted it down.

"Remember," he said. "Don't make me come back again. I'm serious."

4

J ohn Milton went out into the corridor and followed it to the fire escape that he had used to gain access to the building. The door was still ajar; he pushed it open and climbed down to the ground. The apartment was in a converted warehouse right on the water. Milton had parked his motorcycle between a line of concrete posts that marked the end of North 3rd Street and the beginning of the narrow strip of land that ended with a fence and the river beyond it.

He took off the balaclava and stuffed it in his pocket. He took his helmet out of the top box and put it on his head. He slid onto the bike, switched on the ignition and kick-started the engine. It was a sixteen-mile ride back to Coney Island.

It was cold, he was tired, and he wanted to get to bed.

But he was satisfied, too.

He had staked out the shooting gallery for two days, identified the man in charge of it and then put him under surveillance. He had followed him home the night before and had determined that tonight was the night to act. As Tramon had stopped off at the 7-Eleven, Milton had made the decision to get to the apartment before him so that he could surprise him as he arrived. And it had worked very well.

Milton hoped that he had been persuasive enough.

Milton rode south through Brooklyn Heights, Red Hook and Sunset Park, picked up the Belt Parkway and eventually crossed Coney Island Creek. He saw the struts and parasol of the old abandoned Parachute Jump ride on the board-walk, dominating the skyline ahead of him as he drew closer and closer to the sea. He reached West 24th Street. His building was an ugly, brutal monstrosity that seemed to crouch on one side of the road, facing a similar building set on the opposite side in a fashion that suggested that they might launch themselves at each other. It was arranged in the shape of a short T, with two broad wings on either side of a stumpy protuberance. The central spine was seventeen storeys tall, and the flanks were marked with dozens of stingy windows that did not admit nearly enough light. Trees had been planted around the perimeter of the build-ing, but the winter had stripped the leaves and now they just looked like bare skeletons exposed in the cold.

Milton parked his bike next to a utility pole. He had left a thick lock and chain fastened around the pole. He unlocked it, fed the chain through the wheel, and locked it again.

His apartment was on the fourteenth floor. Milton went in through the door and tried the elevator. It didn't come. He went to the stairs and started to climb.

Milton had done his homework. Most places available in the area at less than a thousand dollars a month were shared, and shared accommodation was something that Milton was not interested in investigating. He preferred his solitude, and he suspected the 'young creatives' who were advertised as already in residence in most of the available apartments would not have taken too kindly to someone like him as their co-tenant.

He had logged onto Zillow and increased his maximum rent to $1,100 a month. That had presented him with a few more options that bore more promise. He had selected one —a one-bedroom apartment—and visited to check it out. The landlord was a Russian who either spoke no English or had no interest in conversation. He had unlocked the door and invited Milton to take a look around with a grunt that suggested he was putting him out by making him come over here. The apartment was tiny: a small kitchenette, a bathroom and a tiny sitting room with scuff marks on the tile indicating the spot where a bed must once have been positioned.

Milton tried to haggle, but the landlord greeted his efforts with a shrug and a sneer that suggested that he was wasting his time. Milton decided not to take offence and said that he would take the place. It was a little expensive for his present circumstances, but, if he was economical in the other areas of his life, he thought he would be able to manage.

Milton was tired as he finally reached the fourteenth floor. He followed the corridor to his door, unlocked it and went inside.

He took off his jacket and hung it and his helmet on the pegs that he had put up on the wall just inside the door. He went to the window and gazed out. He was higher than almost all of the surrounding buildings, so he had a wide and spectacular view across Surf Avenue down to the boardwalk, the beach and the Atlantic beyond. The beach was out of season, so the attractions and the arcades and the restaurants were all mostly unlit. The neon that would have bathed the Ferris wheel was gone, leaving the structure naked and vulnerable standing before the vastness of the night and the sea. The odd car hurried to its destination and, far out at sea, there was the glimmer of lights from a freighter, but, save that, it was quiet and calm.

There was something about the seaside in winter that had always appealed to Milton. It was romantic and sad. Milton's childhood had involved time spent in melancholic places like this and coming here had reminded him of it, just as he had hoped it would.

He took off his clothes, filled a glass with water, gulped it down, and went to bed. The sheets were icy cold, but Milton hardly noticed. It had been a long day and he was asleep within moments of his head touching the pillow.

Milton had set his alarm for six. He would have preferred to have had an extra hour or two of sleep, but he had a busy schedule today and he meant to keep to it.

He dressed in his shorts and a faded old AC/DC T-shirt, put on his running shoes and took the stairs down to the ground level. He opened the double doors and paused in the bright sunlight to push his earbuds into his ears. It was bitterly cold: his breath steamed in front of his face as he pressed play on his phone's music app and set off to the south. He had put a playlist together years ago, and as he heard new songs that he thought would fit onto it, he simply tacked them onto the end. He started today with the Jane's Addiction cover of 'Sympathy for the Devil' playing as he pounded down West 24th Street toward the sea.

He reached the end of the road and took the ramp that brought him up onto the boardwalk. The promenade was much wider than any that Milton had ever seen back home. Strips of weather-beaten boards were laid end to end, a zigzagging pattern interspersed with vertical stripes and bordered to the left and right with metal fences. Victorian-style lamps and benches were set at regular intervals on the side of the boardwalk nearest to the sand, with trees opposite them. The beach itself was broad, the sand running down for a hundred feet to the deep blue of the ocean.

There were a handful of men and women out with him at this early hour. The tractor that the city used to rake the beach was ahead of him to the east, sweeping back and forth to pick up the litter that had been deposited by the overnight tide. There were a few other joggers and an old woman who Milton remembered from previous mornings, always out with the same tiny dog. Milton was passing by the Aquarium when he saw the slender figure of a girl down by the water's edge; she was wearing a wetsuit and looked as if she was ready to go out for a swim. Milton shook his head: he had considered adding a swim after he had finished his first run here, but had decided to postpone it until the Spring when the water was a little warmer. The girl stepped into the water and kept walking out; she was braver than he was.

Milton picked up his pace, Perry Farrell's whoops fading out to be replaced by The Beatles and then The Kinks. He ran toward the huge red-painted lattice that comprised the Parachute Jump, the defunct amusement ride that stretched two hundred and fifty feet overhead and had once been the main attraction for the long-since-closed Steeplechase Park. He ran on, easing into a comfortable loping stride that ate up the distance. He followed the boardwalk all the way to Brightwater Avenue to where the planks descended and were eventually submerged beneath the encroaching sands. He stopped to take a breath and stretch out his legs and then, ready once more, he turned back and retraced his steps.

He was approaching the Aquarium for the second time when he saw the woman with the dog standing by the barrier next to the beach. She was shielding her eyes with a hand and gazing out to sea. Milton slowed and looked in the same direction.

He saw it: an arm waving frantically from a hundred feet off shore.

He veered across to the barrier and slowed to a stop. It would have been easy to miss. The swimmer was way out, beyond the outreached arms of the rocky groynes. Milton couldn't make out the detail from where he was, but he knew it was the girl that he had seen earlier. He heard her cry, a desperate yell that was quickly obscured by the cawing of the fat gulls that whirled on the thermals overhead.

The old woman heard him approaching. "You see that?"

"Call 911," Milton said.

He put his hands on the top rail and leapt over it, landing on the sand and setting off toward the water at a flat sprint. The tide was all the way back, and Milton soon felt his thighs burning from the effort of punching in and out of the loose furrows that had been stirred up by the tractor and its rake. He focused on the girl and aimed directly for her. He could see a little more clearly now. She was struggling to stay afloat, her cries for help louder now that he was closer to her.

"Help me! *Help!*"

She disappeared for a moment, obscured by a wave that rolled right over the top of her.

It was a riptide. Milton could see the channel of churning, frothing water, and knew that she had been caught in it and hurled out farther than she wanted to go. Fighting a rip was pointless. It was best to swim parallel to shore until you were at the edge of the current and then swim back. It looked as if she was fighting it. Milton knew that would kill her.

"Try to float!" he yelled. "Don't fight it. I'm coming."

Milton yanked out the earbuds and his phone and dumped them on the sand. He reached the water's edge and ploughed through it until it was up to his thighs. He dived forward, slicing through the surf and kicking out until he was deep enough to stroke out toward her. He was right: it was a riptide and it was strong, greedily sucking him farther out. The water was cold, too, quickly chilling his bones until they throbbed with a dull ache. He wasn't surprised that she had got into difficulty. He was a strong swimmer, and he would never have chosen to risk coming out as deep as this with the current so strong and the water so cold.

He took a breath and looked forward as he crashed through a breaking wave.

He couldn't see her.

She had been right ahead of him and now she wasn't.

And then he saw her again.

Her head broke the water, arms splashing frantically on

either side of it, before she sank beneath the surface once again.

Milton's lungs were burning, but he pressed again, as hard as he could manage.

He reached the spot where he had last seen her, gulped in as much air as he could take, and dived down, staring into the dim green water for any sight of her. There she was: she was struggling again, trying weakly to kick up, but her legs and arms seemed limp and lifeless.

Milton reached out for her, his fingers brushing against her shoulder and then fastening around her elbow. He dragged her up, righted himself and started to thrust up for the surface. He burst out of the water just as a wave crashed over the top of him, water rushing into his mouth and nostrils. He gagged on it, the salt stinging his throat, swallowed it down and took a breath. He dragged the girl up, locking his arms around her waist.

Another wave rushed out, strong enough to pull them both under. Milton held on tight until the force dissipated and they surfaced once more.

The girl spluttered and then coughed.

"Are you okay?" Milton asked.

"We're gonna drown!"

"No, we're not. Just relax. We need to let it take us a little farther out."

"What?"

"It's a riptide. We won't be able to fight it. You have to trust me."

She started to wriggle, trying to get her legs ahead of her so that she could try to kick them back to shore. Milton gripped her tightly, and she soon kicked herself out.

"You have to trust me," he repeated. "Do you trust me?"

She slumped in his grip. "Yes."

Milton knew what he needed to do. He turned onto his back so that he could keep her head above the water and let the current push them farther out. They drifted another twenty feet until he felt the current slacken. He turned his head to get his bearings and then kicked, stroking the water easily so that they started to traverse parallel to the shore. He looked back to the boardwalk and saw a group of people. Two men were running toward the water; Milton hoped they were wise enough to recognise the rip and stay out.

He drifted west for a minute and then decided to try the current. He turned until his shoulders faced the beach and then kicked. They started to slide back toward the shore. Milton's legs felt empty. He didn't know if he would have the strength to make it all the way back, but there was nothing else for it but to try. It was early in the morning; he had no idea how long it would take the Coast Guard to show up, and that was assuming someone had remembered to call them. The water was too cold for them to stay in it for much longer. They would be dead before a boat could get out to them.

He heard the sound of voices from the shore. There were shouts of encouragement and then splashing as more than one person crashed through the surf to get closer to them. He craned his head all the way back until it was almost upside down and glanced toward the beach. There were two men, both fully clothed, the water up to their chests.

"Nearly there, man," one of them yelled out. "Keep kicking."

Milton did. He closed the distance until he guessed he might be able to stand and put his legs down. His toes brushed against the bottom. He kicked again, and, when he put his feet down for a second time, he was able to stand with the water up to his neck. He put one hand beneath the girl's back and the other beneath her head and struggled through the tide until he was close enough to the two men to pass her over.

"Well done, brother," one of them said, reaching for Milton's hand. He took it and allowed himself to be tugged back toward the beach.

He stumbled out of the surf and collapsed to his knees. He was exhausted. He hadn't realised quite how much it had taken out of him.

The girl was lying on her side. She had been covered with two coats, and bystanders hovered over her anxiously.

"Is she okay?" Milton asked.

The man who had helped Milton out of the water came over to him. "She's breathing," he said. "But she's very cold."

"Get her to a hospital."

The words had barely left his lips as Milton saw the flashing lights of an ambulance on the boardwalk. He slumped back on the sand, staring up into the powdery blue sky. Gulls continued to ride the wind, turning in graceful arcs high overhead. He heard the sound of the ambulance doors as they were opened and closed, and then the sound of raised voices as the medics ran across the sand toward them.

7

M ilton went back to his apartment, stripped out of his sodden clothes, and stood under the shower for twenty minutes. The flow was feeble, but at least the water was hot; he let it wash over him, driving out the cold that had seeped into his bones and washing the salt from his skin. The EMTs had suggested that he ought to go and get checked out, but he had politely declined. He knew the symptoms of hypothermia—shivering, slurred speech, confusion—and he wasn't showing any of them. After that, a news reporter from a local station showed up and asked to speak to him. That was confirmation that it was time to leave.

He shaved away two days' worth of stubble, dried himself off, and—finally feeling a little warmth—dressed in a pair of black denim jeans, a black polo neck and the Red Wing boots that he had picked up from a thrift store on Atlantic Avenue. He went to his dresser and picked up the bundle of bills that he had taken from the dealer. They were held together by a rubber band; he took it off and counted out fifteen fifty-dollar bills. He secured the remainder with the band and hid it inside his pillowcase together with the Beretta that he had taken.

He picked up his leather jacket and his helmet, opened the door and stepped out into the corridor. He locked the door and made his way down to the street. He had things that he needed to do.

Milton walked around the kids' playground that had been erected inside a fenced area at the foot of the block and made his way to West 24th Street again. He had parked his bike on the road, at a diagonal with the sidewalk and in the space between a white van stencilled with the logo for Sebco Laundry Systems and the Honda Civic behind it. It was a Triumph T120 Bonneville. He had seen it advertised on Craigslist and had immediately made an appointment to see it. It was the 1971 model, with chrome pipes, a gold and cream two-tone tank and gold mudguards. The Triumph logo was emblazoned proudly on the side of the tank; Milton had run his fingers over it and had immediately been cast back nearly forty years to a childhood that he could only vaguely remember. His father had had the Bonneville, too, the exact same model; he had lavished attention on it, forbidding Milton to touch it and only driving it at weekends, when he would race around the country lanes near their property. That was where the similarity ended, though. Milton's father's bike was kept in pristine condition; this one had been allowed to fall into almost terminal disrepair.

Milton bought it anyway.

The state that it was in was the only reason that he had been able to afford it, and the prospect of spending the time to bring it back to life was an appealing one. It ran, at least most of the time, and the shabby appearance would, he hoped, make it less likely that anyone would be tempted to try to steal it.

Milton unchained the bike. He lowered the helmet over his head, straddled the seat and then reached down to turn on the fuel. He opened the choke, turned the ignition on and stomped down on the kick-starter. It spluttered once and then twice before it grumbled to life.

He negotiated his way out of the space and onto the road and set off.

It was fresh and bright and Milton enjoyed the ride. He headed east onto the Belt Parkway. It was outside the rush hour and the road was quiet enough for Milton to open the throttle up a little. The engine grumbled but cooperated, and Milton was soon able to push it up to fifty and feel the cool air whipping around him, icy fingers reaching inside the open collar of his jacket. He continued to the east, and, after twenty minutes, he saw the signage for the mall at Kings Plaza and turned off. He left the bike in the garage and took the elevator up to the ground floor.

He went to Foot Locker. He attracted the attention of one of the store assistants.

"I'm looking for a pair of Adidas trainers," he said, with no real idea what he was talking about.

"Trainers? You mean sneakers?"

"Yes," he said. "Sneakers. Sorry, I'm English."

"No problem. Which ones? We have plenty."

"They're special editions." He tried to remember what the guy had said in the meeting he had been to three days ago. "There's a designer," he said, fumbling.

"Rick Owens?"

"That's it. R.O."

"Probably the Mastodon Pro—think that could be the one?"

"The anniversary edition?"

The assistant nodded. "You got good taste, man."

"It's not for me," Milton said. "Do you have any?"

"You might be in luck," he said. "Think we still got one pair. What size?"

Milton struck out. He had no idea what size he needed. "I don't know. It's for a young lad."

"We got 'em in sevens," the man said. "How old's the kid?"

"Thirteen."

"Might be lucky, then. You wanna gamble on it? You can bring 'em back if they don't fit."

"Yes, please," Milton said.

The attendant went into the back and came back with a boxed pair of sneakers. He opened the lid and took them out. They were white, made from textured leather and with a chunky rubber sole.

"This is in milk," the man said, referring to the colour. "You got calf leather upper and goat leather lining. Really nice. You want them?"

"How much are they?"

"Two hundred and fifty bucks."

"Bag them up, please."

8

T he meeting was at ten. Milton left the mall at nine thirty and hurried north, knowing that he had ten miles to cover and only barely enough time to manage it. The traffic on the Belt Parkway was heavy, but he was able to cut through it on the bike and he made it into the grid of dense streets of East New York with five minutes to spare, parking outside St. Barnabas Church at a minute before ten. The blue and white logo that indicated that a meeting was taking place had been tied to the railings outside the church, the little tag fluttering in the cool wind. Milton took off his helmet, jogged through the open gate and went inside. The lady who brewed the coffee for the morning meeting was just stacking up the dirty cups.

"They just getting started," she said. "It's busy, but you got places at the back."

The door was ajar. Milton pushed it open and slipped inside. The woman was right: the room was almost full, with just a couple of spare seats at the back. Milton quietly apologised as he negotiated the narrow space between the woman sitting next to the aisle and the vacant seats to her right. He sat down, sliding the bagged box of sneakers beneath the seat.

There was a table up at the front of the room, where the secretary sat with the speaker who would be sharing his story. The meeting started with the attendees raising anything that they wanted to get off their chests. The man with his hand raised to indicate that he wanted to speak was one whom Milton recognised. He had spoken at the same meeting last week. His skin was a very light shade of brown, and his soulful eyes shone out from beneath heavy brows. He wore a neatly clipped goatee, and his hair was cut short to his head. Milton guessed that he was in his early forties.

"My name is Manny," he began, "and I am an alcoholic."

"Hello, Manny," the meeting responded.

"I just want to check in with something," he said. "You know how much I've been worrying about the place across the road from me and my boy. There was an old woman in there until they had to take her into a home six weeks ago, and, since then, one of the local scumbag dealers took it over and started selling heroin. Druggies going back and forward, all hours of the day and night, the fights, the cops being called but doing nothing about it, my boy finding syringes on the street and then him getting mugged for his sneakers. I mean, that was the last straw—he's only thirteen and they pulled a knife on him, made him walk back across the road in his socks."

The secretary encouraged the man to continue. "But something has changed?"

"When I got back from taking him to school this morning, I saw one of their corner boys outside—I heard him telling the junkies who showed up that the place was closed, and that they needed to go to this new place they'd set up on Ridgewood."

"You think it was the police?" the secretary asked.

"Might be," he said, "but if it was, they ain't never done nothing about it until then, so why would they suddenly do something now?"

"Does it matter?" said one of the other regulars. "They gone."

"I know," he said. "And I don't know how I should be feeling about it."

"You don't feel good?"

"Yeah, of course I feel good about it, but it's more complicated than that. I kinda feel I should've done something to make it happen, but I didn't. They just moved on. I don't wanna sound like I'm ungrateful, but I used to be in the army before..." He waved his hand around the room. "Before this. Before booze. And before I drank myself into the ground, I would've gone over there and sorted it out my own self. I know this is gonna sound stupid, but I kinda feel like I let my boy down. I didn't do nothing. I didn't set him the right example."

"It's your Higher Power," said the woman ahead of Milton. She was particularly fervent in her adoption of the religious underpinning to the fellowship; Milton didn't buy any of that and had always been pleased that it wasn't a prerequisite.

"Yeah," Manny conceded. "Maybe that's what it is. Look, I know it sounds like I'm ungrateful, but I ain't. And I ain't unhappy. I'm pleased they're gone. It's a weight off, believe me." He leaned back and waved his hands. "Ah, fuck it. I'm giving thanks. Good riddance."

Milton listened intently. It wasn't the response that he had been hoping for, and now he wondered whether he should follow through with the rest of his idea.

"Thank you for sharing, Manny," the secretary said.

The meeting proceeded with the share from the morning's speaker. Milton sat and listened, closing his eyes and putting his anxiety to the back of his mind. He concentrated on finding the meditative, peaceful space that he could only find when he was with others who shared his weaknesses.

9

It was usual for most of the men and women who attended the ten o'clock meeting to go for coffee afterwards. Blendzville Café Inc was a small independent coffee shop a short distance away. Milton rode there, parked his bike on the street outside an old building that had been co-opted as a church—the writing on the awning read Triumphant Church of God, Inc.—took off his helmet and went inside.

Some of the others had already arrived.

Manny was at the counter, placing his order. Milton nodded an acknowledgement to the others at the table.

"Can I get anyone anything?" he asked.

"Manny's just got the order," said the secretary. "Get over there. You can add whatever you want to it."

Milton left his helmet on the table and took the bag with the sneakers over to the counter.

"Morning," he said.

"Hey," Manny replied with a smile. "What you want?"

"A coffee," he said. "Black."

"One extra black coffee," Manny said to the barista.

"You got it."

The man took the order, turned to the coffee machine and started to prepare the drinks.

"Thanks for sharing," Milton said.

"For bitching and whining, you mean?"

Milton smiled. "If it's any consolation, I wouldn't have had the guts to do anything either. Maybe I would've called the police, but that's it."

"I didn't even do that," Manny said, his smile fading.

Milton was finding the conversation difficult. He didn't know what was the right thing to say, and saying the wrong thing was evidently going to sour Manny's mood.

"I hope you don't mind," he said. "I have something for you. Well, for your son."

He raised the bag so that Manny could take it.

"What is it?"

"It's… it's a pair of sneakers. I hope they're the right size."

Manny took the box out of the bag and turned it over so that he could look at the label. "Sevens," he said awkwardly. "Yeah, that's his size."

"I'd like him to have them."

Manny shook his head. "I can't take them."

Milton had been worried that his offer might elicit the wrong response. He had been worried that he would appear presumptuous or, worse, patronising, and now he feared that Manny was seeing him as both of those things.

"I bought them for my nephew," Milton explained. "Wrong size."

Manny put the box back in the bag and held it out for Milton to take again. "So take 'em back."

"I can't. I got them back home. In the UK."

"So eBay them."

"I could," he said, "but I'd rather your son had them. It was awful what happened to him. Really—it's fine."

Manny thought about his offer for a moment. Milton had no idea which way he would go: it was obvious that he felt bad about being the recipient of Milton's charity, yet perhaps he would be unable to find the money to replace the shoes himself. Manny could make his son happy by taking the sneakers and giving them to him, but the price would be the admission—as he saw it—that he couldn't provide for him himself, just as he had obviously concluded after he had failed to confront the dealers. Milton didn't want him to view the offer in such a fashion, but it was clear that was what he was doing.

Milton started to speak, but changed his mind and waited.

Manny shook his head. "That's kind of you. Thanks. And I don't even remember your name, man."

"It's John."

"I feel bad about taking them without giving you no money, though. At least let me do that."

"It's fine. To be honest, I'd forgotten I'd even bought them. I'm just glad you can put them to good use."

The barista returned with a tray of coffees.

"All right," Manny said.

10

M ilton took a seat between the secretary and the 'Higher Power' woman. Milton would have preferred to avoid her, but it was the only space left around the table. He kept an eye on Manny and saw that he drank his coffee quickly, said a hurried goodbye to the others and then left. Milton turned to watch him as he set off on foot, heading east on Sutter.

At least he had taken the sneakers with him; Milton hoped, again, that he hadn't miscalculated. It seemed apt to take the money that he had taken from Tramon and use some of it to right at least one of the wrongs that had been caused by his business on Danforth Street. He worried that he had let the pretty symmetry of his forced redistribution get the better of him. Perhaps it would have been better to have skipped that. Perhaps it would have been better to have done nothing at all. Milton was trying hard to be a better man, but he found it difficult to empathise with others and predict how they might react. He was concerned that he had misjudged Manny's reaction and worried that he had made things worse.

It looked as if the woman was about to engage him in conversation when the secretary turned to him. Milton turned and smiled broadly at him, angling his shoulders away from the woman just enough to suggest that she would find a more willing conversationalist on her other side.

The man put out his hand and Milton shook it.

"It's John, right?"

"That's right. And you're Charlie."

The man nodded. His grip was firm and he held it for a little too long.

"How you finding New York?" he asked Milton as he released his hand.

"I like it," he said.

"You been here before?"

"A long time ago."

"Business?"

"A bit of both."

Milton was being economical with the truth, but he could hardly be honest. His visit had been to assassinate a Russian mole who had somehow managed to worm his way into the British embassy. The man had been using a dead drop at Penn Station to pass secrets to the SVR and, once Milton had collected the evidence to confirm his treason, he had garrotted him in the Upper West Side apartment that he called home.

Charlie asked a question and brought him out of his reverie. "What's your business here now?"

"I've been travelling. I wanted to see a different part of New York. Everyone goes to Manhattan. I knew there'd be more to the city than skyscrapers."

"Like Brooklyn?"

"Exactly."

"Where you living?"

"Down in Coney Island."

"Seriously?"

"I've got a little apartment there. It's nothing special, but it's fine for me."

"It's dead in the winter."

"I like it. It's beautiful out of season. And I like that it's quiet. It's peaceful."

"It is that," Charlie said. "Peace and quiet is no bad thing for a drunk."

Milton didn't answer.

"I saw what you did," Charlie said.

"About?"

"The sneakers. That was a nice touch."

"I had a pair I didn't need," he lied. "They would've gone to waste otherwise."

"It was good of you. I've known Manny a while. He might not say, but I know he's grateful."

"I didn't do it for his gratitude," Milton said.

"I'm not saying you did."

"I hope he took it the way it was intended. I was worried that he might think I was taking pity on him."

Charlie sipped his coffee. "Look, you did him a good turn and I'd like to do you one, too, if you'd let me. You're trying to get an idea of what it's like to live here, right?"

Milton said that he was.

"So have you been to see the Giants?"

"I haven't," Milton said.

"You want to? I've got a spare ticket for the game tonight. Playing the Cowboys. Can't get too much more of a typical New York experience than seeing the Giants and Cowboys."

Milton's instinctive response was to say no. He had always had trouble accepting the kindness of others, partly from a reluctance to accept favours that might one day be called in and partly because he didn't think he deserved it. But this was tempting.

"It's the same thing as you and the sneakers," Charlie said, sensing his hesitation. "My business has a box. We got ten seats and one of our guests has pulled out. Last-minute deal. It'll be wasted if you don't take it."

Milton didn't say, but he had followed American football ever since it had been big in the UK during the eighties. He'd been to see a preseason game at Wembley, but this was something else.

"Sure," he said. "I'd love to. How much?"

"Don't be crazy. No cost. The box is already paid for. I've no idea what a ticket would cost, and I wouldn't take it even if I knew."

"That's very kind," Milton said.

"Great. I'll meet you outside gate six. The game starts at eight; if we get there at seven, we could have a chili dog first."

Officer Bobby Carter pulled up outside the precinct building on Sutter Avenue and checked his reflection in the mirror on the back of the pull-down visor. He had been out drinking until late last night and he hadn't had enough sleep. He had awakened on the couch in his den, stinking of alcohol, and had showered for fifteen minutes in an attempt to get the stink of booze and cigarettes off his skin. The effort had failed; he concluded that he was probably still drunk and that the odour of it was leaking out of his pores. Becky had gone out to work, leaving a note stuck to the door of the refrigerator that she would see him when he got back off his shift tonight. Carter had felt a moment of shame; she was heavily pregnant, and he knew that she would be asleep when he got back. He wouldn't see her until tomorrow morning at this rate. The shame didn't last, though. He was able to rationalise it away. He had been busy. He and Shepard had hit a smoke house on Pitkin, climbing up the outside fire escape and using the sledge to smash down the door and get inside. They had cleared two thousand each, plus a good haul of dope that Shep was going to sell to his connection. Shep needed the money now that he was retired and it would come in useful for Carter, too. Two grand would buy a lot of baby clothes.

He locked his car, crossed the sidewalk to the entrance and went down to the locker room in the guts of the building. It was the end of the eight-to-four shift, and the officers who had worked it were ending their tour. Men were taking off their uniforms, some of them showering before getting changed and going out for a beer to help them decompress. Others, like Carter, were getting ready for the four-to-twelve. The day was divided into three shifts: eight in the morning until four in the afternoon; four until midnight; and midnight until eight in the morning. Of the three shifts, the midnight tour usually held the promise of the most serious action. Carter was being rotated to it next week and was looking forward to the fun and games and the opportunities that were always presented.

Carter had been stationed in three precincts during his career, and there was no doubt in his mind about one thing: the locker room in the basement of the precinct house on Sutter Avenue was the loudest and most unruly of all of them. It was a big space, with a long double row of lockers leading to a shower room and, opposite it, a lounge with easy chairs and an old TV. The set had been donated by a grateful storekeeper whose life had been saved after the punk who had slashed him with a machete had been shot in the head and killed by the officers who had responded to the 911 call. There was a separate locker room and shower block for female officers, but the lounge was shared. About a hundred men and ten women shared the space, using the space to play cards, drink beer, and, when they ran into problems at home, sleep. Carter had seen it done out as a target range on one occasion, with playing cards stuck to the wall and officers taking pot-shots with their service pistols. There had been threats of an investigation and terminations after that, but all that had happened was that the atmosphere was dialled back for a week or two. As soon as memories had been allowed to fade, it had returned to how it was before.

That suited Carter. Hanging out with the men and women of the Seven Five before and after his shift was one of the highlights of his day.

Carter was changing into his uniform when he saw the newcomer making his way down into the locker room. He was around six feet tall and had a slender build, with neatly cut hair and nervous eyes. He was carrying his new uniform in the crook of his elbow. He had probably picked it up earlier; the pressed trousers and blue shirt were still shrink-wrapped from the dry-cleaner's. He looked tense.

The rookie found his locker, opened the door, and hung the uniform over the top of it. He looked around. No one paid him any attention.

Carter buttoned up his shirt and went over to the new man.

"How you doing?"

The rookie looked up. "I'm all right."

"Bobby Carter," he said, putting out his hand.

"Jimmy Rhodes."

"First day?"

"Yeah," Rhodes said. "Is it obvious?"

"I know what you're feeling. I been there, years ago. You wanna make a good impression?"

"Something like that."

"Don't worry about it. Everyone in here felt that way once. You're no different."

"Thanks."

Carter grabbed his belt, put it around his waist and fastened it tight. He took his pistol and put it into its holster.

"You got roll call in three minutes. Get your uniform on and go up to the muster room. Don't be late on your first day."

12

C arter climbed the stairs and went into the muster room. There were nine tables arranged into three rows of three, with six chairs to each row. There was a lectern at the front of the room and, behind that, a whiteboard. A projector was suspended from the ceiling and a cork board tacked to the wall held a series of official notices and departmental documents. A pile of summonses had been stacked in a box by the door. The other officers on the shift filed in, joshing amiably with each other, some carrying takeout coffee and slices of pizza wrapped in greaseproof paper.

Rhodes hurried into the room. He saw Carter and gave him a nod. There was a spare seat up at the front and he went to it and sat just as the sergeant arrived. His name was Ramirez and he had a printout in his hand.

"Is that everyone?" he said.

There were grunts from the assembled cops.

He looked out, taking off his glasses. "Where's Anderson?"

"Said his car wouldn't start."

"And Garcon?"

"Sick."

"Again?" He looked down at the sheet. "Wilson?"

Carter could answer that one. "Busted a porn vendor on Atlantic last night. Took a whole load of porno DVDs. He's still vouchering them."

"Vouchering?" offered one of the officers at the front. "That what they're calling it these days?"

"Shut up," Ramirez said. He laid the paper on the lectern and looked out into the room. "Where's Rhodes?"

The rookie whom Carter had met in the locker room raised his hand. "Here," he said.

"We got new blood today," Ramirez said. "Officer Rhodes joins us fresh from an exciting career as a transit cop. I'm sure you'll join me in giving him a warm welcome to the Seven Five."

The other cops turned to look at Rhodes and then gave him a sarcastic slow handclap.

One of the female cops turned to him. "So how did you fuck up?"

"Who said I fucked up?"

"You must've fucked up to have been sent to this shithole. Everyone knows you only get sent to the Seven Five as penance."

Gales of laughter followed.

"Settle down," Ramirez said. "Rhodes, I got something special for you tonight. Carter, put your hand up so Rhodes can see you."

"S'alright, Skip," Carter said. "We've already met."

"You're going to be taking Rhodes's cherry," Ramirez said. "Now, when you bend him over, you make sure to do him gentle, you hear?"

The others laughed. Carter looked over at the rookie and saw that his cheeks were flushed.

"I don't know why you're laughing, Harry," Ramirez said. "You and Hector have got Garcon's sectors tonight."

"The fuck?"

"We're shorthanded, so you two are gonna have to cover. Go and do your jobs. Dismissed."

The officers stood, donned their caps and started to shuffle outside.

Carter brushed the dirt off his cap as he made his way over to Rhodes. "Come on, kid," he said. "Let's get going."

He led the way out into the crowded reception area, where a handful of men and women were being ignored by the sergeant at the desk. They walked through the room and out of the front doors, out into the freezing late afternoon.

"We're over here," he said, pointing to a parked patrol car.

Other officers were emerging, slouching over to their cars so that they could start their shifts.

Rhodes opened the passenger-side door and slid into the car. Carter opened the driver's door and dropped into the seat.

"You got lucky," he said.

"Yeah?"

"You got me, first of all. I been in the Seven Five for eight years. I know the streets. I'll keep you in one piece until you get your feet underneath you. Trust me, you could've had it a lot worse."

"Yeah?"

"Oh yeah. I've seen rookies get given a foot patrol on Pitkin on the midnight shift. That's what you could call a challenging introduction to policing in East New York. Very challenging."

Carter put the car into reverse and pulled back onto the road.

"Let me correct what I said about you being lucky. You *are* lucky, but luck is relative, know what I'm saying? You're luckier than a rookie doing a foot patrol on Pitkin, but *real* luck would have been being posted out to midtown or the Hundred and Twentieth out on Staten Island. Nice easy assignments, the kind of place you can grab a six-pack and drink it down by the water. No one gives a shit if you coop for an hour or two in the middle of the night. It's a bit different out here."

"Yeah?"

"You know what they used to call this part of Brooklyn?"

"No," Rhodes said.

"You got the Seven Seven north-west of here. That was what they called the Land of Fuck. They sprayed that on the side of the precinct house. And this here—the Seven Five—this was the Alamo. It might look like it's changed, and maybe it has. It's not like it was—there's more money now than there was back then, and there's a fraction of the murders that there used to be—but don't let that fool you. This is still a tough posting. You take your eye off the ball and the Seven Five will punish your ass."

13

Freddy Blanco looked at the time on his phone. It was already six, and there was still no sign of his father.

Freddy had been home all afternoon, playing *Madden* on his PlayStation. He had picked the Giants, just like always, and played a match against the Cowboys in anticipation of the game tonight. The tickets were in an envelope on the kitchen counter. He had gone to look at them more than once, sliding them out of the envelope and running his fingers over the glossy surface. The tickets were decorated with action shots of Odell Beckham and Eli Manning, the jump-ball touchdown that had sealed the win against the Eagles the last time the Giants had played at home. Freddy and his father had watched that game on Fox, and Freddy had said—for the hundredth time—how much he would love to go to see a game in person. His father had promised him that they would go one day; he had come home with the tickets the very next day. Freddy knew that finding a hundred and fifty bucks for something like that was difficult for his father, and he noticed that his watch—a second-hand Rolex that had been passed down to him by his own father—was missing. Freddy didn't say anything, but he'd found the receipt from EZ Pawn Corp on Atlantic Avenue and he knew where the money had come from.

Freddy tried not to feel guilty about that. It was easier when he saw that his father was almost as excited about the game as he was.

He looked at the time again. It was a quarter past six. The game kicked off at eight, and it would take an hour and a half to get there.

He opened his father's bedroom door to see if there was anything there that might give him an idea where he had gone. There was a Foot Locker bag on the bed. He opened it and took out the Adidas box from inside. He opened the box and looked down at a brand-new pair of Mastodons, identical to the pair that had been stolen from him by the junkies across the road. The sneakers were white, unmarked, and still had the smell of fresh leather. He reached into the box, took the shoes out and removed the bunched-up brown paper from inside them. The sneakers would have cost two hundred and fifty bucks. He had no idea how his father would have been able to find that much, especially after he had just laid out a hundred and fifty on the tickets for the game. He ran his fingertips over the raised stitching, then turned the shoes over and followed the indentations on the underside of the oversized sole. He took off his beaten-up pair of Nikes, slid his feet into the shoes and laced them up. They were the right size. He didn't know whether he should wear them—he didn't know whether his father had been planning on giving them to him as a surprise—but he didn't want to take them off, either.

Freddy went and stood by the mirror. He was wearing the Odell Beckham Jr jersey that his mother had bought for him at Christmas. It was second-hand, faded and with a small hole where the stitching had come apart, but he had loved it then and he still loved it now. The sneakers looked so white and pure that he wasn't sure if he would ever want to wear them outside the house, but then he thought of what his friends at school would say, and he quickly decided that it was something that he would be able to get over.

He took out his cell and checked the time. Six twenty-five. He forgot the sneakers and started to worry again. He pressed redial, calling his father for the third time, but, once more, the call went through to voicemail.

"Hey, Dad," he said. "It's me. It's nearly six thirty and I don't know where you are. If we don't go now, we're not gonna be there in time and we're gonna miss it. Call me when you get this."

He went into the living room and paced the room, back and forth, watching the minutes tick by. Manny was ninety minutes late. He had promised that he would be home at five so that they could make the journey to Jersey together. The gratitude that he had felt at the replacement of his stolen sneakers curdled and grew sour; it was replaced first by worry, and then—coloured by the memory of what things had been like before and the fear that his father had let him down again—the worry became resentment.

Freddy didn't know what he should do. He went over to the counter, took the tickets out of the envelope and stuffed them into his pocket. His dad had made a sacrifice to buy them, and Freddy wasn't about to let them go to waste. He called again, left a message to say that he was going to go to the stadium and that he would meet him outside, grabbed his jacket and set off. He was halfway to the station when he realised that he was wearing the new sneakers. He paused, wondering whether he should go back and change out of them, but then he saw that it was already 6.35 and he knew that he didn't have time.

He started to jog toward Crescent Street station.

14

<hr>

Freddy caught the J Train from Crescent Street, changed onto the A Train at Broadway Junction and rode north. He got off at Penn Station and bought a round-trip to the Meadowlands. He changed again at Secaucus Junction and pressed himself into the busy subway car for the final ten-minute ride to the stadium.

It was five to eight when he climbed to street level and emerged into the usual display of pageantry and excitement that marked a Giants game. The atmosphere was taut with excitement; the Cowboys were in town, and although the G-Men were favoured, everyone knew that it was going to be a coin flip as to who came out on top.

He made his way under the track and came out on the approach to the stadium. There were stalls offering Giants merchandise and hawkers pushing knock-offs at a fraction of the price. There were carts that had been wheeled up from Lyndhurst and Rutherford to serve dogs and burgers and pretzels. Late taxis arrived from Manhattan, disgorging men in suits and brightly coiffed women, who made their way through VIP entrances to be whisked directly to their skyboxes. The crowd pulsed and throbbed as they drew nearer and nearer to the gates and the prospect of the game that would shortly begin inside. Scalpers tried to hawk tickets, cops watched with disdain, and those without tickets stood around and jealously watched those who did. Freddy hurried along until he reached gate eight. He stopped for a moment so that he could frame a picture of an electronic scoreboard: "New York Giants vs Dallas Cowboys. Today. 8.05 p.m."

He took out his phone and called his father again. There was no answer.

He put his back to the wall of the stadium and looked out at the dispersing crowd. Most of the fans were already safely inside the stadium and the hubbub was dying down. The scalpers lowered their prices, the touts packed up their counterfeit shirts, vendors closed up the carts with the cheap dogs and pretzels and popcorn and began to push them away so they could count up their takings. The kids without tickets took out their phones and then slouched away. A fat security guard, broad shouldered and with his belly straining against the buttons of his blue shirt, stared at Freddy until the boy had to look away.

Freddy heard the closing chords of the national anthem and then a roar from the crowd.

He took out his phone again and looked at the screen, as if that might hurry along a response from his father.

Still nothing.

He stuffed his hand into his pocket and took out the tickets. He sold one to a scalper for twenty bucks—the man wouldn't offer more—and used the other one to get inside.

He made his way through the turnstile and into the guts of the building, then followed the concourse around until he found the gate he wanted. He showed his ticket to a waiting steward and then climbed up the last few steps to the open doorway that offered access to the stadium.

He stood there, his mouth open.

All he could see was the wide-open expanse of grass. It was a beautiful, pristine green, so vivid and bright that it was almost phosphorescent. The gridiron was painted a bright white, and the logos of the Giants and the NFL were hyperreal. Freddy gazed up at the vast structure that encircled the field, the rows of concrete and iron and the dazzling hi-def screens that glittered and popped with replays and ads and exhortations for the crowd to get behind their team.

Fireworks went off and music blared as the teams emerged from a covered walkway and spilled out onto the field.

"Popcorn!" called out a vendor as he moved down the steps toward him. "Out of the way, kid."

Freddy looked up at the vendor, a boy in his late teens with acne and braced teeth, and worried that his obvious nervousness would mark him out as someone who shouldn't have been here. He stepped aside and, as he did, noticed the two empty seats at the front of the section. He checked his ticket, descended the steps, and then checked again. He tugged down on the hem of his handed-down OBJ jersey, aware that it looked dirty and out of date compared to the jerseys of the kids around him, and shuffled between a family and the seats in front of them as he made his way to the empty spaces.

15

Milton took the train from Coney Island to Jay Street. He changed from the F to the A Train and rode north to Penn Station. He went to the nearest ticket machine and paid $7.75 for a return trip to Meadowlands. He changed at Secaucus Junction and transferred to the Meadowlands service. He walked the rest of the way to the stadium. It was a new building, a typically soulless carbuncle that had been dropped into this otherwise thankless part of New Jersey. Thousands of people were disembarking from their trains and beginning the slow walk to the stadium, hands shoved deep into the pockets of thick coats in an effort to ward off the cold. A few brave souls, their common sense loosened by early tailgating, were shirtless, their bare skin painted in Giant blue.

Milton crossed underneath the track by way of a wide tunnel and emerged in the broad approach that ended with the stadium. He made his way to gate six.

Charlie was waiting for him.

"Cold enough for you?"

"Freezing."

"They're forecasting a ton of snow later this week —you hear?"

"I did."

"Don't worry. You'll be warm tonight. They keep the suite very pleasant. Let's get inside, shall we?"

Charlie led the way through the turnstiles and into the concourse of the huge MetLife Stadium. Milton loved football and baseball, but he had always preferred the old stadiums compared to the blandly efficient replacements that had been erected in the dynamited wreckage of their predecessors. He had been to the Bronx to watch the Yankees and had been cowed by the sheer vastness of it, everything angled toward the most efficient ways of extracting even more money from the spectators. He always found the new places to be flavourlessly corporate, and he quickly came to the conclusion that this place would be no different. There were the lines of identical concessions, the antiseptic cleanliness and the hollow ambience that one might expect to find at an airport terminal. Never mind. The football was what he was here for, and this evening's game promised to be a good one.

Charlie led the way to a line of elevators, and they got into the first empty car and rode it up to the fourth floor. The lobby that met them opened up to a long corridor that stretched away to the left and right, with doors on the left-hand side marked by chrome numerals. Charlie led the way to number 22. A stencil on the frosted-glass doors announced the suite belonged to Rapid Semiconductors, Inc. Milton had never heard of the company before.

"This is us," Charlie said. He opened the door and ushered Milton inside.

It was impressive. The suite was split into two distinct areas: a bar area with granite countertops and dark wood panelling, and then a spacious living room with comfortable leather furnishing. There were sliding glass windows at the other end of the room that overlooked three rows of exterior cushioned suite seats with teak arms. The bar area was loaded with food, the boxes and packages all conspicuously branded with the Giants logo, and a large flat-screen TV showed the pre-game show.

They were the last to arrive. There were eighteen other men and women in the private suite, and it was obvious from the way they greeted Charlie that he held a senior position in the company.

"How we doing?" he called out.

A young man raised a pint of beer. "They're looking after us, boss. You want a drink?"

"No, thanks." Charlie smiled. "We're good."

He led the way to the sliding doors and the three rows of five seats outside. Milton followed him. The cold hit him at once, his breath steaming in front of his face. The seats were separated from those belonging to the suites on either side by glass panels embossed with the MetLife logo.

"Boss?" Milton said.

"Yeah," Charlie said.

"Is it your company?"

"It is. I've done okay for a drunk." He nodded back in the direction of the suite. "There'll be a bit of drinking going on in there tonight. Just saying."

"They don't know about you and the fellowship?"

"No. You okay with that?"

"Yes," Milton said. "I've got plenty of time under my belt by now. I'll manage."

They both looked down on the field as the teams came out for their warm-ups.

"Should be a good game," Charlie said.

16

The first couple of hours were quiet. Carter drove, working their way around the sector so that he could give the rookie the heads-up on the areas where they usually found the most trouble. Rhodes was quiet and attentive, seemingly hanging on Carter's every word. Carter wanted him to loosen up a bit and, when he told Rhodes to relax, the rookie apologised, said that he would and then quickly reverted to the same intense state of concentration as before.

Carter shook his head, but he got it. He remembered his first day on the job, eight years earlier. He had been nervous, too. The academy was necessary, but it didn't prepare you for a life on the street. Theory was one thing, but theory went out the window when the rubber hit the road. You needed instinct and smarts to make it as a cop in the Seven Five, and no classroom was going to teach you that. You either had it or you didn't, and the street would find out one way or another.

Carter had been partnered up with Landon Shepard until last week. Shep had decided to retire. He was older than Carter and had been struggling with arthritic hips that his doctor was prepared to say were caused by the strain and stress of being a cop. Carter had chided him, trying to argue that it was a minor ailment that wouldn't have prevented him from holding down a job in construction, the line of work that Shep's father had gone into. Shep had dismissed the suggestion; there were plenty of cops in the precinct who would have loved to pick up a minor injury that meant that they could retire, too. Disability was no bad thing if it meant that an officer couldn't run for more than a hundred yards or hold out his gun; small ailments like that would always be enough for the city to agree to a retirement, especially after notice had been drawn to them. If that officer got into a scrape and a member of the public was put at risk because he or she wasn't one hundred per cent fit, the financial fallout from a legal case would always beat how much it might cost to pension off the cop and train a replacement.

So Shep had applied for retirement. He had gone before the medical review board. They'd taken a look at the notes that his doctor had provided, done their own examinations and then recommended that the application be approved. His wife, Alice, had a career as a dental hygienist and they had already paid off the mortgage on their house. Carter had been upset when Shep told him that he was going to call it a day, and had spent the better part of a week's worth of patrols trying to persuade Shep that it was a dumb idea. He hadn't had any luck, though, and, in the end, he had been forced to admit defeat. The retirement had been made official and Shep had started to draw his pension.

"I need a drink," Carter said. They were on Belmont. He pulled over and parked outside Whitey's bodega. "You want anything?"

"I'll get a Coke," Rhodes said, reaching into his pocket for the money.

"Put it away," Carter said. "I got it. You want anything else? A sandwich? A pack of smokes?"

Rhodes opened the bag that he had brought with him to the car and took out a Ziploc bag with a sandwich inside it. "I'm good," he said, holding it up.

"You made your own sandwich?"

"I didn't know how it would work," Rhodes said, a little sheepishly.

"You don't need to do that," Carter said with an amused shake of his head. "Don't bother with that tomorrow. I'll show you how it gets done, okay?"

Carter's phone vibrated in his pocket. He took it out and looked at the screen. His wife had texted him.

"You okay?" Rhodes asked.

"It's my wife," he said. "She's just reminding me that I agreed to go up to Kmart after I finished tonight to pick up a crib."

"You've got a baby?"

"Not yet. Got one on the way."

"Congratulations," Rhodes said with a bright smile. It was the most natural reaction that Carter had seen from him all day.

"Thanks," Carter said. "You got kids?"

"No," he said. "It's just me."

"No woman?"

"Not right now. When's the baby due?"

"Two weeks. A little boy. She's as big as a house now and she ain't too keen on going outside, so I promised I'd go and get the crib. It's the last thing we need before the nursery's done. Wasn't like I was going to forget." He put the phone back in his pocket and unclipped his seat belt. "I'm gonna get a beer, too. You want one?"

"What? Come on," Rhodes said. "We're on duty."

"You're not gonna bust my balls about that, are you? I'm thirsty. You must be the same. Wait here."

He got out of the car. It was cold outside of the warmth of the cabin, and he zipped his navy-blue jacket all the way up to the top as he glanced up into the dark skies. The kid looked like he was going to be okay. He'd have to bring him along carefully, get him started with small indiscretions and then see how far he could push him before he got too uncomfortable. Carter had been brought along the same way when he had started. It had been Shepard who had broken him in, and Carter had returned the favour with a few of the rookies that had followed after him. It took a while, sometimes, to realise what was possible as an officer working the street. Carter had picked it up quickly, and it hadn't taken long before he had been bringing opportunities to Shepard and pushing him beyond where he had previously decided he was comfortable. It was Carter who had found the hook-up with Acosta, and that had proved prosperous ever since

He looked back at the car. Carter would give Rhodes his real education, show him a little at a time, demonstrate the benefits that would help put a little extra weight in his pay packet, make his shifts more comfortable and more interesting. Getting him to take a drink on the job was where he would get things started.

17

The drama of the game meant that Freddy was almost able to forget the fact that his father had let him down. The Cowboys were up by six as the game moved into the fourth. Dak Prescott was having an efficient game, and Dez Bryant was feasting on the secondary no matter how many defensive backs were assigned to cover him. The crowd was still in the game, but every Giants' three and out and every punt was greeted with a dip in the intensity of the noise and the growing acceptance that the Cowboys were going to hold on.

The seat to Freddy's right was empty, a reminder that his father should have been there with him and was not. There was a big guy on Freddy's left. He was with his wife and, Freddy gathered from overhearing their conversation during half-time, he was a firefighter based at one of the firehouses in Lower Manhattan. He was huge: well over six feet tall, solid muscle, and with tattoos visible on his throat and on the top part of his chest that was visible because he wore his jacket half unzipped, despite the bitter cold.

He must have noticed that Freddy was looking at him;

he glanced down at him, shook his head, and said, "Ain't looking good, is it?"

Freddy said that it wasn't.

"What would you do now, kid?"

"Get the ball to Odell."

"They got Carr and Scandrick on him most snaps," the man said. "Can't get him the ball if he ain't open. He's good, but he ain't *that* good."

"Sure he is," Freddy said. "They just gotta throw it up to him and let him do the rest."

The big man laughed. "If you say so, kid."

Freddy felt defensive on behalf of his favourite player, who was, he was sure, more than good enough to beat a couple of halfway decent corners even if they doubled him. He turned back to the field, self-consciously awkward about talking to someone he didn't know, and was saved from having to make any further excuse by the ringing of his phone. He took it out of his pocket and checked the display. It was his father. He pressed "accept" and jammed the phone against his ear.

"Dad?"

"Where are you?"

His father's words were slurred, one tripping over the other, each emerging with effort. Freddy could picture his face: his eyes would be heavy-lidded, every blink slow and ponderous; he would be licking his lips, as if they were dry; his cheeks would be flushed. He knew what his old man looked like when he was drunk, and he was definitely drunk right now.

"Freddy?" he said again. "Where are you?"

"At the game."

"Oh shit. It's tonight?"

"Of course it's tonight!"

"I forgot," he mumbled. "Goddamn it." He coughed. "You went anyway?"

"I wasn't gonna waste both tickets," he said. "I been looking forward to this for weeks, Dad. I waited until six thirty. What did you think I was gonna do?"

There was no reply. Freddy could hear the sound of voices, a raucous background of shouted conversations and laughter, with music playing across everything.

"What happened to you?" Freddy said, keeping his voice down so as not to be easily overheard by the firefighter or the other fans around him.

"I forgot," Manny repeated.

"What do you mean you forgot?" he said, unable to keep the heat from his voice. "We spoke about it this morning. We were gonna leave at six."

"I'm sorry, son. I'm..."

"Where are you now?"

"I'm... I'm..."

He didn't finish the sentence. Freddy heard the hum of the background noise and the staccato interruption of a woman's high-pitched holler, and he knew. He knew exactly where his father was and what had happened to him: Manny had gone to Mike's Pub, got drunk and forgotten him. It used to happen all the time—it was the reason that his mother had left them—but he had been making an effort lately, and Freddy had started to wonder and hope that he might have got it under control. It made the disappointment of hearing him like this so much worse.

"Did you..." Manny started to say. He cleared his throat and started again. "I'm sorry, Freddy. I'll make it up to you."

"Bye, Dad," Freddy said.

He ended the call and put the phone away.

He swallowed. He felt a tightness in his chest and had to blink to keep back the tears that were welling in his eyes.

Freddy had been distracted from the game by the call and, as he wiped the back of his hand across his eyes and looked out at the gleaming green field, he noticed a streak of motion arcing up from the line of scrimmage. There was a collective groan as Manning was crushed by a defensive end but then an intake of breath as the crowd saw that he had been able to toss the ball up. It curved up through thirty yards and then started back down to earth, racing from its apogee, picking up pace and converging with the flanker who had won separation from the cornerback who had failed to cover him. There came a deafening explosion of noise as the receiver hauled the ball in and high-stepped into the end zone.

Freddy was caught up in the roar of noise and the sheer, untempered joy of the moment, the fans around him surging out of their seats and pressing up against the railing, their hands and voices raised in communal celebration. The receiver was Odell Beckham; Freddy could see the flash of his blond highlights as he tore off his helmet and tossed it high above him. He trotted into the centre of the end zone and launched the ball at the crowd. For the second time, Freddy watched it laser through the air, losing momentum and falling down toward him. He knew that he was going to catch it even before its momentum declined and it started to fall. It was as if Beckham had thrown it to him out of all the thousands of others who had just witnessed his excellence. Freddy reached out his hands, his fingers splayed out and pointing up, and felt the ball slap against his palms. He tightened his fingers around it, feeling the rough texture of the pigskin and, as he drew it down to his chest, he caught the smell of the leather.

He felt hands on his shoulders, a whoop of joy, the firefighter clapping him firmly on the back. He clutched the ball tightly, suddenly worried that someone would try to take it from him, but, as he saw a man in his early twenties turn around and reach up for him, the firefighter reached out a warning paw. The younger man grinned, stuffed his hands in his pockets, and turned back to watch the teams as they set up for the extra point.

"Keep it close to you," the man said. "You got guys here who'll grab it off you and stick it on eBay."

"Thanks," Freddy said.

"'Get the ball to Beckham,'" the man said, repeating what Freddy had suggested. "What do I know?"

Freddy grinned.

"And good catch, kid," he added with a broad smile. "Those are nice hands."

18

I t was nine and Detective Aleksander Polanski was still working. He had been investigating a sergeant down in the Seven Seven who had demanded that a patrol cop have a threesome with him and his wife and had then accused her of falsifying her time sheets when she refused. The patrol cop had resigned from the NYPD and was bringing a ten-million-dollar lawsuit against the city. Polanski had been given the case and told to see whether there was anything in it. He had discovered, very quickly, that the sergeant was a sleazebag with a previous history that made the allegations look very credible indeed. Polanski had just finished interviewing other cops from the precinct and had compiled a list of behaviour that made for depressing reading: crude sexual remarks during roll call and propositions to other female cops, who had switched to the graveyard shift to get away from him. Polanski had enough dirt on the man to bring his investigation to a close and recommend suspension and formal charges.

He was taking a break from the paperwork when his

phone rang. He took it out of his pocket and saw a number that he didn't recognise.

"Hello?"

"It's me."

It was González.

"What's up?"

"I gotta get out, man. Tonight. Right fucking now."

"Hold on." He pushed away from his desk and went out to the stairwell.

Polanski climbed halfway down the stairs so he could be sure that there was no one on the landing below him.

"I'm here," he said.

"Didn't you hear me? I gotta get out, man."

He was frightened.

"Calm down, José. Take a breath. What's the matter?"

"It's too hot. He knows. I'm telling you, I gotta get out."

"All right," Polanski said. "Tell me. What do you mean he knows?"

"I can tell. The way he's been looking at me, the things he's been saying—it's like he can see right through me."

"You've seen him tonight?"

"He came by the shop and he *never* comes by the shop. He's gonna kill me, man, I swear."

"Okay," Polanski said, reaching for a pen and paper. "Where are you now?"

"The payphone on Pitkin near Van Siclen. You gotta bring me in. You promised. You said if I did what you said, you'd get me the fuck out of Brooklyn."

"I did. And I will. You'll give evidence?"

"You make sure I don't get capped, I'll give you chapter and fucking verse, man. Everything."

"What about the cops?"

"They came in last week—well, one of them did. Took his pay-off, just like always."

"You feel like giving me some names?"

"No," González said quickly. "Not until I know you can get me out of here. You do that tonight and I'll give you everything."

That was the deal. Polanski had no interest in pushing González for more right now, especially when he was close to getting what he needed. "You taped him?" he asked.

"Sure I did. Just like you said."

"Got the recorder with you?"

"It's safe. It's in the shop."

Polanski felt his stomach churn with a mixture of anticipation and nervousness. The sexual harassment case was nothing compared to the investigation he had been running in the Seven Five. This was big: corrupt cops on the payroll of a serious player in the local drug market. It was the closeness of it, the culmination of months of careful, diligent police work. He was almost there. *Almost.* He just had to stick the landing.

He made sure that he had a little assurance in his voice. "Okay. Well done, José. Let's meet."

González was right on the edge. "Not in Brooklyn. I don't want it to be anywhere near here."

"I wasn't going to suggest Brooklyn," Polanski said, as measured as he could manage. "We've got a safe house in New Brunswick. An apartment. It's miles away and no one knows about it. I'll give you the address—you ready?"

Polanski recited the address and checked that González had noted it down correctly.

"You gonna be there?" González asked.

"I'm on my way. Are you leaving now?"

"You want the tape or not?"

"Yes," Polanski said.

"So I gotta go back. It won't take long."

"Be careful," Polanski said. "In and out, that's it."

"I just want this to be over," González said.

"It's almost done, José. Get moving. Get the tape and then get over to the safe house. I'll see you there."

———

Polanski put his phone away and climbed the stairs again to the second floor. He grabbed his jacket and headed for the open door to Sergeant Haynes's office.

"Sarge," he said, "you got a moment?"

Richard Haynes was Polanski's supervising officer and had been responsible for his transfer to the bureau. He had been partners with Polanski's father and had been a friend of the family for almost as long as Polanski could remember. He had visited the family home in Irvington for Sunday lunch every week after his first marriage had blown up.

Haynes had served thirty years on the force, and—at least the way he told it—had been drafted into Internal Affairs against his own will by a district commander who hadn't taken kindly to a prank that went wrong. Despite an initial reluctance, he had thrived in the bureau. He had quickly risen to a position of seniority, stressing that his officers must be unimpeachable and encouraging their integrity with incentives that made them less vulnerable to the temptation of what could be had on the street. When Polanski had run into the trouble that had isolated him within his precinct, Haynes had stepped in and offered him a transfer and the chance to do what he called 'good work'.

Haynes looked up. "Sure," he said. "What's up?"

"I need the safe house in New Brunswick."

"When?"

"Tonight. I'm bringing in a CI."

"Which investigation are we talking about?"

"The Seven Five."

Haynes raised an eyebrow. "You better shut the door."

Polanski did as he was told.

"I don't know anything about this, do I?" Haynes asked him.

"No, sir. That's deliberate on my part. I thought it was a long shot. I thought the CI was gonna flake on me and I didn't want to bother you with it until I knew it had potential."

"Who's the informant?"

"José Luis González. He's got a stereo shop on Atlantic."

Haynes shook his head. "Don't know him. And you think he *does* have potential?"

"Yes," Polanski said. "For sure. He's been looking for a way out for weeks. He's convinced Acosta is through with him—they had a falling-out; my guy doesn't think Acosta trusts him any more. And you know what Acosta is like when that happens. We've seen it before."

"Yeah," Haynes said. "Those people end up in the river with their throats cut."

Polanski nodded. "And those are just the bodies we find. González knows what'll happen to him. I said I'd help him get away if he helped me."

"And what does he have?"

"He's been acting as Acosta's bagman. Acosta gives González the money to pay off the cops that Acosta's been running."

"Do we know who they are?"

Polanski shook his head. "He won't name them until he's sure he's safe. But he said one of them came in for his money last week and that he's got him on tape. So long as González isn't full of shit, I might have the way to get into that precinct. You know what they're like down there, sir. We've been looking for a way to get inside for months. Maybe this is it. González says he'll bring the tape in with him. I'll listen to it and make a call. Maybe we can make a move on the bad guys tonight or tomorrow."

"You speak to me first, all right? The commissioner's gonna hate this. I'm old enough to remember what it was like down here in the eighties. The Seventy-Fifth was overrun back then. If the press run with this, say it's getting back to how it used to be, there's gonna be hell to pay."

"I know. And I will—call you, I mean."

"Where you meeting him?"

"The safe house in New Brunswick. I just need you to clear it for me."

"All right," Haynes said. "I'll call ahead. You go bring him in."

19

Carter's phone rang as they were waiting for a red light on Belmont. He took it out of his pants pocket and looked at the display. It was Shepard. He accepted the call and put it to his ear.

"What's up?"

"We've got a problem," Shepard said, his voice throbbing with tension.

"Calm down. Take it easy."

"I can't calm down. We got a big fucking problem."

"What are you talking about?"

"It's González. He's speaking to IAB."

"Hold on."

The light was green. Carter pushed down on the gas and slid the car over to the side of the road.

"You okay?" Rhodes asked him.

"I've just gotta take this," he said, holding up his phone. He gave an exaggerated shrug and mouthed, "My wife."

Carter opened the door, stepped outside, and closed the door again. He turned his back to the car.

"I'm back," he said. "What about González?"

"He's a rat."

"What are you talking about? What do you mean?"

"I'm telling you, that fucking spic just called Internal Affairs. No kidding. He said he taped you when you went to get paid last week."

"What the fuck? He *taped* me?"

"I just heard. Polanski's bringing him off the street. There's a safe house in New Brunswick. González's going there tonight. He's taking the tape."

Carter felt a shudder of panic.

González could fuck them.

"Shit," he said. "*Shit*. How long's this been going on?"

"I don't know."

Shepard found a little assurance to balance Carter's rising panic. "We can fix this. It's not too late. I went straight to the shop. I'm outside. González is here. He just went in. Where are you?"

"On patrol. Van Siclen and Belmont."

"You gotta haul ass over here. We can't let him hand that tape over."

Carter balled his fist. "I'm with the rookie."

"So get rid of him. Be creative. We gotta fix this."

"All right," Carter said. "I'll think of something. Stay on him. I'll call back."

He ended the call and put the phone back into his pocket. He went over to the car, opened the door and slid into the driver's seat.

"All okay?"

"It's my wife," Carter said. "The contractions have started. I need to get out of here."

"Shit," the rookie said. "What do we do?"

Carter started the engine and rolled the patrol car into

the street. "I'll take us back to the precinct. I'll get my car and go home."

"What about me?"

"You go back out on patrol."

"Do I gotta tell anyone?"

"I'll speak to Ramirez and take care of it. They won't have anyone ready to ride with you. Just take it easy for the rest of the shift. Drive around, get a feel for the precinct. We can pick it up again when I get back."

It was half a mile to the station house and then another mile to González's stereo shop on Pitkin. The diversion was unwelcome, but there was nothing that Carter could do about it. He had to dump the rookie and get changed out of his uniform before he went out again. Shep was good, but the longer they left González alone, the better the chances that he would get away from him. González knew Shep; if he made him and bolted, it would be game over. And that couldn't happen.

20

Milton and Charlie made their way out of the stadium and into the slow-moving crowd of people that was gradually moving along to the station.

"So?" Charlie said as they shuffled along.

"It was great," Milton said.

"What you think of the atmosphere? Compared to what you got back home?"

"It was different," Milton said. "A football game—"

"Soccer."

"Fine," Milton conceded. "It's a little more..." He searched for the right word. "Tribal."

"A better chance of getting kicked in the head?"

"Not so much these days," Milton said. "But yes."

It was true. It was a very different experience. Milton had been a season ticket holder at West Ham years earlier, and he remembered the throb of energy in the crowds before and after the matches, and the threat of violence whenever they played Chelsea or Spurs or—most of all—Millwall. Milton's urge for violence had always been smoth-

ered and suppressed because of his job, the requirement
that he play his part and only unveil his true nature in those
cataclysmic moments of release when he fulfilled his
mission. He had been too professional to surrender to the
base desires of the crowds as they raced down terraced
streets, chasing rumours of dust-ups with rival crews, but
there had been an unbridled hum of energy to it that he had
found exhilarating. That had been missing tonight. By
comparison, it was antiseptic. The toilets were spotless. The
food was decent, if bland. The crowd was, save a few excep-
tions, polite. They cheered when they were asked to cheer
and booed when a replay on the vast HD screens suggested
the referees had erred. It was, he decided, all a little sterile.

They were approaching a line of fast-food vendors that
had pushed carts up to the station in an attempt to snag
trade from those who were not already full from the more
professional outlets that were licensed by the stadium.

Charlie saw that Milton was looking at them. "Hungry?"
he said. "Wanna get a dog?"

"Let me," Milton said.

Milton had loved getting hot dogs from the East End
wide boys who arrived in catering trucks and set up on
Green Street. He could still remember the sizzle of the pork
sausages on the hot plate, the spit and hiss of the grease and
the smell of the onions. He started toward one of the
vendors.

"Nah," Charlie said. "Not here. Over there."

He pointed to a vendor who was advertising foot-long
Hebrew National all-beef hot dogs.

"The food here was better before the new stadium," he
said as they made their way over to the stand. "You had the
old dudes who pushed their carts up here, kept their
wieners in boxes of hot water and fished them out when you

wanted one. Pretty sure there wasn't much meat in the dogs, least not the cuts you'd want to eat, but they'd drop it in a fresh bun and it sure tasted better than what they got now. The foot-longs they got here, though, they're still pretty good."

Milton got into line and, when he reached the front, he ordered two dogs. The vendor picked out two and put them into fluffy buns that were already half-wrapped in foil.

"Now you add mustard and a dollop of sauerkraut," Charlie instructed when Milton handed one of the dogs over. "No ketchup. Makes you look like a rube."

They joined the crowd again, the pulse and eddy as it flowed toward the tunnel that led beneath the tracks.

"Where you going now?" Charlie asked him.

Milton took a bite and swallowed. "The late night meeting."

"Which one?"

"There's a meeting at the Community Center on Glenmore."

Charlie looked over at him askance. "But you went this morning."

"Yeah," Milton said. "I go twice sometimes."

"Shit," Charlie said with a rueful smile. "Now I feel inadequate."

"It's all that drinking in the box," Milton said.

"Really? I—"

"I'm kidding," Milton said with a smile.

His reassuring denial wasn't strictly true. He didn't want to say anything to Charlie, but there had been something about the box and the booze that had been passed around that had wormed inside his defences. The others were young and they all seemed so relaxed and happy, without the awkwardness that he had struggled with in a room full of people he didn't know. A drink would have made it all so much easier. But he had resisted. Having Charlie there—with the promise of the crushing shame that Milton would have felt if he had taken a drink in front of him—had been enough of a reason for him to say no. But he had been tempted, and, whenever that happened, he got himself to a meeting as quickly as he could so that he could shore up his defences once more.

21

C arter made his way down to the locker room and changed out of his uniform and into his street clothes. He left his service pistol in the locker and replaced it with his personal Glock. He started to close the door, paused, and, on a whim, reached up and took the flick knife that he had confiscated from a corner boy on Pitkin whom they had rolled last week. He put the knife in his boot, shut and locked the locker door, and hurried up the stairs.

Sergeant Ramirez was loitering at the desk. He was about to say something when he saw Carter's face and changed his mind. "Shit," he said. "Becky?"

"Yes," Carter said. "She just called. It started an hour ago."

"So get the fuck out of here."

"Thanks, Sarge."

"What about Rhodes?"

"I sent him back out in the car again. He'll be okay. It's quiet. And he's got his head on straight."

"I'll call him," the older man said. "Don't want him shitting his pants his first day."

Carter's phone buzzed in his pocket as he hurried out the door. He took it out, expecting a text from Shep, but it was the reminder that he had set for himself: GET CRIB. He would have to postpone that particular trip. There wouldn't be time for that tonight.

The station house was separated from Sutter Avenue by a row of parking spaces. There were patrol cars parked alongside the personal rides of the officers based there, and Carter jogged along the line until he got to his Ford F-150. He got inside the truck, started the engine and drove onto the street. There were white clapboard houses on the other side of the road and the Golden China restaurant, where he often grabbed takeout when he was working late shifts. He turned the wheel and ran the stop sign at the corner of Shepard Avenue, following the residential street to the north. He turned right onto Pitkin, racing up to fifty and drawing doleful glances from the locals gathered on the sidewalk outside of Crown Fried Chicken.

His phone rang. He put it on speaker.

It was Shepard. "He's on the move."

"Where?"

"Just crossed Milford."

Carter thought fast. It was a standing joke between them that González, despite owning a car stereo shop, didn't drive. "If he's going to New Brunswick, he'll get the PATH from the World Trade Centre."

"Might be headed for Euclid."

"Stay with him. I'll come around on Pine Street and park."

He approached Atkins. González Auto Sound was on the other side of the road, inside an old bus depot that González had converted with the proceeds of his early dealings with Acosta. Carter thought of being inside the shop last week; the fact that González had recorded the delivery of Acosta's payment filled him with anger. He accelerated, flashing across the intersections of Montauk, Milford and Logan until he saw Shep and, two hundred feet ahead of him, the distinctive figure of González. He was big, with broad shoulders and a heavy roll to his walk. His skin was a light chocolate brown. His long black hair was tied up in braids, spilling out from beneath a bandana to run down his back.

Carter slowed right down to the speed limit.

"I see you," he said into the phone. "I see him, *too.*"

Shepard turned to look out into the street just as Carter went by him. "I got you."

González crossed Fountain Avenue.

"He's definitely going to Euclid," Carter said. "I'll go around so he doesn't see me and park. Just stay on him."

"And then what do we do, Bobby?"

"You know what we do."

"I know that. I mean do we tell Acosta?"

Carter gave that a moment's thought. In an ideal world, he would have preferred to talk it out with their patron, but this wasn't an ideal world and they didn't have the luxury of time. "We can't," he said. "If González hands himself in, we're finished. We do this right and Acosta ought to thank us. Because you know they won't stop with us. They'll want to round the whole gang up, including him. Fuck, we'll ask him for a bonus."

22

F reddy waited on the platform at Penn Station with all the other spectators from the game. He needed the A Train headed to Far Rockaway. The quickest way to get home would have been to change at Broadway Junction so that he could take the J Train to Crescent Street. But, as he waited, he heard an announcement that the J Train was suspended thanks to an incident on the line. He went over to the map and worked out an alternative route: he would take the A down to Euclid and walk the rest of the way.

He couldn't stop thinking about the game. There was something magical about a game under the lights: the grass seemed a little greener, the atmosphere felt more alive, and there was a simple pleasure in sitting down and watching the game in frigid winter cold. He had taken off his gloves so that he could grip the pigskin a little tighter, and he brushed his fingers across the stippled exterior and thought, for the hundredth time, what his friends at school would say when he showed the ball to them. OBJ, after making that catch, had launched the ball into the stands and he had grabbed it. What were the odds of that?

He thought of his father. What would he say when he showed him?

Thinking about Manny brought him down. His dad should have been with him. He should have seen him catch the ball. He should have been there to slap him on the back and celebrate with him. But he wasn't. Freddy felt his mood beginning to sour and, to ward off the moment when he would have to figure out what he was going to do next, he lifted the ball to his nose and let its pungent smell fill his nostrils.

There was a blast of warm air as the train approached through the tunnel. It rumbled out of the dark mouth, the brakes squealing as it slowed down and stopped.

Freddy stepped into the car and found a spare seat. He sat down, watching the other passengers as they embarked from the busy platform. He could smell the alcohol from those in the highest spirits. There was one man who caught his eye more than the others: he was of average height and build and had dark hair. He wouldn't normally have stood out save that Freddy noticed his eyes: they were a pale, almost icy blue, and, as the man glanced into the busy car, Freddy found that they were staring at each other. He looked down, at his sneakers, and, when he looked back up again, the man had started to talk with the man standing next to him.

The train rumbled into motion, heading off again.

23

M ilton and Charlie had chatted amiably for the first fifteen minutes, but they only knew each other a little and, as they exhausted what they could say about football, they had run out of things to say. Charlie took out his phone. Milton glanced over his shoulder and saw that he was reading the report of the game that had been hastily posted to the website of the *Post*.

He was happy to sit back and enjoy the ride. It was warm despite the air-conditioned car, and he found his eyelids growing heavy. He allowed them to close and let his thoughts drift. He had enjoyed a pleasant couple of months since he had left Manila, and he allowed himself to replay the memories that he had stored up. He had started in Vietnam, visiting Hanoi and then the Mekong Delta before heading north to Halong Bay and the rice terraces of Sapa. He'd spent a week travelling to Cambodia to see Angkor Wat and then turned to the north, traversing Myanmar to visit the Buddhist shrine at Kyaiktiyo. He had ended up in Thailand, spending a week amid the raft houses and waterfalls of Kanchanaburi before finishing with another week on the island of Ko Lanta.

The trip had been exactly what he had needed after the beatings he had taken in New Bilibid prison. It had allowed his body to heal and, after just a few days in the sun, his skin had taken on a deep tan and the bruises had been hidden, soon to heal completely. More important than his physical well-being was the opportunity to disentangle himself from the raging torrent of his thoughts, stirred into confused life by Fitzroy de Lacey and the sleights of hand that he had arranged in order to trick Milton into visiting Manila. Milton's dark side, normally suppressed by meditation and his regular AA meetings, had been prodded into wakefulness and there had been nothing that he had been able to do to pacify it. The killer in him had been roused and then unleashed; the ease with which he had slipped back into it, as if pulling on a comfortable pair of shoes, had frightened him. Milton had spent hours rereading the Big Book, concentrating on the Steps and renewing his faith in their power to bring him peace of mind.

"Hey," Charlie said.

Milton opened his eyes.

"You asleep?"

"Just resting my eyes," he said.

"What's your stop?"

"Euclid."

"It's next."

Milton looked up as they flashed out of the blackness of the tunnel and into the artificial brightness of the subway station.

"You had a good time?"

"Better than that. Loved it. I'm very grateful."

Charlie waved his gratitude away. "It was nothing."

Milton reached out for the metal rail and pulled himself upright. "This is me."

The train slowed down and then stopped.

"I'll see you at the meeting tomorrow night?"

Charlie offered his hand and Milton shook it.

"I'll be there."

He stepped down onto the platform. The chill enveloped him at once, a reminder of how cold it was and how much colder it promised to get. He did up his coat. The train pulled away and soon it had disappeared into the maw of the tunnel, leaving Milton to stare across the empty track to the lines of dirty beige tiles and the single word—EUCLID—repeated over and over.

He made his way to the stairs and trotted up to the mezzanine.

24

F reddy needed to use the restroom when he got off the train. He went to the mezzanine and followed the signs. The men's room was inside a wooden door with a metal kick plate that had been dented and scratched by years of misuse. He pushed the door open and went inside.

The restroom had a line of five porcelain basins along the left-hand wall with a long horizontal mirror above them and then three urinals. On the opposite wall were five cubicles. The first cubicle was missing its door, the toilet in the second one was blocked—Freddy couldn't get out of it quickly enough—and the floor in the third and fourth was covered in urine, and Freddy wasn't about to walk in that in his new sneakers. The cubicle at the end was empty and reasonably clean. He went inside. The door was spring-loaded and it closed by itself. He put the football on the cistern, unzipped his pants and urinated.

His mind drifted back to his father. He was nervous about going home. His dad might be angry with him for going to the game alone, but Freddy knew he would be okay with anger; at least he would be able to talk to his father if he was angry. But his stomach lurched as he thought about the more likely scenario: that his father was drinking again. There had been many occasions over the course of the last year when Freddy had had to care for Manny after he had gotten drunk. He had done things that a child should not have had to do: undressed him and put him to bed; helped him go to the toilet; washed his soiled clothes; cleaned up the mess that always accompanied his worst excesses.

But lately his dad had been really trying, and things had gotten better—so much better. Freddy had been hoping that those bad days were over. He never wanted to go back to them, ever.

He zipped up, went to the basin, washed his hands and went to the door.

It opened suddenly, catching him on the shoulder.

A man barged inside. He looked Dominican, like him. He was big, wearing a Patriots jersey beneath a leather jacket, and his hair was long and unkempt, reaching down from underneath a bandana to beyond his collar. He looked unwell, and he stumbled past Freddy without apologising and made straight for the nearest basin, where he bent over, held on with both hands, ducked his head down between his arms and vomited. Freddy guessed that he was an addict; he had seen plenty of those in the house across the street from them. Rubbing his shoulder, he turned on his heel, slipped out the door, and made his way quickly to the exit.

The station was quiet save for two men who were paying their fares. The sight of the man at the basin had made him think unhappily of his father again, and he felt his forehead crease with anxiety. Freddy spared the men no attention as he pushed through the turnstile and made his way into the chill outside.

Carter and Shepard hurried into the station. González was ahead of them. Carter knew that they had to move quickly. The longer they waited, the more difficult it would be to get to him. If they let him get onto a busy train, it was going to be impossible to take him out without causing a fuss.

They watched as González diverted, crossing the space to a door marked "Men."

"It's our lucky day," Shepard said quietly, inclining his head toward the turnstiles. "You see the booth? She's asleep."

"What about the cameras?"

"Not working."

"Sure?" Carter asked.

"One hundred per cent."

González shoved the door and went inside. Carter watched as a young boy in a Giants jersey came out. The boy rubbed his shoulder and turned to look back into the restroom with a look of annoyance on his face.

"Ready?" Shepard said.

The kid went by them.

"I'll do it," Carter said. "Stay on the door."

He waited a moment, looked left and right, and then made his way across the mezzanine to the men's room.

The restroom was filthy. González was bent over the basin, leaning heavily on his arms. Carter smelled the stink of his vomit. He reached down into his boot and took out the flick knife.

"What's up, José?"

Startled, González looked up at him in the mirror. He looked away again, but not quickly enough to hide the fear in his eyes.

"Hey, Bobby," he said. "Small world."

"You okay? Looks like you've been sick. What's up?"

González spat a mouthful of phlegm into the dirty basin. "Had fried chicken from Ramon's place. Fucker never cooks that shit properly."

"You sure that's it?"

He smiled nervously. "Yeah. That's it. Why you say that?"

"Don't look like you're pleased to see me."

"Just surprised is all."

"Where you going?"

"What? Now?"

"Yeah, José. Now."

"Got girl problems. You know Hector's woman? I been seeing her. She's—"

Carter cut him off. "Don't bullshit me," he said with a grin.

"It's true."

"No, it isn't."

"What you mean?"

"I mean you're a lying, traitorous piece of shit."

Carter pressed the button on the shaft and the blade sprang out of the knife.

González straightened up, but, before he could move away from the basin, Carter moved in tight and drove the blade into his side. González gave a grunt of surprise and pain. He tried to back away, but he had nowhere to go. Carter stabbed him again, and then a third and fourth time. González stumbled and Carter slid in behind him, yanking back on his head to expose his neck. The blade sliced through González's flesh, opening his throat from one ear to the other. Thick, dark blood spilled out.

González clutched at his neck, gurgling as his breath bubbled out through the gush of blood. He slumped to his knees, his eyes rolled back, and he fell sideways to the floor. Carter knelt down next to González and quickly frisked his body. He took out his wallet from the pocket of his jeans, moved to his leather jacket and found a small digital recorder. He wiped the wallet, put it back in the pocket again, and put the recorder into his pocket.

González's breathing grew shallow and then stopped. His legs twitched once and then they, too, were still.

Carter stood up and stepped back, looking down at his hands: they were covered with blood. Stepping over González's legs, he went to the second basin in the row, turned on the taps and rinsed the blood away as best as he could. He glanced in the mirror and saw that his jacket was stained, too. He took it off and folded it so that the blood was hidden.

Satisfied, he stepped over González one last time, opened the door, and went back outside.

"Done?" Shepard asked.

"Done. We clear?"

"No one around. You find the recorder?"

Carter tapped his pocket and nodded. "We need to book," he said.

25

F reddy was thirty seconds down the road before he realised.

The ball.

He had left it in the cubicle. He had been so worried about what he would find when he got home that he had clean forgotten about it. If someone else found it, they'd take it for sure. He turned around and retraced his steps, then broke into a jog. Catching that ball was the best thing that had happened to him for months, and he was damn sure he wasn't going to lose it now. He hadn't been away for long; the odds of someone getting to it first were slim, but he didn't want to take any chances.

One of the gates was open. The woman in the booth had her eyes closed and might even have been asleep; he hurried through and headed for the men's room, and then stopped in his tracks.

There was a man standing by the door to the bathroom. He was older, black, and wearing jeans and a heavy jacket. He had greying hair that was receding all the way to the back of his head, deep lines on his face and a beard that was flecked with white. Freddy was bad at judging age, but, if pressed, he would have guessed that the man was in his fifties. He recognised him from before: it was one of the men he had passed as he had left the station a few minutes ago. There was something weird about the way he was standing there, as if he was guarding the door. It made Freddy uneasy. He diverted to the map of the subway on the wall and pretended to study it.

A few moments later, he heard the squeak of the restroom door as it was opened and then a snatch of conversation, too quiet for him to make anything out. He heard footsteps on the tiled mezzanine floor and stood stock-still, as though he was concentrating on the map. The footsteps went by and he heard the turnstile as it rattled around.

Cautiously, Freddy turned away from the wall and looked back. There were two men: the black guy and a white guy. They had their backs to him. The white guy wasn't wearing a jacket; it looked like he was carrying it under his arm.

Once they were out of sight, he turned and made his way over to the restroom. He put out a hand, swung the door open, and stepped inside.

Milton climbed up to the mezzanine. He saw the sign for the men's room, crossed over to it and pushed the door open.

The first thing he saw was the body.

It was a man. He was big and well built, with light brown skin and black braids that fell out from beneath a bandana to snake around his head on the floor. He was wearing a leather jacket, a New England Patriots jersey, loose-fitting trousers and a pair of crocodile-skin cowboy boots, visible up to the ankle where the hem of his right trouser leg had ridden up. He had fallen over onto his right-hand side, resting on his arm as if he had just lain down for a nap.

The door was on a spring-loaded hinge; it bumped into Milton's shoulder as it closed. He stepped farther into the room until he could take a better look at the body. The front of the jersey was sodden with blood. There were rips in the fabric—Milton counted ten without giving it a close inspection—and blood had run down and pooled over the floor, spreading out in thick rivulets that covered the grout between the tiles. Milton knelt down next to the body. His eyes were open, staring blankly ahead. There was an ugly gash that ran from one ear to the other, a line that opened his throat right across his larynx.

Milton thought quickly. Out of habit, he had scoped out the security at the station; the ticket clerk had seemed to be sleeping, and he didn't believe that there were any cameras outside that would have recorded his presence. The mezzanine had been quiet, too, and he wouldn't have made much of an impression upon anyone who had seen him. He looked down at the body again. The last thing that he wanted was to be involved with the police. He could just leave. That was an option. Someone else would discover the dead man. He could leave it to them.

But what if he *was* seen? How would he explain his behaviour? He wouldn't be able to.

He would have to call it in.

He heard a sound from the direction of the cubicles.

He paused and listened.

He heard it again.

A quiet, half-strangled sob.

He felt the tingle of adrenaline as he turned back to face into the restroom.

"Hello?"

Nothing.

There were five cubicles. Save the first, each cubicle was shielded by a green wooden door.

The first cubicle was empty. He clenched his right hand into a fist and tried the second door, pushing it back with the fingertips of his left hand. That stall was empty, too.

He moved to the third and then the fourth.

"Hello? Is anyone there?"

Still nothing.

He pushed the door to the last cubicle. It opened.

There was someone inside.

A young boy, crouching down on the floor to make himself as small as possible.

"Hey," Milton said. "It's okay. You don't need to worry."

He was wearing a Giants shirt, a pair of denim trousers and a pair of white sneakers. Milton doubted that he was any older than thirteen.

"Hey," he said, putting out a hand. "It's okay. Relax."

The boy stood. He was clutching a football to his chest.

"Were you in here when..." Milton let the words drift off, their meaning still obvious.

The boy shook his head.

"What's your name?"

He said nothing.

Milton put out his hand. "I'm John."

The boy shrank away.

"Take it easy. I'm on your side." Milton's attention was drawn to the ball and the Giants jersey. He stood between the boy and the body, blocking as much of it from view as he could. "You just been to the game?"

The boy looked at him, his eyes wide with fear; Milton thought he saw a tiny inclining of his head.

"Me too. You a Giants fan?"

The boy nodded, more noticeably this time.

"What about the ball? Is that for real?"

"Yeah," the boy said in a quiet voice. "OBJ threw it into the stand."

"After he caught that bomb? And you caught it?"

He nodded.

Milton put out his hand again. "Like I said, I'm John. What's your name?"

"Freddy," he said quietly.

He reached out and tentatively took Milton's hand.

"All right, Freddy. We need to get out of here, okay? There's no need for you to look. You just close your eyes and I'll guide you to the door and then we'll be outside. Is that going to be okay with you?"

The boy swallowed and nodded.

"Come on, then."

Milton gently pulled the boy by the hand to set him moving, making sure he stayed between him and the dead body in the event that he opened his eyes. Milton had seen dozens of dead men and women before, many of them in that state because he had, for one reason or another, been given their files and the order to terminate them. He was inured to the sight of death and blood, but he found—to his slight surprise—that he didn't want the boy to have to look. He concentrated on guiding him to the door, opening it and then gently ushering him outside.

The restroom was unheated, but it was still several degrees colder as they stepped out onto the mezzanine. The ticket clerk was still dozing inside her booth, swaying gently back and forth with her eyes closed. Milton told the boy that he could open his eyes now and, still holding onto his hand, he led the way to the booth so that he could report what he had found.

26

Milton and the boy were shown through to a small office in the station where they were told to wait until the police arrived. The clerk—Milton saw from her name badge that she was called Felicia—evidently had no idea what she was supposed to do. She had gone into the restroom despite Milton's insistence that she would be better to just call the cops and, when she emerged again, she looked as if she was going to be sick. Finding a dead body in your place of work was not, perhaps, something that she had been trained for.

"Felicia," Milton said in a kindly voice, "do you know what to do?"

"I ain't got no clue."

"You need to call the police."

"Yeah. The police. I'll do it now."

"Before you do, you need to make sure the body isn't disturbed."

"How do I do that?"

"Do you think you should close the station?"

"Close the station?" she exclaimed, as if that was the

single most ludicrous thing that she had ever heard. "Are you crazy? I can't close the station. They'll fire my ass before my feet can touch the ground I go and do something like close the station."

"Then maybe you could lock the restroom door? The police will be unhappy if anyone gets inside before they come."

"Yeah," she said. "Lock the door. That's what I'll do."

Milton watched through the window in the office door as she went over and turned a key in the lock. She found a free-standing out-of-order sign and placed it on the floor in front of the door. She seemed pleased with this little flourish of individuality and, when she returned to the office, she bustled around with the self-importance of someone who has remembered that she was in a position of authority.

"Felicia," Milton said, "could we get a warm drink for the boy? He's had a shock."

"Sure," she replied. "But I only got coffee."

"Is that okay?" Milton asked.

Freddy had retreated into himself once more. He sat on a plastic chair in the corner of the room, cradling the football.

"Freddy?"

He nodded his head.

"Thank you, Felicia," Milton said. "And one for me too, please."

———

Felicia was in the process of pouring hot water into the two china mugs that she had found when the police finally arrived. A uniformed officer knocked on the door; Milton could see the woman through the window. Felicia hurried across to open the door and let the officer inside. There was another one outside —this one older and male—speaking into his radio.

"Got a call about a dead body?"

The sight of the police officers seemed to reinvigorate Felicia's confidence. Perhaps it was the uniforms, the feeling that reinforcements had arrived, but she bustled forward and put out her chest. "I called it in," she said.

"Where?"

She pointed to the restroom. "In there."

"Door locked?"

"Uh-huh."

"Could we have the key, please?"

She went over to her desk and, after a moment spent fumbling through loose papers during which Milton was concerned she might somehow have misplaced the key, she found it and handed it over. The police officer handed it to her partner and waited with them as he went to check the room.

"What's he gonna find?" she asked.

"Body on the floor. Lot of blood."

"Did you find the body?"

"No, I did not," she said. She pointed at Milton and Freddy. "They did. They came out and told me. But I went and checked that it was true and I called you."

"Sir," the police officer said, "that true? You found it?"

"I did," he said. "But I think you'd better speak to him first." He pointed to where the boy was sitting in the corner.

"The kid? Why?"

"He went in first. He found the body—I found him."

"And he's not with you?"

Milton shook his head. "No."

"What's your name?"

"John Smith."

"So how do you fit into it?"

"I was going to use the bathroom. I opened the door and saw the body. The boy was in one of the cubicles."

"Right. Have you spoken to him?"

"Just briefly. He's scared."

"You know his name?"

"Freddy."

"Last name?"

"Didn't ask for that."

The office was tiny, and it would have been impossible for the officer to speak to Freddy without Milton being able to hear what she said. She knelt down so that she was at his level and put a hand on his shoulder.

"I'm Officer Farley," she said. "You're Freddy, right?"

He nodded.

"What's your last name, Freddy?"

"Blanco."

"How old are you?"

"Thirteen."

"You out on your own tonight? It's pretty late."

He nodded.

"He's been to the Giants game," Milton offered.

Farley turned to look at him. "I got this, Mr. Smith." She turned back. "Were you in the restroom?"

Freddy nodded.

"Tell me what happened."

"I needed to pee. I came out and saw..."

"Go on."

"I saw the man coming in."

"The man? Do you mean the victim?"

"Yes. I saw him come in. He started barfing at the sink, and then I left."

"But you found his body? How'd that happen?"

"I left this in the bathroom." The boy tapped a finger against the football that was clutched to his chest. "I got out to the street, realised I'd left it and came right back inside."

"And then?"

"Found the man on the floor."

"Anything else?"

"Like what?"

"You see anyone else?"

"Two men. One of them, a black guy, was waiting outside the door. I thought it was strange. Then a white guy came out of the bathroom and they left."

"You get a good look at them?"

"I..." The words trailed off.

"Did you see them, Freddy?"

Freddy shook his head. "Not really."

"You saw them or you didn't?"

"I only saw the black guy, really" Freddy said.

"And?"

Freddy shrugged. "That's all. I was trying not to look at them."

The office door opened and the second officer came inside before Farley could ask Freddy anything more. Farley glanced across at him. "So?"

"So it's like they said. It's a guy, Latino, looks like his throat's been cut. It's messy. We're gonna need homicide down here."

27

Carter dumped his soiled jacket in the back seat and drove them both away from the station. At the corner of Fulton and Marcus Garvey Boulevard, he pulled over, wiped the knife with a rag to remove the blood and his prints, got out of the car and dumped both items in a dumpster outside Royal Bengal Fried Chicken & Grocery. He would be more careful with the recorder—he'd toss it off the bridge on the way home.

He got back into the car and followed Fulton to the west until he reached Nostrand Avenue. The Mystery bar was between two hair salons: one that advertised itself for men and women and another that promised the best hair extensions in Brooklyn. He pulled over outside the bar and switched off the engine. He reached back for his jacket and held it out: there were big splashes of blood right in the middle of it.

"Motherfucker," he cursed. "Just bought this last week."

"So buy another," Shepard said.

He had another lightweight jacket in the truck, so he took that and put it on, then got out and led the way into the bar. It was run by an ex-cop called Cousins who had worked the precinct three years ago, cashing out his pension and buying the bar. He had a clientele of cops from the surrounding sectors, a group of regulars who came here knowing that they would get a good deal on their booze and an atmosphere of peers who would keep whatever was discussed inside private.

Cousins was behind the bar and raised a hand in greeting as Carter and Shepard came inside and took a table at the back of the room. Shepard went up to the bar to get a couple of beers and Carter took the opportunity to check his phone for messages from Becky. She had sent a text two hours ago reminding him to get a crib and then another asking where he was. He tapped out a reply to that message, telling her that he was having a drink with Shep. She would know that would mean that he would be home late and wouldn't wait up for him. Carter would grab the crib on the way into the precinct tomorrow. No problem.

Shepard came back with the beers and handed one of the bottles to Carter. He took it, held it up, and touched it against Shepard's bottle.

We got lucky," Carter said. "You didn't see anyone?"

"Just some kid."

"And you're sure the cameras don't work?"

"Haven't worked for weeks," Shepard said. "You know Carl Rivera?"

"Sure," Carter replied. "Dumbass. Sells weed on Pitkin, least he used to."

"Transport cops busted him inside the station last week," Shepard said. "I know someone who knows him. Had to let him go because the cameras weren't working."

Carter held up his bottle again and Shepard clinked it once more.

He took a swig of his beer. "What do we do about Carlos?" he said, wiping his mouth.

Carter had been thinking about that on the drive across Brooklyn. "We gotta tell him. We can't not."

"We should've spoken to him before. Him and González were tight."

"We had no choice," Carter said, annoyed with his friend's concern. "If González had gotten to the cops, we would all have been in the shit. We would've been the first to get rolled up. And you think Carlos would just let that happen? You think he'd take the chance that we'd talk? No. He would've done us both. And González could still have spilled on him, too. He's gonna be pissed with González, not with us. We did what we had to do."

"Who were you riding with today?"

"A rookie," Carter said. "It was his first day."

"What you tell him?"

"That the baby was coming. It's fine—I'll say it was a false alarm."

Shepard grinned at him. "You remember your first day?"

"You gonna bring that up again?"

Carter remembered it well. They had sent him out on a foot post. He was on the corner of Liberty and Fountain with his thumb up his ass. He got a ten-two call over the radio, but he didn't know the codes, so he just ignored it. He got back to the station at the end of the tour and the sergeant and a few of the other guys, including Shepard, were waiting for him at the front desk. The ten-two was an instruction to get back to the station house. The sergeant held up the license plate for his car and handed it to him. A drunk driver had slammed into the back of his prized Camaro and crushed it against a wall. The plate was all that was left of it.

"Your face," Shepard said. "I'm never gonna forget it."

Carter allowed himself a smile and finished the rest of his beer. "I got to get out of here."

"You don't want another?"

"Some of us are still working," he said. "I got another shift tomorrow, and we'll need to see Carlos before. I'm tired. I need to get some sleep."

"Pussy," Shepard said, but he raised his bottle in a friendly salute, said he was going to stay for another and that he would get a cab home. He told Carter to call him when he had spoken to Acosta.

Carter said that he would. He zipped up the replacement jacket and went out to the truck. It was cold and getting colder. The forecast for snow looked about right. They said a big storm was coming. He hoped the baby came before that happened, or getting to the hospital might turn into more of a challenge than it might otherwise have been. He opened the door of the truck and got in. No sense in worrying about that now.

There was no sense in worrying about González, either. They'd done what they had to do and they'd done it well. They were in the clear.

He started the engine and pulled out onto the empty street. He had a long drive home ahead of him.

28

The uniformed officers had a patrol car parked on the street outside the entrance to the station. They led Milton and Freddy outside, opened the rear doors, and invited them to get inside. The front of the car was separated from the back by a wire cage, and he knew, as the door was pushed shut, that he wouldn't be able to open it. There was no suggestion that Milton was being treated as a suspect, but he had a long-ingrained aversion to places that he couldn't easily leave. He had an aversion to authority, too, and he was finding the experience unsettling. He had begun to wonder whether it might not have been a much better idea to have slipped out of the restroom and disappeared into the Brooklyn night. But, as he had that thought, he remembered Freddy in the car beside him. The boy had the ball in his lap and his hands were clasped over the top of it, his fists clenching and unclenching as he struggled with obvious anxiety. Milton's unease was irrelevant in comparison to Freddy's. He had promised to help him, and that was that. He had to stay. He was going to do the right thing.

The officers got into the front of the car and they set off, heading west on Pitkin.

"Where's the station house?"

"Sutter," Farley said. "Five minutes."

They turned onto Essex Street and then onto Sutter Avenue.

"Freddy," Farley said, "you want to give me your dad's number again? I'm not getting anything when I try it."

Farley had already tried to call the boy's father three times, but had no luck. Milton saw a flicker of unease pass across the boy's face, but he repeated the number and waited in silence as Farley put it into her phone and called again.

"Nothing," she said. "Is he usually this hard to reach?"

"Don't know," the boy said with a shrug. Milton could see that he was withholding something.

"Never mind," the officer said. "I'll keep trying. If he doesn't answer, I'll just drive over and get him."

Milton looked out at the darkened streets, almost deserted at this late hour, and settled back in the seat to wait for them to arrive. They would want him to give a statement. He would do that, and stay with Freddy until his father arrived, and then he would be on his way.

———

The precinct house for the Seventy-Fifth Precinct was on Sutter Avenue, but Milton and Freddy were driven around to a yard at the rear of the building. There were other patrol cars, and officers stood outside the doors talking over cups of coffee that steamed in the cold. The patrol car pulled into an empty space and Farley got out to open the door for them. Milton got out first and then Freddy slid across the seat to join him.

"This way," Farley said, pointing to the doors.

They went inside, making their way along a dingy corridor until they reached the main room of the station house. Farley pointed to a bench where they could wait, and then left them to go and speak to the desk sergeant. Milton took his place on the bench next to the boy and casually looked across the room. The information desk ran across the front of the squad room, facing the entrance corridor. The wall behind it was fitted with a large number of pigeonholes for sundry forms. There was a blotter on top of the desk with a PC terminal behind it. There were filing cabinets to the right and, on a low bench, a TV screen played back footage from the security cameras around the building. A widescreen TV had been affixed to the wall and Milton watched as it cycled through a series of promotional videos for the NYPD.

Milton turned to the boy. "You okay?"

He was clutching the ball to his chest as if that might help him through the next few hours.

"Do you know where your father might have gone?" he asked.

Freddy shook his head.

"Is it unusual?" Milton pressed. "Is he often out of touch like this?"

"No," the boy replied.

"What about your mother?"

"She don't live with us no more," he said tersely, and looked away.

Milton would have tried to get a little additional information from him, but he noticed that Farley had returned with another woman. She was dressed in a pantsuit and carried a small leather pouch. Her dark hair was parted and swept back tightly behind both ears. She had a severe aspect, everything underlined by flinty eyes and a mouth that didn't look as if it was accustomed to regular smiling. Milton guessed that she was in her early forties.

"Hello," she said. "I'm Detective Mackintosh. You're Mr. Smith?"

"That's right," Milton said.

"Could you come through here, please?" She made a quarter turn and indicated a door at the side of the room.

Milton paused, looking down at Freddy.

"You're not related, are you?" The question was rhetorical; it was obvious that Milton and the boy were not kin.

"No," Milton said.

"Then don't worry. Officer Farley will look after him until his parents show up. Please—this way."

29

Milton followed Mackintosh into the interview room. It was dark; the detective reached out for the light switch and flicked it on. To call the room that was revealed 'functional' would have been generous: the walls were painted concrete blocks, with vents down toward the floor and a window into an empty observation area in the adjacent room. There was a single desk in the centre of the room with two metal folding chairs facing one another. Milton's attention was drawn to the two cameras on the wall facing him. There was one in each corner, both aimed to cover the table from two directions.

"Take a seat," Mackintosh said.

Milton pulled out a chair and sat down at the table. The detective sat down opposite him. There was a small device with three buttons on the table. Mackintosh took out a pad of paper and a pen from the pouch that she was carrying and laid them out next to the device.

"We'll record our conversation," she said, pointing up to the cameras. "Is that okay?"

"Yes," Milton said, although the thought made him uncomfortable.

She picked up the device. Milton could see that the buttons were labelled START, STOP and RECORD. She pressed the button marked RECORD.

"This interview is being tape recorded at the station house of the Seventy-Fifth Precinct. I am Detective Rebecca Mackintosh. There are no other officers present. We are in interview room three. For the purpose of the tape, could you please state your name and date of birth?"

"John Smith." He gave her the date of birth on his fake papers.

"Thank you very much. The date is the twenty-seventh of November and the time is 23:20, so twenty minutes after eleven in the evening. Okay. So, Mr. Smith, this interview is being tape recorded so should this ever go to court one of the tapes will be sealed and it can be used in evidence should this ever get that far."

"I understand."

"So—John Smith. That's an anonymous-sounding name. That's definitely you?"

Milton found the lurch into a more aggressive form of questioning a little disconcerting. "Want to see my passport?"

"That's all right. Where you from, Mr. Smith? England?"

"That's right."

"Holiday?"

"No. I'm working here."

"That right?"

"I'm a cook."

"Where?"

"There's a place in Coney Island. Red Square."

"I've never heard of it."

"No reason why you would. It's not going to win any awards."

"You got a visa?"

He exhaled. "Want to see that, too?"

"That's okay. No reason not to believe you. Where do you live?"

"Coney Island."

"Near to work?"

"That's right."

"Let's get to it, then. You saw the body?"

"I did. But I think the boy has got more to say about it than I have."

"Yes," Mackintosh said. "You're probably right about that. What happened? He found it?"

"That's what he told me."

"I'll ask him. But tell me what you saw."

"I was coming back from the Meadowlands," Milton said.

"You saw the game?"

"I did. I was coming back."

"Sorry to interrupt," she said, looking down at her hand-written notes. "You live in Coney Island. What you doing getting off at Euclid?"

Milton chewed his lip. He would have preferred a different question.

"Sir?"

"I was going to a meeting," he said.

"What sort of meeting?"

Milton paused. He knew he'd be out of here sooner if he was truthful, and he had nothing to hide. "Alcoholics Anonymous," he said. "There's a midnight meeting at the Community Center."

"You're a drunk?"

"Is that relevant?"

"You might be a witness in a homicide—I'd say it was relevant. Had a drink tonight?"

"I haven't had a drink for a long time."

Mackintosh didn't react. "Go on. Keep going."

"I got to the station and I needed to use the bathroom. I climbed up to the mezzanine and followed the sign to the restroom. I went inside and I immediately saw the body on the floor."

"Describe it."

"He was lying on his side. His head was resting on his right arm. I could see that he was dead."

"How so?"

"He'd been stabbed. There was a lot of blood. When I got a little closer, I saw that his throat had been slit."

"You see anyone coming out of the restroom before you went in?"

"No."

"Anyone outside when you came out?"

"No. The station was empty. There was just the woman in the ticket office."

"She says she didn't see anything."

"She was asleep," Milton said.

"And the security cameras weren't working. Looks like all we've got to go on is what you saw."

"And the kid," Milton added.

"What did he say about it?"

"That he went in to use the bathroom. He left as a man was going in, then saw a guy go in after him and another guy hanging around outside the door. Freddy went out of the station, and then came back again to pick up a football he'd forgotten."

"A football?"

"He'd just been to the game. He went back for the ball, saw the same two guys he'd seen earlier walking away from the restroom, and then when he went inside he found the body."

"Lucky kid," the detective said. "A little earlier and it might not have gone so well for him."

"What else do you want to know?"

"I think we're done for now," she said. She looked at a counter on the remote control and added a note to her pad. "Terminating interview at 11.30 p.m."

She reached over and pressed STOP.

"We're done?" Milton asked.

"Stick around the city for a while, would you? Don't go anywhere."

"I'm not a suspect?"

"No. Not right now you're not. I'm happy for you to go, but I don't want you going too far—like back to England—until I've got to the bottom of this. Might have more questions for you, too. That reminds me—what's your address?"

Milton provided his home and work addresses, plus the number for his cell, and followed the detective out of the interview room.

30

Freddy was still sitting outside. Milton went over to him and sat down. Mackintosh diverted to the information desk.

Milton overheard Mackintosh as she spoke to the desk sergeant.

"Where's Farley?"

"In back."

"She was supposed to have called his parents. We can't leave him here on his own."

"We've both been trying," the sergeant said. "Just getting voicemail."

Milton went up to the desk.

Mackintosh heard him approach and turned to face him. "Can I help you, Mr. Smith?"

"I'll stay with him," Milton said, "until his parents get here."

"It'll be social services if they're not here soon."

"I don't mind waiting. Is there anywhere I can get him a drink and something to eat?"

Mackintosh looked doubtful.

"*Look*," Milton said. "He's scared. And he seems comfortable with me. He shouldn't be in here on his own."

She shrugged. "Sure. Knock yourself out. Vending machine around the corner. Cans of Coke, chips, candy bars. Machine doesn't always work, though."

"Thank you, Detective," he said.

Milton went over to the boy and sat down next to him.

"How you doing, Freddy?"

"They say they wanna talk to me," he said.

"They do. They'll want you to tell them about what you saw."

"Didn't really see nothing," he said, although Milton could tell that he was underplaying it. He was frightened. He probably wanted to go home. That was understandable. Milton would have felt the same.

"You hungry? Thirsty?"

Freddy nodded.

"You want some candy? They say there's a machine over there."

"Sure."

Milton got up and followed Mackintosh's directions to the vending machine that had been set up just inside a corridor that led off the main area. The stock had been allowed to dwindle without being replaced, and the choice was meagre. Milton punched in the numbers for two Hershey bars and two bottles of Arizona iced tea, collected them from the slot and took them back to Freddy.

"Thanks," the boy said as Milton handed him one of the bars and one of the iced teas. He unwrapped the chocolate, broke off a piece and hungrily stuffed it into his mouth.

"You like the Giants, then?" Milton asked him.

"Uh-huh," Freddy said with a nod, his mouth full.

"I like the Dolphins."

"Dolphins suck," Freddy opined as he unscrewed the lid of the bottle.

"You don't like Tannehill?"

The boy took a slug of the iced tea. "He ain't no Eli Manning."

Milton could see that Freddy was relaxing a little. The chocolate and the iced tea and a conversation about something that was obviously close to his heart had all served to distract him from the horrors that he had been forced to witness. Milton opened his bottle. He lowered his head to take a sip just as Freddy crossed his legs. Milton's attention was snagged by the shoes that he was wearing.

"Nice sneakers," he said.

Freddy reached down and brushed his fingers against the appliqué stripes on the sides of the sneakers as if rubbing away a smidge of dirt that wasn't there. "They're new," he said.

"Adidas?" Milton asked.

He nodded. "Mastodon Pro. Special Edition."

Milton frowned. "Did you have a pair like that before that were stolen?"

Freddy took a half turn and then shuffled an inch or two away from him as if his question had frightened him. "How'd you know that?"

"I think I know your father," Milton said. "His name is Manny, right?"

Freddy swallowed and nodded. "How you know him?"

Milton didn't know how much he should say. It was possible that Freddy didn't know that his father attended the fellowship. The last thing he wanted to do was give him something else to worry about tonight.

"He used to be a soldier," he said instead, remembering

what Manny had shared during the meeting. "I did too. We have quite a bit in common."

It was a vague answer that didn't really address Freddy's question, but the boy let it slide.

"Do you have any idea where he is?" Milton asked him.

"I don't know," Freddy said with a weary shrug. "I spoke to him at the game. Sounded like he'd gone out drinking. But maybe he has his phone switched off. I don't know." He took another swig of his iced tea. "How long you think they're gonna keep me here? I just want to go home and go to bed and forget all of this ever happened."

"I'll have a word with them," Milton said. "It might help now that I can say I know your father. Wait here, all right?"

Milton went up to the desk. Mackintosh was still there, leaning against it, her phone pressed to her ear. She finished the call and put the phone away as she saw Milton approach.

"What is it, Mr. Smith?"

"What's the plan for the boy?"

"I need to talk to him, but I don't want to do that without a responsible adult in the room. And I can't get through to his father."

"I know him," Milton said.

"His father?"

"His name is Manny Blanco."

"You didn't mention that before."

"I only just realised."

"You know the boy, too?"

"I've never met him before tonight. I just know his father."

"How?"

Milton bit his lip. Confidentiality was one of the most important principles of the fellowship, but he knew that he would have to offer the detective more than mere platitudes if he was going to be able to take Freddy home.

"His father is an alcoholic," he said. "Like me. I know him through meetings."

Mackintosh didn't react. "You think he might be drinking now?"

"I didn't say that," Milton said, although Freddy clearly thought that was a possibility. "He's been sober for a long time. It's probably something else. I just wanted you to know that I know him. And, if it'd help, I could take the boy home."

She shook her head. "Can't just let you do that."

"What were you going to do? You can't leave him here all night."

"I hadn't made up my mind," she said. "I was beginning to think I might have to call social services."

"I'm not trying to tell you how to do your job," Milton said, "but you're not going to be able to talk to him tonight. Why don't you take him home? I'll come too. I'd like to help if I can, and I think he'll be more relaxed if I'm there. It's probably nothing with his father. Freddy thinks he might just have his phone off. Take him home, and you can get them both back in here tomorrow."

She looked at Milton, over to Freddy, and then back at Milton again. Finally, she nodded. "Fine," she said. "Tell him to get ready. I'll go and get my keys."

31

M ilton went back to the bench.

"Good news," he began, and then stopped.

He could immediately see that something was wrong. The boy's hands were clutched together tightly, and the blood had drained out of his face.

Milton sat down next to him.

"What is it?"

Freddy unclenched his hands and slowly pointed up to the TV that was showing the promotional videos. It was a recording of a news report.

"...and members of the Patrolmen's Benevolent Association handed out informational bulletins about opioid addiction at the Cypress Hills Community Center during last night..."

Milton turned back to the boy. "What's the matter, Freddy?"

"*Him,*" he said in a whisper.

The reporter was still speaking. *"NYPD officers who have saved lives with the opioid antidote Narcan were among those distributing the community safety bulletins to residents..."*

A uniformed officer was in shot, holding a sheaf of

leaflets in one hand and distributing them to a line of men and women with the other. He was black, in his early to mid-fifties, balding and had a beard that was shot through with silver.

Milton spoke quietly. "One of the men from earlier?"

Freddy swallowed hard and nodded.

"Are you sure?"

"It's him," Freddy said. "He was outside the restroom. I'm sure."

The news report ended and was replaced by a recruitment video.

"Don't say anything else," Milton said. "Don't mention it to anyone."

"I can't just... do nothing."

"That's exactly what you need to do—for now, anyway."

"But—"

"We can talk about it later," Milton said.

Detective Mackintosh came over to them. She had a set of car keys in her hand and had one arm through the sleeve of a thick jacket.

"Come on, then," she said. "I'll run you home."

PART II

MONDAY

32

P olanski looked at his watch. It was twelve-thirty. José Luis González had called him three and a half hours ago. Brooklyn to New Brunswick was not a difficult journey. It should have taken him only an hour to get over to the safe house. Polanski had warned him not to wait too long to set off, but even if he had taken an hour to pack a bag, he should have been here by now.

He looked around the apartment. It was simple and bland, with cheap and functional furniture and walls that still smelled of the whitewash that had been used to clean them up after the last occupant had moved out.

He switched off the lights, went outside and locked the door after him.

He took out his phone and stared at the screen. The last call had been from González, and there had been nothing since.

He called a contact at Central Booking on Schermerhorn Street.

"Has anything gone down in Brooklyn tonight? The Seven Five, maybe the Seven Seven?"

"The usual. What are you looking for, Detective?"

"Any homicides?"

"Hold on." Polanski could hear the tapping of keys. "Yes," the man said. "One homicide. Unidentified vic, male, thirty to forty."

"Latino?"

"That's right."

"Where?" Polanski pressed.

"Body was found in the restroom at Euclid Avenue station."

Polanski stood there in the cold, the phone held to his ear, a sickness in his gut. Euclid was the station that González would have used to start his journey to the safe house.

They had got to him first.

"Detective?"

Polanski ran his fingers through his hair.

"Detective? You still there?"

"Sorry," he said. "I'm here."

"You need anything else?"

"Yeah. Who's on the case?"

"Detective Mackintosh from the Seventy-Fifth."

Polanski thanked the man, ended the call and put his phone away. He stood outside the building for a moment, unmoving, the crisp air upon his face. *Shit. Shit, shit, shit.* Grimly, he did up his coat and walked across the lot to his car. He couldn't give up. He had come too far to do that. He was close to rooting out the corruption in the Seven Five. This was the proof. This murder, it was the proof that he was close. It was a setback, but that was it. He would just have to adapt.

33

Mackintosh led the way through the station and outside to the row of cars that were parked at right angles to the road. She aimed her key fob at a Hyundai Sonata, blipped the locks and invited them to get in. Milton went to the back of the car and opened the door for Freddy. The boy slid inside. Milton went around and opened the other door. He sat in the back, too.

Mackintosh started the engine and adjusted the rear-view mirror so that she could see them both. "Where you headed, Freddy?"

"Danforth Street."

"Up in Cypress Hills?"

"Uh-huh."

"What about you, Mr. Smith? That's the wrong way for you."

"I'll make my own way home once Freddy is inside."

"All right, then." She put the car into reverse and pulled out into the road. She switched to drive and set off, heading east on Sutter. The roads were quiet at this late hour, with just the occasional passer-by on the sidewalks.

"You been to the game tonight, Freddy?" she said as she turned north onto Atkins.

"Yeah," the kid said quietly.

"You get that ball there?"

"Uh-huh."

"He caught it," Milton said.

"From OBJ," Freddy added.

"After his TD? Gotta make you feel good."

Milton turned and saw him give a small smile.

She was a decent interrogator. She was establishing points of similarity between herself and the boy, common ground that she would use to build the foundation for the relationship that she would try to construct. Freddy was too young to see what she was doing. There was nothing wrong with her strategy—she was just doing her job, after all, and Milton had no reason to doubt her—but Freddy's admission that he recognised someone in the precinct made Milton uneasy about anyone there, including her. He would need to satisfy himself that she was on the level.

She turned onto the main thoroughfare of Atlantic Avenue.

"Listen to me, Freddy," she said. "Try not to let what happened spoil how you remember tonight, will you? You start thinking about it, you just get that ball and squeeze it tight until you remember the good stuff. You hear me?"

"Yes, ma'am."

"You can call me Mack," she said. "Everyone else does."

Mackintosh paused, still looking back in the mirror, but then she nodded and turned her gaze back to the road ahead. She turned onto Hemlock Street, turned left onto Danforth and then slowed down as she approached the address that Freddy had given her. "Ten, eight, six—here we are. Four. Come on, I'll see you to the door."

"I got it from here," said Milton.

She shook her head. "I'm coming, too."

Milton opened his door, stepped out and made his way around the car. He opened Freddy's door.

Mackintosh got out, too.

"Come on," Milton said to Freddy. "Let's get you inside."

Milton had not expected to return to Danforth Street. It was an odd alley that extended for two blocks west from Hemlock Street to Crescent Street south of Etna Street. The surface of the road had not been paved for many years and was pocked with uneven stretches and potholes that would have been deep enough to damage car wheels and unseat unwary cyclists. The drug den that he had put under observation was number nine. Milton was pleased to see that there was no sign that it was still being used for dealing; it looked as if his warning had been taken seriously.

Number four was right next to the elevated north–south stretch of the subway that linked the stations at Crescent Street and Cypress Hills. Milton had spent several hours outside it, and the details were still fresh in his mind. It was in poor condition, comprising an extended ground floor that abutted a three-storey building behind it. It had been carved into three separate properties: the first-floor addition, and then the second and third floors of the main building. Freddy made his way to the addition. It was accessed by way of a freshly painted red door that was set back a couple of feet behind a wire mesh fence. Dirty trash cans were lined up between the wall of the property and the fence, and a Dominican flag fluttered listlessly from behind one of the barred downstairs windows.

Freddy crossed the sidewalk and opened the gate in the wire fence that marked the boundary of the property. He had a key, and he used it to unlock the door.

He paused on the threshold, his hand on the handle.

"It's okay," Milton said.

Freddy didn't look back at him. He pressed down on the handle, opened the door and went inside.

"Hello?" Freddy called out.

There was a light on inside. Milton turned back to Mackintosh. The detective was in the doorway, waiting to come inside.

"Dad?" Freddy called.

The front door opened into a living room area. It was tidier inside than the exterior had promised. There was a leather couch and matching armchair, a low coffee table and a modest TV that had been placed on a wooden unit. The TV had been muted and left on, and a rerun of *Law & Order* was playing.

Freddy frowned and made his way through the living room to a corridor that accessed the rear of the property. Milton felt like an intruder, but he followed behind him.

The boy paused at a closed door. He tapped his fist against it. "Dad?"

Milton thought he heard something from inside.

Freddy put his hand on the handle and pushed the door open. He went inside.

Milton and Mackintosh waited.

"Oh no," he heard Freddy sigh.

Milton took a step inside. The stench of alcohol was pungent, and he had to resist the urge to gag. He saw empty twelve-ounce cans on the floor around an overflowing trash can. He recognised the black, green and orange design of Brooklyn Lager. There were at least ten of them.

"Dad," Freddy said.

Milton heard a grunt. He stayed in the doorway, reluctant to go any farther. It wasn't just that he didn't want to intrude, although that was part of it. More than that, he didn't want to see what he knew was just inside the door. Manny had fallen off the wagon, and Milton didn't want to see the results. He had always struggled with empathy—it was one of the characteristics that had made him so successful in his previous career, but disqualified him from having any semblance of a normal life now—and he knew he would have no idea how to react if he was asked to help.

"Wake up, Dad. Come on."

Freddy started to cry.

"Out of the way," Mackintosh said from behind Milton.

He clenched his fists. He couldn't ignore it any longer. He was going to have to take responsibility. He stepped into the room.

The room was lit by a single lamp that had been knocked over so that now it rested on the floor next to the bed. Its glow revealed a sorry sight. Manny was sprawled across the bed, surrounded by more empty cans. He was wearing boxer shorts and a white T-shirt that had been discoloured by beer that had been spilt onto it and then dried. Milton's attention was drawn to his legs, and, in particular, to the fact that his right was missing from the knee down. All that remained was a stump decorated with a pattern of puckered stitches. The prosthesis that had previously been hidden under his trousers had been abandoned by the side of the bed.

Freddy was beside his father, gently shaking him by the shoulders as tears washed down his cheeks.

"Come on, Dad. Wake up. I need to talk to you."

Manny grunted again.

Milton went around to the other side of the bed.

Mackintosh came into the room, too, but she stayed by the door.

Milton knelt down and put his hands on Manny's shoulders.

"I know you," the man slurred.

"That's right," he said. "It's John. From the meeting."

Manny blinked his eyes at the mention of the fellowship. His face passed through confusion to shame and then, finally, anger.

"What you doing in my house?"

"Freddy needs your help, Manny."

"That's right," he said, the words tumbling over one another. "Because I can't look after my own fucking boy, can I?"

Mackintosh cleared her throat. "Hello, sir."

He managed to get an arm beneath him and pushed himself into a sitting position. "Who are you?"

"I'm Detective Mackintosh."

"Police?" He swivelled back to look at Milton. "You brought the police into my house? I ain't done nothing wrong. Just had a couple drinks, that's all. There ain't no crime in that."

Manny swung himself around to the side and put down his left leg, pushing away from the bed. He was either too drunk to maintain his balance or he had forgotten that he wasn't wearing his prosthesis, because he immediately toppled forward and fell into a pile of clothes that had been discarded on the room's single wooden chair. He landed heavily, the chair's legs splaying out and snapping off.

"Dad!"

Milton knelt down, hooked Manny beneath the arms and hoisted him up. The man was a dead weight, the smell of booze pulsing out of him in an almost palpable wave that made Milton want to retch.

"I got you," Milton said, bracing his legs so that he might bear his weight.

"Get the fuck off me," he slurred.

Manny started to struggle. Milton grasped him tightly, afraid to drop him, and tried to walk him back to the bed.

Freddy put his hands over his face in horror and shame. "Dad!"

"Settle down, sir," Mackintosh said.

Milton allowed himself to be distracted. He glanced over at the boy and didn't notice as Manny drew back his fist. Milton turned back just as the punch landed. It wasn't a particularly powerful blow—Manny was much too disorientated for that—but it took Milton by surprise and he let go of him, dropping him back to the floor.

Milton stepped back, rubbing his nose.

Freddy hurried to his father. Manny was sprawled out on the floor, his arms braced on either side as he tried to push himself away.

"Get out of my house," Manny spat at Milton. "Get out!"

Mackintosh slipped by Milton so that she could put herself between him and Manny. Milton noticed that she had popped the retaining clip that held her service pistol in the shoulder holster she wore beneath her coat.

"It's all right," Milton said. "I'm fine. He hardly hit me. He's just—"

Manny tried to stand and lost his balance again. He fell into Mackintosh, his shoulder catching her on the side of the chin. She staggered back, and, as she regained her balance, her hand was on the butt of the pistol.

"Dad," Freddy pleaded. "Stop!"

"Don't get up, Mr. Blanco," Mackintosh said, her voice laced with iron.

Manny had fallen onto his backside with his back propped up against the side of the bed.

Freddy turned to Mackintosh. "I got this," the boy said. "You don't need to do this. I can look after him."

It was delivered with the dull acceptance of someone who was clearly used to finding his father in a state like this. Milton felt a flash of anger: Freddy needed his father badly, but it was Manny who would receive the help. Milton was angry and wanted to say something, until he realised that his anger was directed inward. He saw himself in Manny, and all the people that he had let down when he had drunk himself into similar situations. It reminded him of his own shame.

Mackintosh took her phone out of her pocket and dialled a number. "It's Detective Mackintosh. I'm going to need a patrol car at number four Danforth Street."

"Come on," Milton said. "Is that necessary?"

As he said it, he felt a warm sensation running from his right nostril down onto his lip. He reached up with his fingertips and touched the blood.

"Step back, please, Mr. Smith."

Milton backed into the doorway.

"Freddy," he said, "come here."

The boy reluctantly did as he asked.

"Do you have any other family nearby?"

"My mom. She's in Queens."

"You'll probably have to stay with her tonight—is that going to be okay?"

"She hardly sees me no more," Freddy said.

"But she'll let you stay?"

"I guess. What'll they do with my dad?"

"I think they'll take him to the precinct until he sobers up," Milton said.

Freddy looked up at Milton's face, pointing at his nose. "You won't..."

"Press charges?" he finished for him. "No. Of course not. Nothing bad is going to happen. They'll let him sleep it off and he'll be out in the morning."

Freddy exhaled with something akin to relief. "You're sure?"

"Positive. Can you call your mother?"

He nodded.

"Go on, then."

Freddy left the bedroom and went into the living space. There was a cordless phone on the table. He took it and dialled a number. The call went unanswered for twenty seconds—Milton guessed that Freddy's mother was asleep —before he started to speak. He apologised for waking her and then explained what had happened and that he needed her to come over.

Milton saw flashing lights outside, the pulsing blue suffusing the thin curtains. He heard doors open and close and the sound of footsteps approaching the door. There came a heavy knocking and a voice barked out, "NYPD. Open up."

Milton crossed the room and opened the door. There were two male officers standing outside; they both had their pistols drawn and held ready.

"Everything is fine," Milton said. "Detective Mackintosh

is in the bedroom at the back of the house. The owner of the house is drunk, but she has it under control. So you two can take it easy."

"Excuse me," said the man in the front, bumping Milton aside as he went into the house and hurried to the rear.

The second officer stayed by the door. "Who are you?"

"My name is Smith," Milton said. "I came here with Detective Mackintosh."

The man nodded toward Milton's bloody nose. "How'd that happen?"

"Just a misunderstanding. It's nothing."

"That right? You stay where I can see you."

Milton nodded and turned away from him. Freddy was still talking on the telephone, but the conversation was coming to a close. His cheeks were red and his eyes were wet when he finally finished the call and put the telephone back into the cradle.

"Okay?" Milton asked him.

"She's coming over now. She's mad."

There was a shout from the bedroom and the second officer hurried to the open door.

There was a pen and a pad of paper on the table next to the telephone's cradle. Milton took the pen and wrote down his telephone number.

"If you need me, I'm here. Okay?"

"What about the police? What do I do?"

"They'll speak to you tomorrow."

"And the man I saw? The one in the video?"

"Don't mention it to anyone. I wouldn't even mention it to your father. Let me think about it."

"But you don't think I can trust the cops?"

"We need to work out who we can and can't trust."

Mackintosh and the two officers now emerged from the

bedroom with Manny between them. His hands had been cuffed behind him and his prosthetic had not been attached; he was hopping, supported on either side.

"What about my boy?" Manny slurred. "I gotta look after him."

"Mom's coming to get me," Freddy said.

The news seemed to suck all of the fight out of Manny, and he slumped forward. The officers changed position so that they could bear his weight. "Fuck," he breathed. He looked over at his son. "Don't listen to her, Freddy. You hear me? Whatever she says, all the poison, you don't listen to any of it."

The boy looked away.

"I'll stay until she shows up," Mackintosh said. "He'll be fine." She nodded to the officers and they proceeded to the door, Manny hopping impotently between them. Mackintosh turned to Milton. "I'd like you to go now, please."

"What about Manny?"

"Drunk tank until he sobers up." She indicated Milton's nose. "You going to do anything about that?"

"No," he said. "It was a misunderstanding. Just make sure he's looked after."

She nodded and indicated that he should make his way to the open door. Milton did as he was told. He glanced across at Freddy. The boy looked at him for a moment and then looked down.

Milton stepped outside.

35

It took Milton twenty minutes to find a cab and then another thirty to get home. He gazed out at the deeper darkness out to sea, at the few lights that blinked on ships that were passing out into Jamaica Bay and the broad ocean beyond.

He allowed his thoughts to drift back to what had turned out to be a much more momentous day than he could have anticipated. He kept returning to the boy. Freddy was obviously a smart kid, but the events of the night had stripped away the premature ageing that had been bestowed upon him by his life on the street. The sass and lip were necessary for a childhood spent in this part of Brooklyn but, at the end of it all, they were props designed to mask the fact that he was a thirteen-year-old kid. He was not equipped to deal with the trauma of finding a bloodied murder victim, but, then again, what child would be equipped to handle that?

And then, when he needed his father to help him navigate the aftermath of everything that had happened that night, Manny had not been there. He had stood up his own son to go to a bar and drink himself into a stupor. Milton knew why: Manny was drowning out the voice in his head that told him that he wasn't good enough. Milton would have been angry but for the fact that he heard the same voice, and that his resistance to its siren song was hard won and precarious, always to be defended.

That didn't make things any fairer for Freddy.

Milton wondered, again, whether he bore any responsibility for what had happened. He had tried to do the right thing with the dealer in the shooting gallery on Danforth Street, but now he worried that he had emasculated Manny. He worried that he had compounded the slight by replacing the stolen sneakers that Manny would not have been able to afford to replace. Manny had fallen off the wagon because of the things that he had done. His intentions had been good, but the consequences were damaging. Milton found that he felt stupid and culpable.

He had already decided, but, as he probed the nose that still stung a little from Manny Blanco's drunken swing, he nodded and made it certain: he would help Freddy and, if he would let him, he would help Manny, too. He would protect them both and do whatever it took to make things right.

The driver eventually turned west and arrived in Coney Island.

"Where you want?"

"West 24th," he said.

The driver turned off Mermaid Avenue and Milton directed him to the other side of the road. He paid him and stepped out into the cold. The air was fresh and he could taste the salt. A jet passed high overhead, its lights winking in an endless pattern. There was no one else around: no traffic, and no one on the street. He looked at his watch. Two in the morning. He suddenly felt drained, as if the last drop of energy had been poured out of him. He needed to sleep.

The building loomed high overhead. It was ugly and brutal, but it was in the part of town where he wanted to be and it was cheap enough for him to afford without exhausting all of his funds. It suited him well. He pulled up the collar of his jacket and trudged across the sidewalk, around the perimeter of the children's playground that was littered with debris and dotted with dog excrement, and made his way inside. He had work later. He needed his bed.

36

M ilton awoke at seven. He could have done with more sleep. He came around to a familiar aching in his bones, more and more common when he didn't get his hours in. There had been a time when he would have been able to go out and drink until four or five and wake up feeling reasonably refreshed after just two or three hours of sleep. Those days were long, long gone. There was no way around it: he was middle aged now, and the aches and pains were the badges and banners of his advancing years.

He had to get to work this morning, but he needed his exercise first. He got up, took his running gear from the back of the radiator where he had left it to dry, and pulled it on. He pressed his earbuds into his ears and put his phone into his pocket. He took the stairs to the ground floor and stepped outside. It was bright and clear and bitter once again; if anything, even colder than it had been the day before.

Milton set off, trusting that the exertion would warm him up. He headed south, following his usual route, and made his way to the boardwalk. He skipped through the music on his phone until he found Pendulum and, using the throb of the track to pace himself, he picked up speed.

The run was the same as always: Milton saw the tractor on the beach and nodded a hello to the old woman with her toy dog. He was coming up on the Aquarium when he saw a man leaning against the railing, looking back along the boardwalk in his direction.

The man stepped into Milton's path and held up a hand.

Milton slowed to a walk. He appraised the man as he approached him: he was the same height as Milton and of similar build. His hair was swept away from his forehead in neat waves, and his salt-and-pepper goatee was carefully clipped. He wore a black overcoat, a thick woollen scarf and leather gloves.

"Excuse me," the man said. "Could I have a word?"

Milton stopped and removed his earbuds. "Who are you?"

"My name is Fedorov."

"Do we know each other?"

The man shook his head. "We do not. But you are the man who went into the sea to rescue a girl yesterday morning? Around this time?"

His accent was unmistakably Eastern European: he rolled the R in *rescue*, and the consonants at the end of his words were not voiced.

Milton looked at him more carefully. "Yes," he said. "I am."

"I am her father," the man said. He turned and pointed to the bench by the railing. "Please. Can we sit?"

Fedorov smiled, his arm extended toward the bench. Milton was just getting started with his run and would have preferred to continue. He wasn't interested in being rewarded for what he had done, but he also did not want to appear rude. He decided to accede. It wouldn't take long, and then he would start again. He nodded his head, went to the bench and sat down.

Fedorov sat next to him. "What is your name?"

"John."

"You run here every morning?"

"I do," Milton said.

"The cold weather—it must wake you up."

"Something like that." Milton would get cold if he didn't get started again soon. "What's your daughter's name?"

"Nataliya," Fedorov said.

"How is she?"

"She spent the night in the hospital," he said. "It is a precaution. She had mild hypothermia. They say that if she had been in the water for another ten minutes, she would have died from the cold."

"She wouldn't have lasted for another ten minutes," Milton said. "She was underwater when I got to her."

"Did you see what happened?"

"It was a riptide. It was strong. I'm not surprised she was struggling. I'm a good swimmer, and I could barely make it back. And it was very cold."

Fedorov stared out to sea. "We have winter swimming at home. There is a contest every year. Teams come from all over: Feodosiya, Yalta, Salem, Sevastopol, Balaklava. I used to enter with my brothers. My daughter saw that New York will have a winter swimming contest in January. She wants to enter. She wants me to be proud of her. I tell her not to go into the sea here when there are no lifeguards, but she ignores me. She has learned a harsh lesson. She will not ignore me again."

"Where's home?" Milton said. "Russia?"

A flicker of displeasure passed across his face. "No. I am from the Crimea. We came here after Putin stole it from us."

It was obvious that the subject was a tender one; Fedorov's passion was just below the surface and ready to bubble over.

Milton wasn't interested in the effort of choosing his words carefully. He was getting cold, and he wanted to continue with his exercise. He stood. "I'm glad she's okay."

Fedorov stood, too. "I would like to thank you properly."

"That's not necessary. Really. I'm just pleased to have been able to help."

"No, John. I insist. Please—I own Café Valentin. It is on the boardwalk." He turned and pointed to the west. "You head that way, toward West Brighton. My wife would like to cook for you. And my daughter would like to thank you herself. Please, John. Say you will come."

Milton thought of the things he wanted to do today; he thought of Manny and Freddy Blanco and being with them so that he could offer his help, if they would have it. But Fedorov's gratitude was sincere, and, since he had quit the drink, Milton had always tried to open himself up to new opportunities and experiences. It would be churlish of him to say no.

"Thank you," he said. "That's kind. When are you thinking?"

"Tomorrow evening?"

Milton had no plans. "That's fine."

Fedorov extended his hand and Milton took it. "Café Valentin," he said. "That way. You can't miss it. Shall we say eight o'clock?"

"Perfect."

"Then we will see you then, John."

P olanski slotted his car into the row of parked vehicles lined up outside the entrance to the precinct building. He switched off the engine and sat in the car for a moment, looking at the building and thinking about what it represented. He looked at the letters above the entrance doors: 75th Precinct, Police Department, City of New York. The letters were made from aluminium, and they shone in the harsh morning sunlight. It was as if the department had chosen something that glittered and gleamed in an attempt to distract attention from the iniquity that had characterised this place for so long. But the corruption was still there. Polanski lived in that world. He waded through the same sewage day after day. And he knew: the Seven Five hadn't changed at all.

He had known for months that the precinct was rotten. The NYPD had made progress in clearing out the corrupt officers that had blighted its reputation in the 1990s, but it was a fight that required constant vigilance and it was beginning to look very much as if that fight was being lost. East Brooklyn was better now than it had been for years.

Polanski had seen video footage from twenty years ago when Pitkin and Atlantic and the other streets had been blighted, with buildings that had been allowed to dissolve into piles of masonry in images that would not have been out of place in blitzed London. But Brooklyn had been revived in the years since. The artists came first for the cheap rent, businesses followed because the artists were cool, and then, finally, commuters from Manhattan arrived because they could get their chai lattes and organic sandwiches. The area had gone from dangerous to hip, and now, these days, it was close to bland homogeneity.

That did not mean that the criminal element had moved out. The dealers and crews had become more professional, embedding themselves within legitimate businesses and adapting their offerings to better suit a new clientele with deeper pockets. Heroin and crack could still be had, but there was greater demand for blow and meth. Spice— synthetic marijuana more potent than heroin—was becoming popular. The industry was insidious, less blatant than before but with tentacles that reached across the district.

And, when there was a significant criminal presence, there would always be temptation. Cops who were not paid enough to insulate themselves from the possibilities available to those who were prepared to look the other way would always be vulnerable to it. And the opportunities that came with a gun and a badge opened up even wider possibilities for those more avaricious officers who were prepared to actively seek out illicit opportunities.

Polanski's unit had only recently finished an investigation into half a dozen corrupt cops in the neighbouring Seven Seven. The affair had been embarrassing for the NYPD, and even though the mayor had said all the right

things in public as the cops were convicted following a
three-month trial, his private remarks had made it clear that
he did not want to see a repeat prosecution. The man was a
politician, and, like all politicians, he had one eye on his
legacy and the other on how he might get himself re-
elected. The word had filtered out from the commissioner to
Internal Affairs and then to the rank and file. Polanski had
watched with dismay as reports of corruption had
increased. He knew why: the bad cops were gambling that
they had a few months' immunity until the next crackdown,
and, until then, they were going to take advantage.

Polanski had seen it, too. He had been told to soft-pedal
his investigation into the Seven Five, but he wasn't prepared
to do that. He kept digging. He kept turning over rocks and
found more evidence that there was a cabal of corrupt officers who were almost indistinguishable from the Acosta
gang that they were protecting.

And then he had found a man who was prepared to go
on the stand and testify to the truth of what was happening
in the district. A man who was deep within the Acosta crew,
a man who was the bridge between the Dominican gang
and the corrupt officers. José Luis González was going to
name the officers who were involved.

And now he was dead.

Polanski had driven from the safe house straight over to
Euclid Avenue. The subway station had been closed, with a
police cruiser and a CSI van outside. Polanski had been able
to get down into the restroom before the crime scene techs
had finished with their work. The body was still there,
sprawled out in a pool of fast-congealing blood. They had
already been able to identify González from his driver's
license, but Polanski had confirmed it.

They loaded the body into the back of the van and took

it away to the morgue at Kings County Hospital. Polanski had watched it go, and had driven back home to Washingtonville for what little sleep he could snatch before the sun came up again.

A car pulled up into the space next to Polanski. He pulled down the visor and checked his reflection in the mirror. He was tired, and it showed. There was no time to worry about how he looked. He knew that González had been killed by the police—either at their hand or at their behest—and the longer they had to cover up what they had done, the more difficult it would be to follow the evidence back to them.

He opened the door and stepped outside. It was cold. The forecast was for another freezing day, and Polanski shivered as he shut and locked the door. He crossed the sidewalk and went inside.

Polanski went to the desk sergeant and asked whether Detective Mackintosh was at the precinct yet, but, before the sergeant could answer, he glanced up as a woman wearing a leather jacket came down the steps into the main room.

"Hey, Mack," the sergeant called out.

The woman paused and then diverted to the desk. "What's up?"

"Got someone who wants to see you."

Polanski raised his hand in greeting. "I'm Aleksander Polanski."

"Yeah?"

"I'm from Internal Affairs."

She couldn't prevent the curl in her lip. "That right?"

"Can I talk to you, please?"

She shrugged. "Sure. Shoot."

He shook his head. "Not here."

"Why not?"

She was bubbling with hostility; it wasn't unusual, and Polanski had long since learned not to take it seriously. They called IAB the Rat Squad. Attitude from the rank and file came with the job.

"You got the homicide at Euclid?"

She nodded.

"The vic was one of my CIs. He was coming in last night."

Polanski watched Mackintosh's face; she understood what he had said, and, more importantly, she understood the implications. Polanski was IAB, charged with investigating dirty cops. González was his informant, which meant he must have been passing information about dirty cops. And then he had been murdered.

She shook her head and sighed. "Fuck."

"Yeah," Polanski said. "Fuck."

She unzipped her jacket. "What are you doing now?"

"Nothing."

"There's a possible witness," she said. "A kid. I'm going to go and see him now. You want, you could ride up to Cypress Hills with me and tell me whatever it is you think I need to know."

38

Milton showered and changed into his work gear. He went back down to the street, got onto his bike, and rode north.

Milton had worked at the restaurant ever since he had arrived in Brooklyn. He needed the money, but it was more than that. It lent structure and order to his day. His experience had taught him that he needed a routine. It was an important buttress against boredom; when he was bored, he had more time to think about the things that he had done in his past. Those thoughts always led him back to pain and the drink that he had relied upon to salve it. He had worked as a cook before, in London and in Juarez. He had seen the help wanted ad for this job on Craigslist, had applied and— after a perfunctory interview on the phone—had been given the job.

The restaurant was on the corner of Coney Island Avenue and Kathleen Place. It was called Red Square and was the first in what the owner rather optimistically hoped would eventually be a chain. It majored in Eastern European cookery, including dishes from Russia, the

Ukraine, Uzbekistan and the rest of the Caucasus. The menu was full of choices that were intended to be authentic. Guests were welcomed with glasses of *kvass*—the fermented beverage made from pumpernickel bread that was also present in a summer soup called *okroshka*—before they were shown to their tables and invited to choose from all manner of smoked fish, salads, hot and cold soups, and robust stews cooked with beef or pork.

Milton parked his bike on Kathleen Place and went into the restaurant through the rear door. He took off his jacket, changed into his smock and made his way to the kitchen.

The chef-patron was a man named Vadim, who made much of a life that had seen him emigrate to the United States from Moscow by way of China and Uzbekistan. His original plan to offer higher-end dining at prices that matched had been shelved by lack of interest from the clientele, and he had fallen back upon the ploy of offering plentiful food at cheap prices. The weekday lunch specials started at five dollars for a main course and twelve dollars for a choice of three plates.

Milton was in charge of the *samsa*, pastries that were stuffed full of chicken and vegetables. He also had the *pelmeni* dumplings, pork and lamb fillings wrapped in unleavened dough. He went into the pantry to collect the ingredients that he would need and then returned to his station.

Vadim was waiting for him at his counter.

"Smith," he said, "you are late."

"No, I'm not. I was here two minutes early."

Vadim dismissed Milton's rebuttal with a wave of his hand. "We have busy day," he said with gruff disdain. "Wedding party coming in at noon and we have man down."

Milton knew all about that. The woman who worked the

station next to him had quit in tears last week. Her name was Natalia; she was an emigre from St. Petersburg, slight and pretty and with a mischievous glint to her smile that Milton found very attractive. Milton had watched as Vadim had continually talked her down, denigrating the quality of her cooking and, eventually, even the way that she looked. One of the other chefs had explained that Natalia had turned down Vadim's clumsy advances and now she was being punished for it. The last straw had been an explosive volley of insults as Vadim had tasted the perfectly good *okroshka* that Natalia had delivered to the pass. She had turned her back in tears and started back to her counter; Vadim had thrown a plate at her, the crockery narrowly missing her head and shattering into pieces as it caught the edge of the range. Milton had been ready to intercede, but Natalia had caught his eye and shaken her head. She had taken off her smock, set it on the counter, and left. She hadn't returned; Milton didn't think that she would. If Vadim had any shame at the way he had treated her, he didn't show it. Instead, he had railed at how it was impossible to find staff upon whom he could rely. He delivered these declarations with one eye on Milton, as if daring him to react. Milton did not, although he was sorely tempted.

Milton put the ingredients down on the counter. Vadim was still watching him, his brawny arms folded across his chest. It was as if he was looking for a confrontation.

"You standing there watching me isn't going to make me go faster," Milton said.

Vadim snorted derisively, but he took the hint. He turned and went out to the front of the house.

Milton took a knife from the block and started to dice an onion.

39

Mackintosh led the way out of the station house and down to the line of cars outside. She blipped the lock on a Sonata, indicated that Polanski should get in, and went around to the driver's side. Polanski opened the door and sat down. He looked across the cabin as Mackintosh opened the driver's side door and lowered herself into the seat.

Polanski had never come across Mackintosh before. That, he thought, was a good sign. Notoriety within IAB was not something that a decent, ethical detective would encourage. He guessed that she was in her late thirties. She was attractive, with thick brown hair that she tucked behind her ears to fall all the way down past her shoulders. She wore hardly any make-up, and her eyes were bracketed top and bottom by thick lashes. He would have liked to see her smile, but that looked unlikely; her face was set in a scowl as she reached to the dash to start the engine.

"I don't want to step on any toes," Polanski began, "but there's one thing we need to get clear right at the start: this is my case."

"The fuck it is," said Mackintosh as she turned onto Essex Street and headed north. "It's got nothing to do with you."

"Yes, it does. González was my CI. He was coming in last night."

"So?"

"He had evidence about officers from the Seven Five working with the Acosta gang."

"Bullshit," she said.

"He has evidence of officers from this precinct taking money from Acosta."

"Who?"

"He was going to tell me last night."

She stopped for the lights at the corner of Essex and Atlantic.

Polanski pressed, "I'm taking this investigation."

The lights went to green and she pulled out, turning right. "No, you're not," she said. "It's a homicide on my patch. I got the call. It's my case. You want me to take it up the chain?"

Polanski exhaled. "Knock yourself out. We both know what'll happen if you do that."

They drove in silence, turning onto Crescent and heading north toward Cypress Hills. Polanski felt his temper bubbling and distracted himself by looking out of the window. East New York had worked hard to improve itself since the nineties, but it was still a dive. Fulton Street was still an easy place to score drugs, and, although the murder rate had been drastically cut, it was still one of the most dangerous areas in New York for mugging and burglary. Polanski had worked a number of cases in the Seven Five and the neighbouring Seven Seven, and he knew from experience just how much temptation was laid in the paths of the men and women who tried to police it.

"Look," Polanski said. "How about this? We compromise. We do it together. It's your case, but I tag along. And you keep me in the loop all the way through."

She said nothing. They passed beneath the elevated track of the J Line and then turned right onto Danforth Street. Mackintosh pulled over at the side of the road and switched off the engine.

"What do you say?" Polanski pressed. "You agree?"

She turned to face him. "Fine," she said. "But I wanna tell you something first. My brother was a cop. He loved it. I say 'was', past tense, because he was investigated by IAB after a hooker he arrested said he planted drugs on her. He didn't. I know my brother—he was a good cop and he didn't do that. She set him up. But they investigated him anyway, decided he did what she said he did, and had him fired."

"I don't know the case. But if we did investigate him—"

"I haven't finished," she said. "You want to know what happened next? He signed up to be a security guard at Macy's, but he hated it. So one day, just before Christmas, he drove out into the woods at the back of his place and ate his gun."

Polanski's heart dropped. "I'm sorry—"

"So you can understand," she spoke over him, "how I couldn't be less thrilled about the prospect of running my investigation in tandem with someone from the Rat Squad."

Polanski felt like responding, but he bit his tongue. There was no profit in getting into an argument with her. He gave it a moment and then said, "Tell me why we're here," instead.

"There was a witness last night. A local kid—Freddy Blanco—he found the body."

"He see anything?"

"Two guys outside the restroom just before he went in and found the dead guy."

"So he saw the killers?"

"Sounds pretty likely. But he's a kid. Thirteen. Couldn't interview him last night, so I said I'd talk to him this morning."

"All right."

"There's a bit more," she said. "There was a second witness. An English guy—says his name is John Smith, but I'm going to double-check that. He was at the station too, went into the restroom, saw the body and found Freddy. I interviewed him last night. Didn't see anything. Turns out Smith knows Freddy's father—they go to AA together. The old man wasn't answering his phone, so I brought the kid and Smith here. Blanco senior had been drinking all night and was totally out of it. He went for Smith, took a swing at him. He spent the night in the drunk tank and Freddy went to his mom's."

"But he's here now?"

"Yes, and Manny—that's his old man. I called earlier. They let him out at six."

Polanski reached for the door handle. "Let's do it."

They both stepped out into the cold.

"Let me do the talking," Mackintosh said.

"No," Polanski said. "This is my case, too. You can lead, but if I have questions, I'm gonna ask them."

Mackintosh looked as if she was about to argue, but she did not. Instead, she set off, locking the car with a casually aimed blip from the key fob. She crossed the sidewalk and opened the gate.

40

Mackintosh knocked on the door. Polanski waited behind her, close enough to hear the sound of approaching footsteps.

The door opened to reveal a man. He was dishevelled, wearing a stained T-shirt and a creased pair of cargo pants. His eyes were bloodshot and he smelled of alcohol.

"Yes?" he said.

"Hello," Mackintosh said. "You remember me, Manny?"

He nodded.

"How you feeling?"

"Like shit." He reached up and scrubbed his eyes with the heels of his hands. "Look," he said. "I'm sorry about last night. I don't remember much of it, but Freddy told me. I've been working hard to stay clean and sober, but I relapsed."

"You don't have to apologise to me," Mackintosh said. "It's your boy you let down."

"I know it," he said. "I feel awful. It's not gonna happen again."

Mackintosh gestured with her hand. "This is Detective Polanski," she said.

Manny nodded.

"Is Freddy here?"

"Yes."

"You kept him off school?"

He nodded again.

"Could we come in and talk to him?"

Manny stepped aside to let them both in. He was fidgety. Polanski noticed the beads of sweat on his brow and the way he clenched and unclenched his fists.

"We won't be long," Mackintosh said with a soothing smile as she led the way inside. "Where is he?"

"In his room."

"Has he said anything to you about what happened last night?"

"A little. Is it true?"

"The murder? Yes, it is. He found the body."

"Jesus," Manny said. "I should've been with him. He shouldn't have to..."

"There's no point beating yourself up about it," Mackintosh said. "It happened. The best thing we can do now is get his statement. I just need to speak to him so I can understand what he saw. Once that's done, we'll leave you both in peace."

"But if there's a trial? Won't he have to testify?"

"There's a long way between where we are now and a trial."

Manny Blanco fetched his son.

Polanski looked over at the boy. He had taken a seat opposite them and was looking down at the floor.

Mackintosh took out a digital recorder. "I'm going to tape the conversation—is that all right, Manny?"

He nodded.

"Freddy? That okay?"

The boy nodded, too.

Mackintosh thumbed the recorder on and spoke into the microphone. "This is Detective Mackintosh with Detective Polanski. Interview location is Number 4 Danforth Avenue, which is the home of interviewee Freddy Blanco. Also present is his father, Manny Blanco. Both have indicated that they agree to my recording this interview." She laid the recorder on the table between them. "All right, Freddy," Mackintosh said. "Just for the record: where had you been last night?"

"I went to the Meadowlands. The Giants game."

Mackintosh evidently decided that they could dispense with most of the evening and cut straight to the most important moments. "You were coming back home afterwards. You took the train down to Euclid, where you got off. Then you stopped off at the bathroom. That right?"

Freddy nodded.

"Can you speak for the tape?"

"Yes," Freddy said.

"Why don't you tell me and Detective Polanski what happened next."

"I went in, used the bathroom, then I left."

"And then?"

"There was a guy... the guy..."

"The victim?" Mackintosh finished for him.

"Yes," he said. "He came in just as I was leaving. I bumped into him."

"What was he doing?"

"He looked like he was sick. He went over to the basin and threw up."

"Then?"

"I left."

"Did you see anyone else?"

"Two men."

"Get a look at them?"

"One black and the other one white. They were coming into the station."

"Go on."

"I had a football with me—I'd been to see the Giants. I left it in the stall so I went back to get it."

"How far did you get before you realised?"

"I was on the street."

"So how long before you went back?"

"Two or three minutes?"

"All right. Keep going."

"I went back inside, went through the gate and back to the restroom. The same two guys I saw earlier were there."

"They see you?"

"I don't think so."

"You get a look at them?"

"Not really. The black guy was older. Had white in his hair—the same as his beard."

"The other one?"

"He was inside, then he came out. White. Younger. That's all."

"That's a good start. Did you see their faces?"

He paused. "Not really. Didn't get a good look."

"So you think you'd recognise them again?"

"I don't know. I can't..." The words trailed off.

"It's okay. We don't need to worry about that now. Keep going."

He stopped, swallowing on a dry throat.

"Go on—what happened next?"

"I went back inside. I saw the guy. I..."

"Then?" she said.

"I didn't know what to do. I was scared. I thought the two men might come back. I couldn't move. I just stood there."

"For how long?"

"Don't know. A minute? Maybe longer."

"And then?"

"Mr. Smith came in."

"Yes," Mackintosh said. "John Smith."

Polanski noticed that Manny flinched at the mention of the name and wondered what had happened here last night.

"I spoke to him," Mackintosh said. "What did he do after he found you?"

"Took me outside. We went to the token booth and told the woman what happened. She called the cops."

Polanski looked over at Mackintosh and raised an eyebrow; she nodded in return and he took over.

"Let's just go back to the two men," Polanski said. "You didn't really see either of them?"

Freddy left a beat. "No."

"You absolutely sure about that?"

"I only really saw the black guy." He spoke firmly now, as if his previous hesitation had been an aberration.

"Would you remember him if you saw him again?"

"Don't know," he said. "Maybe."

"Because I might ask you to take a look at a few photographs if that's okay? Not today, but maybe tomorrow. You can tell me if any of the photographs I show you look like the guys you saw. You think you could do that?"

"Okay."

"You all done?" Manny asked.

"You got anything else?" Mackintosh said to Polanski.

He shook his head.

"Then we're done," Mackintosh answered. "For now. But I'd like Freddy to come to the precinct house this afternoon so that I can take a full statement. Do you think you could bring him along?"

"Yes," he said.

"All right, then. Thanks for answering my questions. You've been brave, Freddy."

The boy nodded, but didn't reply.

Manny showed them to the door.

"About last night..." he started.

"Forget it," Mackintosh said. "Smith said you go to meetings?"

"Yeah."

"Then get back to them again. Stop drinking. You've got a kid who needs you. Don't fuck it up like that again. You hear me? We good?"

Manny Blanco nodded.

"Bring him to the precinct this afternoon. Four o'clock. I'll see you then."

She turned, opened the gate and headed for the car. Polanski followed. He glanced back; Manny had already closed the door.

Polanski got into the Sonata next to Mackintosh.

"What do you think?" she asked him.

"About the kid? He's scared."

Mackintosh nodded. "That's not unreasonable. He found a dead guy; probably lucky he didn't get killed himself. I'd be scared too."

"What about the father?" Polanski asked.

"I'd say he was repentant," she said.

"What happened last night?"

She allowed herself a smile. "He was out of his mind. Punched Smith in the face. I doubt he can remember a thing."

"So what do we do?" he asked. "You think we need to call social services?"

Mackintosh shrugged. "No," she said. "I've seen junkies and alcoholics before; usually they don't give a shit about anything other than themselves and where they're gonna get their next drink from. He wasn't like that. He was upset. And the house was neat and tidy. It was clean. I had time to look around last night: they had food in the fridge." She glanced across. "What would you do?"

"The same. I'd give him a chance to show he's serious about looking after his kid. Have another heart-to-heart with him when he comes in. Make up your mind then."

She nodded. "You're right. You wanna sit in?"

"If I'm back in time."

"Where are you gonna go?"

"I want to speak to Smith."

Mackintosh took Polanski back to the precinct so that he could pick up his car. He set off again, driving south on the Shore Parkway, gazing out at the grey expanse of water. He'd been to Coney Island with his kids in the summer, but it was winter now and everything was different. The sky was bleak, with a vault of iron cloud punctuated with openings of powder blue that were quickly covered over as the clouds rolled across. There was a little passing traffic and the occasional pedestrian on the sidewalks on either side of the broad avenues.

He checked the GPS for directions and parked on Coney

Island Avenue between an Enterprise car rental franchise and a business that rented ugly stretch Hummers for weddings and other occasions. It was raining as he stepped out of his car, a persistent drizzle of the kind that threatened to seep into the fabric of his clothes and chill his bones. He didn't have an umbrella, and he cursed his forgetfulness as he pulled up the collar of his jacket to provide a little protection from the elements. The forecaster on WNYC had predicted snow tomorrow, but, as Polanski glanced up into the rain, he wondered whether the prediction might have been a day too late. It felt cold enough to snow right now.

The restaurant was fifteen blocks from the sea, but the air was heavy with the smell of salt. Polanski made his way along the street, avoiding the attention of a huckster in a fur coat and a rabbit hat who was offering a black goop that he promised was caviar from a foldable outdoor table.

Red Square wasn't impressive. The restaurant looked pitiful: the owner had tried to bring Russian influence to bear, but his budget hadn't stretched far enough to do it properly. The sign looked authentic, with Cyrillic flourishes on the letters, but everything else looked gaudy and trashy. There was a fibreglass statue of Lenin next to the entrance, but the local seagulls had signalled their disdain for it with a splattering of droppings that no one had ever bothered to remove.

Polanski stepped beneath the building's canopy and looked through the dusty windows. The place was empty save for a cleaner, who was nonchalantly running a vacuum cleaner between the tables. Polanski tried the door. It was open.

He went inside.

41

Milton was busy. Vadim had done a deal on two large sacks of beetroot and he wanted the vegetables to be turned into *borscht* that could be frozen before they could spoil. Milton had peeled and boiled two big bags of potatoes, sautéed carrots and onions until they were soft, shredded six cabbages and then added everything to a pot to cook. He had washed and boiled the beets and now he was peeling and slicing them into match- sticks that he could add to the soup. He had plastic gloves on his hands to prevent the beets from staining his fingers purple.

The doors to the kitchen opened and a man Milton did not recognise came inside. He was shorter than average, with russet-coloured hair that was thinning at the crown. He had a well-groomed ginger beard that was flecked with white, and wore a pair of spectacles with oval frames that looked both expensive and a little prissy. He wore a suit and was carrying a rucksack over his shoulder.

"I'm looking for Mr. Smith," the man called out.

Milton took off the gloves and went over.

"Yes?"

Vadim turned to him with a sour expression on his face.

"You're Smith?" the man said.

"That's right," Milton said.

"Who are you?" Vadim asked, asserting his ownership of the kitchen—and the people who worked there—with typically arrogant bluster.

"Detective Polanski," the man said. "NYPD. Who are you?"

Vadim paused. "I am owner," he said, but with a little less of the bombast.

"I'd like to talk to Mr. Smith," Polanski said.

"Fine," Vadim said. He turned to Milton. "Finish *borscht* after. You make time up over lunch."

"Can we go somewhere quieter?" Polanski said to Milton.

"This way," Milton said.

There was a covered alley at the back of the restaurant. Milton opened the door and indicated that Polanski should go through. He followed, closing the door behind him. They kept the trash cans in the alley. The garbage hadn't been collected for several days, and the air was funky with the smell of rotting food. Milton was able to ignore the stench, but he could see that Polanski was taking some time to adjust.

"Christ," he complained.

Milton took out his cigarettes and lighter. He offered the pack to Polanski, but he declined. Milton took one out of the pack, put it to his lips and lit up.

"This is about last night?" Milton asked.

"That's right."

"I spoke to Detective Mackintosh. Are you working with her?"

"Sort of. Mackintosh is in homicide."

"And you're not?"

"I'm Internal Affairs."

Milton stifled his surprise; he drew down on his cigarette, turned his head and exhaled into the alley. His immediate thought was what Freddy had told him last night: that one of the men he had seen was a cop.

"What does Internal Affairs have to do with this?" he asked.

"Can't tell you that, Mr. Smith. I'm looking into what happened last night. That's all I can say."

Milton could tell that there was no point in pressing him too hard. "You want me to go over it all again?" he said instead.

"Not all of it," Polanski said. "I've read your statement. There are just a few things I wanted to circle back on. That okay?"

"It's fine. Ask whatever you need."

"You saw the body?"

"Yes."

"What were you doing there?"

"What do you think? It's a restroom, Detective."

"And you were just passing through the station?"

"I was coming back from the Giants game."

"Same as Freddy?" Polanski said.

"Yes," Milton said. "Have you spoken to him?"

Polanski nodded. "This morning."

"Was his father there?"

"Yes. I understand he took a swing at you."

Milton reached up to touch the bruise on his face. "It was nothing," Milton said. "Was Freddy okay with his mother?"

"As far as I know. She brought him home this morning when his old man got out of the drunk tank."

Milton probed gently, aware that he was asking the questions and that that wouldn't last forever. "What did Freddy say?"

The detective wrinkled his nose at the continuing stench. "Ah, fuck it," he said, gesturing to Milton's cigarette. "I will have one. Anything to take the smell away."

Milton took his pack from his pocket and gave it to Polanski. The detective took a cigarette and Milton lit it for him.

"The kid," Milton said, prompting as delicately as he could. "What did he say?"

"Can't tell you that," Polanski rebuffed.

"He had a rough night," Milton said, still trying to nudge a little more out of him.

"He did."

Milton could see that Polanski wasn't going to give him anything else.

"Look," he said, "you heard what the boss said: this is coming off my lunch hour. I don't want to rush you, but I need to get back. Do you have anything specific you want to ask me?"

"Did you notice anyone coming out of the restroom before you went inside?"

"No," he said. "The station was quiet. And if you're wondering whether I could've seen whoever it was who stabbed your victim, the men who killed him were probably already out of the station before I got there."

"So the kid found the body and just stayed there?"

"He hid. I don't think that's unusual. He's thirteen."

"I guess. Freddy tell you anything else?"

Milton could see that Polanski's curiosity had been piqued by something that Freddy had—or had not—said that morning. Had he mentioned that he had recognised one of the likely killers in the precinct last night? Milton hoped not, but there was nothing that he could do. He wasn't prepared to mention it until he had a little more information, specifically about Polanski and whether or not he could be trusted.

"Mr. Smith?" Polanski pressed.

"No," Milton said. "Freddy was frightened. We spoke about the football. He caught a ball that one of the players tossed into the crowd. That was the best thing that happened to him last night—it went downhill after that."

"And that's it?"

"Pretty much."

Polanski dropped the cigarette to the ground and trod on it. He reached into his jacket pocket and took out a card. He took out a pen and scrawled something on the reverse.

"Here," he said, handing it to Milton.

Milton looked down at the front of the card: Aleksander Polanski, Detective, Internal Affairs Bureau—Brooklyn North, 179 Wilson Avenue, Brooklyn. There was a telephone number and email. He flipped it over and saw that the detective had written down a second telephone number.

"That's my cell," he explained. "If you remember anything about what happened, give me a call. All right? Day or night."

"I will."

"Thanks for the cigarette."

Polanski picked his way around the discarded trash and clumps of rotten food and made his way back down the alley toward Surf Avenue. Milton watched him go. He was a good judge of character, but he found it difficult to get a solid read off the detective. He was brusque and jaded, but that wasn't unexpected given his line of work. A friend of Milton's from long ago had ended up in the military police, and he had complained of the unpleasantness of investigating fellow soldiers, and the reputation that attached to men and women whose jobs required them to do that. He expected that it was just the same for cops who prosecuted other cops. That might explain Polanski's surliness.

The fact that Internal Affairs was involved in the investigation lent further credibility to what Freddy had said about recognising a cop as one of the two men he had seen outside the bathroom. Milton needed to know more about why Polanski was involved. He needed to know more about Polanski, too.

He dropped his own cigarette to the ground and put it out with his toe. He looked at his watch: he had been outside for twenty minutes. Vadim was a bastard and would deduct more than that from his lunch. Milton went back inside, washed his hands in the bathroom, and went back to work.

42

Back in the kitchen, Vadim had given Milton two additional dishes to prepare: the *solyanka* soup and *vareniki*. The latter were small handmade dumplings, and he started by cracking a dozen eggs into a bowl, adding sour cream, and then whisking them together. He added flour and continued to whisk. Milton covered the dough with a bowl so that it could rest for an hour and had just gone to wash his hands when his phone buzzed in his pocket. He wiped his hands and took it out. He didn't recognise the number.

"Hello?"

"Is that John?"

"Hold on."

Milton recognised Manny Blanco's voice. He tossed the dishcloth onto the counter and made his way to the open door that led into the alley where he had spoken to Polanski earlier.

He closed the door and leaned against the wall. "I'm here," he said. "You okay?"

"Yeah. I just wanted to say I was sorry."

"You don't need to apologise. I've been there. It happens."

"Freddy said I hit you. Did I?"

"You hardly touched me."

"Shit," he said. "I'm so sorry. I feel like a total douche."

"Forget it."

There was a pause.

"You still there?" Milton asked.

"I can't believe I fucked up so bad, man. That thing with Freddy? He told me what happened. He told me you helped him. And then I go and throw you out of the house. I am a total fucking screw-up."

The regret and shame were strong. Milton remembered what that felt like and knew where it might lead. He tried to nudge him away from it. "Did the police speak to him today?"

"This morning," Manny said.

"Who was it?"

"Two detectives. Mackintosh and Polanski. I wondered whether..." He stopped, the words trailing away.

"What is it?"

"I'm worried, John. I don't want him getting caught up in something like this, but there's nothing I can do to stop it. What if it goes to trial? What if he has to stand up and give evidence? How am I going to protect him then?"

His voice was fraying; Milton could tell that Manny was close to losing it. "It might not come to that."

"What if it does?"

"You want to talk about it?"

Manny continued as if he hadn't heard him. "I'm worrying myself stupid here."

"Are you at home?"

"Yeah. We both are."

"Stay put. I'll be over in half an hour."

Milton went back inside. Vadim was standing by his station.

"What are you doing?" he blustered. "You have work!"

"I'm sorry," Milton said. "I've got to go."

Vadim gaped at him. "You can't just *go*."

"I know. And I'm sorry. I might not be back for a day or two. You want to fire me, I can't say I'd blame you."

Vadim's face slowly reddened and, instead of stepping aside, he came forward until he was within an arm's reach of Milton.

"You come here asking for a job. I give you one. I don't check your visa—"

"And?"

"And now you think you can just quit, leave me swinging like this? Take advantage of me? No way, man. No way."

Milton knew what was coming. Vadim telegraphed it: the bunched right fist, the slight shuffle forward with his right step to balance his weight more evenly, the clenched jaw.

Milton didn't react. He stood his ground. He looked straight into Vadim's eyes. He knew the effect that would have: his eyes were pale blue and cold as ice, empty of feeling or empathy, but full of the promise of unshackled violence should that prove necessary.

"Don't be silly," he said.

A flicker of doubt passed across Vadim's face. He took a step back; his arms fell loose at his sides, and his fists unclenched.

Milton stared right through him.

"You're fired," Vadim said.

Milton took off his apron and handed it to him. "Thanks for the job."

He went to the locker room, grabbed his jacket, and made his way outside to his bike.

43

Livonia Avenue ran underneath the elevated section of track that took the train into New Lots Avenue station. Carter pulled over and parked next to number 923. Both sides of the street were given over to businesses, with this side home to a deli, Ace Dry Cleaners, State Car and Limo Services, a fried chicken joint and Shakira Nails and Hair. Next to the nail bar was Omar's, a bodega that provided a front for the drug operation that ran out of the back room and second floor.

Carter switched off the engine.

"He better be grateful," Shepard said.

"Relax," Carter said, placating his ex-partner as best he could. "He will be. But you go in there with attitude, you're gonna change the atmosphere. You know what he's like. So let's chill, okay? Just take it easy."

Shepard was nervous. That was reasonable—it had been a crazy night. Taking González out the way they did had been risky, but, the way they had figured it last night, what choice did they have? If they had let him get on the train, they would have relinquished any control that they had left over the situation. And if he had made it to the safe house, that would have been game over, not just for Acosta, but for them, too. Internal Affairs would have had him, and who knew what he would have been able to tell them? Too much, that was for sure. No. They'd had no choice. They needed to act, and they had.

Carter opened the door and stepped out into the cold. The block was a mixture of business and residential, with half of the businesses active and the other half boarded up. Acosta ran this part of his Brooklyn business out of the bodega. Carter had found it for him. Scouting for new locations for his empire was another of the services that he and Shepard provided.

The store had been run by Pedro Omar, a Puerto Rican businessman with whom Carter had become friendly. Omar's store was on a block of empty lots that had been targeted by the city for eminent domain takeover, no doubt so that more expensive apartments could be built for the hipster city workers who were beginning to make their way into the neighbourhood. Carter—who regularly drank and played cards in the back of the store—had put together a deal that helped Omar out. He had introduced Omar to Acosta and, instead of the fifty grand that the city was offering, they'd struck a deal that paid him seventy-five. Carter and Shepard got paid twice: once by Acosta for finding him a new place to sell his product and then again by Omar for giving him a more profitable exit out of his business.

The store was perfect. There was a third-floor apartment across the street that Acosta had bought to store most of the product, reducing the risk of having a rival hit the bodega in an attempt to rip them off. Another bonus was the McDonald's adjacent to the bodega; it had a large parking lot that always had spaces and was perfect for customers who were driving in to get their drugs.

He paused at the door.

"Ready?" he said to Shepard.

Shepard nodded that he was.

Carter opened the door and went inside.

44

The bodega was typical of the area: dilapidated but functional. It carried stock and had staff who kept it open between the hours of seven in the morning and ten at night. If it was to be an effective front, it had to look as if it was legitimate. Carter went inside first, nodding to the black kid who was manning the till. He worked corners for Acosta on the weekend and worked the till during the week; he recognised Carter and returned his nod of acknowledgement with a point of a finger toward the door at the back of the ground-floor space.

Carter led the way. There were, in fact, two doors: one was wooden, insubstantial and thin, but it served as a means of hiding the two-inch-thick steel door that was at the other end of a short passage. The wooden door was unlocked, and Carter pulled it back and went inside. The passage beyond was secure, with the heavy door and the dome of a camera fixed to the ceiling. There was a buzzer on the wall and Carter pressed it. He looked up into the camera, knowing that he was being observed, and waited until the latch slid out of the strike plate and the door handle was pressed down. The door opened into the room beyond; Carter went inside.

The room was half the size of the bodega. There was a long table with six chairs, a television and an expensive sound system, a leather couch and a refrigerator that was stocked with bottles of beer. There were four people in the room: a man and a woman sat at the table, taking money from large sports bags and counting the bills out into piles; a second man was leaning against the wall, drinking beer and watching a college football game on the TV; and a third man was stretched out on the couch, a joint held between his fingertips. Carter raised his hand to the man on the couch, and he returned the gesture.

The man's name was Carlos Acosta. He was wearing a purple suit and a purple shirt that was open at the collar. He wore shaded glasses with faint purple lenses and a purple cap was perched on his head. He had a blond goatee that stood out against his dark skin, and the hair visible beneath the cap was bleached a similar peroxide blond. He was slender; Carter had done a double-take the first time he had been introduced to him, guessing that he could only have weighed a hundred and twenty pounds. It was difficult to imagine how someone so physically insignificant could inspire such fear throughout the district and such loyalty from the pure-bred gangsters who worked for his operation.

"Yo, yo," Acosta said, unfolding himself from the couch and standing. He put out his arm and bumped fists with both Carter and Shepard.

"How you doing, Carlos?"

"Doing good. You two been busy?"

Carter nodded. He swallowed on a dry throat.

Acosta went over to the refrigerator. He took a beer and

gave it to Shepard. "You're not on duty yet, are you?" he said to Carter.

"No," Carter replied. "I start at four."

"Would it have made any difference?"

"Nah," Carter said, returning Acosta's grin as he caught the bottle that Acosta tossed over to him.

There was a bottle opener on the table. Carter looked at the piles of money as he reached down to take it. There had to be fifty or sixty grand there, at least, maybe even more. And that was just the money that would have been collected from the night before. Carter knew how the game worked: Acosta sent three of his best lieutenants out every night at midnight, and they would each visit the dealers who pushed product through Brooklyn and Manhattan. Then they would return, deposit the money here, and it would be counted and sent away to be washed through Acosta's legitimate businesses: restaurants, a car rental place, and, until recently, José González's car stereo shop.

The operation was vulnerable once you knew how it worked. It would have been easy enough to hit the lieutenants as they made their way back to the bodega with bags full of cash. Carter had considered it before he had become more familiar with Acosta, and had discounted it for the same reason everyone else discounted it: everyone knew what Acosta would do to anyone who ripped him off. It wouldn't make any difference if whoever was responsible was a cop.

"Anything you two wanna tell me?"

Carter looked up. Acosta was watching them both.

Shepard looked over at him. Carter's throat felt as dry as sandpaper. "Okay," he said. "Yeah. There is something."

"You gonna tell me what happened to González? Because I heard he wound up dead last night. Had his throat cut in the bathroom at Euclid station. You know anything about that?"

"Yeah," Carter said. He looked at the three others inside the room. "Alone?"

Carter had no interest in talking about what they had done in front of the others. He didn't know them as well as he knew Acosta, and he didn't want them to have information that they could use to snitch on them to straight cops should they ever find themselves in need of an out.

Acosta dismissed the others with a lazy wave of his hand. They got up and left, glowering at Carter and Shepard with distaste.

Carter waited until the door was closed. "We killed him."

"Now why would you do something like that?"

"He was a rat," Shepard said. "He was on his way to sell us out."

"Yeah?" Acosta said. He turned to look at Carter. "That right, Bobby? He was a rat?"

Carter swallowed again. He knew González and Acosta had grown up together in Crown Heights, and, at least until recently, they had been like brothers.

"I got a call from my contact in Internal Affairs," Shepard said. "They said they'd been putting the screws on González for weeks and they turned him. They said he was going in last night."

"They tell you he had evidence against you two dumb fucks, too?"

Carter felt a hollowness in his gut.

"You didn't know I knew, did you?" Acosta said.

"No," Carter said.

"How long you been holding out on me?"

"We only found out last night. If I'd known before then, I would've told you."

"You didn't think maybe you should've told me first thing you heard?"

"He was on his way to hand himself in," he said. "There wasn't time."

"You find out anything else last night?"

"Like what?"

"Like the evidence he might've had."

Carter's fists were clenched so tight his nails were digging into the flesh of his palms.

Acosta stared at him. Carter had no idea which way it was going to go. He knew that his gun was in his locker at the precinct. Shepard had a .32, but it wouldn't help them if Acosta decided that they had to go.

"He had me on tape," Carter said. "I went in to get our money. He taped me."

Acosta kept eyeing him. "You got the tape?"

"Yeah," Shepard said. "You can relax, Carlos. We got it. It's been destroyed."

Carter couldn't keep it in. He stepped up to Acosta and jabbed him in the chest with his finger. "I didn't hear you telling me that there was something about him we had to be careful about."

Acosta took a step back, paused, the same blank and remorseless look on his face, and then, in an instant, it was gone. He grinned at Carter. "I'm fucking with you." He chuckled. "Fact is, I didn't know. He was fooling me just like he was fooling you, and I knew him practically all his life. So, yeah, I feel pretty stupid about what happened. You did what you had to do. You did good."

He leaned in for a hug, his thin arm around Carter's broad shoulders and bringing him in close so that he could pound him on the back.

"You did it at Euclid?" he said as he disengaged. "In the bathroom?"

"That's right."

Acosta laughed, a braying that sent shivers up Carter's spine. "Appropriate for that piece of shit."

The tension in the room evaporated.

"I'm serious," Acosta said. "You saved me a lot of hassle. He wouldn't have stopped with the two of you. He could've rolled up a lot more than that. So, yeah, you did good—and I wanna say thanks properly." He went over to the table, took two bundles of bills and tossed them over.

Carter caught them. "You don't need to do that," he said, even as he eyed the bundles greedily.

"Sure I do. You've been loyal to me. I reward loyalty. Go on—take it."

Carter kept one and gave the other to Shepard. They were thick with bills. It was difficult to estimate, but he guessed there was ten grand in each bundle. He opened his jacket and pushed the bundle into his inside pocket.

"Thanks," he said.

Acosta waved his hand airily. "Forget it." He took out another bottle of beer and popped the top. "Now—what'll happen next? You think they got anything out of González before?"

"My contact says not much. He was holding it back until they agreed to a deal to get him immunity."

"No names were mentioned?"

"None. That was part of his insurance."

"And you'll keep an eye on it?"

"Of course," Carter said. "It's IAB. It's us they're going after. We'll take it easy for a bit."

"And we'll have to change up where you get your money each week." He stroked his chin. "You know the Chinese restaurant on Pitkin. Happy Wok? My cousin owns it. It's clean, nothing there to tie anything back to me. You go in there, same time as before, and you order takeout. He'll make sure your cash is in the bag. That sound like it might work?"

"It sounds perfect," Carter said.

"All right, then."

Carter looked at his watch. It was an excuse: he knew he had plenty of time before he had to report for roll call, but he was finding it increasingly claustrophobic in this small room. It wasn't hot, but he could feel the slickness of the sweat on his back, across his palms and between his fingers.

He closed his fist and held it up; Acosta bumped with him, then did the same to Shepard.

"Good work," he said again as they went to the door. "I mean it."

"See you around," Carter said, waiting for the door to be unlocked and opened for him.

———

Carter went outside into the short space between the two doors, opened the wooden door all the way and stepped out into the relative normality of the bodega. The men and the woman Acosta had dismissed were waiting there, and they filed back inside without a word to them. There was an old woman at the desk, trying to negotiate a discount on the basket of shopping she had collected. Carter didn't dawdle; he walked straight out, crossed the sidewalk and then the street and, finally, slipped into the car. He had started the engine before Shepard had crossed over to join him, and, as soon as his ex-partner was inside with him, he put the car into drive and pulled quickly away.

"Fuck," Shepard breathed.

"Tell me about it."

"I thought he was gonna pop us."

"Me too." Carter realised he was driving aimlessly. "He's a sadistic fuck. He enjoyed that. You see the way he smiled at me?"

"Where we going?"

"You wanna get a drink? I need to get my nerves under control before I go in for my shift."

"Sure."

Carter turned the wheel and headed north. He'd drive them to Callahan's. They could get a beer and something to eat. He needed something to calm the unsettled feeling he still had in the pit of his stomach. Acosta was a scary dude, and Carter didn't scare easily. He paid well, though. Carter reached up and patted the bump on his jacket where he had stuffed in the bundle of cash. That was just as well. It was the only reason Carter would consider putting himself in close proximity with such an unpredictable, capricious, devious piece of shit.

45

M ilton rode north until he arrived in Cypress Hills again. He rolled to a stop on Danforth Street, opposite the Blanco household. He took off his helmet and noticed that a black garbage bag had been left next to the trash cans outside the house. He guessed that it contained the detritus from the night before.

He crossed the sidewalk, opened the gate and knocked on the door. Manny answered it and stood aside to let him in. Milton saw that his assumption was correct: the house had been scrupulously tidied.

Manny saw the mark on Milton's face. "Please say I didn't do that."

"It's just a bruise," Milton said. "Forget it."

"I'm so sorry," he said, the colour rushing to his cheeks. "I'm really, really sorry."

"Forget it," Milton said, uncomfortable with raw emotion. "You don't need to apologise."

"Of course I do. You saw me at my worst."

"Have you been to a meeting?"

"Haven't been able to. I had to tidy up—the police came.

I didn't want the place looking like a mess. They spoke to Freddy and now I don't want to leave him on his own."

"Where is he?"

"In his bedroom," Manny said. "On his PlayStation. I wanted to talk to you before I go and get him."

"That's probably for the best. Look—do you want to go to a meeting?"

Manny nodded and then looked as if he was going to start crying.

"There's one tonight. Seven. I go to it sometimes."

Manny shook his head. "What about Freddy?"

"Bring him. You know what he needs now? He needs to see you trying again. He needs you to be strong, Manny. You've got to show him you're not going to give up."

"I know."

"It's Al-Anon. Seriously—you should bring him. It'll help him understand."

Manny nodded and limped over to the kitchen counter. "I'll think about it." He inclined his head towards a coffee maker. "You want a drink?"

"That would be nice."

Milton watched as Manny worked, setting up the filter basket, filling it with coffee grounds, pouring a carafe of water into the reservoir. He was wearing his prosthetic now, and Milton might not have noticed without the knowledge that it was there. There was a limp, but it wasn't obvious.

Manny turned and Milton couldn't look away from his leg in time. "You didn't know about my leg?"

"I didn't."

"That's the reason I had to leave the Rangers. Medical discharge." He chuckled humourlessly. "No one wants a one-legged soldier."

"What happened?"

"Kandahar," he said, as if that was all the information that Milton would need. "There were four of us out on patrol near the airfield. Two Brits, me and a translator. We were in a Land Rover. Roadside bomb. We got flipped over. The door sheared off and ended up taking half my leg with it. And I was lucky. Both of the Brits had their tickets punched."

Manny spoke in the same matter-of-fact way that Milton had heard in other soldiers who had suffered similar injuries. It was part of the job; Manny had just been unfortunate. But, nevertheless, it went a long way toward explaining why he had resorted to the bottle: bitterness, a sense of grievance, an angry lament for opportunities lost. Milton understood now why Manny had reacted the way he had about the sneakers. He would have felt like a failure.

Milton wanted to apologise, but, as he tried to find the words to broach the subject, Manny interrupted him with his coffee.

"You were there last night?" Manny asked him as he passed him a mug.

Milton nodded. "I found him in the bathroom. It was pure coincidence. I only realised that he was your son when we got to the station. I saw the shoes he was wearing."

"I should've been there," Manny said. "But I fucked up. I was angry. I couldn't deal with what was going on across the road. Then Freddy gets into trouble with them; they steal the sneakers he saved up so long to get. It was so unfair. Made me feel so useless. I do okay with the leg most of the time, but it just made me remember how I felt when they brought me back here. Like I was half the man he needed me to be. My old man, he would've gone over there with a shotgun. I didn't have the guts to do that. Probably couldn't have, the way I am now."

"I get it," Milton said.

Manny didn't hear him, or ignored his reassurance. "So I got myself into a mess. It seemed like everything I was doing to stay sober was a waste of time, so I went to the bar down the street and started drinking. I forgot about Freddy. Forgot about my boy." He started to sob. "We were supposed to go to the game together, and I clean forgot it. If I'd been there, maybe none of this would've happened."

"You can't second-guess it," Milton said. "You messed up. We all do. Now you just accept it happened and make sure it doesn't happen again. And what happened—it is what it is. Freddy's involved now, for better or worse. I am, too. We just need to get him the support he needs."

"What do you mean, 'we'? This isn't your problem, is it?"

"I'd like to help."

"How?"

"I have experience in this kind of thing."

He glanced at him, momentarily wary. "Police?"

"No. Army, just the same as you. But I've been able to help people in bad situations before."

He was about to respond, but he stopped, his mouth hanging open. "Hold on," he said. "The guys. Across the road. Was that you?"

Milton could have lied, could have denied it, but lying felt wrong. "Yes," he said.

"What did you do?"

"I watched the house. I worked out who the top guy was and I followed him home. I was there when he got back on Saturday night. And we had a chat about the location of his business."

"A chat?"

"I can be persuasive, Manny."

"Jesus," he said. "What were you doing in the army? Special Forces?"

"I was in the SAS," he said, hoping that would be enough to forestall any further questions.

Manny looked glumly down at the floor.

"Look," Milton said. "I didn't do it because you couldn't. I did it because I *could*, and because it was the right thing to do. That's it."

"That's not enough. You don't even know us."

Milton paused, finding the right words. "It's the ninth step," he said. "I'm trying to make amends for things I did a long time ago. This is how I choose to do it. Either way, whatever happened happened. It's done. There's no point beating yourself up about it. You have to think about Freddy now. You've got to work out the best way to get him through this."

46

P olanski drove back into Brooklyn. He thought about what he had heard from Freddy Blanco and John Smith. It was obvious that something was being held back. He didn't want to push the boy too hard for fear of making a difficult situation even worse, but he knew that they would have to speak to him again.

He drove to the bureau, parked his car and made his way along the sidewalk to the entrance.

Haynes was just on his way out.

"Can I get a minute, Sarge?"

"Sure," Haynes said. "I was just going to get a coffee. You want one?"

There was a café across the road, and Haynes indicated it with a nod.

"No, thanks," Polanski said. "I've got too much going on."

"You don't got five minutes for a coffee? Come on."

Polanski couldn't really say no. Haynes had been his patron for as long as he'd been in the bureau, and that was almost as long as he'd been in the NYPD. He was the reason that Polanski was still a cop at all.

Polanski had come out of the academy and been assigned to the Seven Seven, a precinct every bit as challenging as the Seven Five, perhaps even worse back in the day. There had been a shortage in the borough command office, and Polanski and the other rookie who had been assigned to the precinct were sent there to pitch in. Polanski had been put on the switchboard and told to answer the phones. There had been one midnight tour when a call had come in, a cop saying that he needed a tow truck to come and get rid of an abandoned car. Polanski had called a twenty-four-hour towing company and had forgotten all about it. The next day, though, the owner of the company had come into the station house, found Polanski and handed him two twenty-dollar bills. It was a gesture of thanks, the man explained, and a reminder that he was always looking for jobs.

Polanski, who had fancied himself as having an entrepreneurial bent, continued to refer business to the company and had continued to receive a similar reward for every job passed on. It was only when the bureau began an investigation into another cop in a neighbouring precinct that culminated in the arrest of the business owner that things started to look tenuous. It turned out that the owner had been running the same scam with cops the length and breadth of Brooklyn, and, in exchange for a pass, he gave all of them up.

Haynes was working at the bureau and had recognised Polanski's name. He had seen to it that his part in the scam was suppressed, but only on the condition that he transfer to the bureau to work with him. Polanski remembered the conversation that he'd had with Haynes and his father. The two older men had sat him down after dinner one Sunday and told him how it was going to be: he would transfer or resign. Polanski had pleaded to be allowed to stay where he was, but both men had decided that would be impossible. He had demonstrated that he could not be trusted on the street. He would have to do his penance, working with Haynes to root out graft and corruption. In the end, after he had thought about it, he realised that was no choice at all.

Polanski followed Haynes to the coffee shop and found a table. Haynes went to the barista and ordered, then brought the coffees back and set them down.

"So?" he began. "What happened with your CI?"

"That's what I want to talk to you about," he said. "There was a murder last night. In the restroom at Euclid station. Did you hear?"

Haynes shook his head. "No, I didn't."

"The dead guy was González."

Haynes paused. "Your informant?"

Polanski nodded.

"You're kidding?"

"I wish I was. I'd been working on him for the last three months. I had to push hard to get him to trust me. I promised him a new identity, full immunity, the whole nine yards. All he had to do was give me Acosta and whoever he's been working with in the Seven Five and that would've been that."

"He was ready to give them up?"

"That's what he told me. I just had to get him off the street."

"Jesus. Did you tell anyone other than me?"

"No."

"Do you think you've been followed?"

"No. I would've noticed."

"What about your phone?"

Polanski stared at him. "You think it's been tapped?"

"Maybe. I've seen it happen. These are cops, Aleks. They know what they're doing."

"What do I do now?"

Haynes put the cup down. "You got anything else?"

Polanski nodded. "I got a kid who might have seen the killers. He's thirteen. He saw two guys just before he went in and found the body."

"He get a good look at them?"

"He says he didn't, but I don't know if I buy it. I think he's scared."

"What's his name?"

"Freddy Blanco. Lives with his old man up near Cypress Hills."

"So work on him. Maybe you can get back to them that way."

Polanski nodded.

"And be careful," Haynes added. "Get a different phone. And don't talk to anyone else about this. Cops talk to cops. You know that. We got detectives in the office who know the guys at the Seven Five. Keep it close to the vest—it's safer that way."

Milton rode to Sutter Avenue and the station house for the Seventy-Fifth Precinct. He parked his bike and walked the area. The precinct house took up the entire block. It faced onto Sutter and was bounded on either side by Essex Street and Linwood Street. There was a line of cars in front of the building, parked at right angles with the road. There was a yard at the rear of the building, accessed by gates on both Essex and Linwood. Even with the parking in the front and at the rear of the building, there was still not enough space for the patrol cars and private vehicles used by the staff to get to work. As a result, the police had taken over vacant lots of land in the nearby vicinity. There were police cruisers parked on a lot on the other side of Essex Street, and others were jammed nose to tail into spaces that were barely big enough for them.

Milton went back to the station house. The first floor was built in brick, with the second and third floors accommodated within a dun-coloured concrete block that was larger than the building beneath it and seemed to have been lowered atop it. The windows were narrow and the ones at ground level were barred. The entrance was through two sets of adjacent steel-plated double doors beneath large shining metal letters that read 75th PRECINCT – POLICE DEPARTMENT – CITY OF NEW YORK.

Milton turned his attention to the buildings on the opposite side of the road.

There was a white clapboard house, free-standing from the rest of the block and separated by two narrow alleys. The door was protected by a wide awning and the windows were protected by decorative grilles. The neatly tended plants outside the property suggested that it was occupied, and Milton quickly dismissed it as unsuitable for his purposes.

There was a second house to the right of the first. It, too, showed obvious signs of habitation from owners who cared about their property: this one was separated from the street by a recently painted gate and a whitewashed wall topped with ornamental spikes. Milton dismissed that property, too.

Next was a large block of four buildings. The three to Milton's right had been turned into apartments and looked in good order. The property on the left of the block was mixed use. The ground floor, 1013 Sutter Avenue, was the Golden China takeout. The two floors above the yellow awning that advertised the restaurant looked to be in a state of some disrepair. The window frames were rotten with faded and peeling paint, the glass in two of them replaced by plastic sheeting. The pediment at the top of the building was stained and crumbling, and the telephone wires that ran to a pole on the other side of the road had worked their way loose and hung limply.

It looked promising.

Milton walked north on Essex Street. There was a one-storey brick building behind the block that contained the Chinese restaurant. It was derelict, with metal sheets fixed over the windows and blocking the doorway. There was a narrow alley between it and the building to its right, and Milton walked up to it. A decorative gate blocked the way ahead, but it was open and Milton was able to walk through. The alley was the width of a car and, beyond the derelict building, it allowed access to the yards at the back of the buildings on Sutter Avenue. They were demarked by a crumbling brick wall, and Milton was able to haul himself up so that he could see over the top of it. Each of the buildings was equipped with an external fire escape, a zigzagging ladder that climbed all the way to the top with landings on each floor.

The yard behind the restaurant was in an awful state: it had been concreted over, but weeds had pushed through the cracks. Trash had been dumped there too, with empty cardboard packaging and cans and trash cans that overflowed with rotting food. A plump rat, gorged on the fetid remnants, slunk away as Milton approached.

A door to the restaurant had been propped open. Milton could see into the kitchen and could hear the sound of a radio, Iggy and the Stooges playing 'I Wanna Be Your Dog'. He saw motion from inside and heard the sound of conversation; the staff were busy preparing the food for the evening.

Milton went to the fire escape. The ladder wasn't extended all the way down to the ground, but he was able to pull himself onto the first-floor landing by clambering atop one of the large industrial bins that was shoved up against the side of the window. He climbed to the second and then the third floor. The window that faced onto the landing was broken and covered with plastic sheeting that had been stapled to the frame. Milton pried his fingers between the plastic and the wood and pulled; the frame was rotten and the staples popped out easily. He tugged the sheeting back until there was a large enough gap for him to look inside. It was dark; he took out his phone, switched on the flashlight and shone it inside. The room had evidently been damaged by fire at some point in its recent history. The floor and walls were blackened, and soot was spread across the ceiling.

Milton tugged the sheet a little more until he had opened it enough so that he could slide inside.

He passed through the room and carefully opened the door. There was a second room beyond, larger than the first, and, as Milton crossed to the other side, he was able to look down on Sutter Avenue and the station house directly opposite. He was a little to the left of the entrance, but he had an excellent view of the building and the approach to it in both directions.

Milton had seen enough. He lowered himself to the ground and went back to Sutter Avenue again. With a final glance at the precinct house, he checked the map that he had saved on his phone and set off to the north. The camera store was four miles away.

48

Milton returned to Sutter Avenue an hour later. The gate at the mouth of the alley was still open. He pushed it aside and went through. He reached up and placed the bag containing the things that he had purchased on the top of the wall. After checking that he was unobserved, he reached up and hauled himself over. He grabbed the bag and dropped down into the garden on the other side. He made his way across the yard, clambered onto the bin and then scaled the fire escape to the third floor. He climbed inside and crossed the two rooms to the window that looked down onto the precinct house.

Milton opened his bag and took out the equipment that he had purchased: a digital camera with a decent zoom lens, a tripod, extra memory cards, and a pen flashlight. His purchases came to a little short of a thousand dollars and he had paid for them with some of what was left from the money he had taken from the dealer.

He took out the camera and tripod. The window was high enough that he would be difficult to spot from the ground, yet it offered a good range of vision. Milton set up the tripod and fixed the camera to it. He put his eye to the viewfinder and looked down at the entrance to the station house. The door opened and two men in uniform stepped outside. They paused between two cars, conversing easily.

Milton centred the shot, adjusted the focus, and fired off a burst.

The men got into separate cars. Milton took photos of each vehicle, ensuring that he was focused on their license plates.

The cars drove away.

The two cops were white. Milton wasn't looking for a white cop. He took out his phone and navigated to the website for NBC New York. He found the video report of the event at the Community Center that he had watched in the station last night. He hit play and then paused the video at the moment the black cop was staring into the camera. He copied the screen and parted his fingers to zoom the image.

He looked down at the image: he was looking for a black man, mid- to late-fifties, with a receding hairline and a beard that was almost as white as it was black.

Milton had a couple of hours before he had arranged to meet Manny and Freddy at the meeting.

He put the phone down where he could glance at it and settled down to wait.

49

Bobby Carter parked his car outside the precinct house and went in through the big double doors. He went down to the locker room and got changed into his uniform. The other men were drifting in and out, and the officers from the eight-to-four would be here soon. The atmosphere was the same as it always was: they related tales of what had happened on yesterday's shifts, predicted what might happen today, all of it underpinned by banter and joking. Carter had been around long enough now to be a well-liked and respected presence in the locker room. The younger cops looked up to him as a leader who knew the ropes and wouldn't be shy of helping them out should they need advice; the veteran cops had seen enough action with him over the years to know that, if they ever got into trouble and put out a ten-thirteen over the radio—*officer needs assistance*—Bobby Carter would be one of the first to respond and was exactly the kind of guy you wanted on your side.

He was a little anxious. He knew that the murder would come up in the meeting today. He was confident that he and

Shep had been careful and that they hadn't left any loose ends that might lead homicide back to them, but you could never be completely sure. This would be the first chance he had to gauge the state of the evidence.

Carter pulled on his pants, did up his shirt and grabbed his hat from the shelf where he kept it. He fastened his service belt as he made it up the stairs and into the muster room to answer the three-thirty roll call. Rhodes was already there with the rest of the shift. Carter took the seat next to him.

"How you doing, kid?"

"I'm good," Rhodes said. "Are you a daddy?"

"False alarm," Carter said with a shake of his head. "She thought she was having contractions. Turns out it was indigestion—go figure, right?"

"So it could happen any time?"

"Today, tomorrow, next week—who the fuck knows? I told her she better be sure next time."

Sergeant Ramirez came into the room and made his way to the lectern that faced the chairs.

"You ready for your second tour?"

"Sure," Rhodes said.

"What'd you do yesterday after I booked?"

"Stayed out. Just drove around the sector. Nothing much happened."

Ramirez clapped his hands to bring the men and women to order.

Carter shuffled in his chair.

"All right," Ramirez said. "You probably heard we had a murder last night. Guy had his throat cut in the restroom at Euclid." He looked into the small crowd and pointed in the direction of one of the female officers. "Farley was first on the scene. And Mack has got the case. Mack—you wanna?"

Carter turned and saw Rebecca Mackintosh. She was a straight shooter, the sort of cop who would take arrests from those other cops who couldn't be bothered to write them up themselves. She was ambitious and had padded her résumé with dozens of collars that she'd run for others who didn't have the same burning drive. Carter remembered when she had been transferred into the precinct. He had given her plenty of arrests himself, and she had parlayed all of those little wins into a swift promotion to detective. She wouldn't have been his choice for lead dick on this particular case, though; she was much too keen and efficient for his tastes.

"Thanks," she said, taking Ramirez's place at the lectern. "Like he said, it was at Euclid. It was nasty. Looks like we want two guys. One black, the other white."

Carter listened, his stomach tightening. "How'd you know that?" he said, his throat suddenly dry and scratchy. "You got a witness?"

Heads turned to look at him and Carter suddenly wished the floor would open up and swallow him. Mackintosh looked over at him, too, and nodded. "That's right, Bobby. We caught a break. There was a kid there. He saw two men near the bathroom as he was going in, then he found the victim."

"So he can ID them?"

"We're looking into that. There was another guy, too. Turned up afterwards. English guy, works in a kitchen down in Coney Island. He found the kid. Didn't get much from him, though. He said he didn't see anything."

"You interviewed the kid?"

"This morning. Farley brought the kid and the English guy back to the precinct last night, but we couldn't get the kid's old man. We're not gonna interview a minor without a responsible adult, so I drove him home and went back today.

I don't wanna get into the nitty-gritty—it's too early for that. But what I'm saying is that I want you all to keep your eyes open."

Rod Marinelli spoke up. "Who was the vic?"

"José Luis González. Used to have the stereo shop on Atlantic."

Marinelli nodded. "He put a stereo in my Buick five years ago."

"He was well known," Mackintosh said. "From what I know, he was well liked, too. No reason why someone would do him like that—with a knife, made it look very personal, like it was more than just a simple beef. But someone knows something. Put the word out. Speak to your snitches. We've done better with murders the last eighteen months. We don't want this one hanging around."

"Amen to that," Ramirez said.

Ramirez continued with the rest of the briefing, but Carter hardly heard another word. It was all he could do to stay in his seat. He needed to get away, to speak to Shep, to try to figure out how exposed they were. He was furious with himself. How had they left a witness?

Rhodes elbowed him in the ribs.

"What?"

Ramirez was looking at him. "Wake up, Bobby. Jesus. What is it? You look like you've seen a ghost."

"Sorry, Sarge. I got no sleep last night. Becky thought the baby was coming the entire time."

"Wait until you got the baby," Farley offered. "Sleep? What the fuck is sleep?"

There was a ripple of laughter; Carter waved it off.

"I got nothing else," Ramirez said. "Find out who killed González. Dismissed."

Carter got up so quickly that he sent the chair skidding back behind him.

"You okay?" Rhodes asked.

"Yeah," he said. "I'm good. Just need to speak to my wife before we get out there. I'll see you in the car?"

"You got it."

50

C arter went out to the yard at the rear of the station. It was empty. He took out his phone and called Shepard.

"Hey," Shepard said. "I was asleep. This better be—"

Carter spoke quietly. "We got a problem. About last night—a kid found González."

"So?"

"The kid saw us outside the bathroom just before he found the body."

There was a pause. "What?"

"What I said. He saw us outside."

"No," Shepard said, the grogginess all gone. "I don't buy it. I didn't see no one. I was careful."

"Not careful enough. I've just had roll call. Farley took the call. The kid was coming out. He saw González go inside, then he saw us. He remembered he'd left something and went back, saw us again, then found the body.

"Fuck," Shepard said. "There was a kid looking at the subway map. I didn't think he was... Fuck."

"Yeah, Shep, *fuck*. There was an English guy, too. He

went in after, saw the body and found the kid in one of the stalls."

"What are we gonna do?"

Carter took a breath to compose himself; they would get nowhere fast if they panicked. "Okay," he said. "There's no point making this any worse than it already is. What's done is done. We just need to figure out what happens next."

"Did the kid get a good look at us?"

"He said a black guy and a white guy. Mackintosh didn't say anything else."

"Mack's got the case? This gets better and better."

Carter ignored that. "She didn't interview him last night —says they couldn't find his old man. Took him home and went back to see him this morning. Saw the English guy, too."

"I'm guessing, seeing as neither of us have been arrested, we're in the clear for now."

"Maybe," Carter said. "Until they get the kid to help them put together a composite and they think it looks familiar."

"We can't think like that, Bobby."

Carter ran his fingers through his hair. He felt tired.

"What about this other guy?" Shepard said.

"I don't think we need to worry about him. Mack said he came later. We were long gone by then."

Shepard said nothing. Carter waited for him to break the silence.

"So what do we do?" Shepard asked.

"I'm going to look into it. I get on with Farley. I can speak to her."

"And Mack?"

"You think it's a good idea to start showing too much interest around her?"

"She's sharp," Shepard agreed. "Won't be easy to get anything out of her without her getting itchy about it."

Carter agreed. "So we go at it another way. I'll find out where the kid lives."

"You let me know and I'll keep an eye on him. See what happens."

"And if we get the sense that he's a problem?"

"You have to ask?" Shepard said.

Carter knew that he was right. They couldn't take chances.

"What about the other guy?" Shepard asked.

"I'll find out what I can," Carter said. "Might be that we want to look at him, too. Mack mentioned he worked in a kitchen in Coney Island. I'll ask around. Someone's gonna remember a Brit."

"We need to talk about this," Shepard said. "Properly. What are you doing after your tour?"

"I was gonna go home. You know how close it is to the baby coming."

"Come for a beer. Becky won't mind if you're an hour later. She'll be asleep anyway, right?"

"All right," Carter conceded.

"You think you'll be able to go out when the kid is born?"

"I said all right, Shep."

"I'll come pick you up at the precinct. I'll drive you home afterwards."

51

Milton rode to the Tillman Senior Center on Mother Gaston Boulevard. The meeting started at 7 p.m., and he arrived with ten minutes to spare. The men and women who attended the meeting were gathered in the lobby of the building, drinking their mugs of coffee and eating pastries. It was an Al-Anon open meeting, a chance for relatives and friends of alcoholics to attend with them.

Milton waited at the door until he saw Manny and Freddy. The boy was clutching his father's hand. He was nervous. Milton wasn't surprised by that at all. It was daunting to see so many people that he didn't know, but, more than that, there was an unfamiliarity to the proceedings and what he might learn about his father. Manny bringing Freddy with him was an acknowledgement that Manny had a problem that needed serious help; he was admitting it, underlining it, and there would be no way it could be ignored or brushed aside any longer.

Milton got two cups of coffee and a Coke and went over to where the Blancos were standing.

"What happens now?" Freddy said to his father and Milton after he had sipped from the plastic cup.

"The people here have problems with alcohol just like I do," Manny explained quietly. "Most of the time, we just listen. Someone will talk about their story, the things that have happened to them, and then people will say how what they've heard has made them feel."

Milton had been to Al-Anon meetings in London; newcomers were encouraged to learn from members whose personal situations most closely resembled theirs. The goal was for them to begin to understand how much they had in common with the others who had been affected by someone else's drinking, regardless of the specific details of their personal situation.

Freddy stared up at his father. Milton thought he looked younger than thirteen. "Are you gonna say anything?" he asked.

Manny looked over at Milton, as if for guidance, and Milton inclined his head a little in encouragement.

"Yeah," Manny said. "Probably. I got a lot to get off my chest. I let you down, Freddy. I wanna start making that right."

"You don't have to tell anyone that," Freddy said, indignant at the thought of his father embarrassing himself in front of these people.

"It's okay," Manny said. "No one judges. Everyone's got the same issues. I'm the same as all the rest."

The secretary came out of the main room and announced that the meeting was just getting started.

"Ready?" Milton suggested.

Manny bit his lip; his eyes were wet and he looked as if he was about to cry.

"It'll be all right," Milton said.

He took a gulp of air.

Freddy reached for his father's hand and smiled at him. Manny took another lungful, tried to fake a smile, and nodded. He led the way into the room.

52

T he three of them took seats at the front of the room—a little uncomfortable for Milton, who preferred the back—and they sat and listened to the share of a woman about the same age as Manny who had two teenage girls at the meeting to hear her speak. The woman told a tale that Milton had heard many, many times before: she had separated from her husband and had struggled to bring her daughters up on her own, relying more and more on alcohol until she was drinking first thing in the morning and hiding bottles of vodka around the house. Milton saw a flash of movement in the corner of his eye and looked over to see that Manny had reached over to hold Freddy's hand.

The woman finished her story and the chair invited others to speak. Both daughters went first, explaining how their mother's drinking had affected their lives, but then telling her that they both loved her, were grateful to her for what she had done for them and proud of her for admitting that she had a problem. The woman started to cry, and both girls went up to hug her. Milton looked and saw that Manny was crying, too.

The shares continued. Manny didn't say anything, and Milton thought that he had decided to stay silent until the secretary looked at his watch and asked whether anyone else wanted to say something.

Manny raised his hand. He explained that he had been coming to meetings for a while and had said that he had thought that he was doing well. He said that things had got on top of him over the past few days and that he had fallen off the wagon. He said that he had let his son down when he had needed him the most. His voice was clogged with emotion, and he was unable to go on. Freddy reached over and took his father's hand. Manny took a breath and then continued. He said that he had brought his son with him today so that he could see how seriously he was taking his problem, and so that he could tell him, with the others as witnesses, that he was going to stop drinking for good. He told him that he was never going to let him down again.

Milton usually found the meetings to be peaceful and meditative places. He rarely found that he had an emotional response to the stories of the others who shared, but he found that there was a catch in his throat as he joined the room in thanking Manny for his share. He tried to work out why that was. He felt some complicity in Manny's relapse; he was already doubting the good sense in involving himself in their business—closing the drug den and replacing Freddy's stolen sneakers—and worried that he had catalysed Manny's drinking by making him feel inadequate as a father.

That, though, was not the reason why he had found the story difficult to hear. It was more personal than that: Milton had started to feel lonely. It had taken him months to admit it to himself, but, after what had happened to him in Manila, he couldn't pretend any longer. He had ignored his instinctive caution and flown halfway around the world because someone he had known once, a long time ago, had told him that he was a father. It had turned out not to be true, and his gullibility had cost the life of the woman who had lied to him—and had almost cost the life his own, too.

Milton had sublimated it all. He couldn't allow himself the luxury of thinking that a normal life was something that he could ever have. He was a killer, with blood on his hands, and there were people in the world who would have dearly loved to see him murdered in as painful and inventive a way as possible. To bring anyone else into his orbit—a partner, or, even worse, a child—would be the ultimate act of selfishness. His life was full of paranoia and suspicion, and he could see no change to that. He couldn't ask anyone else to share that with him. He had brought it upon himself; it was his burden to bear.

———

The meeting finished and they shuffled along with the others into the lobby.

"Who wants to go to Dave and Buster's?" Manny asked.

Freddy was open-mouthed with excitement. "Seriously?"

"Seriously."

Manny grinned at his son, and Freddy enthusiastically bumped fists with him. Milton smiled; he remembered how excited he had been when his parents took him to McDonald's when he was growing up and this, he guessed, was similar.

"John?"

"Sorry," Milton said. "Miles away."

"You wanna come with us?"

Milton had nowhere that he needed to be, and he found that he was growing more and more comfortable with the Blancos. He also wanted the opportunity to talk to them both about the best way to handle Freddy's involvement in the murder investigation.

"I'd love to," he said.

53

C arter was distracted for the first three and a half hours of their shift. He kept flashing back to the previous night and the knowledge that they had left a witness. It was unprofessional and, more than that, it was dangerous. Mackintosh was one thing, but, as he allowed the thought to fester, he realised that Acosta was worse. They had always sold themselves to him as smart operators who got things done with the minimum of fuss and with no possibility of exposure for him. They were problem solvers.

This time was different.

They might have solved one problem, but, in doing so, they had created another. Acosta was ruthless. It was impossible to rise as high and as fast as he had risen without being able to move decisively, to be able to put aside everything for the sake of building and then protecting the business. Carter knew about the rivals who had sought to keep him down and the upstarts who had tried to usurp his throne. He knew where the bodies were buried; in three cases, he had buried the bodies himself.

Rhodes must have sensed that something was on his mind, for, after a failed attempt to start a conversation as they set off, he had been largely quiet. They listened to the dispatcher on the radio, the squelches of static that book-ended each call to assign officers to incidents. Carter looked over at him and felt resentment. Rhodes was at the start of his career, with every option open to him. Carter had chosen his path and now he was destined—or doomed—to follow it. He was yoked to Acosta. It was true that he had made a lot of money, but most of that had been spent. There was only one way to leave Acosta's employment, as González had discovered. Carter was trapped.

He knew the resentment was irrational, but still he let it stew. Rhodes's naivety, his stupid questions, his blindness to the reality of life on the street—it made him angry, and he decided to do something about it.

They were cruising west along Pitkin when Carter saw the guy. They were fifty feet away from him. The man was standing on the corner of Elton. He was a big guy in a leather trench coat with a black beanie on his head and dreadlocks spilling down his back. Carter knew who he was.

"Pull over," Carter said, pointing to a spot behind an AT&T truck.

Rhodes did as he was told, pulling out of the flow of traffic and slotting in behind the van.

"There's a guy on the corner up ahead," he said. "Big black guy. See him?"

"Sure."

"His name's Otto. Pushes weed on the street. I've arrested him half a dozen times in the last month, but the fucker don't take no for an answer and keeps coming out here. Looks like we're gonna have to remind him not to do that no more."

"What do you need me to do?"

"Back me up," he said. "Otto's a runner. Soon as he sees me, he's gonna book. We're gonna have to chase him down. Ready?"

Rhodes nodded.

Carter opened his door and immediately started to run. Otto was looking the other way, and Carter was almost on top of him before he noticed and started to sprint in the opposite direction. He turned onto Elton Street and headed south. It was a rough street, with decaying houses on either side and cheap cars parked outside them. Otto had been a marine in a previous life and had complained once that he'd been shot in the leg during a tour of Iraq. Whatever the truth of that, he walked with a limp that became even more pronounced as he tried to run. Carter reeled him in, catching him as he reached the church that was halfway between Pitkin and Belmont. He grabbed his coat and flung him into the railing at the side of the church. Otto crashed face first to the ground; Carter dropped onto him, planting his knee in the centre of his back, grabbing his right wrist and yanking it up behind his back.

"Why are you running, Otto?"

"Because you gonna roll me again," the man said, grunting from the pain.

Otto took the opportunity to struggle, trying to free his wrist. Carter took his pistol and pressed the barrel against the back of his head.

"You fucking mutt," he said to Otto. "Keep still."

He frisked him with his left hand, going through the pockets of his jacket and dumping the contents on the ground. He found a thick roll of dollars fastened with an elastic band and a double handful of small clear plastic vials, each with a red cap, about an inch long and the width of a pencil, similar to the vials that stores used for perfume samples. Instead of perfume, though, these vials each contained a half gram of off-white nuggets with jagged edges.

"Crack, Otto? I told you I didn't want to see you selling this shit again."

Carter took the vials and put them in his own pocket. He guessed that there were forty of them, and he knew that each would retail for twenty bucks. He would be able to offer those to his dealer at a discount and take seven hundred dollars for himself. He guessed that the roll of bills amounted to about the same again. He would clear a grand, and all he'd had to do was chase down a one-legged dealer. Easy money, just like always.

Rhodes caught up with them both.

"You okay?" he gasped.

"We're fine," he said. "Just finishing up."

He pulled the gun away, removed his knee from Otto's back, and stood. Otto turned over so that he could look up at them, but he made no effort to get up.

"Go home," Carter said. "I don't want to see you here when we come by later."

———————

Carter got back into the car and waited for Rhodes to join him.

"What happened back there?" the rookie said.

"What do you mean?"

"You let him walk. You said he was dealing."

"He was dealing."

"So why didn't we arrest him?"

It was time for some home truths. "You know how many drug dealers work this part of Brooklyn?"

"I've got no idea."

"Dozens. Let's say there are fifty I know of and probably three times that who I don't. They ain't hard to find. We could cruise up and down this street and find another in five minutes flat. We could arrest our friend back there, add the new guy… we could have three of them back there in no time. You know why we don't do that?"

Rhodes shook his head.

Carter took out the roll of money that he had confiscated from Otto. He reached into his pocket again and took out a handful of the crack vials that he'd taken.

"What are you doing?"

They were going to have the conversation at some point, Carter decided. It might as well be now.

"How much good do you think arresting them would do—I mean *really* do?" It was a rhetorical question, and he waved his hand to forestall an answer. "Look what we got: overcrowded jails, prosecutors who are so busy they don't know what day it is. Add in unreliable witnesses and you got a messy situation. Now let's say we arrest Otto and take him back to get charged. There's a ton of paperwork that we gotta fill out. He gets an interview. We deal with some lawyer, a precinct crawler who knows how to make us look bad and gets him out with minimal effect. Otto is back on the street tomorrow like nothing has happened. Back on the same corner, selling the same shit to the same shitbirds."

"So?"

"*So*," Carter went on, "there's a better way. Rather than go through the hoops, eventually you figure out that it's easier to let the suspect go. Maybe you work him over with your stick a little or, if you're feeling generous, you give him a warning. The dealer is grateful, and maybe you can go back to him later and turn him so you can work up the chain to his supplier. Take the *supplier* down and you take out a dozen dealers all at once, not just one."

Rhodes listened quietly. When Carter was finished, he pointed to the crack and the money. "And *that?*"

"Listen, kid," he said. "Let me ask you a question. How much do you figure to clear after tax this month?"

"Two and a half."

"And you think that's fair for the amount of shit you're gonna have to go through to get it?"

"That's the job. I knew what the pay was like going in. No point bitching about it now."

"But you've got no idea what life on the street is like, do you? This ain't the subway. This is Brooklyn."

Rhodes didn't answer.

Carter didn't know whether he had gotten through to him or not. He reached up, took the money and the crack and put it in the glovebox. He looked at the kid. Rhodes had watched as he put the money and the drugs away. His face was eloquent with the confusion that he was wrestling with: he was sucking and biting the left-hand corner of his top lip, and his forehead was furrowed with a deep frown.

"We got more talking to do," Carter said. "Drive."

54

The nearest Dave and Buster's was in midtown Manhattan. Milton tried not to watch the meter as they crossed the Brooklyn Bridge and headed into the jungle of glittering spires and minarets of the financial district. He knew he had to stop worrying on Manny's behalf, but the cab was going to cost them sixty bucks for a round trip and, given Freddy's excitement about their destination, Milton guessed that it wasn't somewhere that they visited very often. That meant it was probably not going to be a cheap meal. He wondered whether there was any way that he could help defray the evening's expenses without offending Manny or making things worse and concluded that there wasn't.

Milton had never heard of Dave and Buster's, but, as he learned quickly in the back of the cab, it had made a mark for itself by combining the basics of an arcade, sports bar and burger restaurant under one roof.

The place was full. The main floor was a restaurant that could also be turned into a sports bar, and Milton guessed that there was room for at least two hundred customers.

There was a staircase up to the second floor, where Milton guessed—given the pulsing lights and the clamour of noise —the arcade could be found.

Freddy started for the stairs as soon as they entered.

"After we've eaten," Manny said, smiling, as he anchored his son with a restraining hand.

The place was full despite the capacity and they were given a table at the back. Milton looked at the menu and picked the Buffalo Wing Burger. Manny was about to order the Maker's Mark Burger, but realised his error and changed it so that it came without the bourbon sauce. Freddy picked the cheeseburger with sautéed mushrooms. They added extra waffle-cut French fries and three sodas. The waitress took their order and disappeared into the kitchen.

Milton cleared his throat. They had to have the conversation. It would be better to get it out of the way now so that they could enjoy their meal.

"So," he said. "Did the police come back this morning?"

Freddy nodded.

"What did they ask?"

The waitress came back with their drinks.

Freddy waited and then said, "They wanted me to go through what happened last night. What I saw."

"Did you tell them?"

He took a sip of his Coke. "I told them what you said I should tell them."

Manny leaned forward. "What?"

"You didn't say anything about the man in the precinct?"

"What?" Manny said. "What does that mean?"

"No," Freddy said. "I didn't say."

Manny held up a hand. "Hold up," he said. "Let's run through that again. He didn't tell them what?"

Milton took a sip of his drink to give himself a moment

to compose what he wanted to say. He knew that it had the potential to wreck the evening before it even began.

"John? What is it?"

"Freddy and I were waiting in the precinct house last night," Milton said. "They have a TV there. Freddy was watching it and there was video of a man. A police officer. Freddy thinks it was one of the men he saw outside the restroom."

"*What?*"

"I don't think it," Freddy corrected. "I know it. It *was* him. For sure."

Milton took his phone out of his pocket, opened his photos and swiped to the screenshot from the video.

Manny stared down at it. "Him?"

Freddy nodded. "That's the man I saw. He was standing outside."

"You didn't tell me," Manny protested. "Why didn't you tell me?"

"He's telling you now," Milton said, trying to prevent another flash of Manny's temper. "I told him to keep it to himself."

Manny eyeballed him dubiously. "Why would you do that?"

"Think, Manny," Milton said calmly. "Freddy saw the guy who wound up dead as he was leaving. He saw two guys come into the station: one black and the other one white. He went back, saw the black guy outside the door and then him and the white guy leaving. Then he went into the restroom and found the body. It has to be them. And he thinks that one of the two men was a police officer. We need to think carefully about what we do with that information. What if the other man was an officer, too? We don't know what that man looks like. And then go a little further: what if others in the precinct are involved? At the moment, there's no reason for that man to think that Freddy can implicate him. Freddy hasn't said that he's seen anything. But if Freddy says that he does recognise someone, and if that man finds out, if it happens before we're ready, we won't know who we can trust."

Manny took a ten-dollar bill from his wallet. "Freddy," he said, "go up and play on the machines for five minutes. Come down after that—your burger will be here soon."

Freddy took the money. He paused, as if caught between his excitement about the machines on the floor above and his unwillingness to leave the table while his father and Milton talked about him.

"You want me to change my mind?" Manny said.

"Okay," Freddy said.

"Five minutes, no more."

Freddy promised that he would be back and almost skipped to the stairs.

Manny waited for his son to leave and then said, "So what do we do? Do nothing? Pretend he saw nothing?"

"That's an option," Milton said. "It's not one I like."

"He's not your son."

"No," Milton said. "That's true. And you'll have to help him decide—not me."

"Maybe it's best if he says nothing. Let it all blow over. Whatever happened, it has nothing to do with us. Someone else's problem."

Milton took a sip of his soda and then wiped his mouth with his napkin. "Let me lay out the alternative," he said. "What if the bad guys decide they can't take the risk? Freddy's a witness. They can't be sure that he won't recognise them later. Maybe they wait. Maybe they come back in a month, when you've forgotten about it."

Milton didn't want to draw the line between the dots for fear of scaring him, but Manny had no difficulty following where Milton's reasoning was going.

"I don't know," he said. "I don't know what to do."

"So talk it out," Milton suggested.

"All right," Manny conceded. "Let's say we decide Freddy can tell the detectives what he saw. Which detective? How do we know who to trust?"

"The officers who came to see you this morning—you remember their names?"

"Mackintosh and Polanski."

Milton nodded. "Polanski came to see me on his own this morning. That said a lot. He tell you what department he works in?"

Manny shook his head. "Just said he was a detective."

"Internal Affairs. He wouldn't tell me why he was involved, but I can guess."

"He's investigating the cop Freddy saw."

"Maybe," Milton said. "Whether it's that or something else, there's an investigation going on that has something to do with the murder. If we're going to trust anyone, it'd be him."

"But we don't know anything about him," Manny protested.

"No," Milton agreed. "Not yet. I'm going to get to know him a little better and then we can decide."

Manny groaned. "You don't have to do this. You've already done enough."

"I'm a witness, too," Milton replied. "I was there. Whoever it was Freddy saw outside the bathroom, they're going to have questions about me as well. Did I see them, too? That'll make them nervous. The way I see it, I'm in this almost as much as Freddy is. So it's in my interest, too."

There was truth in that, but Milton was playing it up. Manny didn't make it obvious if he realised.

The waitress returned, laden down with their food. She distributed the plates around the table. Manny glanced up at the staircase just as Freddy started down it.

"All right," Manny said. "If there's anything I can do…"

"Don't say anything yet," Milton said. "Not to anyone. Let's see what I can find out; then we can decide."

55

C arter was hungry. It was eleven thirty, and the shift still had another thirty minutes left to run. They were on Pitkin, approaching the bodega on the corner of Sheffield Avenue. He told Rhodes to pull over and wait.

He went inside. The proprietor, a wizened old Dominican named Juan, nodded a greeting. Carter returned the gesture, went to the shrink-wrapped sandwiches in the chiller and grabbed two. He added a six-pack of beer and, going to the counter and pointing at the shelves behind him, added a packet of Marlboro Red. Carter made a show of taking out his wallet but, just as he knew that he would, Juan wagged his finger in mock disapproval.

"Thank you," Carter said, going back outside into the cold.

He opened the car and tossed one of the sandwiches across the cabin to Rhodes. He got in, closed the door, opened his own sandwich and took a big bite.

"Let me put you straight on a couple of things," Carter

said through a mouthful of salami. "There are some facts you need to understand about working a precinct like this."

"Yeah?" Rhodes said, his own mouth full of sandwich.

"You been on the street long enough, you're going to figure out that there are two kinds of cop: grass eaters and meat eaters. Meat eaters take advantage of being police. Maybe they hear about a house that's being used for selling drugs, and they go in and bust the place up. They arrest the bad guys, but, before anyone else shows up, maybe they take half of the money they find lying around in the place and voucher the other half. They share that money out among each other for a job well done."

Rhodes wiped his mouth with the back of his hand. "The other kind?"

"Grass eaters," he said. "They know what goes on and they accept the pay-offs that get tossed their way for being cops."

"What are you?"

"I ain't finished yet. Eventually, the grass eaters get eaten by the meat eaters. That's just the way it always goes. You work in the Seven Five long enough, you're gonna get so much shit thrown at you all the ideals they drilled into you in the academy are going to start looking pretty fucking silly. Maybe you're on the midnight tour, you pick up a whore and she spits in your face. Then maybe you chase down a dealer and he turns and takes a shot at you. You scrape up a drunk you found in the gutter and he pukes all over the back of the patrol car when you take him to the drunk tank and you gotta clean his shit up. Those things happen again and again and, soon enough, you see a pile of money on the table after you've busted a place and you think to yourself, maybe I do deserve that. What's the point in vouchering it?

It all goes back into the city funds; none of it comes back to us. So who cares if I help myself to half of it? It's what you might call a victimless crime."

"I don't know, Bobby. What happens when you get caught?"

He ignored the question. "You don't *have* to dip your hand in," he said. "But let me give you a word of advice. Everyone is on the take. This precinct, the Sixty-Ninth, the Seventy-Seventh, the Seventy-Ninth—shit, you go down to some quiet precinct on Staten Island and I guarantee you dollars to doughnuts that old cop who looks like he's done everything right for all of his thirty-year career, he's been feathering his nest when no one's looking, too. You can pretend like none of that happens if you like, but you'd be wrong, and, worse than that, guys are gonna start looking at you in a different way. They ain't gonna trust you if you don't take your share. Maybe they think you're the kind of cop who'd rat on other cops. I ain't saying you would, I'm just saying that's the way it is."

"I just got this job," Rhodes said. "Last thing I want is to get myself in trouble. I ain't got nothing else to go to."

Carter didn't know if he was getting through to him or not. He pointed to the half-eaten sandwich that the rookie had in his hand. "Take that sandwich," he said. "I didn't pay for that. Same as I didn't pay for mine or the beers or the smokes he gave us."

Rhodes had just taken another bite. "For fuck's sake, Bobby," he said, lowering the sandwich from his mouth as if he had just found something unpleasant inside.

"You know why he gave us all that for nothing?"

"I don't wanna get into this."

"Why?" Carter pressed.

Rhodes sighed and relented. "Because he wants us on his side."

"'Because he wants us on his side,'" Carter repeated. "Exactly. And let's say we go by there every night. How much you reckon all that would have cost if we'd bought it? Twenty bucks? Five nights a week, that's a hundred bucks he's sending our way. Four hundred bucks a month. Nearly five grand a year."

Rhodes had been about to take another bite of the sandwich, but now it just hovered there, an inch away from his mouth.

"Eat it," Carter said. "It's a shitty sandwich, kid. All I'm saying, this is just the way it is. Internal Affairs could take the view that we get paid an extra five grand a year to keep an eye on that particular store. Maybe they'd say that was corruption. Maybe they'd say we were taking advantage of the fact that we were cops. But everyone does it."

He reached forward, opened the glovebox and took out the cash that he had lifted from Otto.

"Put that away!" Rhodes protested.

"No one's looking," he said. "And what they gonna do if they are? We're cops. Relax."

Carter licked his thumb and peeled off four twenties, then held them up.

He reached across and pushed them into Rhodes's button-down pocket. He didn't resist.

"A sandwich or a hundred-dollar bill—it don't matter. The principle's the same. You eat grass or you eat meat. Your choice. But I know what I'd recommend."

Rhodes's hand hovered above his pocket, but, after a long moment when Carter didn't know which way he was going to go, he shook his head and lowered his hand to the wheel.

"There you go," Carter said. "There you go."

Rhodes put the remains of the sandwich on the dash and put the car into drive. They still had another twenty minutes left before their shift was over. He glanced into the mirror, touched the gas and drove out into the quiet street.

56

The rest of the tour passed without incident. Rhodes was quiet; Carter assumed that he was thinking about their conversation and the money that was still inside his breast pocket. Carter was pleased with how the kid had reacted. He had been reluctant, perhaps even hostile to the idea that they might profit from Otto, but that hostility had quickly subsided. Rhodes had pretensions to probity and still had the idealism that they bred into the rookies during their time at the academy, but that would pass. It always did. Ideals were fine, but they never lasted once they were stood against the realities of life. Brooklyn would do that to you. Tonight had been the rookie's first lesson. There would be other lessons, but this would be the one that he remembered. Carter remembered when his own cherry had been popped. He'd had similar conversations with other idealistic young cops over the years, and the outcome had been the same every time: they took, just like he took.

They drove up to Dumont Avenue. It was five to midnight, so Carter told him to turn around and head back to the precinct. Rhodes did as he was told, turning right on Sutter and cruising to the east.

They were rolling through the intersection with Linwood Avenue when Carter saw Shepard's car parked next to the precinct. He indicated that Rhodes should park the patrol car next to it.

He opened the door and stepped out into the freezing cold night.

Shepard got out of his vehicle, and Rhodes stepped out of the cruiser.

"This is Shepard," Carter said, turning to the kid. "Shep, this is Rhodes."

"The rookie?" Shepard said, his voice slurred and dripping with unsubtle sarcasm.

"That's right."

Carter could see that Shepard had already been out drinking. He was unsteady on his feet. Carter knew that he would make Rhodes feel uncomfortable, just because he had taken his old place as Carter's partner and because it was an easy thing to do. Carter didn't know Rhodes well enough to feel protective of him, but he knew that Shepard could be a dick after he had been drinking and he found, a little to his surprise, that he didn't want the rookie to form a bad impression of him by association.

"How was the tour?" Shepard asked Rhodes.

Carter wondered whether he would mention Otto and the money that they had taken, but he didn't. "Nothing to write home about," he said instead.

"Yeah? You think it's easy, do you? Working the precinct more straightforward than you thought it was gonna be?"

Carter could see that Shepard was rushing along the road to antagonism, and he didn't want that. He stepped between Shepard and Rhodes and clapped the rookie on the shoulder. "I'll see you tomorrow," he said. "Think about what I said, okay? It'll make everything easier."

Rhodes paused, a response caught on his lips, but he let it pass. "You okay?" he said, nodding to Shepard.

"He's just drunk. I'll help him get home."

Rhodes gave a nod and made his way inside the building.

Carter turned to Shepard. "What the fuck?" he said. "You've been drinking?"

"Don't get your panties in a bunch," Shepard said. "I needed a drink. Settle my nerves."

"You shouldn't have come here," Carter said. "I don't know what I was thinking saying this was a good idea. Get in the car. Come on—get in, you fucking reprobate. Move."

Carter opened the passenger-side door and pressed down on Shepard's shoulder until he gave in and dropped down onto the seat. Carter shut the door and took a moment to compose himself. He had to hold it together.

"What do we do?" Shepard said as soon as Carter was inside the car.

"We do nothing," Carter said. "We behave just like we always do."

"But—"

"No, Shep, no buts. *Think*. They got nothing on us. That's a fact. If the kid had seen something, if he had been able to identify either of us, you think we'd be here like this? No. We would've been arrested by now. We'd be sitting in an office and they'd be yelling in our faces about how they had us dead to rights, how we ought to protect ourselves by ratting the other one out. You know it, I know it—and it ain't happening. Think, Shep. What does that mean?"

"That they don't have nothing."

"That's right. They don't got squat. So you and me need

to play it cool, don't do anything to draw attention to ourselves, and make a few quiet enquiries to make doubly sure that we're in the clear."

The suggestion registered with Shepard. "You speak to Mackintosh?"

"What am I gonna say, Shep? 'I was just wondering if you could fill me in on that murder you're investigating down in Euclid?'"

"Nah," Shepard said, "that's not—"

"Give me a little credit, Shep. I'm gonna go back tonight when it's quiet. I'll have a look through her murder book and see if there's anything we need to look out for."

Shepard nodded. "You wanna get that drink?"

Carter shook his head. "You've had enough for one night, partner. I'm gonna drive you home, you're going to bed and you're gonna sleep this off. And then, in the morning, when you've got your head on straight, we can talk again. All right?"

"Sure, Bobby."

He slumped back in the seat and closed his eyes. Carter pulled out into the road, swung the wheel and headed east, setting off toward Port Washington. It was a ninety-minute round trip. He would take him home and then come back when the station was quiet.

He found that he was in a better mood than he had been earlier. He had worked with Shepard for years and they had made a good team. He had been unsettled when Shepard had told him that he was going to hand over his shield and his gun, but now, he realised, he was happy with the way things had played out. Rhodes showed promise, and truth be told, Carter didn't miss Shepard's drinking. He and Shepard would still work together, but it wouldn't be a bad thing to bring along a little new blood. The kid hadn't returned the money that Carter had given him. He would be pliable, just like they all were. He'd bring him along one step at a time.

Carter reached forward, switched on the radio, and worked through the presets until he had Q104.3. The station pumped out classic rock, and, as he headed through Elmont, Dire Straits' 'Sultans of Swing' faded out to be replaced by the beginning of 'Dazed and Confused' by Led Zeppelin.

Carter drummed his fingers on the wheel. He exhaled and tried to relax. It was fine, he told himself. Everything was okay. They were going to be fine.

57

T he top floor of the derelict building was cold. Milton had been in the room for two hours, ever since he had returned from Manhattan, and he wished that he had brought a warmer jacket. He had his hands thrust into his pockets and the coat was zipped all the way up to his throat, but he was still cold. It was an inconvenience that he was able to overlook. His work was important. He would dress more appropriately if he had to return here tomorrow. For now, though, he would just have to suck it up. He had conducted surveillance in locales far less hospitable than this.

He had been busy. He had noted down the makes and registrations of the cars that were parked in the narrow space below his window, most of them slotted in so that their hoods pointed out into the street. The cars were plain and unprepossessing, the kinds of rides that a municipal cop on a decent salary might be able to afford. Milton noted down two Fords, an old Lexus, a Nissan, a Chevrolet, a Toyota and a BMW. He hoped that he would be able to identify the man he was looking for without having to rely upon the plate of his car, but, if that was the only way, he had a few ideas. An old trick he had used when he had been working for the Group was to visit government emissions check sites and run a search on the plate. That often listed the shop that had serviced the car; Milton would then have visited the shop and either bribed the owner to give him the owner's information or broken in and found it for himself.

He looked down into the street. A car had been waiting outside the entrance to the precinct for ten minutes. It had backed into an empty space so that the hood was facing him. It was a maroon Honda CR-V. Milton had photographed it as it arrived, making sure that he had the plate. It was directly below a streetlight and the glow reflected off the glass, rendering it almost impossible for Milton to see inside. He thought that there was a single occupant, but he couldn't be sure. There was nothing unusual about it, but Milton noted that it was there and photographed it anyway.

Patrol cars from the four-to-twelve shift started to return to the precinct at five to midnight. Some of them parked at the front of the building. Others drove on to Essex Street and then went around so that they could get to the yard at the back. Milton photographed them all, making sure that he recorded the identification numbers that were painted above the trunk, on the rear wings and repeated on the front and back plates.

Milton checked his watch. It was a little before midnight. His breath was steaming in front of his face.

A patrol car pulled up and backed into the space next to the Honda. The doors opened and two uniformed cops got out. The driver's door of the Honda opened and a third man emerged.

Milton caught his breath. He held the camera steady,

stared into the viewfinder and cranked the zoom as far as he could.

Milton was confident: the man who had stepped out of the car was the same man that Freddy had picked out in the video. He was black with a salt-and-pepper beard, around six feet tall, probably in his fifties, well built and dressed in jeans, a leather jacket and a pair of Timberland boots. Milton didn't recognise the two officers. One of them looked to be in his early forties and evidently knew the black man from the hug that they exchanged. The final man was the youngest. Milton guessed that he was five ten, two hundred pounds, late twenties. He took off his hat and Milton saw a full head of boyish blond curls.

The older cop and the black man in civilian clothes disengaged from their embrace and started to talk. The younger cop said something and the black man turned and spoke sharply to him; Milton was too far away to hear what was being said, but body language made it very clear that the younger man did not share the same chemistry with the older man as the other cop did. The black man's gait was unsteady and he emphasised whatever it was that he was saying with declaratory finger prods and wide gestures, overcompensating in the way that drunks often do.

Milton held the camera steady and took photograph after photograph, the shutter clicking as he pressed down the button again and again.

The two cops spoke and the younger one took his leave and made his way into the precinct.

The remaining cop put his arm around the shoulders of the black man and ushered him back toward the Honda. He opened the door and pressed down on his shoulder, impelling him into the cabin, and then shut the door behind him. He paused there, turning around so that Milton could see his face clearly. He held down the button and shot a dozen pictures, a sequence of him as he turned away and then made his way to the driver's side.

Milton focused on the car and made doubly sure that he had a clear shot of the license plate.

The engine started; the car pulled out into Sutter Avenue and then swung around to the east and drove away.

Milton flicked the camera's selector so that he could look through the photographs that he had taken. He had a good range, with clear views of the three men and the car.

The cop had driven away in his uniform and in the other man's car. Milton guessed that he would be back and, clapping his arms around his torso to try to keep warm, he resigned himself to another wait.

58

C arter drove Shepard back to Port Washington, made sure that he got into his house, and then turned back. He returned to Sutter Avenue, parked the Honda, and went into the building. It was one thirty in the morning and it was much quieter than usual. He made it through the main room and into the offices without being seen by anyone other than the desk sergeant, whom he greeted with a raised hand.

He went into the back, but, instead of going down to the locker room, he went up.

The detective's office was upstairs. It had last been decorated in the nineties, and it was sorely in need of attention. It was accessed through a pair of double doors at the top of the stairs, the doors supposed to offer privacy and security but perpetually wedged open with door stops. There was a photocopied sign on the opaque glass—CRIME PREVEN-TION, with a large rip in the paper—and then two cabinets, three boxes perched precariously atop the cabinets and a plastic documents box balanced atop those. Junk from the main office was stored in the short antechamber that opened into the main room: folders, more boxes, an old rotary fan.

Carter continued on, passing a closed door that was marked ROLL CALL and on into the main office. It was a large space that seemed smaller thanks to the amount of furniture that had been forced into it. Each detective had a desk with an old terminal-style PC, the desks arranged with degrees of organisation or chaos that spoke volumes to the personalities of the detectives who had claimed them as their own. There were more filing cabinets, cork boards with posters and notices, and a water cooler that burbled incessantly. The walls were painted a drab municipal green and bore yet more paraphernalia: an American flag, with 'United We Stand' and '9/11' written across it; a sticker from the Detectives' Endowment Association that read 'Overworked and Underpaid'; a blown-up reproduction of the NYPD police shield; wanted posters, most of them offering cash rewards for unsolved homicides. There were no windows, and the illumination was provided by eight large square apertures in the ceiling through which flooded harsh UV light.

There were eleven desks for the seven detectives and three sergeants who made up the complement. Their commanding officer, Captain Donald Winter, had a small office at the end of the room. The office was empty, just as Carter had expected that it would be. He crossed the room, sat down at Mackintosh's desk and looked down at the items laid out before him. Most homicide dicks still kept a murder book: a collection of interview transcripts, follow-ups, crime lab reports, victim information, sheets of paper that were hole punched and filed in plastic files. Mackintosh was no different. There was a collection of files on the desk in which she kept her papers. Carter sat down and selected the file with the legend GONZÁLEZ, JOSÉ LUIS written on the tab. He opened it and quickly thumbed through the papers inside.

The main report noted that the victim, identified as José Luis González, had been found in the men's room at Euclid Avenue subway station. The dead man's address and next of kin were noted, together with the assumption, still to be confirmed by the pathologist, that the cause of death was that his throat had been cut. The body had been found by a young boy who had reportedly entered the restroom minutes after the supposed time of death. He had seen two suspects outside the door just before he went inside. A second witness, an older man, had then entered the restroom, seen the body and found the boy hiding in a toilet cubicle.

Carter gritted his teeth in frustration, but read on.

The man was identified as John Smith, with an address on West 24th Street in Coney Island. Smith had said that he hadn't seen anything out of the ordinary as he approached the bathroom, nor anything as he exited with the boy as they went to report the murder to the woman working in the station's token booth. This woman—identified as Felicia de la Cruz—also reported that she had seen nothing amiss that evening, and that her position in the booth meant that she did not have clear sight to the door that led into the bathroom. Smith said that she had been asleep. Mackintosh had asked Ms. de la Cruz whether there was any video coverage and she had reported that the cameras had been out of order for several weeks.

Carter took out his phone, swiped across to the camera app, and photographed the relevant pages.

Mackintosh wasn't as scrupulous about order as Carter had expected, and he shuffled through a collection of hand-written notes that had yet to be typed up and filed properly. He found one note, halfway through the slim pile, that recorded the name and address of the youngster who had seen the two suspects outside the restroom. His name was Freddy Blanco, his age was reported as thirteen—the detail was circled in red pen—and his address was listed as 4 Danforth Street, Cypress Hills.

Carter photographed the page and put his phone back into his pocket. He replaced the file where he had found it, made his way out of the office and went down to the locker room. He changed out of his uniform, dressed in his street clothes, and went back up to the ground floor. The desk sergeant was occupied with taking the details of a hooker who had been brought in by police officer Joyce Rogers, and neither he nor Rogers noticed him as he made his way through the room to the steps and the door outside.

He got into his car and took his phone out of his pocket. He swiped through the photographs that he had just taken, and skimmed through Mackintosh's notes once again. He was tired and ready for bed, but he wanted to check out the address he had just found. He drove north to Atlantic and then followed Crescent Street to Danforth.

He slowed and stopped at the side of the road as a late-running train rumbled above him on the elevated track. Number four was on the corner of Danforth and Crescent. It was an old building that looked in need of restorative work, surrounded by a wire mesh fence and with a rickety old fire escape that clung to the wall and offered access to all three floors. It was late, and there was no sign of light or any kind of activity through the barred ground-floor windows or the windows on the second and third floors.

Carter waited for a moment, just watching. He wondered whether he would need to return here. The kid had said that he hadn't gotten a good look at them, but how realistic was that? Carter knew that he would have to talk it out with Shepard once he had sobered up. They had two choices: trust that the kid really hadn't seen them, or tie up the loose end and ensure that he would never be a problem for them. Carter didn't like the idea of going after a kid, but he liked the idea of an Internal Affairs bust or a problem with Acosta even less.

He would think about it. At least he knew where the kid was. That gave him options.

He put the car into drive and set off. He wanted his bed.

PART III

TUESDAY

59

"Time to prepare for the worst snow in years, New York. As you probably know, we've been tracking a very unpleasant storm and, if we're right, it's going to hit the area tonight. The National Weather Service is warning residents of the upper Midwest, the Northeast and the Middle Atlantic of widespread heavy snowfall and possible blizzard conditions in the coming days, so you might want to keep those warm clothes out and make sure you've got everything you need to get around in the snow. How much snow are we talking about? Well, we're talking about a lot."

Milton pulled the duvet up around his chin as he listened to the forecast on the radio.

"If you live in or around Washington, Baltimore or Philadelphia, you could see as much as a foot of snow later today or early tomorrow morning. A winter storm watch has been issued for those areas. But things are likely to be more severe for us who live in and around the Five Counties. We're predicting snowfall of one to two feet. Things look pretty heavy with a significant winter storm for much of the I-95 corridor."

Milton reached up and pulled the curtains aside. The

sky was dark and grey, but there was no sign of any snow yet.

Time to move. He rolled out of bed and got into his running gear before he gave himself a chance to change his mind. He followed his usual route along the boardwalk, passing Café Valentin and reminding himself that he had promised to visit Alexei Fedorov and his family that evening. He continued to the eastern end of the boardwalk and, for a change, turned left and followed 15th Street up to Brighton Beach Avenue and then followed that for two and a half miles to the west all the way back to his apartment.

He showered, shaved and dressed in his jeans, a T-shirt and a thick sweater. He went into his tiny living room and took the camera out of its bag. He ejected the memory card, slotted it into a reader and pushed that into his laptop's USB port. He transferred the photos that he had taken last night and then looked through them. There were more than five hundred. He worked through all of them, finding the ones toward the end of his vigil that showed the Honda CR-V that had pulled up at the precinct house and waited, the patrol car that had pulled up alongside it at the end of the four-to-twelve shift, and the three men who had met outside the vehicles and the conversation that had ensued. He also had pictures of the cop who had driven away with the drunken black man, and pictures of him as he had returned ninety minutes later. Milton had snapped him getting out of the Honda, going into the station house, coming back outside in civilian clothes, and then getting into a big Ford F-150 pickup. Milton had close-ups of his face and the license plate of his truck.

Milton scrolled back and looked more closely at the black man. He had thirty good shots of him, several offering a clear view of his face. He took out his phone and compared him with the man in the video whom Freddy had identified.

It was the same man.

He selected the best photographs of all three men, emailed them to himself, and closed the laptop. He called Manny's number, left a message on the machine to say that he was coming over, grabbed his leather jacket and made his way down to the street and his motorbike.

60

M ilton parked the bike outside the Blanco house, opened the gate and went up to the door. He rapped on it and turned to look out into the street as he waited. The drug den was still vacant. A man came out of the adjacent house, descended the steps to the sidewalk and went over to a white panel van that had been graffitied with a crude drawing that resembled Pac-Man.

"John."

Milton turned back. Manny was standing in the open door.

"Good morning," Milton said.

"Come in. It's freezing."

Milton stepped into the house and went through into the living room as Manny shut the door behind him. Freddy was sitting on the couch, a bowl of cereal balanced on his lap as he watched something on the iPad that he had propped up against the arm of the chair.

"Hello, Freddy," Milton said.

The kid looked up and smiled. "Hello, Mr. Smith."

"It's John," Milton corrected. "Call me John."

"I got your message," Manny said. "What's up?"

"I've got some photographs for Freddy to look at," Milton said. The kid looked up again. "Would you do that for me, Freddy?"

"Photos of what?"

"People."

"Okay."

"Put the iPad away," Manny told his son.

Milton went to the table, sat down and took out his phone. He selected the photographs that he had culled from the collection that he had taken last night.

Manny looked down at them. "Is that the precinct house?"

"Yes," Milton said. "I found a place where I could watch them without being seen."

He turned the screen around so that Freddy could see it. "Do you recognise any of them?"

The boy came closer and looked at the image.

He froze.

"Freddy?"

"Him," the boy said. He pointed, his finger quivering.

Milton looked down at it, too. He was pointing at the black man in the Honda.

"You're sure?"

"That's him. He was outside the restroom. That's the man I saw."

"Are you *absolutely* sure?" Manny said.

"Yeah. Definitely."

"What about the other two?" Milton said.

Freddy stared at the screen. He shook his head. "Don't recognise them."

"Let's look through a few more," Milton said, reaching for the phone and swiping right to bring up the next image.

Freddy did as he was told and looked through the remaining images. He shook his head again. "I don't know the other two," he repeated. "But I didn't... you know, I didn't really get a good look at the second man.

"All right." Milton pocketed the phone. "That's fine. Well done."

Manny stood awkwardly, reaching down to rub the place where his stump and prosthesis met. "What now?"

"I find out some more about him."

"Like?" Manny asked.

"His name would be a good place to start. It wasn't in the video or on the website. The other guys, too. I'd like to know who they are."

"You think one of the others is the other man he saw?"

"It's possible."

"What about us?" Manny said. "What do we do?"

"Nothing," Milton said. "Whatever you would have done if this hadn't happened. Freddy's not going to school?"

"I've said he's sick," Manny said.

"But I'm not," Freddy protested.

"I don't want you out of my sight until we figure out what to do," his father said firmly. He turned to Milton. "You agree?"

"Actually, I think school might not be a bad idea. If he feels up to it—"

"I do," Freddy interrupted.

"—then it might help keep his mind off what happened."

Milton walked over to the door and gave a gentle incline of his head. Manny noticed the gesture and followed him. "And I'm not sure it's clever to make it look like he's frightened," Milton said in a low voice. "It might make someone think that he has something to hide."

"I don't know," Manny said.

"You're his father," Milton said. "I'm just telling you what I'd do. But it's your call."

"I'd rather walk him to school myself when he goes back," Manny said. He looked at his watch. "I was going to go to a meeting this morning and then I've got to get to work."

"You want me to take him?"

"You don't have to do that."

"I don't have anything else to do," Milton said.

Manny paused, considering it. "You wanna go in?" he called over to his son.

"I told you I did."

"Get your things. John says he'll take you."

61

Freddy went to Grover Cleveland High School. It was in Ridgewood, Queens, a bus ride to the northwest. The boy led Milton up to the corner of Etna and Crescent. There was a bus stop there; Freddy turned and saw the B13 bus rumbling toward them, so they bolted for the stop and flagged it down just in time.

They took empty seats next to each other and caught their breath as the driver pulled away from the stop.

"How long does the bus take?" Milton asked.

"Twenty minutes."

"You don't have a closer school?"

"There was Franklin K. Lane, but they closed it down. They had a shooting there. And I don't mind the bus. I usually read or listen to music."

They sat in silence for a minute as the bus swung hard left onto Jamaica Avenue and then right onto Cypress Hills Street, passing through the middle of the park. They went by an enormous cemetery, with white headstones lined up in neat lines for hundreds of feet, nestled beneath the sheltering boughs of ancient oak trees.

"You think my dad is gonna be okay?" Freddy asked him.

"I can't say that," Milton said. "But he's trying as hard as he can."

"What about you?"

Milton smiled. "What about me?"

"How do you do it? You seem like you've got it together."

"You might be surprised."

"But you don't go out and drink."

"No," Milton said. "Not for a long time. But it's not easy. It takes hard work. And I go to a lot of meetings."

"Do you have anyone to help you?"

"No," Milton said. "It's just me."

"You don't have any children?"

"No," Milton said. "No one."

"You don't get lonely?"

Milton shrugged. "Sometimes."

Freddy didn't hear him. He stared out at the sign for Machpelah Cemetery and the fresh rows of headstones that came into view. "I'm gonna help my dad," Freddy said. "I know he's trying. I'm gonna do everything I can to make it easier for him."

"He's lucky to have you," Milton said.

———

Grover Cleveland High School was a huge building. Milton waited at the gates on Himrod Street and watched as Freddy made his way along the path that led to the main entrance. The boy looked a little smaller and a little younger as he disappeared inside and Milton found, again, that he was impressed by how he was handling a frightening episode. Milton rededicated himself to helping him and his father find their way out of the mess that they had been unfortunate enough to find themselves in: he would get to the bottom of what had happened, and he would make it right.

62

Milton took a taxi back to Danforth Street, collected his bike, and set off to Union Garage, a motorcycle store in Cobble Hill. It was accommodated within an old industrial space and had a mural of an American eagle painted above the door. Milton went inside and waited for the clerk.

"I'm looking for a tracker," he said. "Something robust."

"Waterproof?"

"Yes," Milton said.

"Follow me, sir."

The clerk led the way deeper into the shop until they reached an aisle that was set aside for accessories. He took a box from the shelf and handed it to Milton. The front of the box had a clear window, and Milton looked inside to see a small black device, around two and a half inches by two inches.

"That's a Spot Trace," the clerk said. "You get advanced theft-alert tracking for whatever you stick it on. Cars, bikes, boats—whatever you like."

"How does it work?"

"You get a text or an email if it moves. Or you can follow them on Google Maps in real-time."

"Does it store data?"

"Sure does. The website records movement for the previous month. Hundred and twenty bucks apiece."

"I'll take two," Milton said.

Milton headed back to the station house on Sutter Avenue once more. He parked in the same spot as yesterday evening, made his way into the derelict building and back up to the window where he could surveil the precinct house. It was midday when he took up his position again. He had stopped in a 7-Eleven to pick up a sandwich and a bottle of water and to use the restroom. He was ready to stay up here and watch for as long as it took.

He had been waiting for four hours when he saw the officer who had driven the black man home and then returned to the precinct last night. He arrived at the precinct in the same Ford F-150, backing the big truck into the narrow lot so that it was perpendicular to the building and aligned with the other cars that were already there. Milton watched as the cop got out of the truck and disappeared into the building, and then settled back down to wait a little longer.

Another five minutes passed. Two more cars pulled up and parked. The second, a grey Ford Fusion, backed into the spot next to the first cop's car. Milton watched and saw a younger man with a shock of bright blond hair step out, lock the car and then make his way into the precinct. He recognised him, too: it was the officer who had been in the patrol car with the first man.

He reached into his pocket and took out the GPS trackers. He took out the industrial-strength double-sided tape that had come with the units, tore off the backing strips and stuck a piece on each one. He switched the trackers on, went to the back of the room and climbed down into the yard. He jumped down the last few feet and hurried around the block to Sutter Avenue.

He idled for a moment, waiting for a female cop to lock her car and head into the building. Milton looked up and down the street and, satisfied that he was alone, walked toward the Ford truck. He took out the first tracker, peeled off the backing from the adhesive tape on the back of the case and, with a final check that he wasn't being observed, reached down beneath the rear fender and pressed the device against the chassis.

Milton went to the Fusion. He checked up and down the street again and, still satisfied that he was not being watched, secured the second tracker.

He continued walking away from the cars and the buildings.

He had been quick: setting the trackers had taken less than thirty seconds.

———

Milton went back to his vantage point. He took out his phone and navigated to the website of the company that manufactured the trackers. He set up an account and entered the serial numbers of the two units; within moments, he saw a map of East New York with two overlapping blue dots outside the precinct house on Sutter Avenue.

He saw the two cops from last night go out on patrol together at ten minutes past four, but the older man—the drunk—did not show again. He surveilled the station for another two hours, until his phone showed six and the leaden clouds above had grown darker in the fading light. He was cold and he had an appointment to keep. Content that the two trackers were functioning, he climbed down into the yard and went back to his bike.

63

He went home and found a clean shirt for dinner. He washed and changed, then looked out of the window: it was dark, the moon and stars hidden by the cloud banks that had moved in off the ocean. He collected his camera bag, locked up and descended the stairs to the street.

It was a cold night, with the promise of snow in the air, and he zipped his leather jacket all the way up to his chin to ward away the chill. He made his way south and then turned to the east, passing on the other side of the same landmarks that he saw every morning during his run. They looked different at night; the Wonder Wheel and the Parachute Jump loomed high overhead, their struts and joists like skeletal silhouettes against the light from the neighbouring streets that bled up into the darkness.

He reached Brighton Beach Avenue, the main drag that was closed in by the elevated tracks of the subway overhead. The signs of the businesses that he passed changed from English to Cyrillic. There were restaurants and stores that offered counterfeit goods at knock-down prices, fake electronics and racks of designer frames from optometrists. The young men displayed their masculinity by wearing thin jackets that would have offered minimal protection from the cold, but their elders—grizzled men and haughty women—wore fur and wool coats, fur-lined *ushankas* on their heads and solid boots. They knew that the storm was coming, and they were ready for it.

Milton slowed to look around. This was Little Odessa, the New York home for an expatriate community of Russians who had fled their homeland through fear of the regime or in hope of finding better circumstances in the land of the free. Milton continued along the road, passing shuttered stands that would normally have offered fruits and vegetables, and plate-glass windows through which Milton could see empty racks with stained ice beds that would be replenished with fish in the morning.

He turned onto 4th Street, passing between Roksolana Wholesale and a deli. He parked the bike, bought a pack of cigarettes and then continued down to the boardwalk, the narrow road crowded by large brick apartment buildings on either side. He climbed the stairs to the boardwalk. Café Valentin was on the corner, accommodated in the ground floor of the last of the apartment buildings and equipped with a wide awning that would have allowed for *al fresco* dining were the weather to be amenable.

Milton checked his watch: he was five minutes early. He took out a cigarette, smoked it, checked his watch again, and made his way to the entrance. He pushed open the doors and went inside.

The restaurant was pleasant. It lacked the utilitarian efficiency of chain outlets and the glitz and sparkle of the establishments that might have been found in a more well-to-do area, but it did not suffer for that. It was warm and cosy, and busy despite the fact that it was cold and inhospitable outside.

Alexei Fedorov was drying wine glasses behind the bar. There was a bell above the door and it tinkled as Milton came inside. Fedorov put the glasses down on the counter, raised his hand in greeting and made his way across the room.

"Mr. Smith," he said.

"John—please."

"Then, John, it is good to see you. May I take your coat and your bag?"

Milton removed his coat. Fedorov hung it on a hat stand in the corner of the room and gave the camera bag to a waiter to store in a cupboard behind the bar.

"It is cold," he said, his arm on Milton's elbow as he guided him into the room.

"Very," Milton responded.

"It will be colder tonight. The snow is coming."

Milton looked around as he was led to a table with a dozen people sitting around it.

"My family," Fedorov said, indicating the table with a broad sweep of his arm.

The party comprised all ages. Fedorov introduced them all. The man and woman at the far end were very elderly and introduced as Fedorov's parents; the two men and two women of similar age to him were his brothers and sisters; and then the four kids, their ages ranging from perhaps ten to their late teens, were his children. Milton recognised one of them: a girl, in her mid-teens, looking at him shyly. It was Alexei's daughter, the one he had rescued from the sea.

A woman near to the head of the table stood and smiled at Milton. "*Musafir,*" she said, bowing her head.

"I'm sorry," Milton said. "I don't understand."

Fedorov stepped forward. "*Musafir* means guest. It means you are welcome here."

"Thank you," he said. "Are you Mrs. Fedorov?"

"I am," she said. "My name is Svetlana."

Milton returned her warm smile and bowed his own head. "It is very kind of you to invite me."

"Thank you," the woman said. "For our daughter."

She turned to the table and gestured to the girl Milton recognised. She stood, a little bashful, and came around so that she was close enough to offer her hand.

"Thank you for what you did," she said.

"My pleasure," he said, giving her a smile that he hoped might be reassuring. "How are you feeling?"

"My pride is hurt," she said, her English a little more natural than her parents'. "But I am fine. I wanted to thank you. You saved my life."

"It's nothing," he said.

Fedorov nodded solemnly. "You're never going to swim there again, are you?"

"She says it was strong current," said Svetlana, defending her daughter from the edge of her husband's tongue.

"It was," Milton said. "It was difficult to see and very powerful. It was difficult for me to get back again, and I'm a strong swimmer. I wouldn't blame yourself."

"It is not about blame," Fedorov said. "She did what I told her not to do. And she is lucky to be alive because of it. This is a lesson."

"Hush, Alexei," said his wife. "She knows she was wrong. You don't need to tell her again."

Fedorov looked as if he was caught between rebuking his wife for chastening him or laughing at the spectacle of the family's drama being played out in front of the dour newcomer. He chose the latter, his face breaking into a wide grin as he came closer to Milton and clapped him heartily on the shoulder.

"Come," he said. "We will eat and drink. We have a lot to thank you for."

Milton sat with Alexei on his left and Fedorov's mother on his right.

A waiter appeared with a tray of empty shot glasses and a bottle. The man worked his way around the table, distributing the glasses and then reaching down to fill them.

"*Samohon*," Fedorov said. "Home-brewed vodka. It is distilled from wheat or rye. We add chili peppers to give it more kick. We start with a toast."

Milton winced awkwardly.

Fedorov noticed. "What is it?"

"I don't drink," Milton said.

The man reached Milton, reached down and filled his glass.

"You do not?" Fedorov said, as if the suggestion was the most preposterous thing he had heard all day.

"No," Milton said. "I don't."

Fedorov looked as if he was about to protest, but his wife shushed him. "Would you prefer cranberry juice? Orange juice?"

"Cranberry would be fine," he said. "Thank you."

The menus were handed around. Milton glanced at his.

"You speak Russian?" the old lady asked.

"No," Milton said.

The old lady laid her finger against the menu. "The menu is Russian, but this is not Russian food. The Russians never *had* any food. They steal it from us, the Lithuanians, the Estonians, the others."

"Us? Crimeans?"

She nodded. "Have you eaten our food before?"

"Never," he said. "What would you recommend?"

She took the menu from him and ran her finger down the long list of items. "Artem," she called out to the waiter, who was evidently another member of the family. "Mr. John will have the *cheburek*."

"Mother," Fedorov chided her.

"It's fine," Milton said. "I need all the help I can get."

He had been operational in mainland Ukraine before and had half-expected the menu to include the warming *varenyky* and *borscht* that he had enjoyed in Kiev, but the food that was brought out for them was not familiar to him. The Black Sea peninsula was temperate, and the food represented that: there were sweet and sour pastries, flatbreads, grilled and stewed meats, stuffed nightshade vegetables, all redolent of the spices and flavours that might have been expected from Turkish cuisine.

Milton's dish turned out to be the specialty of the house. The *cheburek* was a slender, deep-fried pocket of meat and mushrooms. It was large, filling his generously proportioned plate, and the edges were decorated with a neat crimp that had clearly required a skilful hand.

"You like?" the old woman asked.

"I do," Milton said. "It's delicious."

"It is almost the national dish for the Tatars," Fedorov explained. "It reminds us of home. How much do you know of our people?"

"Not much, I'm afraid."

"We have a thousand years of history in Eastern Europe," he said, with evident pride. "But we are a minority. When Putin stole our land, many of us feared what might happen next. We came here, and now we see it as our duty to preserve our culture. That is what we do here, at the Valentin. We speak Tatar. We serve Tatar food. During Ramadan, we do not serve alcohol. We have Tatar musicians here three times a week. And we welcome our guests—our *musafi*—with the hospitality that our people have always cherished."

It was an awkward speech, but one which Fedorov had evidently delivered before. The adults around the table raised their glasses and one of the men—Milton suspected that he was Fedorov's brother—proposed a toast that Milton could not understand. Glasses were raised and the toast was solemnly observed.

Milton cleared his plate, enjoying the warm atmosphere that pervaded the group. It was evident that the family was close: Fedorov's parents conversed affectionately, his father—who didn't speak any English—reaching out regularly to touch his wife's hand; the siblings shared raucous stories, slipping between languages to suit whatever it was they wanted to say; the children were polite and well-mannered, with good-natured ribbing at one another's expense. The shot glasses were filled and then refilled, but no one put pressure on Milton to drink and he found it easy to relax. The evening was more enjoyable than he had anticipated, and he was glad that he had made the effort to come.

The first course was finished and the plates were cleared away.

"You do not drink, John," Fedorov said. "Do you have any vices?"

"I smoke," he said.

"That is good." Fedorov reached into his pocket and took out two cigars. "Would you smoke one of these with me?"

Milton thought of the cheap packet of cigarettes in his jacket pocket. "That would be nice," he said.

"Come." Fedorov stood. "We go outside. We smoke and talk."

64

Milton retrieved his leather jacket, put it on and stepped out onto the boardwalk. He followed Fedorov as he crossed over to the bench next to the railings that guarded the short drop down to the sand. He looked back and saw the tall apartment buildings that backed onto Café Valentin and the Tatiana Grill. The beach stretched away, the first few feet lit by the tall lamp that stood above the bench, the illumination quickly swallowed up by the darkness. There was a big freighter in the channel, turning right to the open Atlantic.

Fedorov joined him on the boardwalk. He held a bottle of vodka in his right hand and the two cigars in his left.

He dropped down onto the bench next to Milton. He held up the bottle of *samohon*. "Are you sure?"

"Yes. But thanks."

"My wife says I drink too much," Fedorov said. "I tell her to mind her own business." He took the cap off the bottle and raised it. "*Za nashu druzhbu*. To our friendship."

He put the bottle to his lips and took a generous swig. He put the bottle down on the bench, took out the cigars and found a cutter in his pocket. He inserted the head of the first cigar and made a neat cut just before the cap, leaving enough space to avoid tearing the wrapper. He gave the cigar to Milton and then set to work on the second. Milton held the cigar beneath his nose and inhaled it.

"It is from Nicaragua," Fedorov said. "Very good."

The tobacco was pungent. Fedorov took out a lighter and thumbed flame. Milton put the cigar to his lips and puffed on it as Fedorov lit the end.

Fedorov waved a hand at the boardwalk and the blackness all around them. "Odessa is not so different from this," he said. "Both are on the sea. Odessa has no boardwalk, like here, but it has a promenade along the water. My city is beautiful. I doubt I will ever have the chance to return."

He put the bottle to his lips and drank again.

"You say you are a cook, John?"

"That's right."

"But you haven't always done that."

"No," Milton admitted.

"You were a soldier, I think."

Milton was surprised by his perceptiveness. "Is it that obvious?"

"Perhaps only to those who know what to look for. I was a soldier for many years. I think you and I have much in common."

Milton drew down on his cigar.

"Where did you serve?" Fedorov asked him.

"Here and there," Milton said, and then, when Fedorov looked at him expectantly, he added, "Gibraltar. Helmand. Northern Ireland. Other places."

"Helmand? I was there, too."

"With the Soviets?"

He nodded. "In 1989, just before Gorbachev ended

things. I was young. I saw things that no one should ever see."

"So did I."

Fedorov put the bottle to his lips again. Milton heard the calling of a gull, high overhead, and the shushing as the tide gently ran up and down the beach.

"What did you do after the war?" Milton asked him.

"I went back to Sevastopol, married my wife and started my family. The Crimea is beautiful, John. Have you been?"

"No," Milton said.

"We lived in the Riviera, near Yalta. It is warm and pleasant. A good place to bring up my children. I would have stayed there forever if it wasn't for Putin and his thugs. If I was a younger man, I would have fought them, but I have family now and I am old. It is the same for my brothers. We were all in the military. We left together and came here. We put our assets together and bought this place. We have been fortunate."

"It's very nice," Milton said. "And the food was delicious."

"Then you must make sure to return. Whenever you wish. You just need to say that you are a friend of Alexei and you will not need to pay."

"That's very kind, but it's not necessary. Tonight has been more than thanks enough."

"Nonsense," Fedorov said, drinking again. He held the bottle up. "Are you sure? Just a taste?"

Milton could smell the alcohol on Fedorov's lips and could see that he was fast becoming drunk. "Thanks, but no."

Fedorov nodded and put the bottle down. "You know, what you did for my daughter, it means more to me than perhaps you understand."

Milton didn't respond and waited for Fedorov to find the words to continue.

"We lost our son a year ago," he said. "He was called Dmitri, after my father. He was eighteen years old."

"I'm sorry," Milton said. "What happened?"

"Drugs." Fedorov drew down on his cigar, held the smoke in and then blew it out, to be dispersed in the wind. "We lost him. There were kids at his school. Bad kids. Dmitri started to go out with them. There was one friend, a Dominican boy called Diego, they grew close. Diego was a drug addict. He liked the heroin. He gave it to Dmitri, and he liked it, too." Fedorov paused, the caws of the gull competing with the susurration of the waves. Fedorov drank again, and then continued. "My son hid it from us. We didn't know until it was too late. He was given heroin that was contaminated with fentanyl. It made it more powerful. His body, it could not stand it, and it killed him. I found his body in an apartment in Bath Beach. I had to kick the door down. The police said he had been there for three days. He was curled up on the floor as if he was asleep."

"I'm sorry," Milton said. "That's terrible."

Fedorov continued as if he hadn't noticed that Milton had spoken. "The police said there was nothing that they could do. I disagreed. I found the dealer who sold him the heroin." He took another slug of the vodka. "My brothers and I met with him one night. Let us say he never sold it to anyone else."

The atmosphere had changed. Fedorov was a little drunk, but the earlier ebullience had given way to a darkness that Milton found disconcerting.

Milton stood. "I should be going," he said. "I've got a busy day tomorrow and I haven't slept properly for a while. I'll say goodbye to your family and then I'll be off."

Fedorov stood and immediately lost his balance. Milton caught his arm and held him up. He could feel the tight muscle of his bicep.

"Thank you," Fedorov said with a chuckle. "I think this bottle is a little stronger than usual."

He released himself from Milton's grip, crossed to the restaurant and opened the door. A slant of warm light painted a golden stripe across the boardwalk. Milton followed. It was cold and growing colder. The snow couldn't be far away now, and he had business to attend to.

65

Milton made it back to the precinct house at eleven fifty. He knew that the cop with the truck was on the four-to-twelve tour, and, if his routine was anything like it had been the previous night, he guessed that he would be leaving for home at a little after midnight.

He found a spot on the other side of Linwood where he could leave his bike and put himself out of plain sight by hanging around behind a large dumpster that had not been emptied for some time.

He took off his helmet and rested it on the seat, then leaned against the wall that separated the sidewalk from a parking lot and took out his phone. He navigated to the app that he had downloaded after purchasing the tracking devices and fired it up. He was rewarded with a map of Brooklyn, with Sutter Avenue running across the centre of the screen. There were three dots highlighted on the map: the first, in red, was his position, to the east of the precinct house; the second two, both blue, winked on and off just a short distance to the west.

He lit a cigarette and waited.

PART IV

WEDNESDAY

66

Milton watched the patrol cars as they arrived back at the station house for the change of shift. His position was a decent distance from the entrance to the precinct, but he was close enough to see the faces of the men and women as they got into and out of their cars. It was just before midnight when the patrol car with the same license number as he had seen yesterday arrived. It slowed and then backed into a space that had just been vacated by a departing Altima. Milton waited patiently, observing as the two cops that he had seen last night got out of the car and then went inside together.

The younger of the two men re-emerged first. He paused beneath the tree that leaned out into the street, did up his jacket, and then went over to the Fusion. He opened the door, slid inside, and backed out into the street. Milton glanced down at his phone and saw the first of the two blue dots sliding smoothly along Sutter as the Fusion pulled away. Milton had already decided that he would leave that officer for another time. He had tagged his car for the sake of thoroughness; his partner was the one who had conversed with the black guy that Freddy had recognised. The odds were against the younger cop being involved, but Milton was thorough and he could be investigated later.

The second officer emerged a moment later. He passed along the sidewalk behind the parked cars until he came to the Ford F-150.

Milton straddled the Bonneville, rolled it off its kick-stand and gripped the key.

The engine of the F-150 started with a loud grumble. The lights flicked on and the cop revved it, then drove out of the parking space and onto the road.

Milton turned the key and kick-started the engine.

The NYPD didn't allow its officers to live in the areas that they patrolled, so Milton was ready for a reasonable ride, maybe up north to Westchester. But, as he let the Ford pull away into the distance, he saw that the driver was headed east. Milton followed, keeping the Ford almost out of sight. There was no need to take chances. The tracker was active, and Milton could easily rely on the map on his phone if he lost sight of the truck.

The Ford followed the Belt Parkway east, continuing on through Valley Stream, Wantagh and West Babylon. Milton stopped trying to guess where they were headed. The roads became quieter, and, as they headed to Smithtown, he dropped back even farther, confident that he would be able to track the lights of the truck if it took a sudden turn.

They approached the coast at Stony Brook and Milton knew that they must be close to where the truck was headed. They headed into Setauket, following the road until they reached a series of large houses. Milton saw the flash of the brake lights as the truck slowed. He slowed, too, switching off the headlamp and drifting across to the side of the road behind a parked car. The truck rolled off the road and onto a sloped driveway. The engine continued to run for a moment, but then it was switched off. The lights flicked off and the driver got out. He paused next to his truck, reached up and stretched his arms, and then went inside.

Milton waited for ten minutes. He saw a light flick on in one of the downstairs windows and then flick off again.

He started the engine, switched on the headlamp and rolled ahead. It was a very nice house. Big. It looked like it was sixty or seventy years old and had been built to mimic the Queen Anne cottages that still persisted in the Hamptons. It was two storeys tall with projecting gables to the front and the side. The roof was hipped and the structure was clad in white clapboard. There was a wraparound porch to the front and left-hand side, with turned porch posts and elaborate balustrade spindles. It had small sash windows on the upper floor and larger windows on the ground floor.

Milton memorised the address—87 Shore Road—and took a series of photographs of it with his phone. He decided that he would return tomorrow. He continued past the property, retraced his path along adjacent roads, and headed back toward the city and his own apartment.

He was halfway home when the first flakes of snow started to fall. He glanced up into the sky; the stars were hidden beneath an impenetrable vault of cloud. The flakes were fat and ponderous, the headlamp picking them out in its golden light. They started to fall more heavily, reducing visibility and settling on the road despite the layer of salt that had been spread earlier in the evening. Milton slowed down, bleeding twenty miles an hour off his speed and concentrating hard on the way ahead.

67

M ilton slept in until eleven. He awoke and closed his eyes again, aware, as he slowly came around, that something was different. It took him a moment to realise what it was: it was the noise from outside the window, or rather the lack of it. The buzz and hum of activity was missing. Instead, there was a sense of a smothering, muffled quality to the sound that reached him. He pushed his duvet aside and—flinching from the sudden frigidity of the apartment away from the warmth of his bed —he stood, parted the curtains and looked outside.

The snow that had started on his ride back to Coney Island must have fallen all night. Everything was covered. The cars that were parked at the foot of the block had seen their sharper angles smoothed out and replaced by gentle curves and lines. The road itself had been cleared, with ridges on either side where a snow plough had forced its way through, but the snow had continued to fall and the grey of the asphalt was invisible, covered by a whitening carpet. Flakes were still falling, but they drifted down lazily, as if the storm was taking a moment to gather its strength.

Milton took out his phone, navigated to CNN's website and tapped to play the last bulletin.

"The biggest snowstorm to hit the north-eastern United States since 2006's epic nor'easter left behind over two feet of snow, widespread power outages and significant travel disruptions. The weather quickly deteriorated in cities such as New York City and Boston by the Wednesday morning commute as the system continued to strengthen, eventually turning into a powerful blizzard. Snowfall rates exceeded two inches an hour, making travel almost impossible for a time. There have been five reported fatalities and—"

Milton closed the page and went into the bathroom. He showered, standing under the warm water and scrubbing the sleep from his eyes. He brushed his teeth, dried himself and dressed. He collected his laptop and set it up on the small table.

He opened a browser, navigated to Google Maps and typed in the address of the house that he had tailed the officer back to last night. Shore Road traced the outline of a bulge of land that formed the southern shore of Setauket Harbor. The officer's property was in a prime spot. Milton dragged the Google Street View icon to the road and scouted the area. He remembered the houses that he had seen last night, and was able to match the relevant property to the one he had photographed on his phone. Now he had the benefit of the bright sunlight that had accompanied Google's camera car when it had visited the town. The houses were all neat and tidy, their owners evidently house-proud judging from the freshly painted picket fences and the neatly clipped lawns.

Milton opened a second window and opened up Zillow. He looked at the prices of comparable houses in the area. There were twenty properties on the market, and none of them were priced at less than $400,000. A house on View Road, similarly close to the water, was being marketed for $600,000.

The Ford F-150 he had tailed last night was on the drive of the property in the Google photograph, its license plate blurred out. Milton opened another browser window and Googled local Ford dealerships. The officer had been driving the F-150 XLT with the crew cab; the same make was available for a touch over $50,000.

Milton looked at the Setauket real estate prices and the cost of the truck and couldn't help thinking that both would normally have been beyond the reach of a patrol cop. Other possibilities? He could have benefited from a windfall. A bequest from a wealthy relative, perhaps. It was possible, but unlikely.

Milton was more certain now than before: the officer was involved in something, and the dead man in the restroom had been a threat to whatever that was.

68

M ackintosh had spent the morning and the early afternoon working on the case.

The autopsy report had come back on José Luis González. The coroner reported that the body was that of a well-nourished male around forty years old. The body weighed 160 pounds and measured 72 inches from crown to sole. The section headed 'Evidence of Injury' was extensive: there were multiple stab wounds to the torso, with associated wounds to the hands and forearms that Mackintosh knew would have been defensive as González tried to fend off his attacker. The coroner had concluded that the fatal wound was the incision across the man's throat. The wound began on the left side of the throat, an inch from the left ear, and continued for six inches to a point diagonally adjacent to the tip of the right ear. The wound passed through the skin, the subcutaneous tissue, and into the musculature beneath.

Mackintosh reviewed the interviews that she had taken on the evening of the murder and had started to put together a list of follow-up questions that she wanted to put to the kid and to John Smith. She was especially interested in him. There was something about him that she found curious. His attitude had been matter-of-fact, an iciness that was unusual given the scene that had greeted him when he went into the bathroom. Most witnesses, when facing a murder scene that was as bloody as this one, would have been frightened. Most would have required coaxing and gentle persuasion to extract the details of what they had seen. Smith had not been like that at all. For a man who professed to be a cook, he had answered her questions with smooth efficiency. It was the kind of matter-of-fact response that she would have expected from an officer. It was incongruous, and she determined that she would dig into his background a little more.

She entered his details into the National Crime Information Center. It was an electronic clearinghouse of crime data that recorded details of crimes and criminals across the continental United States. There were twenty-one separate databases; she logged into the Violent Persons file and requested a search on John Smith, adding in additional identifying details that would, she hoped, filter the flood of responses that she anticipated would be generated by such a common name. The data would take time to be returned, but she put a reminder in the murder book for herself to check tomorrow.

There was something about John Smith that was off, and she meant to find out what that might be.

69

Milton opened his laptop and navigated to the website of the tracking company. He browsed to his account and clicked on the tracker that he had attached to the Ford F-150. The tracker was in motion, heading west along the Northern State Parkway. Milton glanced up at the time in the top right of the window: it was 3.35 p.m. The officer was heading back into Brooklyn for his 4 p.m. shift.

Milton closed the laptop, grabbed his coat and headed down the stairs.

The ride was challenging, to say the least. The main roads had been cleared and gritted, but the smaller connecting streets and avenues were often treacherous. Milton rode slowly and deliberately, aware that there was likely to be ice hidden beneath the snow that covered everything.

The snow started to fall more heavily again as he

merged onto the Southern State Parkway. It was a three-lane route, eastbound and westbound traffic separated by safety rails and a grassy median between them. It had been ploughed thoroughly, and, as Milton passed beneath the Wantagh State Parkway, he saw a big yellow snow plough rumbling in the opposite direction.

He returned to the property on Shore Road and checked his watch: it was five in the afternoon. Darkness was falling quickly and the internal lights of the houses that faced the harbour twinkled brightly. Milton pulled over a quarter of a mile from the officer's property and walked the rest of the way. It was bitterly cold. Snow was falling lightly again, blown into his face by gusts of icy wind that rushed in off the water. The area was quiet. The harbour, to his right, was a wide-open space, the opposite shore marked out by a sparkling of lights that ended at the open channel leading out to the ocean. The bank comprised a thin strip of scrub, mostly covered over with drifts of snow that had been tossed there by the municipal snow ploughs, and then a line of poles that bore telephone and electricity cabling. Milton walked along the side of the road, his hands thrust deep in his pockets, his eyes on the houses that he passed.

He reached number 87, the number denoted by a small mailbox fixed to a wooden post that emerged from the drift. The property shared a driveway with number 85, the second house set back another fifty feet from the road. The driveway was empty and the house looked unoccupied— dark, with no lights shining from any of the windows. He had no idea whether the officer lived alone or with family, but it appeared as if Milton had been fortunate.

He looked left and then right and, happy that he was alone and unobserved, he crossed the road and hurried up the drive. There were two tracks just visible in the drift that would have been left by the Ford as it pulled out onto the road an hour or so earlier. Milton followed those, careful not to leave footprints.

The side of the property that ran adjacent to the shared driveway would be visible to anyone in the second house fifty feet farther on. Milton turned off the drive and tramped through the drift across what would have been the front lawn. He left footprints here, but there was nothing that he could do about that. The snow continued to fall and would eventually erase the evidence of his trespass. He continued across the lawn until he reached the steps that led up to the veranda. He paused, listening carefully, but could hear nothing: no television, no radio, no voices or any other sign that someone was at home.

The steps had been shovelled clear of snow, and Milton climbed them and stepped forward into the shelter of the porch. The main entrance to the house was through a tall door, the frame painted green and with a large pane of glass in the centre. Milton walked around to the right, but that side of the house was overlooked by the property at number 85. He went back to the front: despite being visible from the main road, it was still—given the lack of traffic and the fact that it wasn't overlooked by the neighbours—the easiest way to get inside without being seen.

Milton knelt before the door and examined the handle. The door itself looked as if it was original but, at some point in the recent past, it had been fitted with a new spring bolt lock. Milton reached into his pocket, took out his wallet, and slid out a YOUR NAME HERE card that had been sent to him in the mail. He wedged the card into the narrow gap between the door and the frame, held it flush against the frame and then worked it down until the edge was against the smallest part of the lock. He pushed the card in and bent it away from the doorknob. He felt the latch slide back and, pressing a little more forcefully, he turned the handle and opened the door.

He went inside and closed the door behind him.

70

Milton took out his phone and switched on the flashlight. He was in a front hall. There was an open passage ahead, a door to the left and a flight of stairs leading up to the right. There was a small table just inside the door with a cordless telephone and a small pile of unopened correspondence. Milton shone his flashlight on the envelopes as he shuffled through them: some were for Robert Carter; others were for Rebecca or Becky Carter. They looked like bills. Milton photographed them and then left them where they were.

He opened the door to his left and went into the living room. The windows were shuttered and he was able to shine his flashlight without fear of the light being seen from the outside. There was a couch and a matching armchair, an LCD screen mounted on the wall and an old vinyl record player on a sideboard. There were magazines spread out on the coffee table that sat before the couch: there was an issue of *American Baby*, the pregnant woman on the cover smiling at the camera as she sat on a swivel chair. Milton filed away the possibility that Robert and Rebecca Carter were expecting a child.

The living room offered access to the dining room through a set of double doors that looked as if they were usually left open. Milton passed through them. There was a dining table with six chairs, a dresser that displayed a set of plates, and a large potted plant in the corner of the room. There was a framed picture on the wall that looked like it had been staged during a wedding: the Carters, Milton assumed, with Rebecca wearing a white dress as she perched on the hood of a yellow New York cab, her husband in a tuxedo as he held her hand. Milton photographed it. There was nothing else of interest.

Milton continued through the open door, passed along a narrow corridor that offered access to a small pantry and stepped into the kitchen. Once more, there was nothing out of the ordinary: appliances that looked brand new, clean surfaces, a small table with two chairs, a bunch of flowers in a bright yellow vase.

He went upstairs. The layout was as he had expected: three bedrooms accessed from the hall and a family bathroom. The first bedroom, at the front of the house, was around fifteen feet by fifteen feet and was evidently used as the master suite. Milton went inside and searched it quickly and efficiently. There were two free-standing wardrobes: one was filled with a woman's clothes and the other with a man's. Milton concentrated on the latter, taking out the piles of shoes at the bottom of the wardrobe and feeling for anything that might suggest a false floor or a hidden compartment. He found nothing. He went to the bed. There were bedside tables on either side: the one to his left held a copy of a Naomi Klein book and a collection of aromatherapy bottles. The table on the other side of the bed had a Kindle, a trailing cable used to charge an iPhone, a copy of *Sports Illustrated* and a scattering of change. Milton opened the table's drawer and found a nest of cables, a runner's watch with a heart monitor that was worn on a strap, an old-fashioned alarm clock, and more superfluous cables. Nothing of interest. Milton dropped to his belly and looked under the bed, then lifted the rugs on either side and tried the floorboards in the event that one of them was loose. None of them were.

The other bedroom at the front of the house was in the process of being turned into a nursery. The walls were painted pink and a mobile had been fixed to the ceiling above the spot where a crib might be placed, animals with friendly faces twirling gently as Milton nudged them with his shoulder.

Milton crossed the hall to the rear of the house. There were two more rooms: a bathroom and a further bedroom that had been turned into a study. Milton eliminated the bathroom first. There was nothing of interest save for a bottle of pills in the wall-mounted cabinet. Milton held them up so that he could photograph the label: ROBERT CARTER, Xanax, 0.5mg tablets.

Milton went into the study. It was around thirteen feet by fifteen feet and dominated by a large antique desk. There was a roller chair with leather cushions behind the desk, and Milton sat down in it as he searched. There was more correspondence in the name of Robert Carter. Nothing of note was apparent to Milton, but he photographed it all anyway. The computer on the desk was on; Milton tapped a key to wake it and was presented with a photograph of the man he now knew was Carter fishing off the side of a boat. He tapped again and was presented with a box to enter a password. Milton ignored it.

He was about to leave the desk when he noticed a framed photograph that had been allowed to fall forward. He picked it up and had his first success: the picture in the frame was of the white man he now suspected of being Robert Carter and the black man he had been with the night before last, the man whom Freddy had seen outside the restroom. The two of them were on a boat—it appeared to be the same as the one that Milton had seen on the screensaver—and were both holding up bottles of beer, the photographer catching them in an easy moment of shared laughter. There was nothing to identify the other man, but, on a hunch, Milton turned the frame over and flicked the clasps that held the mount in place. He slid it away and took out the photograph. Someone had written on the back of the print: Me and Shep, June '15, Jamaica Bay. Milton took a picture of both sides of the photograph and then replaced it in the frame and left it as he had found it, face down on the desk.

There was a rug on the floor. Milton wheeled the chair to the side of the room and pulled it back. It was obvious that one of the boards was loose; it wasn't flush with the others, and, as Milton looked at it more closely, he saw tiny splinters protruding from the shorter edge. The board had, at some point, been worked up with a screwdriver. Milton took a metal ruler from the desk drawer and used it to gently pry the board up so that he could get his fingers beneath it. He pulled carefully, removing the board and revealing the space beneath. He shone his phone's flashlight down and saw that a small stash was kept there. He took out a metal box, two passports and a bundle of bills inside a plastic Ziploc bag. He reached down again and felt the familiar lines of a pistol. He removed it: a Sig Sauer P226 and, as he reached down a third time, a box of 9mm ammunition.

He opened the passports. The first was in the name of Peter Marino and the second was in the name of Alissa Marino. Robert Carter's picture was in the passport for Mr Marino. The picture for Mrs Marino was the same woman that Milton had seen in the framed picture downstairs. He photographed both documents and then put them back in the bag.

He took the money and riffled through it. It was a collection of fifties and twenties; Milton estimated ten thousand dollars. Ready money, he thought. Just in case. He put the cash back in the bag, too.

The pistol was in excellent condition, but the least interesting of the items that he had taken from the stash. He replaced it and the ammunition beneath the floor.

The box was the final item that he examined. It was small, only a little larger than Milton's wallet. It was hinged at the top and would, once unlocked, open to allow access to what could only have been a very small compartment. The front had an alphanumeric keypad and the rear was printed with the manufacturer's details: it was a CodeBox product, in their junior line. Milton guessed that Carter used the box to keep a key, which would then offer access to a locker or storage container that he kept off-site. There was nothing that Milton could do with the lock. He would have been able to call Tech Ops at Vauxhall Cross if he was still working for the Group, and they would have been able to send back the manufacturer's override code, but that wasn't an option for him now. And, even if he could have relied upon Tech Ops to help him open the box, and if he was right that the box was used to hold a key, he would have no idea how to find the lock that the key opened.

He replaced the items—the box, the money and the passports—in the hiding hole, put the loose board back in place and covered it over with the rug.

He took out his phone and the card that Polanski had given him at the restaurant. He dialled the number as he made his way back down the stairs.

The call connected. "Hello?"

"It's John Smith," he said.

"Hello," Polanski said.

"I need to see you."

"It's late. I was about to leave."

"It's urgent."

"Can't wait until tomorrow?"

"No," Milton said. "It's about González. I know who killed him."

71

The Brooklyn North division of the Internal Affairs Bureau was at 179 Wilson Avenue, just to the north of Bushwick. The building looked almost ecclesiastical in design. It was on the corner of Wilson and Dekalb and it was large, constructed in heavy red brick with decorative insets that framed the vertical rows of windows in a design that Milton thought looked unfortunately phallic. The roof was embellished with crenelations and there was an ornate portico held up by four ugly concrete pillars. The building was separated from the sidewalk by an extraneous set of iron railings, and someone—a protestor, Milton guessed—had decorated the railings with pink and white tinsel and one single word: HOPE.

There were two entrances. The first was beneath the portico, although it didn't appear to be open. The second offered access to a smaller building that was connected to the main office by way of a single-storey addition. There were bars on the window and the glass in the double doors had been stencilled with the shield of the NYPD and the legend 'Patrol, Borough—Brooklyn North'.

There was a bike store and a store offering refurbished cellphones to the right of the building. Opposite was a Chinese restaurant, a store advertising liquor and wine, and a small independent coffee shop. Milton was in the coffee shop, sitting on a stool, a coffee on the wooden counter before him. He was next to the window and able to watch the comings and goings on the street outside.

He didn't have very long to wait.

The double doors of the bureau office opened and Polanski stepped out. He paused, looking left and right, then, stepping carefully on the icy surface, he crossed the street and came into the coffee shop. Milton raised his hand and Polanski saw him. The detective walked over to him.

"Thanks," Milton said.

"This is all very mysterious. You couldn't come into the office?"

"Didn't think that would be safe."

"Really? Why's that?"

"Because I think you have a big problem."

Polanski looked as if he was about to reply, but he did not. Instead, he sat down and spread his hands. "Okay," he said. "I'll play along. Who killed González?"

"I need you to give me some assurances first. I'm not here for myself. It's someone else—I'm trying to keep them out of trouble."

"Assurances? For who? The kid?"

Milton didn't answer. "Are you investigating officers in the Seventy-Fifth Precinct?"

"I can't talk about that."

"Then we have a problem. I need to know I can trust you."

He raised his eyebrows. "I'm a detective, Mr. Smith. You can trust me."

Milton had no way of confirming that Polanski was on the level. What could he do? There was no one to ask, no references that he could take. All he had was his instinct. Milton was a good judge of character and had told enough lies and been lied to enough times that he trusted his gut when it came to deciphering truth from falsehood. He would have to rely upon it now, but the complication here was that it was not simply his own future that was in play. Freddy was inextricably caught up in the very same mess, and the accuracy of Milton's assessment of whether Polanski was honest and dependable would have consequences for him, too.

But Milton didn't have a choice. They needed help, and they had no other options. Who else was there? Mackintosh worked in the Seven Five. She could be involved with Carter. Polanski worked in the bureau. He rooted out the bad apples. That wouldn't make him popular with other officers, and it was that unpopularity that set him apart.

Milton had given it plenty of thought and it was what it was: Polanski or no one.

He spoke quietly. "The other night, at Euclid. Freddy Blanco said he didn't get a good look at either of them."

Polanski nodded. "That's what he said."

"That's not true. He did. He saw one of them waiting outside the restroom door, like he was guarding it. Later, when we were at the precinct, he saw the same man in a promo video."

"Who was it?"

Milton waved his question aside. "You've got to get Freddy and his father out of Brooklyn first. It's not safe for them here."

"You're making this conditional?"

"You want Freddy to take a risk like that, you've got to

make him feel safe about doing it. I'm about as uncomfort-able as I'm prepared to get right now. That's not negotiable."

Polanski frowned. Milton was not going to budge from his demand. If Polanski couldn't accommodate it, they were done and he would have to think about another way to make things safe for the Blancos.

"Detective?" he pressed.

"I can do that," he said. "There's some preparation to do first, but it's possible."

"When?"

"I can start figuring it out in the morning."

"Call me when it's arranged," Milton said. He finished the lukewarm coffee, stood and pushed the empty cup into a trash can.

Polanski stood, too. "I'll need to take a statement," he said. "From you and the kid."

"Let me speak to his father."

"You haven't done that yet?"

"I've been solving your murder for you," he said. "I'll talk to them next."

"When are you going to talk to them?"

"Tonight," Milton said. He did up his jacket.

Polanski nodded to the window. A blizzard had begun, with thick snow reducing visibility to just a handful of yards. The street outside was almost impossible to see. "Look at that," Polanski said. He indicated Milton's helmet. "You're not riding in that, are you?"

Milton had no interest in small talk or the detective's concern. "Call me when you've got somewhere for them to go."

He grabbed his helmet and stepped out into the cold.

72

The blizzard was so thick that Milton couldn't see more than ten feet ahead of him. Polanski was right: he would have been insane to try to ride the Bonneville to Danforth Street. He pushed it the short distance to a parking lot that he had seen as he had arrived for the meeting. It was on Himrod Street, a gap in the block that was protected by a tall wire mesh fence with a gate next to a building denoted as the headquarters of Christian Ambulette, Inc. There was an attendant on the gate. Milton handed the man a twenty to cover twenty-four hours' parking and wheeled the bike inside. He found a space, chained his helmet to the wheel, nodded to the attendant as he left and headed to the subway.

Milton spotted the tail as he walked the short distance from Himrod Street to Central Avenue station. Counter-surveillance was a matter of instinct as much as technique, and noticing that he was being followed had always been something that he was very good at doing. The man was wearing a padded jacket, his hands shoved deep in the pockets. He followed Milton down into the station and took a seat in the same car as him, albeit at the opposite end. He had turned to glance at him and, for a moment, the man had been caught staring back. He caught himself, trying hard to look nonchalant as he glanced down at the floor and started to fidget with a ring on his finger.

Milton took the M Train to Myrtle Avenue station. The man waited until just before the train departed and disembarked, too. Milton transferred to the J Train headed for Jamaica Center. The man got into the same car.

The quickest way to Danforth Street was to disembark at Crescent Street station, but Milton did not want to lead his tail there. He looked at the line map above the door and changed his plan.

He turned away so that his tail would not be able to see what he was saying, took out his phone and called Manny.

There was no answer.

He tried again, this time letting the call go through to voicemail.

"It's John Smith," he said. "You need to get out of the house. Go somewhere with a lot of people and call me."

He ended the call, but, rather than putting the phone away, he switched to video and hit record. He held the phone on his lap, angling it back into the car. He let it run for thirty seconds and then stopped it and reviewed the footage, pretending to be scrolling through email. The guy was there, staring right down the car at him.

The train rolled into Cypress Hills. Milton made no effort to elude his tail as he disembarked. Instead, he looked for any sign of a second or third tail. It was almost impossible for one person to follow someone who was trained to look for the signs of surveillance; a three- or four-person team was ideal, able to switch the pursuer at regular intervals so that the mark did not notice. Milton couldn't see anything to make him suspect that he was the subject of a more organised pursuit. The guy was on his own.

Milton came out of the station and started to walk. The quickest way to get to the Blancos' home was to go south on Hemlock Street, but, instead, Milton went east on Jamaica Avenue. It was five thirty now, and the blizzard had driven all but the most determined pedestrians and drivers back home. It was bitterly cold, the wind whipping into his exposed flesh, the snow sticking to his face. Milton trudged on. The road continued beneath the elevated section of track. There was a large cemetery behind iron railings to Milton's left and shuttered buildings, all of them defaced with graffiti, to his right.

He walked on for a hundred yards until he reached a large brick building that offered a point of entry into the cemetery. It, too, was derelict: the ground-floor windows were boarded and the glass in the windows above had been knocked out. The inscription above the gates read MAIMONIDES CEMETERY.

Milton turned off the sidewalk where the railings curved back and hid there, concealed by a large oak tree.

He heard the man's footsteps crunching through the icy crust.

73

He came around the corner and Milton grabbed him by the lapels of his padded coat, swinging him off the sidewalk and manhandling him through the gate and into the covered archway that led into the cemetery beyond. There was a dumpster there, with black bags stacked up outside it, and the man staggered, tripping over the trash. He fell onto his knees, putting his left arm down to stop himself from sprawling flat on his face.

Milton advanced on him in time to notice the man's right hand snake into his open jacket. His head was at the level of Milton's waist, just the right height for Milton to drive his knee against his jaw. The man spun away, crashing against the side of the dumpster, a knife glinting in the dim light as it landed in the dirty snow.

The man was face down in the snow. Milton reached down, grabbed him beneath the shoulders, and hauled him upright. He slammed him against the wall, knitted his fist in a handful of the man's hair, and ground his face into the brick.

"What do you want?"

"N-n-nothing, man," he stammered.

"Why were you following me?"

"What you talking about?"

Milton drew the man's head back a few inches and then slammed it against the wall once more.

"Why were you following me?"

"I was gonna roll you."

Milton crashed his head into the wall again.

"Don't lie to me," he said. "You've been following me from Brooklyn. I saw you on the subway."

"I don't—"

Milton pushed the man's head, flattening his nose against the rough brick.

"Last chance. Who are you working for?"

"Fuck... you..."

Milton turned sideways and pivoted, using all of his momentum to send the man across the archway so that he crashed into the opposite wall with as much force as possible. He bounced off the brick, lost his balance again and fell down onto his backside.

Milton collected the knife that he had dropped and reached down for the man's collar. He dragged him into the cemetery, out of sight of the street, and then got down on his knees next to the man. He wrapped his left arm around the man's forehead and pulled back, exposing his throat, and then laid the blade of the knife against his skin.

Milton leaned down close enough to speak into the man's ear. "I want you to think about something for a minute. I saw you on the train. I'm trained to notice people who are following me. And if I'm trained to do that, what else do you think that says about me? What else do you think I'm trained to do?" He angled the blade and pressed;

the sharp edge sliced into the first few millimetres of skin, enough to draw a little rivulet of blood that gathered on the metal. Enough to focus the man's attention. "Who sent you?"

"Acosta," he said, the three syllables tripping over one another in his haste to get them out.

"Go on."

"He told us to follow the cop."

"Which cop?"

"The detective from the Rat Squad."

"Polanski?"

"Yeah," he said eagerly. "Polanski."

"How long have you been on him?"

"Since Monday."

"How many of you?"

"Two."

Milton thought: Monday was the day after the murder. If they had been on him for as long as that, they had everything.

"Tell me about Acosta."

"You don't know who he is?"

"Tell me."

"He runs East New York, man."

"Drugs?"

"Yeah, and everything else."

"And what did Acosta tell you to do?"

"He wants you dead, man. He wanted me to do you."

"Tonight?"

The man managed a nod. "We told him you'd gone back to see the cop. He said you had to go."

"Where's your friend now?"

"Gone to see the kid."

Milton felt a judder of panic, and, momentarily

distracted, he let his guard down. The man jerked his head back and butted Milton in the nose. Milton fell back, releasing his grip and dropping the knife into the snow. The man turned, reaching down to collect the blade and then flashing it in a wild forehand swipe that tore into Milton's jacket, tearing the leather across the stomach. The man snarled, his teeth as white as the snow, passed the knife from hand to hand and feinted once and then twice. Milton took a step back, his mobility restricted by the deep drifts. The man lunged forward, jabbing the blade at Milton's gut, but Milton had anticipated it and circled his right forearm, his wrist jarring against the underside of his attacker's wrist and blocking the thrust. The blow unbalanced the man and, as he staggered, Milton disarmed him and then ghosted behind him, snaking his left arm around his throat, his trachea at the crook of his elbow. Milton grasped the biceps of his right arm with his left hand, placed his right palm against the man's shoulder and then forced his elbows together, applying pressure to the neck on both sides. It was a blood choke, and Milton had it clamped on tight. The man struggled, but, with blood flow to his brain severely curtailed, his body went limp within ten seconds. Milton maintained the choke, tightening his grip, holding it in place for thirty seconds, then forty. He released the hold after a minute, and the man fell flat on his face and lay still in the snow.

Milton took a moment to gather his breath. The snow was churned up from the struggle. It was preternaturally quiet, the snow already settling on the man's prone body.

Milton dragged the body around behind the dumpster. He opened the lid, hauled the body up and shoved it over until it fell head over heels and landed amid the bags of garbage. Milton wiped the knife so that his prints were removed, tossed that in too, and then pulled the lid closed again.

And then he started to run. It was difficult: his feet plunged into the snow up to his ankles, slowing him down, and he struggled through the drift onto the road, where he could pick up a little more speed.

He reached Hemlock Street again and turned to the south.

It was obvious what Acosta was thinking. He was rattled. He was concerned enough to order Milton's death.

He was insulating himself.

No more witnesses.

Milton would be the first to go.

And Freddy would be next.

Milton's feet almost slid away from underneath him as he started to sprint.

I t took Milton four minutes to reach Danforth Street. The house was at the opposite end of the street, so he took a right turn and kept running hard toward the elevated track on Crescent Street. The house on the corner was as he remembered it. The gate and the front door behind it were shut; there was light visible from the window to the right of the door, a glow that shone through the narrow space between the edge of the curtain and the frame.

Milton looked up and down the street. It was quiet, the snow smothering the sound of the city. Milton looked down the street and saw a car turn out of Hemlock Street and drive slowly toward him. The car slowed and rolled into a space on the opposite side of the road. There was a street lamp behind it, and the glow was enough to silhouette the two figures in the front seats. Milton thought he could make out a third figure behind them, too.

He hurried across the sidewalk to the house, pulled the gate open and knocked on the front door.

Nothing.

He knocked again, louder and more vigorously.

This time, he heard footsteps and a gruff, "Hold on, I'm coming."

Milton heard the sound of a car door opening. He turned and looked back up Danforth Street to the parked car. The rear door was open and a man was stepping out. The passenger door opened, too, and a second man emerged.

Milton turned back to the house, raised his fist and was about to knock for a third time when the door opened. Manny looked out at him.

"What's going on?"

Milton didn't answer, but quickly stepped inside. He moved Manny back into the room with a hand on his shoulder and then closed and locked the door behind him.

"What are you doing?" Manny said. "What's wrong?"

Still Milton didn't answer. He went to the window to the left of the door and moved the curtains aside. The window was barred. Milton glanced through the dusty glass. The car was out of sight, the angle too acute for him to see it. The snow fell in a thick veil. He couldn't see either of the men who had stepped out.

"*John*," Manny urged.

Milton closed the curtains and turned to Manny. "Where's Freddy?"

"Playing on his PlayStation."

"I need you to listen carefully," Milton said. "We're about to get a visit. It won't be a friendly one."

"I don't understand."

Milton was about to respond, but, before he could, he heard the sound of footsteps crunching through the snow.

"Are all the windows barred?"

"Yes," Manny said.

"Is there any other way inside?"

"There's a door that goes into my room. I never use it."

"Locked?"

"Yes."

Milton quickly assessed the layout of the property. This area, containing the living room and kitchen, was at the front, facing onto Danforth Street and accessed by way of the main door. A central hallway led deeper into the building, with the bathroom and Manny's bedroom on the left and, he assumed, Freddy's bedroom on the right.

"Does Freddy's room have any windows?"

"No."

"Go there now."

They both heard the creak of the gate as it was pushed back on its unoiled hinge.

Manny didn't move. "Not until you tell me what's happening."

The curtains were thin and the light from the street lamps outside bled through. They saw the outline of a figure framed within the glow, and then it moved away.

"I went to see Polanski," Milton said. "A man followed me. He tried to kill me."

"What does—"

Milton cut him off. "It looks like the men that Freddy saw outside the restroom are working for a local drug dealer. His name is Acosta. He's trying to make sure that what happened doesn't cause him any trouble. That's why he tried to get me out of the way. Freddy is next."

The colour drained out of Manny's face.

There came the sound of three firm knocks on the front door.

Rap.

Rap.

Rap.

"Go to his room. Shut and block the door and get under the bed."

"What about you?"

"Just go. Now."

His mind flashed back to London, a little over three years ago. He thought of Elijah Warriner, the kid in the East End, and what had happened to his mother after Milton had let his guard down for a moment.

There was no way he was going to let the same thing happen again.

No way.

Not again.

"*Go!*"

Manny hobbled down the corridor and turned right into Freddy's bedroom. He shut the door behind him; Milton could hear his voice as he spoke to his son.

Milton looked around the room for anything that he could use as a weapon. He went to the kitchen. It looked as if Manny had been interrupted in the process of preparing dinner. A pan of water was boiling on the stove and a sheaf of spaghetti was on the counter next to a can of chopped tomatoes and a bowl of sliced mushrooms. There was a knife on the chopping board. Milton ran his finger against the edge. It was blunt. No good.

Rap.

Rap.

Rap.

Milton found a coffee mug in the cupboard to the right of the stove and scooped up some of the boiling water. He took a bag of sugar and poured in enough to fill a quarter of the mug.

"Hello?"

The voice came from the other side of the front door.

"I saw you go inside. Open up."

Milton took the mug of hot sugared water and got down low, below the windows. He crawled across the room to the door, raised himself, and then pressed up against the wall between the window and door.

"Who are you?" Milton called.

"Police," the voice said. "Open the door, please."

"What do you want?"

"What's your name, sir?"

Milton quietly reached up and unlocked the door.

"Manny Blanco."

"Open the door, please, Mr. Blanco. I want to speak to you about your son."

"Hold on."

Milton heard the door mechanism creak gently and watched as the handle very slowly descended.

Milton stood behind the door with the mug in his left hand. He felt the welcome pulse and throb of adrenaline. He closed his eyes and revelled in it, accepted it, dismantled the bulwarks against it that he had erected ever since he had left the service. He had built them to protect himself and the people he met, but there had been times when he had needed his old instincts and habits.

Like now.

Milton waited for the right moment. He reached for the handle with his right hand and yanked, opening the door to reveal a man in the doorway. Milton assessed instantly: the man was shorter than he was, slender, and dressed in black jeans and a black jacket. He was holding a pistol, the muzzle pointed down. Milton flicked his left hand so that the scalding water splashed across the man's face. He had used the combination before; the sugar caused the water to adhere to the skin, exacerbating the burns that it caused. Homemade napalm. The man screamed and clamped both hands to his face, letting the pistol fall to the floor. Milton scooped it up and then kicked him in the gut, bouncing him out into the snow. He slammed the door and twisted the key in the lock.

He heard a crash from the rear of the house: the sound of an impact, and then another, and then the unmistakeable sound of splintering wood.

Milton checked the gun: a 9mm Glock. He dropped to one knee, clasped the weapon in both hands, and extended his arms. He could see down the corridor from where he had positioned himself, and, although he would also be visible to anyone at the other end of the house, he would have the benefit of preparedness and surprise.

He heard footsteps from Manny's bedroom and then watched as a finger of light was cast into the hallway. The finger widened as the door to the bedroom was opened farther, and then it was interrupted by the shadow of the man who must have forced the door into the house.

Milton took a breath, sighted down the pistol, and put a pound of pressure on the trigger.

The man was little more than a silhouette, a shadow in the gloom, but Milton waited until he was almost all the way out of the doorway and then squeezed a little more.

The Glock barked and leapt in Milton's hands. He had anticipated the kickback and absorbed it, then aimed and fired a second time. The first round had found its mark, although it was too dark for Milton to see exactly where it had struck the man. The intruder's body twisted, presenting a narrower target, and the second round went wide, crunching into the frame of the door.

The man staggered back into the room.

Milton stood, the gun still clasped in both hands, and took a step forward.

The door closed and the light that had shone from the lamp inside was immediately extinguished.

He heard a grunt of pain.

Milton reached the corridor.

"John?" Manny called.

"Stay there."

Milton stalked along the corridor, the gun held in steady hands. There were threats to the front and rear; and, although both intruders had been wounded, they were still to be definitively accounted for. And he remembered the third man in the car.

He heard the sound of footsteps in Manny's bedroom.

He paused at the side of the door, reached out with his left leg and gave a gentle prod with his foot.

He flinched from the sound of the gunshots: three quick rounds, the door splintering as they burst through the panel where he would otherwise have been standing.

They were at a stalemate. The man might have been shot, but, if he was still inside the room, he would certainly be aiming at the door just as Milton had done. Milton wouldn't be able to sight the man without making himself a sitting duck.

"Get out," Milton called. "I know I hit you. Leave now and I'll let you live."

"Fuck you!"

Milton clasped the pistol and held his breath. He thought he heard the sound of scuffling feet and then the sound of a door creaking on unused hinges.

Milton stayed where he was. He heard the sound of an engine from the front of the house. He heard the crunch of tyres on compacted snow and then that stopped, the engine still running. Milton sensed what was about to happen and flattened himself against the floor. There came a tremendous boom and then the glass in the window to the left of the door in the front room was blown out. A second boom followed immediately thereafter and the window to the right of the door received the same treatment. Fragments of glass and shot peppered the ceiling and walls. Chunks of dislodged plaster dropped to the floor.

Milton checked himself: no damage.

He heard the sound of a muffled scream from Freddy's room.

"Stay there," Milton called out. "It's okay."

He heard the sound of car doors opening and closing, a raised voice, and then the whine of an engine as tyres slipped and skidded across an icy surface.

Milton kicked open the door to the bedroom and went in gun first, swivelling through ninety degrees as he cleared the room. It was empty. There was a stripe of crimson on the carpet and the door to the street was hanging partially open, the door frame splintered where the lock fitted into the jamb. Milton crossed the room and opened the door just in time to see a car slide out of Danforth and turn hard left onto Crescent. It was a black Jeep Grand Cherokee; Milton tried to make out the plate, but the thick snow made it impossible to read.

The car found traction on the gritted surface and picked up speed toward the corner of Ridgewood Avenue.

Milton had no way of giving pursuit. He had to let it go.

He went back inside, crossed the room and went to the door to Freddy's bedroom.

"It's John," he said. "Open up. We've got to get out of here."

Milton heard the sound of movement and then a scrape

as something was removed from behind the door. Light fell onto his face as the door opened. Manny was standing there, the chair he had used to jam the door handle behind him.

"What happened?" His eyes slipped down to the Glock that Milton still held in his right fist. "I-I—"

"Get your coats and shoes," Milton instructed, cutting him off. "We have to move. Right now."

75

A taxi approached. Milton stepped into the street and waved it down. He told the driver to take them to Essex Street station. The driver agreed and they set off, no one speaking. The driver switched on his radio and switched over to Lite FM. 'Hazy Shade of Winter' by The Bangles was playing.

It would have been quicker to tell the driver to take them straight down to Coney Island, but Milton did not intend to be sloppy. He spent the drive to the west watching for any signs of surveillance. The roads were quiet, and that made it easier to observe the traffic around them. He was content that they were alone, but was still not willing to take chances.

They crossed the Williamsburg Bridge into Manhattan and then travelled the short distance to the Essex Street MTA station. Milton paid the driver and they got out. He shepherded them quickly down the steps and into the subway station. He bought three MetroCards and led the way through the turnstile and down to the platform. They took the J Train and rode it south to the end of the line. The trip to Coney Island took forty minutes, and Milton was vigilant throughout. He was confident that they had not been followed in the taxi, but, even if they had been tailed, it would have been difficult for the tail to continue down into the subway without him noticing. Their car was almost empty, too, and no one else went all the way with them.

The train pulled into the station, sliding into a platform between the trains that were lined up to commence their trips to the north. They had a wide view of the area from the elevated track: Milton looked out at the skeletal frame of the Ferris wheel, the struts of roller coasters and the tall vertical towers that hoisted thrill-seekers high into the air and then plunged them back to earth. The neon signs of the Foxy Club and Shooting Gallery were smeared across the dirty, snow-slicked windows of the car.

Milton led the way through the station, down the ramp and through the turnstiles and out onto Stillwell Avenue. The tracks and the canopy for the station were overhead, and Milton put them to their backs as they set off to the south. They followed the quiet street between garishly graffitied walls and shuttered storefronts. Milton checked behind them to ensure that they were alone; he was happy that they were.

They turned left on Surf Avenue, the taste of salt brought to them on the breeze.

"Where are we going?" Manny asked. He had been quiet for most of the journey, clutching Freddy's hand and regularly looking over at Milton as if he would be able to divine how much danger they were in by the changing expression on his face.

"I have a friend here," Milton said. "He'll be able to keep you safe until this is fixed."

"A friend?"

"He owes me a favour."

76

It was eight by the time they reached Café Valentin. The restaurant was open. Milton pushed the door and went inside, Manny and Freddy following closely behind him.

Manny reached for Milton's arm. "Who are we here to see?" he asked.

"A friend," Milton repeated. "Wait here. I need to speak to him."

The restaurant was quiet. Three of the tables were occupied: there was a couple at one, a single diner at another, and a family of four at a third. Alexei Fedorov was standing behind the bar, looking out into the room. He saw Milton as he approached, his face breaking out into an open and welcoming smile. He stepped out and clasped Milton's hand with both of his.

"John," he said, "this is a surprise."

"I'm sorry to bother you."

Fedorov smiled at Milton and put his hand on his shoulder. "You are not bothering me. What can I do for you? You want something to eat?"

"It's not that. I need a favour."

"Of course. What is it?"

"My friends need somewhere to stay." Milton stepped to the side so that Fedorov could see Manny and Freddy standing just inside the threshold of the restaurant.

Fedorov appraised them. "Who are they?"

"Manny and Freddy Blanco. They've found themselves in a little difficulty. They've had to leave their home and they don't have anywhere else to go."

"What kind of difficulty?"

"Would you mind if I didn't say?"

Fedorov smiled and shook his head. "No, of course. That is fine. Privacy—I understand. What do they need?"

"A room for a week or two. I'll pay, obviously."

"No, you will not. I have somewhere. We have a few apartments that we rent. My brother Sergei, he is in charge. A tenant moved out last month and I have not been able to fill it. It is nothing special—a studio. Would that be okay?"

"I'm sure that would be perfect."

"Then I should meet your friends."

Milton led the way between the tables back to them, Fedorov following close behind.

"This is Manny and this is Freddy."

Fedorov smiled. "Good evening to you both. My name is Alexei. You are both very welcome here. Come—I get you something to eat."

Fedorov led the way to one of the empty tables. He pulled back a chair for Freddy and then signalled to the waitress that she should bring over three menus.

"John," Fedorov said, "you will eat?"

"Yes," Milton replied. "That would be very kind. I just have a phone call to make, and then I'll be back."

Fedorov nodded, took one of the seats and began a

conversation with Manny. Milton could see the hesitation in Manny's responses, but Fedorov was charming and ebullient and he had no doubt that Manny's caution would quickly subside. Freddy was watching cautiously; Milton caught his eye, gave him a smile that he hoped would be reassuring, and then made his way to the door.

77

Polanski pulled into his driveway. He opened the door, stepped out, and almost lost his footing on the slippery surface. He opened the door and stepped into the warm hallway.

"Hey," he called out, "I'm home."

He heard the sound of footsteps approaching from the living room, and his wife, Laura, opened the door. "Hush," she chided him. "The kids have just gone to sleep."

"How was your day?"

"Challenging."

"I forgot. They cancelled school?"

She nodded. "I spent all afternoon trying not to lose my patience when they started arguing about whose turn it was to pick what they watched on Netflix."

"I'm starving," he said.

"There's meatloaf in the oven. Should still be warm."

He went through into the kitchen.

"And get me a glass of wine, would you?" she said after him. "There's one open on the side."

He took a glove from the oven's handle and opened the

door. The smell of cooked meat, onions and breadcrumbs drifted up and filled his nostrils. He reached down for the dish and took it out as his phone buzzed and vibrated on the counter.

He put the dish on a metal trivet, removed the glove and took up the phone.

He didn't recognise the number.

"Hello?"

"It's Smith. Call me back on your landline."

The call went dead.

It had sounded as if Smith was outside; Polanski had heard the sound of a passing car.

They had a cordless phone hooked up to the landline. Polanski took the handset from the cradle and, reading the number off his phone's display, called Smith back.

"It's me," he said as the call connected. "What's going on?"

"We need to be careful with which phones we use," Smith said. "Yours might be tapped."

"Don't talk crazy."

Smith ignored him. "I went to see the Blancos after I saw you this afternoon. The house was attacked while I was there."

"What do you mean it—"

"Two men tried to get inside," he interrupted. "When they couldn't, they shot out the windows."

"Are you okay? The kid?"

"We're okay. They didn't get what they wanted, so they left. The Blancos are with me now. I've taken them somewhere safe."

Polanski found that he was nervously drumming his fingers on the counter. "Where?"

"It doesn't matter. They're okay." Smith paused. "But it's

worse than that. I was followed after I met you this afternoon. Just one guy—I spotted him early and I lost him on the subway."

"How can you be sure?"

"I haven't told you everything about what I used to do," he said.

"Military?"

There was a pause. "Can we just say that I've been trained to notice when someone's following me and leave it at that? There was hardly anyone on the street tonight. I saw one man behind me who stuck to me like glue all the way to the station. He got on the same train as I did and then he followed when I transferred to another one going back in the opposite direction. That's the easiest counter-surveillance trick in the book—the only reason someone would behave like that is if they were following me. But one man is easy to lose. And I lost him."

"Why would he be following you?"

"Come on," Smith said impatiently. "You're not thinking. He wasn't on me before we met. I notice when people are following. He could only have picked me up at the coffee shop. That means it wasn't me they were watching—"

"It was me," Polanski finished.

"Yes," Smith said. "You need to be careful. It's very likely that you're under surveillance. They might be watching you right now."

"That's why you want this on a different line?"

"Are you sure you can trust your cell?"

Polanski didn't answer. He looked down at the phone on the counter as if it were suddenly untrustworthy. He thought back to Sunday night. González had called him on his cell. Haynes had raised the possibility, too: could Acosta have tapped him? Was it possible that he was being followed?

"Oh shit," he said.

"Is your family safe?"

Polanski went to the window and parted the blinds. He peered between the slats. Their house was part of a small development that was accessed along Cartwheel Close. The main road was shielded by a screen of trees that had been planted at around the same time that the houses had been built. There was an entrance from the road that opened out into a wide parking area, with each house allocated two bays each. They used the bays to park the cars that wouldn't fit onto the driveways. There were cars there tonight, but none that he didn't recognise.

"Polanski?"

"Yes," he replied, staring at his reflection in the darkened window. "We're fine. And I can't see anyone outside. Where are you? Where are the Blancos?"

"I told you—they're safe."

Polanski felt as if he had lost control of the situation. "Can we meet?"

"When?"

"Tomorrow."

"Be on the boardwalk at noon. Outside Luna Park."

"I'll be there."

"Be careful," Smith said. "This is going to get worse before it gets better."

PART V

THURSDAY

78

P olanski took the half-empty bowl of Apple Jacks and put it in the sink to be washed up. Both of his boys were sitting on the floor in the TV room, watching their usual cartoons. Their routine was always exactly the same: he was up first at six so he could take a shower while the others were still sleeping; he dressed and then woke the boys, taking them downstairs for their breakfast while Laura woke and showered. He would usually take his oldest, Nathan, to school and his wife would take their youngest, Ben, to day care. The routine was going to be different today: the TV was saying that schools in the area were closed.

His wife came down the stairs. "Can I have a word with you?" she said.

He got up and walked across the room. Laura had gone to the window and was looking out into the street. Her lips were pursed and she was frowning with concern.

"What is it?" he said.

She gestured out of the window. "You see that car over there?"

Polanski looked. The parking bays outside the house were emptying out now as their neighbours—several of them cops, like Polanski—set off for the drive south to the city. There was one car, a red Acura, that was parked in the bay that usually housed the Porsche Cayenne that was the pride and joy of the Grahams. Buddy Graham was a cop in Manhattan and left before Polanski every morning.

"You mean the Acura?" he asked.

She nodded. "It was there yesterday, too."

"You sure?"

"Definitely. The same two guys in it, too. They just sat there for an hour, looking at the house."

Polanski stared out at the car. There were two men in the front. He was too far away to make them out or to read the plate.

He went into his study and opened the gun safe. He didn't like carrying his service Glock when he was off duty, so he typically swapped it for his sub-compact Colt Mustang XSP. He took the pistol, checked that it was ready to fire and, satisfied, put it into the pocket of his jacket.

"What are you doing?" Laura asked him as he came back into the living room.

"I'm gonna check them out," he said. "I won't be a minute."

Laura bit her lip anxiously, but Polanski walked by her and made his way to the hall before she could object. He opened the door and set off across the snow-covered lawn to the parking lot. He looked at the two men in the car. The driver was white, with dark glasses obscuring his eyes. The man in the passenger seat looked bigger, with a shaven head and tattoos visible on his neck and down one arm.

Polanski walked straight at them. He put his left hand into his jacket pocket and took out his badge.

The car pulled out of the parking space and turned hard left, heading to the access road that led to Cartwheel Close. The passenger stared out of the window at him as they drove past. He put his index and middle fingers together like the barrel of a gun, pointed them at Polanski and then cocked his thumb in the manner of a hammer. He brought his thumb down two times.

Polanski reached for his weapon, his fingertips tracing the shape of the butt as the car swung sharply onto the main road and accelerated away in the direction of the stores on Brotherhood Plaza. He waited until it was out of sight. He was breathing quickly and he had a kernel of fear in the pit of his stomach. It was not a subtle threat; whoever the two men were, they worked for Carlos Acosta and they were warning him to back off.

He took another moment to compose himself and then went back to the house.

"Who were they?" Laura asked.

"It's nothing."

She turned away so that the children couldn't see her face. "Don't bullshit me," she said in a tense, low whisper. "What were they outside for?"

"I don't know," he said. "I think it might be to do with a case I'm working. I need to run the plate."

He knew how pointless that would be as soon as he said it; the car was probably stolen, and there would be nothing to trace it back to Acosta.

"Are we in danger?"

"Can you speak to your mother? Maybe take the kids up there for a day or two."

"What about school?"

"They cancelled it again today. Just as well."

"Jesus, Aleks. What's going on?"

"I need to figure it out, baby. Speak to your mother. She'll be pleased to see you and the kids."

"How long?"

"Not long. A couple days. Three, max."

"For fuck's sake," she mouthed before she took a breath, composed herself, and turned to the children with a smile on her face. "Who'd like to go and surprise Grandma?"

Polanski went back to the front door and looked outside. He looked at the tracks that the Acura had left in the snow; save those, there was no sign that it had ever been there.

He felt sick as he made his way out to his car.

79

L aura's mother lived in Bloomingburg. It was twenty-five miles to the north-west, and Polanski followed his wife as she took Sarah Wells Trail to Hamptonburgh and then the interchange with Route 17.

Polanski had been watching carefully, and he was as convinced as he could be that they had not been followed. They reached Exit 121. Polanski sounded the horn and flashed the lights, indicating that he was going to turn off, and took the exit for Scranton. He watched the car with his wife and kids until the turn took it out of sight. He felt conflicting emotions: he was happy that they would be safe, but he couldn't ignore the fear that accompanied the fact that it had been necessary for them to leave home.

Montclair was fifty-five miles away. Polanski switched on the radio and listened to the news as he started the drive to the south.

Richard Haynes lived on the outskirts of Montclair. Polanski had called ahead from the interstate and the older man was waiting for him as he pulled up outside the house.

"What's up?" he said as he welcomed Polanski inside.

"We got a big problem."

"About?"

"The investigation into the Seven Five."

"Nothing we can't fix. Go and sit down in the conservatory. Let me fix a couple coffees."

Haynes and his wife had built a conservatory on the side of their house and it was obvious that Haynes had been in there this morning when Polanski had called. He had asked whether it would be possible to speak away from the office. Haynes had said that he had a day off to go visit a couple of old bureau buddies, but that wasn't until later and that he should come and visit. Polanski sat down and looked around the pleasant room. It was warm, with newspapers spread out on a low table and pictures of Haynes and his family hung on the wall. There was a desk in the corner that Haynes used to take care of domestic paperwork. The conservatory looked out onto the garden, and Polanski could see a snowman in the centre of the space. Haynes had two grandchildren, and he knew that they often came to visit. The snowman, and the riot of scuffed prints in the snow, was evidence that they had been here recently.

"Here," Haynes said, bringing over two mugs of coffee. He handed one to Polanski.

"Thanks."

The older man lowered himself into his chair and sipped his drink. "So," he said. "What's the problem?"

Polanski explained. He started with what had happened to González, going over the ground that they had already covered in the aftermath of the murder. He continued, explaining that Freddy Blanco had changed his story; now he said that he *could* identify one of the shooters, and that his father was insisting that they be rehoused before he went on the record. He described what had happened when Smith had visited the Blancos yesterday afternoon and then what had taken place outside his own house that morning.

Haynes listened intently, encouraging him to fill in the parts that he would otherwise have skimmed over.

"The kid hasn't said who it is he recognised?"

"No," Polanski said. "They want to get out of Brooklyn first."

"Can't blame them for that."

"Smith said that he was followed after we spoke. He's sure he wasn't followed before the meeting, so the only thing that makes sense is that they've been watching me."

"And you think it's Acosta?" he said when Polanski was done.

"Who else?"

Haynes nodded. "I agree," he said. "No one else makes sense."

"I met him in the coffee shop outside the office. What if they had someone in there with us? They could've heard what we were talking about. Smith had just told me that the kid was ready to testify. An hour later and they try to break into his house. It feels like it's my fault."

"Why didn't you bring Smith into the office?"

"Because I'm concerned Acosta's getting help from the bureau. I just keep going back to Sunday. Someone knew that González was coming in."

"I've been thinking about what you said," Haynes said. "Maybe he told someone."

Polanski shrugged. "Maybe. But that would have been a dumb move, and González was smart. I don't see it."

"Then who did you tell?"

"You."

Haynes smiled. "I promise it wasn't me."

"I know that. But I keep wondering about my cell. Or maybe the office is bugged. I know that sounds hysterical."

Haynes stood. "No, it doesn't. I told you—I've seen it before."

"So what do I do?"

Haynes went over to an old-fashioned Rolodex on the desk. He opened it and flipped through the cards inside. He took one out and held it up. "I have an idea."

"Who's that?"

"The special prosecutor," he said. "Maybe it's time to call for reinforcements."

80

Haynes made the call and then said that he would cancel his visit so that he could come to the meeting, too. Polanski protested, but, secretly, he was pleased. He had started to feel as if he was out of his depth, and Haynes had years of experience and a contacts list to die for. He was also calm and measured, and, as Polanski drove them both into Manhattan, he started to relax.

They took the Holland Tunnel beneath the Hudson and then headed south to Rector Street. He parked his car and they walked to the vertiginous office at number two. The building's purpose was not obvious from the outside; Haynes had called on the way into the city and explained that they would need to take the elevator to the twenty-third floor. Polanski waited nervously next to Haynes as the car ascended. This was a big moment and he couldn't be sure that they were doing the right thing.

The doors opened and they stepped out into the small lobby. There was an empty desk and, behind it, a sign on the wall reported that they were in the right place: Office of the New York State Special Prosecutor for Corruption.

There was a door to the right of the lobby. It had frosted-glass panels that he couldn't see through and, when Polanski pushed it, he found that it was locked.

He knocked on the glass.

Nothing.

"They'll be here in a minute," Haynes said.

There was a row of seats against the wall. Both men sat down. Polanski folded his hands in his lap and stared down at them. Haynes had laid it all out as they had driven south. The special prosecutor was the best option available. The prosecutor had state-wide jurisdiction and was responsible for felony narcotics investigations and prosecutions in the five boroughs. The office was granted wide powers to deal with narcotics-trafficking organisations and had the ability to track offenders across jurisdictional boundaries that might otherwise prove difficult. More important than that, it was independent and had no overt ties to either IAB or any of the Brooklyn precincts that Acosta might have corrupted.

He heard the click as the lock was turned. He looked up to see a shadow in the frosted glass. The door opened and a woman smiled at him.

"I'm Beth Winters," she said. "Sergeant Haynes? Detective Polanski?"

Haynes stood. "Hello."

"Thanks for coming in. Mrs. Harris will see you now."

81

Haynes went first and Polanski followed. Winters —a lawyer, Polanski guessed—led them through an open area where a dozen men and women worked at a series of open desks. They were all dressed similarly, a little shinier and more impressive than the staff who filed in and out of the IAB building in Brooklyn every day. Polanski felt a twist of unease in his gut. He knew what it was, even as he also knew it was ridiculous: being in here made him feel like a rat. Cops who worked with Internal Affairs must have felt the exact same feeling as he did right now. He was stepping outside of his own office. Just being here was an admission that he felt that he couldn't trust the men and women with whom he worked. It made him feel uncomfortable, almost traitorous. He knew that he was doing the right thing, that this was a necessary and unavoidable measure that he had to take, but that didn't make him feel any better about it. That they were here at Haynes's suggestion made it more tolerable, but he would still rather have been almost anywhere else.

Winters led them to a line of three conference rooms at

the other end of the floor. They had glass walls, and they were all occupied. She went to the room on the left, nodded to the woman waiting inside and opened the door so that Haynes and Polanski could go through.

The woman stood. Polanski recognised her from the TV.

"Richard," she said warmly to Haynes, moving in closer so that he could lean down and place a kiss on her cheek. "This is a pleasant surprise."

"It's good to see you," Haynes replied. "I'd rather it was under better circumstances, though."

"Detective Polanski?" she said, turning to him.

"Yes."

"Thanks for coming in. You want some coffee?"

"That'd be great," he said.

Haynes had given him the low-down on the drive down from Montclair. Barbara Harris had been a prosecutor for twenty years. She had cut her teeth in the DA's office as assistant district attorney, taking care of misdemeanour and felony prosecutions. That, he had explained, was where he had come across her for the first time. She had been appointed to be the special prosecutor by the city's five district attorneys, and Haynes had suggested that her tenacity and drive was because she was the first woman in the role. There had been resistance from the rank and file, but that resistance had been destroyed as she brought in a string of high-profile busts, men and women who had previously been impervious to prosecution. Haynes said that she had shrewd judgement and a willingness to throw the full authority of her office behind cases regardless of the risks involved. He had warned him that she was also known for a waspish temper and a sharp tongue. Polanski felt the perspiration running down his back as he took the seat opposite her.

Harris smiled at Winters and nodded down to the tray that had been left on the table. It bore a coffee pot and four cups. Winters poured and passed cups across the table to Haynes and Polanski. Polanski reached for a bowl laden with sachets of creamer and packets of sugar and attended to his drink, glad to have something to occupy his hands.

"Thanks," Harris said to Winters. "I'll call you if I need you."

"Nice to meet you, gentlemen," Winters said as she left the room, closing the door behind her.

Harris smiled at Haynes. "An unexpected call," she said. "You said you needed my help."

"It's a case that Aleksander's been running," Haynes explained. "We've come up against a serious problem. We wouldn't be here otherwise."

She turned to Polanski. "So—how can I help you, Detective?"

He had been working on how he would get started for the entirety of the drive into Manhattan, but, now that he was here, sitting at this shiny conference table with the skyline of the city out of the window, he forgot all of his prepared lines.

"I know this is probably difficult," she said. "But whatever you say stays here—you have my word on that. You can speak freely."

His throat was dry, but he began. "I've been running an investigation into corruption in the Seventy-Fifth Precinct."

"Corrupt cops?"

"Yes," he said.

"I thought the Seven Five was cleared up?"

Haynes shook his head. "There's a group of cops who've been working both sides for years. Aleks has been looking into it. He's been close to a bust for a couple of weeks."

"So why have you brought it to me?"

"I'd been cultivating a CI," Polanski explained. "José Luis González. He was working as the bridge between the cops and the Dominican gang they've been representing. I leaned on González a little, offered him immunity if he'd wear a wire and go on the stand when we brought the case. It took a lot of leaning, but he went for it. He called me on Sunday and told me that he wanted to come in. He was sure that the Dominicans were onto him. I said fine—provided he brought me the evidence he had, I'd take him off the street. We agreed to meet at a safe house, but before he could get there, he was murdered in a bathroom at Euclid subway station."

"I read about that," she said.

Polanski nodded and took a sip of his coffee. "I couldn't figure out what had happened. It wouldn't've made any sense for González to have told anyone at his end that he was coming in."

"Wife?"

"Wasn't married. No girlfriend, either. And he was smart. The gang he was working with don't mess around."

"Which gang?"

"The Acosta crew."

She nodded. "Why doesn't that surprise me?"

"No way González would've taken the risk of talking about it."

"Go on," she said. "What then?"

"Homicide got involved. They had a witness. A thirteen-year-old kid who said he saw two guys outside the restroom right around when González was killed. I went down with homicide and spoke to him. Turns out that the kid thinks he recognised one of the men he saw."

"Who?"

"Kid won't say until Aleks has got them into a safe house outside Brooklyn," Haynes said.

"He's scared," Polanski added.

"I don't blame him," Harris said.

Polanski took another sip of his coffee. Harris waited patiently for him to continue.

"Last night," he said, "someone tried to break into the kid's house."

"Is he okay?"

"Yes, but it could've been different. And now it looks like I've been kept under surveillance, too. There was a car outside my house yesterday and then first thing this morning. It's Acosta. He's trying to close me down."

"So?"

"I've been thinking around it all week, but I can't get it out of my head."

"Someone in your office tipped the bad guys off?"

He nodded. "The investigation has been kept under wraps. It's just me on the case, no one else. And no one save us knew that we were running González."

Harris looked over at Haynes. "You been telling the bad guys?"

"No, ma'am," Haynes said with a smile.

Harris steepled her fingers on the glass table. "So what are you two proposing?"

"I heard you're running an investigation into Acosta," Haynes said.

She smiled. "You heard that, did you?"

"Is it true?"

"We might be."

"So give Aleks an office and some resources here. He can come at him from a different angle. He gets you the cops, maybe you can flip them and then you get Acosta, too."

She turned to Polanski. "You think you can do that?"

"The kid will go on record and identify the officer he saw. But, like I said, I need to get them somewhere safe."

"We can help with that," she said.

"If we could get that fixed, I'll get him to go on the record. Then we put the officer under surveillance. Give me two guys. If I can get into him, maybe we roll him up and get the others."

"You won't be able to follow him with two. I'll give you four."

Polanski felt a shiver of anticipation. "Thank you," he said.

Harris reached for the coffee pot and refreshed all of their cups. "If you're right," she said, "if there is a rat in the bureau, we need to get you out of it without them knowing that you're working for me. You got any ideas how we could do that?"

"That's easy. I've got vacation coming up. Two weeks. We're supposed to be going to Hawaii. I could cancel it, move everything here and go at them hard."

"Two weeks?"

He nodded.

"That okay with you, Haynes?"

"Absolutely."

"Then I think we can give you that."

"Is that a green light?" Haynes asked.

"It is," Harris said. "Do it. Go and get them."

82

P olanski met Smith in Coney Island at noon, just as they had arranged. The snow had covered everything, erasing the separation between the promenade and the start of the beach, the demarcation indicated only by the railings, which were themselves covered by snow. The sky was grey and dark despite it only being noon; the forecast predicted more snow before the day was out. It seemed as if it would never end.

Smith was leaning against the wall that separated Luna Park from the boardwalk. Polanski raised his hand and Smith pushed away from the wall and trudged through the snow to meet him. He had a half-smoked cigarette in his hand and blew a jet of smoke into the air before switching the cigarette to his left hand and putting out his right for Polanski to take. They shook.

"Were you followed?" he asked.

"No," Polanski said. "But you were right. They were tailing me. They were at my house yesterday evening and this morning."

They set off to the east and Polanski explained what had happened since they had seen each other yesterday afternoon. He said that his wife had reported seeing an unusual car outside the house, and that the car had been there again when she looked outside this morning. He explained how he had sent his family away and how he had taken his concerns to Haynes.

"You trust him?" Smith asked.

"I've known him for a long time. I do."

He went on to explain that he and Haynes had concluded that the only way to continue the investigation against Acosta was to bring in the special prosecutor.

"What will she do?" Smith said once Polanski had explained that Harris had, indeed, taken the case.

"I'll be able to work in Manhattan, away from Brooklyn. And she'll give me a small team for surveillance. I'll have the manpower I need. I need to know who to investigate. I need to speak to the kid."

"And I need some more background."

"Okay."

"Start with Acosta. Who is he?"

Polanski nodded. He had studied Acosta for so long that he knew his biography as if he were a close friend. "He was born in Santiago in 1973. Family emigrated to New York in 1980 and he was raised in Queens. Started dealing around 2000. At least that's when he was busted the first time. Moves pretty much everything and anything: party drugs, heroin, coke, crack, dope. He runs his gang like a business. The guys we've busted from the crew say he calls it La Corporacion. Gets his recruits from his family, from friends and from friends of friends around East Brooklyn. His brother, Savio, is his second in command. His sister, Elsa, makes sure the product gets delivered. I heard a rumour that his mother does his accounts for him. And Carlos works just like the Colombians worked: he puts some of his guys in to import and package the drug, others to move it around the city and keep it safe, and then he's got the corner boys and vendors who move it on the street. On top of that, I've heard rumours that he's put together teams to take down rivals and anyone he thinks might be able to threaten him."

"Like the guys who went after the Blancos."

"Maybe. The DEA has him down for a dozen homicides over the last eighteen months, but you can probably double that once you add in the ones we don't know about."

"And how does he tie in with the dead guy?"

"González was deep in his gang, but I flipped him," Polanski said. "Took three months. Three fucking months. He had a business on Atlantic Avenue, where he said the cops on Acosta's books used to come and get their monthly pay-offs. I persuaded him to record a meet. He was coming in the night that he was killed. He had evidence of one of the cops taking the money and he was going to testify against him."

"You don't know which cops?"

"He wouldn't give me anything until we had him somewhere safe."

Smith took another cigarette from a packet in his pocket. He offered it to Polanski. "No, thanks," he said, waiting for Smith to put the cigarette to his lips and light it. "Now you," he said. "Who did the kid see?"

Smith reached his left hand into his pocket and took out his phone. He clasped the cigarette between his teeth and swiped through the photos until he found the one that he wanted. He handed it to Polanski and invited him to look.

It was a screen-grab from a video. "What is this?"

"There's a TV in the precinct house. They run promotional stuff on it. The night they took us there, they had something running about these cops who were handing out anti-drug leaflets. It was an extract from a report on the news. I found the original."

Polanski looked down at it.

"Him," Smith said. "You know who he is?"

"Landon Shepard. He used to work the Seven Five. Retired last month, I think. Why?"

"Because he's one of the men Freddy saw outside the restroom. He's your killer—or one of them."

"He's sure about that?"

"Swipe right," Smith suggested.

Polanski did as he was told. The next image was a photograph that Smith had taken of a photograph in a frame. It showed two men—one black, the other white—on a boat. The black man was Shepard. He was holding a big bluefish. Polanski swiped left and looked at the previous picture again.

"Swipe right again," Smith said.

Polanski did and saw what he guessed was the back of the photograph. He read aloud: "'Me and Shep, June '15, Jamaica Bay.'"

"The white guy is Robert Carter," Smith said. "I think he goes by Bobby."

"He does. He and Shepard used to be partners in the Seven Five."

"You have anything on either of them?"

"They've both had complaints made against them over the years, but nothing ever stuck. But if I was guessing on the types of officers who might end up working with someone like Acosta, they would be toward the top of my list."

They kept walking. "Shepard was waiting at the precinct for Carter at midnight on Monday. He was drunk. They had what you might describe as a vigorous discussion and then Carter drove him off. I've got photos—you can see them if you want."

"You were spying on them?"

"I wanted to see if I could find Shepard—the precinct seemed like the best place to start."

"What—you were just standing outside?"

"There's a derelict building opposite. I was on the top floor."

Polanski looked at him with a curiosity he couldn't hide. "You're not really a cook, are you?"

"I am."

"So what did you do before?"

"This and that," Smith said.

"Law enforcement?"

"No."

"So that leaves military, like I thought."

"Once upon a time. Does it matter?"

Polanski held out the phone with the picture of the framed photograph still showing. "How did you get this?"

"Probably best you don't ask," Smith said with a shallow smile.

"Did you break into his house?"

"Like I said—best you don't ask."

"Jesus," Polanski said. They walked on in silence for a moment. Polanski looked down at the phone and swiped right, moving into the surveillance pictures that Smith had taken. He saw Shepard and Carter and a third man, this one in uniform like Carter. "That's James Rhodes," he said, pointing. "He's a rookie. Straight out of the Academy. I checked him out when he got posted to the Seven Five. I'm guessing he's been assigned to work with Carter."

"He didn't stick around long. I got the impression Carter wanted to speak to Shepard alone."

Polanski held up the phone. "Can you email me these?"

"Sure," he said. "What else do you need?"

"The kid. We need to take a proper statement and get him to identify Shepard."

"He'll do it. You got a safe house?"

"I'm working on it. I can do it, though—it'll happen. Where are they now?"

"With me."

"Where?"

"They're safe."

Polanski could have pressed for their location, but there was no point. He doubted that Smith would tell him until he was ready and, he noted to his mild surprise, there was something trustworthy in the man's gruffness that he found reassuring.

"What are you going to do now?" Smith asked him.

"I'm going back to Manhattan. I'll take care of the safe house and then I want to get surveillance started on Shepard and Carter. The sooner the better. What about you?"

"I'll be with the Blancos," he said. "Fix it so that they can get out of New York and then call me."

They were by the stairs that led down to Beach Walk. Smith nodded his farewell, broke away from Polanski and descended the stairs. Polanski turned around and started back to where he had left his car. He could see their footprints, two sets that made their way back to the shuttered rides of Luna Park. It was cold, with a chill wind blowing in off the sea and a crispness in the air that augured yet more snow. Polanski's feet were cold in his boots, frozen after trudging through so much snow. He shoved his hands deep into the pockets of his coat and continued on. He was excited. The week had started badly, but Smith's revelations promised an improvement. He was keen to get back to the island so that he could get started.

83

Detective Rebecca Mackintosh got up close to the dumpster, rose up and looked inside. The body was still there. The dead man hadn't been touched so that the technicians could take their photos of him in his final, ignominious resting place. He was in an undignified position: he was upside down, his weight borne on his shoulders with his arms stretched out; his legs were split so that she could look down between them and see the man's face. He had been frozen there by a combination of the cold and rigor. Mackintosh could see what must have happened for him to land in that position: he had been killed outside the dumpster, hauled up the side and pushed over the sill. He had gone in head first, with his legs toppling over the top and bracing against the opposite wall of the dumpster.

The body had been found by a homeless junkie who had clambered inside the dumpster in an attempt to find somewhere to shelter from the cold. The woman had seen the man, unmoving and frozen solid, had called it in and then had tried to get away so that she didn't have to deal with the cops. She was stoned, though, and had already blabbed about the gruesome discovery to the man who described himself as her husband. The responding officers had asked around and the woman had been located. Mackintosh would talk to her later. She certainly wasn't a suspect, but if she had been in the area, then perhaps she might have seen something.

The man's wallet had fallen out of his pocket. They had fished it out in an attempt to identify him. His name was Alejandro del Cabral and he had a state ID card. She had been able to check the picture on the card against the man's upside-down face and was reasonably sure that they were one and the same. The wallet held a driver's license, a small paper fold containing a white powder that Mackintosh knew would be confirmed as cocaine, and three hundred dollars in paper bills.

The photographer arranged a small stepladder so that he could stand on it, look into the dumpster and snap his pictures. Mackintosh didn't want to get in his way, so she stepped back. The snow around the dumpster had been churned up by the stampede of people who were already involved in investigating the discovery: the homeless woman, the responding officers from the Seven Five, Mackintosh, the photographer, the CSI technicians. There was a line of vehicles parked on the street outside the arched entrance to the cemetery. A uniformed officer had been posted there to keep people out. The officer had already had to move on a TV crew from ABC7 after the presenter had blocked the way inside while shooting a hasty report.

Mackintosh shivered in the cold, snowflakes settling on the hood of her coat and her shoulders. Two murders in a week. One just outside Cypress Hills station and the other at Euclid, no more than a mile and a half between them. She wondered whether they might be linked. It was possible. The Euclid murder had presented nothing of interest since she had spoken to the two witnesses. She had no leads, not even a hint of a lead, and now they had another killing to clear. They put each homicide on a board in the office. There had been ninety-nine murders in the whole of Brooklyn so far this year, with six in the Seven Five. They had solved four of those murders, a clearance rate that the city saw as just about acceptable. These two were unhelpful. And Mackintosh had landed both of them.

She trudged through the snow to the patrolmen waiting by their car.

"Anything? Witnesses?"

The first man shook his head. "We asked up and down the street. No one saw a thing."

"What about video?"

"Here? Most of these buildings don't have anyone in them."

"What about the station?"

The man shrugged. "I guess…"

"Go and ask them," she said.

"You think they'd even be working?"

"Go and ask."

She turned away as the cop muttered to his partner. She checked her watch: three in the afternoon. It was cold and dark, the sky grey and impassive for as far as she could see. Another big fall of snow was forecast, and that would soon cover any evidence that they might otherwise have found. Every day that went by made it less likely that they would be able to solve the murder. More likely the killer would be able to get away.

Two murders in less than two miles in the space of five days. She'd had decent numbers all year, but now they were going to shit. She just needed to catch a break.

84

Carter was getting changed at his locker when Rhodes came down the stairs and joined him.

"Hey, kid," Carter said. "How you doing?"

"I'm good," Rhodes replied.

"Gonna be a cold one tonight."

Rhodes reached into his bag and took out a Thermos. "I've come prepared," he said, with a little of the goofiness that Carter had come to associate with him.

"So have I." Carter grinned, taking a hip flask from his bag.

Carter took off his sweatshirt and jeans and pulled on his uniform. The rookie did the same. Carter watched him as he strapped on his belt and checked his weapon. The kid had relaxed after the first couple of days. Carter had continued to gradually introduce him to what life on the street was really like, the kind of activity you could indulge in without bringing down any unnecessary trouble, and the kid's initial hesitation had been replaced by what Carter took to be a curious acceptance. It was too early to be sure, but, if he had been forced to guess, Carter would have said that the kid had the ethical flexibility to make a decent patrol cop in this part of Brooklyn. A grass eater, for sure, with the hope that he might be able to introduce a little meat into his diet.

Carter holstered his pistol, fastened the retaining clip, and grabbed his coat.

"I'll see you in the muster room," he said. "Don't be late. Ramirez is in a shitty mood."

———

The sergeant hurried through roll call, picking out a few of the incidents that had made the previous shift just a little less boring than the eight-to-four usually was: there were reports of shots fired in Sutter Ballfields between Schenck and Barbey; a burglary on Bradford Street with the perpetrator climbing up the fire escape and forcing the window; a half dozen fender benders as drivers lost control on the ice; the disappearance of a ten-year-old girl who had failed to come back to her parents' house on Dumont after throwing snowballs in Martin Luther King Jr. playground.

Carter and Rhodes made their way out to the patrol car. Rhodes, who had settled into his role as Carter's driver, slid inside and started the engine. The cabin retained a little warmth from the crew who had used it on the previous shift, and it didn't take long to bring it back up to a hospitable temperature.

Rhodes backed them out onto Sutter and started driving to Sector Ida-John, the area that they had been assigned. They drove slowly along Pitkin, watching the locals struggling along sidewalks that were treacherous with black ice.

Carter looked over at Rhodes. It was obvious that the kid had something on his mind. He had been quiet, drumming his fingers on the wheel and almost starting a conversation before deciding against it and holding his tongue. Carter had waited for him to say what he obviously wanted to say, but, since he seemed reluctant to spit it out, he decided that he would have to give him a little nudge.

"What's up?" Carter asked.

Rhodes glanced over at him. "Nothing."

"Come on," Carter pressed. "You're quiet. What's on your mind?"

"Seriously, Bobby. It's nothing."

"Don't bullshit me. I can see you've been wanting to say something ever since we left the precinct. Spit it out."

Rhodes paused, clicking his tongue against the roof of his mouth. "Okay," he said slowly, as if tasting the word to ensure it was palatable. "Let's say I had an opportunity. Would you be interested?"

"An opportunity?"

"To make money."

"Always interested in that," he said. "Go on. Let's have it."

"I heard something from a friend last night. This guy—I used to work on the subways with him. He drives trains. Based at the Coney Island Complex—the yard down in Gravesend. You know it?"

"I know where it is," Carter said. "It's huge. What about it?"

"They got a card game down near the yard every Friday night. This garage on West Thirteenth, around the back of Stillwell Avenue—owner's the brother of one of the union guys. He lets them set up a table in one of the back rooms. It's quiet. No one goes down there after dark. You got drivers and engineers, they come down and play a few hands."

"You ever been?"

"Yeah," he said. "Couple times."

"So what are you suggesting?"

"We should bust it. It's an illegal game, right? We close it down and... you know..."

"Help ourselves to some of the money?"

Rhodes shrugged. "Why not?"

"You know these guys?"

"Not really. But these guys are all total dicks."

It wasn't hard to see what must have gone down: Rhodes had gone along to play and he'd had a rough time, either beaten fair and square or taken advantage of, and now, whatever had happened, it had left a bad taste in his mouth.

"So?" he pressed.

Carter laughed. "Listen to you," he said. "Two days ago you wouldn't have said boo to a goose, now you want us to rip off a card game."

Rhodes shrugged. "I been thinking about what you said. About meat eaters and grass eaters. Maybe I don't want to be a grass eater no more."

"Good for you, kid."

"You interested?"

"Let me think about it."

85

P olanski watched as the four people filed into the conference room. It was the same room where he had met Harris seven hours earlier; the same coffee pot, refreshed with a new brew, had been left on the table. Harris had moved quickly. Polanski had been given his own desk, together with a new phone and laptop. His old phone had been taken away to be checked over by the techs, and, in an abundance of caution, one of the junior detectives had been assigned to go through the district attorney's records to see whether a wiretap on Polanski's number had been authorised. Haynes and Harris were also arranging for the IAB office in Brooklyn to be subjected to a covert bug sweep carried out by a Manhattan counter-intelligence outfit that Harris had used for a similar purpose during a previous investigation. Polanski had been taken aback by the speed and diligence with which she, and the rest of the office, worked. Their professionalism made the standards he was used to in Brooklyn look slapdash and second-rate by comparison, and it gave him another jolt of confidence that things were finally moving in the right direction.

The two women and two men took seats around the table. Polanski gave them a moment to settle and then spoke.

"All right then," he began. "Let's get started. Introductions, first, I think. I'm Aleksander Polanski. I'm working out of this office for the next two weeks, but I'm based in IAB up in Brooklyn."

The blonde woman to Polanski's right spoke next. "Detective Michelle Walker. Narcotics Gang Unit."

There was an older black man to Walker's right. "Detective Jarvis Moore. Just moved across to the HIT."

"HIT?" Polanski queried.

"Heroin Interdiction Team," Moore clarified.

"I'm Detective Alice Walsh," said the middle-aged woman to the right of Moore. "Narcotics."

"And I'm Assistant District Attorney Mark Mantegna," said the man in the suit next to Walsh. "I work in the trial division. I'll co-ordinate the prosecution. It's your case, Detective, but we want to make sure it gets done right. Anything you need, you come to me. Search and arrest warrants, you want to tap a phone—whatever it is, just ask."

They were easy-going and reassuring with their confidence. Polanski stood and poured cups of coffee for each of them.

"What have you got for us?" Mantegna said. "The boss said you're looking at corrupt cops down in Brooklyn?"

"Corrupt cops on the payroll of one of the bigger drug gangs down there."

"Carlos Acosta," Walker said. "We've looked at him before. He's a bad man."

"Who you want us to look at?" Moore asked.

Polanski had spent the afternoon after returning from Coney Island putting together a list of information on

Landon Shepard. He had compiled it and printed it out; there was enough to fill two sheets. He passed the dossiers to Walker; she took one and passed it on.

"His name is Landon Shepard," he said. "Born in Ozone Park, Queens, in 1961, then moved to Rosedale. Joined the NYPD in 1986 as a twenty-five-year-old rookie. Went through the academy, did well enough to graduate but not well enough to avoid being assigned to the Seven Five as a patrol officer. He's always worked the street, never been interested in making detective as far as I can work out. Retired from the police a month ago. Doesn't seem to have another job to go to."

"Where does he live?"

"He's got a place in Port Washington, up on the water."

"We'll have a look at it," Walsh said. "Get an idea of his outgoings."

"And we can check with his bank if we think he can't afford his lifestyle," Mantegna offered.

Walker had flipped the page and was pointing to a picture of Bobby Carter. "Who's the other guy?"

"Bobby Carter. Used to be Shepard's partner. They rode together for seven years. They're close. Best men at each other's weddings. Carter is godfather to one of Shepard's kids. They're tight."

"But it's Shepard we're going after first?" Mantegna said.

Polanski nodded. "There was a murder at Euclid Avenue station on Sunday night. I was working an informant, a guy who worked as Acosta's bagman, said he was responsible for paying Acosta's friendly cops their monthly fees. He said he had recorded evidence that would nail one of the cops and we'd just agreed on the deal for him to bring it to me. He was on his way to the safe house when he was killed."

"What a coincidence," Walker said.

"He had his throat cut in the restroom. The thing is, there was a witness. A thirteen-year-old kid saw two guys outside. He's identified Shepard as one of them. He didn't get a good look at the other one, but, if you ask me to put my neck on the line, I'm pretty confident we'll find out it's Carter."

"So we put Shepard under surveillance first?" Walsh said.

"I think so."

"Does he know what you look like?"

"We have to assume he does. Acosta's been following me. That's why I'm here and not in Brooklyn."

"I'll have a word with Harris and see if we can add another body to the detail. We get four of us who can rotate the surveillance—that ought to be plenty for what this is. When do you want to get started?"

"As soon as we can. Tonight?"

"No time like the present," Walsh said, and the others nodded their agreement.

"There's one other thing," Polanski said. "The witness needs to be moved out of the area before he'll give us a statement."

"The boss mentioned that," Mantegna said. "It's him and his old man, right? We got them a place in Middletown. It's just been cleared—we can get them there tomorrow."

"Thank you," Polanski said. "That was fast."

"You're in the big leagues now, Detective. We don't mess around."

86

Carter had been thinking about Rhodes's proposal all shift. He was ready to go for it, but he knew that he would need backup. The kid was as green as they came, and he wasn't prepared to bust a joint he didn't know without someone he trusted having his back. And, more than that, he wanted to have it checked to make sure that it was kosher. Carter knew his weaknesses, and impatience was one of them. He wanted to hurry Rhodes along so that he could get him to a place where he could trust him with what life could really be like on the street, and going through with an idea that he had brought up himself was the best way he could think of. But, saying that, he didn't want his enthusiasm to colour his judgment. Shepard had a litany of his own faults, but impatience was not one of them. Carter wanted Shepard to sign off on it before he committed.

They were outside the Happy Wok on Pitkin. Carter said he would go in and get coffees for them both. He got out of the car and went inside. The restaurant was owned by Acosta's cousin. Carter went up to the counter, ordered a box of noodles, said that he was a friend of Carlos and that he needed to make a phone call. The owner grunted and pointed to a phone on the end of the counter. Carter nodded his thanks, picked up the receiver and called Shepard.

"It's me," Carter said. "You wanna make a score?"

"You have to ask? What is it?"

"It's the rookie. He's put an opportunity our way."

"The *rookie?*"

"I know. Says he wants to play in the majors."

"And you trust him?"

"I checked him out the day after he started. Everything he said, I went over it. He said he worked the subway and he did. I spoke to an instructor I know at the academy. He came back clean."

"You think it's beyond Internal Affairs to put someone in the car with you?"

"No," he said. "I don't. I know they could do that. But this guy? No fucking way. He'd have to be de Niro and Brando all rolled into one, and, trust me, he ain't. I'm not getting bad vibes off him."

"What do you need?"

"He says there's a card game at the subway yard in Gravesend. There's a garage off Stillwell, next to the yard. End of West Thirteenth. The owner's related to one of the union guys from the subway. I'm not doing it without backup. If we think it's worth a look, we can kick the door down and roll them."

"How much are we talking about?"

"He thinks a few thousand."

"You think it's worth the aggravation?"

Carter had considered that. In the old days, when he and Shep had gotten their start, a few thousand would have been a big payday. They had graduated since then, and, normally, the idea of driving all the way over there and taking the risk—however small—of busting a small-time game would have been one that they would have quickly dismissed. But there was more to this than just the take. Rhodes had surprised Carter with the proposal. He had expected to have to bring the rookie along slowly, gradually exposing him to the full range of opportunities that he would be able to take advantage of; going in and busting up a card game was a sudden escalation, and, better, it was one that Rhodes had suggested himself. It would accelerate the process. Carter didn't like having to constrain what he could and couldn't say and do when he was in the car. He wanted a partner who would be just like Shepard. Maybe the kid could be that for him.

"It's not gonna be a big score," Carter said into the phone. "But it's a chance to blood the kid. I don't want to turn him down."

Shepard laughed. "What is it? You think he's gonna take my place? You're gonna make me jealous."

"You're the one who retired."

"You got me. What time does it start?"

"Kid didn't say. But it's eight fifteen now. Gonna be around this time if it's happening."

Carter heard Shepard's long exhalation. He imagined him on his couch, a beer at hand and quite happy to stay where he was all night.

"Come on, Shep. I can't do it with him on my own. I need you."

Another sigh. "Fuck it," Shep said at last. "On my way. I'll see you there."

87

P olanski sat down at his new desk and reviewed the progress that had been made. It was half past eight in the evening and things had moved with a speed that was both unfamiliar and exhilarating. All the frustration and impediments that Polanski had suffered through before taking the case to the special prosecutor had vanished. Assistant District Attorney Mantegna had quickly made the decision that it would be wise to put a tap on Landon Shepard's phone, and, within an hour of their afternoon meeting coming to a close, he had reached out to colleagues in the Bureau of Crime Investigation who supervised electronic surveillance in the Five Counties. The senior investigator from the BCI who was assigned the case had gone to work with similar alacrity, working on an affidavit with the district attorney's office and the captain of his troop. Everything was fast-tracked: it was decided that there was no need to pass the application to Division Headquarters for review, so the DA had submitted the application to a judge, who had quickly granted the court order. Mantegna was now liaising with Shepard's service provider, Sprint, to execute the order and install the tap on his phone. He had come across to Polanski's desk and told him that the work would be done by ten at the latest.

Walker, Moore and Walsh had gone out to begin surveillance. They had taken three cars and were en route to Port Washington. Walker had called to report that they had just crossed the East River on the Throgs Neck Bridge and that they were around forty minutes away from the house given the weather conditions and the state of the roads.

Polanski looked down at the pile of papers on his desk and decided that he could take a moment.

He picked up the phone on his desk and dialled the number for his mother-in-law's house.

"Hello?" It was Laura. "Aleks?"

"Yes," he said. "It's me."

"Thank God," his wife said. "I've been worried sick. What's going on? Are you okay?"

"Everything is fine," he said, gazing out of the window and onto the stupendous Manhattan vista beyond. "You sound worried."

"You think? After what happened this morning?"

"I know," he said. "You don't need to worry. I know it's easy for me to say that, but it's true. You can relax. Everything is under control."

"All right," Laura said after a moment's pause.

"Are you okay? You and the kids?"

"We're good. Mother was surprised to see us, but she's made such a fuss of the kids they haven't had a moment to worry."

"Good," he said.

"You haven't said what's going on. You gotta tell me what's happening."

"I can't. You'll have to trust me, baby. I'm going to be

staying out here for a day or two. There's been a big development in the case I was working. I think it's coming to an end. I just gotta make it happen."

"You in Brooklyn?"

"No. I'm sorry. I can't say anything else."

"How long is this going to take? How long do we have to stay here?"

Polanski looked out at the vista, east across the river toward Brooklyn, and imagined Shepard and Carter and the net that neither of them would be able to see, the net that was slowly closing around them.

"It won't be long," he told her. "Two days. Three at the outside. We're nearly there."

88

Carter could see the subway yard from the Belt Parkway. It was vast, an expanse of open space that contained dozens of lines of track and hundreds of subway trains and cars. The train cars, many crested with snow, stretched away like long silver fingers.

Rhodes turned off at Exit 6N and looped around to Stillwell Avenue and the industrial zone that lay between it and the subway yard. They drove on for another fifty yards until they reached the end of West Thirteenth Street. There was a scrapyard ahead of them, a company that serviced school buses to the left, and a tall mesh fence that demarked the yard to the right.

Carter told Rhodes to kill the lights and roll up to the side of the road ahead of Shepard's Honda. The parking spaces were all taken by yellow school buses, so Shepard had parked in front of them.

Carter did up his jacket, got out of the squad car and walked back to the Honda. Rhodes came, too. Carter got into the front and Rhodes, at Carter's insistence, got into the back.

"All right?" Carter asked.

Shepard was smoking a cigar, tapping the ash out of a narrow gap in the window. "All good."

"How long have you been here?"

"Ten minutes."

Carter turned to look at Rhodes. "Where's the game?"

Rhodes reached across and pointed between the front seats. "Over there."

Carter followed his gesture. There was a building between the garage and the scrapyard. The door was next to a dumpster and a pile of discarded tyres. There was a closed up-and-over roller door that would have been big enough to get a bus inside, and the door was next to that.

"Through there?" Carter said.

"Yeah. You go through and cross the garage. There's a big office at the back. They clear the shit out of the way and set the table up in there. You got privacy. No one knows about it."

"Apart from us," Carter said. "How many players?"

"Ten? Never saw more than that."

Carter looked over to make sure Shepard was paying attention. "So this is how we do it. We go in, say we've had a complaint that there's an illegal game going on and that they're gonna need to shut it down. We say we should probably make arrests, but that maybe we won't need to do that if we get treated right. The usual. You want to add anything, Shep?"

"Nah," he said. "I'm good. It'll be easy. You go in first and flash your badge. I'll back you up."

"Rookie?"

The kid looked nervous. That wasn't surprising. This was a step up from liberating money and drugs from a small-time dealer or accepting free refreshments from business owners. There would be witnesses tonight, and they would be outnumbered. Carter knew that it wouldn't matter. They had their badges and uniforms and guns. No one would be stupid enough to go against them.

"Hey," Carter said. "Rhodes? We good?"

"I'm good, Bobby," he said. "Let's do it."

Carter led the way with Rhodes and Shepard behind him. The garage was a great spot for a game of cards when you didn't want to be disturbed. It was at the end of the street, the entrance almost hidden behind the buses that had been lined up outside it. There was no reason for anyone to come down this way after dark, and especially not on a night like this. He slipped into the gap between two buses and walked on, unfastening the restraining strap on his holster and resting his hand on the butt of the pistol. He didn't think that he would need to take the Glock out—leaving his hand there to draw attention to it was usually more than enough —but he wasn't going to take chances. He glanced back at Shepard and Rhodes. His ex-partner had a hungry glint in his eye, the same expression that Carter had seen on dozens of previous occasions. The rookie was nervous, falling back a little so that they were in single file: Carter, Shepard, then Rhodes.

"You all right, rook?" he hissed.

Rhodes nodded. Carter let it ride.

The door was closed, but, as he put his hand on the handle and pressed down, he felt the mechanism work and knew that it was unlocked. He pushed gently, opening the door slowly and quietly. It was dark inside. He paused so that his eyes could adjust to the gloom. A little light from outside leaked through the door, enough for him to see that the garage offered a wide space, with two darker slots on the ground that he took to be service pits, and large benches and lockers on the periphery. He could hear the sound of music and followed it across the room to another door, slightly ajar, with light seeping around the edges.

He stepped into the darkness.

89

Polanski returned from the printer with a sheet of paper that recorded all of the calls that were made and received on Shepard's cellphone. The sheet contained a version of the official billing records maintained by Sprint about call activity. It included the date and time of each call; the telephone number dialled or the number from which the subscriber was called; whether the call was completed; and the length of the call. Each entry also identified the local cellular base stations that serviced the call. The records didn't record the content of the call, but they had put in a request for that data, too, and they had been told that it would start to be delivered tomorrow.

He sat down at his desk and took out a pen.

Landon Shepard had received fifteen calls on his cellphone today. Most would be mundane—girlfriend, wife, family, whatever—and he would be able to disregard them quickly once the team started to investigate them properly. One line of the record stood out. All of the other incoming calls were identifiable as originating from other cellphones.

Only one of them looked as if it had originated from a landline.

718-566-25412.

Polanski tapped on the keyboard and woke up the PC that he had been assigned. He opened a browser window and navigated to Google. He entered the number and hit return. The search result was almost instantaneous: the number was registered to Happy Wok restaurant on Pitkin Avenue.

That was squarely within the boundary of the Seven Five. Polanski would be able to get the sector map from IAB and find out from the precinct house which officers were assigned to that sector tonight.

He was confident that he could guess.

Bobby Carter.

He circled the number and scribbled a reminder on a Post-it note to check the content of the call when it came in.

He stood, stretching his aching arms and shoulders, and was about to go to the kitchen to refill his coffee when his phone vibrated on the desk. He picked it up and put it to his ear.

"Polanski."

"It's Walsh."

"Go on."

"I'm outside the target's place."

They had decided to be careful with their communications until they knew that there was no interference. They had agreed not to refer to Shephard by name.

"And?"

"There's no one home. All the lights are off, and his car's gone. There are fresh tracks coming down from his drive. Looks like we just missed him."

Polanski looked down at the sheet of calls again, dragging his finger down the list until he reached the entry that he had circled in red.

"I've got his phone records," he said. "He had an inbound call at a quarter past eight."

"We know who from?"

"A restaurant on Pitkin Avenue."

"Bit far away for takeout," Walsh joked.

Polanski looked at his watch. "It's five after nine now. What time did you get there?"

"Twenty minutes ago."

"So he gets this call at eight fifteen and goes out before you got there at eight forty-five?"

"Looks like it," she said.

Polanski felt like he was on the verge of a breakthrough.

"We'll set up here," Walsh said. "He'll be back and then we'll stay on him."

"Keep me posted," Polanski said.

He ended the call.

90

C arter made his way across the darkened garage, aiming for the line of light that was leaking around the edge of the door. The music was clearer now: Eminem's new track playing loud.

Carter could feel Shepard and Rhodes behind him. He reached the door and pushed it open.

He paused, his mouth falling open in confusion.

The room was empty.

"What the fuck?"

Shepard pushed by him and went inside. There was nothing inside: no chairs, no table, no people. There was no one here and there was certainly no card game. The only thing in the room was a boom box plugged into a wall socket.

Dark blue plastic sheets had been spread out across the floor and tacked to the walls.

"Inside."

Carter turned around and looked into the barrel of a pistol. Rhodes held it out in an easy, comfortable, two-handed grip.

"What the fuck?"

"Inside, Bobby. Next to Shepard. Now."

"What the fuck is this?" Shepard said.

"Inside, Bobby. Last time I'll ask."

Carter backed away from the pistol, taking three steps until he was next to Shepard. It looked like a Taurus, not the Glock that the kid had chosen for his service weapon.

"Put that fucking thing down," Shepard said, his voice frayed with anger.

"Come on, rookie," Carter said, trying to maintain a measure of calm. "What are you doing? What is this?"

"He's lost his mind is what this is," Shepard said.

Rhodes levelled the Taurus at them both. "I have a message from Carlos Acosta for you both. He's sorry, but there's nothing else that can be done. The net is closing in and he can't risk you being prosecuted. He doesn't think you'd be able to resist talking if IAB offers you a deal."

"What?"

"The bureau's all over you."

"No," Shepard protested. "We fixed that. You mean González? We took care of it."

"No, you didn't. You just made them more determined. The special prosecutor's involved now. Guy named Polanski has a hard-on for you. Word is, he's not gonna stop."

"Bullshit."

"And you wanna know the worst thing? How unprofessional you two are. There was a kid outside the restroom after you killed González. A *kid*. And he saw you, Shepard. Says he can ID you. They're going to round you both up. Acosta says it'll be soon. A few days. And he can't have that. He can't trust you to keep your mouths shut."

"We wouldn't rat him out," Shepard protested. "You tell him that. We'd never rat on him."

Carter looked at Rhodes and realised that this had already gone too far. The youthful inexperience that he had laughed at was all gone. The rookie suddenly looked much older. His face was straight, without fear or trepidation or even the slightest scintilla of doubt. He held the pistol in steady hands, his weight balanced evenly, with the two of them far enough ahead of him that they wouldn't be able to reach him before he could fire.

"Shepard," Rhodes said, "get on your knees."

"Please," Shepard said. "I've got a family. You don't need to do this. Carlos knows he can trust me. I'd never rat him out."

"On your knees."

Shepard knelt. He was close enough that Carter could hear the creak in his knees, and he remembered—for a moment—the jokes that he had made about how he was old and getting arthritis.

Rhodes switched the Taurus to aim at him and pulled the trigger.

Shepard jack-knifed backwards, his arms spread wide. His blood and flesh splattered onto the sheet.

Carter felt his bowels loosening.

The acrid smell of gun smoke quickly filled the room.

Rhodes turned the pistol on him.

"Knees, Bobby."

"No," Carter protested. "Please, kid. Think about what you're doing. It doesn't have to go down like this. Let me speak to—"

He saw the flash from the muzzle, heard the crack of the discharge and saw the jerk of the recoil.

91

The locker room was busy with men getting changed after their shifts. Rhodes undressed, wrapped a towel around his waist and went through to the row of showers. He put the towel on a hook, cranked the faucet and stood under the hot water, letting it work away the chill that had seemingly seeped into his muscles during his shift. He closed his eyes and allowed himself to think about where he had been and what he had done.

Before he was real police, Rhodes had been a transit officer for five months. He hadn't expected much of his job, but it had only taken him a week to decide that it wasn't for him. His assignment was on the midnight shift. He got on the N Train at Coney Island and rode to Manhattan and back again. Each officer was issued a radio but, since most of the line was below ground, they were pretty much useless. There had been plenty of occasions when Rhodes would have called for backup, but it was a waste of time. He dealt with passengers who were drunk or high, collared muggers who rolled vulnerable passengers for their valuables. He'd confronted dealers pushing coke and crack as they passed through the cars; groups of kids playing music out of their phones as loud as they could and threatening the other passengers who told them to stop; couples who had sex on the benches; men who exposed themselves to women; women so drunk that they were sprawled out and oblivious to the perverts who felt them up. The worst, by far, were the jumpers who ended themselves by leaping out in front of the trains that rushed through the stations. Rhodes had never understood why someone would decide that was a good way to put an end to things, and that was a conclusion that came to be reinforced when he attended to a man who had jumped beneath a train only to survive the impact. His legs, though, had not been so fortunate; they had been severed at the knees and were eventually found in the tunnel twenty feet away. The man died on the gurney as they tried to get him out of the station to the ambulance on street level. Others died more quickly, their bodies torn and mangled, leaving behind blood and guts that had to be cleaned away.

He had started drinking in an attempt to erase the grim certainty that his life was headed along the same dismal line to irrelevance that had tormented his father before he had vanished one night, leaving his mother to raise him and his brother on her own. Booze had led to a resumption of a high school weed habit and then, quickly thereafter, cocaine. It was everywhere. He could try to ignore it, but what was the point? Rather than bust the dealers who pushed their merchandise on the trains, he started to accept payment from them in exchange for letting them get on with their business. It was money at first—twenty bucks here, fifty bucks there—but then he took payment in kind. The contents of small folds of newspaper, little triangles that he opened with reverent hands, were all that he needed to banish the tedium of his working hours and the depression of a lonely existence in his one-bedroom studio apartment in Queens. After coke came K2, synthetic dope that laid him out for hours at a time. It erased hours and, when he didn't have to report for work, whole weekends. In his increasingly rare moments of clarity, he knew that he was pathetic and that, if left unchecked, he was headed for an early grave. But he didn't care.

Rhodes worked up a debt that he had no hope of paying, and, after he had been beaten up by his dealer and a couple of his goons, he had started to think that the only thing for him to do was to quit and move away. That was when Acosta came into his life. His dealer had sold his debt to him. It turned out that Acosta had put the word out that he was looking for someone to fill a very particular role, and that Rhodes was just what he had in mind.

Five thousand dollars was all it had taken for him to buy him. Five grand for a badge. Rhodes had still entertained thoughts of running, especially when he realised who it was who now owned the debt he owed, but things had spun off in a direction that he could never have anticipated.

Acosta had arranged for him to be picked up after his shift one night. The car took him to the strip club on Atlantic and Grand where Acosta did most of his business. He had been welcomed with a drink and a gram of cocaine, and Acosta had made him an offer: he wanted a tame cop on his books, someone he could trust entirely, and he wondered whether Rhodes could be that man. The terms were generous: the debt would be extinguished and, on top of that, he would pay him ten grand a month. All he had to do was accept the place at the police academy that Acosta would arrange for him, and, when he graduated, accept the offer of an assignment in the Seven Five, where he would be Acosta's eyes and ears inside the precinct house. The ten grand was in addition to his salary as a rookie cop, such as it was, but there would be further remuneration related to the information and favours that he was able to relay to Acosta.

There was one stipulation: he had to get clean. No more drugs. He had agreed. He had gone cold turkey, getting a friend to lock him in the back of his van for two days until he had sweated out the drugs and the temptation, focussing on the prospect of a way out of his shitty job and a means of obtaining the money that he would only have been able to dream about before.

He turned off the faucet, grabbed his towel and wrapped it around his waist.

He took his watch out of his shoe, where he had left it. Midnight. He had an appointment to keep.

PART VI

FRIDAY

92

Rhodes made his way out of the precinct and got into his Ford Fusion. The car was parked next to Bobby Carter's big truck. Rhodes entertained the thought that Carter would never drive the truck again, but the thought did not detain him for very long. What had happened to Carter was of his own doing. Acosta was a fair man. If you did well, you were rewarded. If you were negligent, then you had to accept the consequences.

Carter and Shepard had been unforgivably sloppy.

He was about to start the engine when Sergeant Ramirez came out of the doors and raised a hand for him to stop.

Rhodes rolled down the window.

"Hey," he said.

"I just heard," the sergeant said. "He left you holding your dick again. What did he say?"

"His wife. She's in labour."

"Again?"

"For real. He said he didn't have time to come back and get the truck"—Rhodes nodded to the big Ford to his left

—"so he was going to get a cab to take him straight to the hospital."

Ramirez shook his head and smiled. "All right. It'll calm down when the baby's here. You have a good night—I'll see you tomorrow."

Rhodes raised his hand in farewell, started the engine and backed out into the street.

———

Prospect Park was the largest open space in the borough, and, at half past midnight on a night with the weather as bad as this, it was almost deserted. Rhodes drove south until he reached the zoo and then pulled over to the side of the road and slid up behind the Audi that was waiting there.

He crossed the distance between the two cars, opened the nearside rear door of the Audi and slid inside.

Carlos Acosta was sitting on the other side of the car. He smelled of patchouli oil, a scent that reminded Rhodes of insect repellent. He was wearing a gaudy Rolex Daytona with a cheetah print dial. It was ostentatious, in bad taste and very expensive.

"How'd it go? You all good?"

"All good," Rhodes said. "No problems."

"Tell me."

"They bought it. I said there was a card game and I wanted to hit it. Carter said yes. Said he wanted to be the one to take my cherry."

Acosta laughed—a braying, ugly sound. "And?"

"He called Shepard for backup. They went in. Didn't come out."

"You did good," he said.

Acosta reached forward and tapped the driver on the

shoulder. The man reached into the glovebox and handed back a thick wad of bills.

Rhodes took the money. He had been promised a twenty-thousand-dollar bonus: ten grand for Carter and ten for Shepard. The wad was thick and heavy, and he had no reason to count it. Acosta had never stiffed him before, and to suggest that he thought it was even a possibility would have been a dumb move.

"You tell 'em the reason it was going down like that?"

"I said you were disappointed. Said they'd been sloppy and you couldn't trust them no more."

Acosta shrugged. "And that's the truth. I don't take no pleasure in it. It's just business."

Rhodes knew that was a lie. Carlos Acosta was a killer, and every chance he had to kill was a reminder to himself and to everyone else of what he was capable of doing. It was a reminder of the things that he had done to haul himself out of the gutter, and the lengths that he would go to, to keep from going back there.

Rhodes and Acosta had that in common. Rhodes knew that Acosta had seen his own story in him.

Scrappiness. Determination. Ruthlessness when that was needed.

And Rhodes knew, too, that Acosta took pride in a job well done. He had anticipated the consternation and confusion that would infect the Seven Five now that one of their serving officers and another man who had only recently retired had just disappeared off the face of the earth. They would know, of course, that the two had been murdered. Internal Affairs would suspect that Acosta was behind it. But they would never find the bodies. And no one would be able to make Acosta for the crime. He was above it all, omnipotent, able to erase people and problems with the impunity of a god. That would frighten them, and fear was good for business.

"What about the clean-up?" Rhodes asked.

"Don't worry about it. They're probably in the furnace now."

"What happened to the kid?"

Acosta's mood shifted.

"That's the other thing I want to talk to you about," he said grimly. "We got another problem. You know I sent Savio and the others to keep an eye on Polanski?"

"Sure. You said."

"The English guy, Smith, he went to see him on Wednesday. One of Savio's guys was in the coffee shop where they spoke. He said the kid could ID one of the guys who took out José. That's why they had to go. I told them I wanted the kid and the English dude dead. I ain't taking no risks on this one. They gotta go. So Savio told Alejandro to follow Smith while he took Diego and Matías to go and take care of the kid. They get to the house. Savio goes inside and he has boiling water thrown onto his face. Matías goes in through a back door and gets shot in the shoulder."

"Who did it? The father?"

"He's on one fucking leg," Acosta said, waving his hand disdainfully. "No, it ain't him. They said it was Smith."

"What about Alejandro?"

"We didn't hear nothing from him. All day Wednesday —nada. And then, yesterday morning, we hear that a body's been found in a dumpster in the cemetery up near Cypress Hills station. Police are saying that it's Alejandro. Choked to death."

Rhodes stayed silent. He didn't want to speak until Acosta had finished.

"It's obvious, man. Smith kills Alejandro, figures out

what's going down and books to the kid's house before Savio gets there. He's waiting for them. Takes them out when they get there. And that boiling water he used? He put sugar in it, too. You know what sugar does in hot water? Turns it into motherfucking napalm, man. That's my baby brother. He blinded him."

Rhodes was disquieted. This should have been simple, and now it wasn't. "And the kid?"

"He ain't there no more. His old man, too. They gone." He clicked his fingers. "Whoosh. They in the wind. Smith must've moved them."

"But all the kid can do is say that he saw Shepard or Carter or both of them. With them dead—"

"I know that," Acosta interrupted acidly. "He can't do much. But I don't do loose ends. He needs to go, too. Him and his old man."

"And Smith?"

Acosta smirked, the gold cap on his teeth glittering. "I *especially* want him gone. You get me him and I'm gonna make it worth your while. Fifty."

Rhodes let that sink in. "All right," he said. "What about Polanski?"

"Taken the case to the special prosecutor. But there's no case without Carter and Shepard. Where does he look next? You?"

"I'm clean."

"I know you are. So if he's sensible, he sees he's struck out, finds something else to occupy himself, moves on."

"And if he isn't?"

Acosta grinned again. "You *know*."

Rhodes did know. Carlos had already ordered the murder of a cop and an ex-cop tonight. A cheese-eater from the Rat Squad would be no different.

"You need anything else now? Else I better get back. I gotta be sharp tomorrow. They're gonna start asking questions when they can't get hold of Carter. His truck's still parked up outside the precinct."

"Nah," Acosta said. "It's all good."

He held up his fist and Rhodes bumped it.

"Find Smith and the kid," Acosta said. "Bring them to me."

Rhodes opened the door and stepped back outside into the cold.

93

S even in the morning.

Port Washington was on the peninsula along Nassau County's North Shore. It was a beautiful waterfront town just seventeen miles from New York City. It was redolent with money, with locals drawn in by the views of Manhasset Bay, the Manhattan skyline and the Long Island Sound. It was also within easy commuting distance of the city. Polanski had driven along Main Street as he had arrived at six that morning and found antique shops, spas, boutiques, galleries and book stores.

Polanski looked at Landon Shepard's house and wondered how a recently retired NYPD patrol officer could afford a property like that in a place like this. It was a large Dutch colonial on Summit Road, in the heart of prosperous Beacon Hill. Polanski had called up the details of the purchase and found that it had been bought by the present owner a year ago and had been listed for a shade under one and a half million dollars.

Looking at the house made Polanski angry. That Shepard should have a place like this was a slap in the face.

It said that he didn't care, that he had no fear of being convicted for the crimes he must have committed to find the money for the purchase; that he had nothing but contempt for the ability of Internal Affairs to bring him in.

Polanski's mood wasn't helped by the fact that he was tired. He had been up all night. He had been sustained by adrenaline and the prospect that they were close to taking a decisive step to close down an investigation that had obsessed him for so long, but the thrill of the chase had dissipated as hour after hour went by and there was still no sign of Shepard. Two in the morning became three and the house was still empty. Three became four and they all knew that they had a major problem. Mantegna had stayed late to offer support and had suggested that he prepare the paperwork for a search warrant. He had drawn up the affidavits and made the application on an emergency basis overnight. Polanski had the warrant in his hand as he opened the door and stepped out of the car.

Walker, Moore and two uniformed cops from the City of Beacon police followed him along the path to the front door of the house. The curtains were drawn across the windows, but there was no light showing around the edges. There was a pane of glass to the side of the door and that, too, was dark.

Polanski knocked on the door. There was no reply.

"Police," he called. "Open the door."

No reply.

He knocked again. Still nothing.

He turned to one of the uniforms. "Do it."

The officer had a compact ramming device. It was a brute-force tool that was engineered for fast and accurate forced entry. The officer grabbed the two non-slip grips, drew the twenty-pound tool back and then crashed the convex head into the door at the spot where the lock would fit into the striking plate. The lock shattered, the door flew back and they hurried inside with their weapons drawn.

Moore and the two uniforms searched downstairs, leaving Polanski and Walker to check the rest of the house. They found three bedrooms: two were neat and tidy and obviously unused for some time; the third, with an en suite bathroom, looked to be the one that Shepard used. The bed was unmade, an ashtray was overflowing with ash, there was a half-empty bottle of vodka on the bedside table and there were clothes strewn across the floor.

They would take their time to search the property, but, for now, one thing was clear: Landon Shepard was not here.

94

Manny stared at the frozen landscape outside the window of the apartment. It was depressing: the vast open sky, vaulted in grey; the ocean, just visible between the buildings that stood between them and the beach; and the eerie skeletons of the famous Cyclones roller coaster and the Parachute Jump. It was eight in the morning, but it might as well have been the evening for the gloom. He watched down below as a lone pedestrian stopped at a shop selling knishes, emerging with the treat and immediately glancing up as a huge gull summoned others with a hungry cry. The gulls swooped low, sending the man scurrying into cover.

Manny hadn't been down here for years. His father had brought him when he was a child, and then there had been visits with his friends when they would buy beer with fake IDs and drink it on the sand while they watched the girls going by. That seemed like a lifetime away now. He had fought for his country and lost his leg in the process, then been dumped back in Brooklyn with no wife and no friends and no support, forgotten and forlorn. The memories of those happy afternoons might as well have been a million years ago for all the relevance that they held for him today.

The Russian who owned the place had been decent enough to them, although it was clear that he was doing them a favour because of a debt he owed to Smith and not through any sense of altruism. The apartment was small, with one bed that they had to share and just a thin door separating the main room from the toilet, but it was warm and, more important than that, it was safe. Smith had explained that the Russian could be trusted and that there was no reason to think that anyone else knew where they were.

The reassurances were fine, but that didn't make their time any less boring. Freddy had turned on the TV and switched across to *Days of Our Lives* on NBC. He was just staring at the screen without paying attention to it.

"Turn that off if you're not watching it," Manny said.

Freddy hit the remote and aimlessly skipped through the channels, from *The Young and the Restless* to *The Chew* and finally sticking to *Sesame Street* on PBS.

"What's gonna happen?" Freddy asked.

"We're getting out of here," Manny said. "We just have to be patient."

"Where?"

"I don't know. Out of Brooklyn. John said that the police are gonna get us a new place."

"And then?"

"We make a fresh start."

"No," Freddy said. "That's not what I meant. They give us a new place and then I tell them what I saw?"

Manny nodded. "They'll show you some pictures," he said. "You just have to pick out the man you saw leaving the bathroom. That's it."

Freddy was quiet, mulling something over in his mind.

"What is it?" Manny asked.

"What about our stuff?"

"I guess they'll bring it for us," Manny said. He hadn't given much thought to the practicalities.

"You *guess* they will?"

"I've never had to do this before, Freddy."

"And my football?"

"What football?"

"The one that I caught from OBJ. I can't leave it there. Someone might take it."

"It's just a football," Manny said. "No one's gonna take it."

"But what if they do?"

"They won't."

"Will we be able to go back before we go?"

"If the police think it's safe…"

Freddy got up and started to pace. "We gotta go and get it."

"He told us to stay here. We wait until he calls and then we go."

"He didn't say we couldn't go home though, did he? And it wouldn't take long. We could be in and out in thirty seconds. I know where it is—it's in my bedroom, underneath my bed."

Manny looked at his son. He knew they should stay where they were safe, but he couldn't get it out of his head that he had already been responsible for so many disappointments in the boy's life. His ex-wife had plenty to do with the fact that he didn't really have a mother, but if he hadn't been such a shitty drunk, then maybe there would have been a better chance that they would have stayed together. And then, beyond that, there were the small ways in which he had failed him. Missing the game because he was drinking. Not looking out for him when the gangbanger had stolen his shoes. Not having the balls to call the police or threaten the junkies so that they abandoned the den. Failing Freddy, again and again, over and over. Relying on a stranger to do his dirty work for him.

"Come on, Dad. Catching that ball was the only thing I want to remember about what happened on Sunday. I *can't* just leave it."

Manny hesitated. All Freddy wanted was to go and get his football. They could be quick. In and out, like he said. How much harm was there in that?

"Dad?"

"Let me call him," he said.

Manny took out his phone and dialled Smith's number. It rang and rang, but Smith did not pick up before it went through to voicemail.

"It's me," he said. "Freddy wants to get the football he got at the Giants game. We're gonna go back and pick it up. We'll be quick—in and out—and then we'll head back to the apartment. I'll have my phone with me. Call if you need to."

He ended the call and shoved the phone in his pocket.

"We going?" Freddy asked.

"Yeah," Manny said. "Get your sneakers and coat. If we get the subway, we can be back in a couple hours."

Milton was up early. He took the subway to Central Avenue and walked back to Himrod Street. The parking lot was open, and, after showing the attendant his ticket, he paid the fee for the extra day and picked up his bike.

His phone rang. He put the bike onto its stand and took it out of his pocket.

"Hello."

"It's Polanski."

"Morning," Milton said.

"I'm calling about the Blancos."

"Have you made progress?"

"Yes. We've got a place ready for them. It's up in New Haven. Miles away from Brooklyn. They'll be safe there."

"Thank you."

"Will you tell them?"

"Yes," Milton said. "I'll call them after we're done. Have you found anything?"

There was a pause; Milton heard the sound of footsteps

and then, when Polanski spoke again, his voice was a little lower. "No," he said. "We've struck out."

"What do you mean?"

"We can't find either of them. We've been inside Shepard's house, but he's not been back here since around eight yesterday evening."

"And Carter?"

"I just called his wife. He didn't come home last night. He told his partner that she'd called him to say that she'd gone into labour, but she said she didn't."

"So they're missing?"

"Well, we certainly don't know where they are. I want to press on with the statement from the kid."

"I'll speak to them," Milton said. "I'll call you."

He ended the call and, as he looked at the display, he saw that he had voicemail; it must have come through while he was speaking to Polanski.

He put the phone to his ear again and listened to the message. It was Manny. Milton swallowed and then found that he was holding his breath.

"It's me. Freddy wants to get the football he got at the Giants game. We're gonna go back and pick it up. We'll be quick—in and out—and then we'll head back to the apartment. I'll have my phone with me. Call if you need to."

Milton called Manny back at once.

The phone rang through to voicemail.

"It's Smith," he said. "Do not go to the house. Turn around and go back to the apartment. It's not safe. Call when you get this."

Milton shoved the phone into his jacket pocket, straddled the bike and set off.

Manny and Freddy took the subway to Cypress Hills and then walked down Hemlock Street to their old road. Manny felt a buzz of nervousness in his gut as they turned right, and reached down to clutch his son by the hand. His anxiety must have transmitted itself to Freddy, because he had stopped talking about the Giants' big game with Green Bay at the weekend and settled into a pensive silence that was unlike him.

The street was quiet. The cars parked on either side were covered in snow, and piles of it had been dumped on the sidewalk from where the residents had cleared the steps that led up to their front doors. The street was not important enough to be treated, so the snow had been compacted down by the tyres of the cars that had struggled between Hemlock and Crescent.

Manny tightened his grip on his son's hand as they headed toward the elevated track that marked the end of the road. He was struck by a sense of sadness as he saw the consequences of Wednesday's attack: the shattered windows beneath the bars and the listless twitch of the curtains in the breeze.

"In and out," Manny said.

Freddy nodded that he understood.

Manny took his key out of his pocket, opened the gate and climbed the single step. He put the key into the lock, turned it, and went inside. Freddy followed. Manny shut the door.

Milton pushed the bike as hard as he dared. The snow and ice were treacherous, but he knew that he could not take too long. He followed Cypress Avenue through the wide-open spaces that made up the various cemeteries at Cypress Hills, accelerating all the way up to sixty as he broke onto the cleared Jackie Robinson Parkway. He was forced to stop as he hit the traffic that had backed up on either side of a fender bender at the intersection with Jamaica Avenue. A traffic cop was in the middle of the street.

Milton took out his phone and dialled 911.

"I need police at number four Danforth Street, Brooklyn," he told the operator.

"What's the emergency, sir?"

"There's someone outside. I think they've got a gun."

A gap in the traffic appeared and Milton took his chance. He opened the throttle, the back wheel sliding across the ice until the tyre found purchase and sent the bike jerking forward.

96

Rhodes hadn't gone home. He knew that the window for taking action was short and that if he was going to cash in Acosta's offer of fifty grand, then he would have to move decisively. He had driven from Prospect Park to Danforth Street and had been here, waiting in his car, ever since. It was nine in the morning now. He had been outside for eight hours.

And his patience was going to pay off.

He saw them coming down the road toward him. He couldn't believe that they would do something so stupid as to come back here, yet here they were: Manny and Freddy Blanco, walking hand in hand along his side of the street. He was inside his car and watched them in the wing mirror as they drew closer, passed by, and went to the door.

He worked quickly. He reached into the glovebox and took out the Taurus. He rested the gun on the passenger seat so that he could take out his phone and call Acosta. He would be able to detain them, but he would need another vehicle and another couple of men to get them away without making a scene on the street.

Manny Blanco took out his key and put it in the lock. His kid stood behind him, stomping his feet in an attempt to ward off the cold. They went inside.

Rhodes got out of the car, quietly shutting the door and checking up and down the street to ensure that the Blancos had come alone. They had turned off Hemlock, which meant it was most likely that they had arrived on the subway. There was certainly no sign of a car that might have brought them, nor anyone else who might have come to stand watch. As far as Rhodes could tell, they were on their own.

He followed their footsteps to the end of the road. He was at the gate when the door to the house opened. Manny stood there; he looked out at Rhodes and saw his gun as he pulled it out of his pocket and aimed it ahead.

"Back inside," Rhodes said, climbing the step and bustling through the doorway and into the house.

He pushed Manny in the chest with his left hand, hard enough to overbalance him so that he dropped down onto the floor. The kid was behind him, clutching a football to his chest.

Rhodes closed the door behind him. He held up the gun so that both father and son could see it.

"Where's the other guy?" he said. "Smith?"

Manny Blanco looked at the pistol and said quietly, "I don't know."

"Why did you come back?"

"My boy wanted his football," he said.

"Does Smith know you're here?"

Manny shook his head.

"Take a seat," Rhodes instructed, indicating the couch. "No shouting and nothing stupid. I'd rather I didn't have to use this."

"What are you gonna do?"

"Nothing," he said. "We're just going to take it easy and wait. I got a friend who'd like to talk to you, that's all. Just a friendly chat."

97

Milton turned onto Danforth Street and then halted as he spotted a black van outside the Blancos' house. He saw movement from the door and watched in horror as two men frogmarched Manny and Freddy through the gate, across the sidewalk and into the back of the van. Milton was still fifty feet away as the van pulled out. The street hadn't yet been ploughed and was slick and treacherous, but he opened the throttle and closed on the van, fighting to keep his wheels from sliding out from beneath him.

The van turned right onto Crescent Street.

Milton hit the brakes and turned, too. He gunned the throttle, the old bike racing up to forty and then fifty, fast enough to draw alongside the van. He had automatically taken note of the plate, but, now, he needed to stop the vehicle.

Milton glanced through the side window. He saw two men: the driver, nearest to him, and a passenger.

He reached into his pocket and took out the pistol he had confiscated from the dealer.

The driver saw him before he could aim, and yanked the wheel in his direction. The van veered toward him. Milton was riding one-handed and, as he tried to mirror it, the bike caught a patch of black ice. The sudden swerve, together with Milton's lack of control and the icy road, sent the back wheel sliding out. Milton dropped the gun and wrestled with the handlebars but was unable to maintain control. He went down, his shoulder crashing onto the surface and the bike pressing down against his pinned leg. The bike spun through a full rotation, its momentum eventually arrested as the front wheel bumped up against a yellow painted strut that helped suspend the elevated track above.

Milton was dazed, pain pulsing from his shoulder and hip. He pushed the bike off him and looked back for the pistol. It was twenty feet away. He hobbled back to collect it and then stood and turned to face the direction that the van had taken. He just saw it as it completed a hard left turn by Veginos Deli. It disappeared into Etna Street.

Milton had no shot.

"Fuck," he yelled. "Fuck!"

He put the gun away and hauled the bike upright. He tried to kick-start the engine, but nothing happened. He checked the machine quickly, but saw nothing wrong. He tried to start it again, with the same result. He tried the horn: nothing. The battery was faulty.

He heard sirens approaching from the direction of Atlantic Avenue.

Milton checked the battery terminal connections. There was a loose connection; it must have been jarred by the crash of the impact. He tightened the connections and stomped down on the kick-start again.

The engine growled.

He straddled the bike. He had no interest in talking to

the cops. He was carrying an unlicensed weapon that had previously belonged to a drug dealer. He glanced back as he approached the corner of Etna Street and saw the flashing blue lights racing north along Crescent.

He opened the throttle and started forward. He took the turn and kept going.

98

Milton stopped at the McDonald's on Atlantic Avenue and went inside. He ordered a coffee, took it to an empty table and dialled Polanski's number.

"Yes?"

"We've got a problem. Manny and Freddy have been taken."

"What?"

"They went back to the house."

"You said—"

"I wasn't with them." Milton spoke over him. "Listen carefully—you need the details. They were taken out of the house by two men. One of them was late twenties to early thirties, medium height. I didn't get a look at his face. I got a better look at the driver: dark-skinned, a goatee, eyes a little far apart."

"Okay," Polanski said.

"The van was a black GMC Safari, unmarked. I got the registration—do you have a pen?"

"I can use my phone. Shoot."

"It had a New York plate. H54 9KW. It was heading west on Etna Street."

"Got it. I'll get it put out on the radio."

The phone throbbed. "Hold on," he said. He looked at the display. He had another call. "I'll call later," he said, ending the first call and accepting the second.

"Hello?"

"John?"

It was Manny. "Yes," Milton said. "It's me. Where are you, Manny?"

"John—you gotta help us."

"What's happened, Manny?"

"They got us."

"Who got you?"

"We went back to the house. This guy was waiting there. He—"

Manny was interrupted, the phone evidently taken away from him. Milton pressed it to his ear, listening for anything that might prove to be helpful—any sound that might give him an idea where Manny had called him from—but there was nothing, just the background chatter of indistinct voices.

"Mr. Smith," a new voice said, "are you there?"

"I'm here."

"I'm guessing you care about them? The boy, perhaps? You feel a connection with him?"

"I care about them both," Milton replied, his fist clenched tight around the phone.

"Good. I'm glad to hear that. It's up to you whether you see them again."

Milton heard a change in the background noise of the call: it was the rhythmic thump of a bass line, a little muffled as if it was being played in a nearby room to whomever it was who was on the other end of the call.

"What do you want?" Milton asked.

"I'll call you later. We'll speak then."

The line went dead.

99

M ilton rode back to his apartment.

He closed his eyes and tried to put all the information together.

He thought about the call that he had received. He was as sure as he could be that it had been made from inside a building. Whoever had abducted the Blancos had got them into the back of a van; that meant they could transport them with impunity. There would be no reason for them to stop, take them out of the van and then hold them at some halfway house before continuing on to their ultimate destination. The location of the call was, most likely, where the Blancos were going to be held.

Milton took a large-scale map of New York that he had purchased when he arrived in the city and laid it out on the floor. He took a red Sharpie and drew a circle around Danforth Street. The Blancos had been taken at just before nine. The call had come in at 9.45. That meant that they had forty-five minutes to get to wherever it was that they were going. But Milton could amend that figure a little: it was rush hour, traffic was moving slowly because of the adverse conditions and they would have needed a few minutes at their destination to get the Blancos out of the van and secure them. Perhaps that meant they had thirty minutes of travelling time. That would serve as his working assumption.

Milton opened his laptop and navigated to Google Maps. Using Danforth Street as a centre point, he plotted a series of destinations around the points of the compass. He assessed the boundaries of the area that the van would reasonably have been able to reach within thirty minutes, marking each point with a red dot on the paper map. When he was finished, he connected the dots so that he had a rough unbroken circle: it started with the Barclays Centre to the west, included the southern shore of the East River as its northern boundary, continued out to Freeport in the east, and was penned in by Jamaica Bay to the south. The circle contained almost all of Brooklyn save a large slice to the southwest. He regarded it for a moment. That was the beginning of his search area.

He dragged the cursor back to Danforth Street and zoomed in. The van had turned onto Etna Street and headed west. The driver would have been agitated: he would have been full of adrenaline and had just forced Milton off his bike. Milton doubted that a driver as excited as he must have been would have had the presence of mind to engage in subterfuge. If his ultimate direction was north or south, he would have headed to Jamaica Avenue or Atlantic Avenue, respectively. He had turned to the west; Milton would assume that he would continue in that direction.

He took a black Sharpie and drew a second circle that included the parts of Brooklyn to the west, southwest and northwest of Danforth Street. His more focused area included Crown Heights, Bedford-Stuyvesant, Park Slope, East Flatbush and Brownsville.

It was still a lot of territory to cover.

Milton navigated to the website that recorded the movement of the tracking devices that he had bought. He entered the serial number of the device that he had attached to the Ford truck. The website was able to access up to twelve months' worth of journey reports, but Milton did not need to go back that far; he had attached the trackers on Tuesday afternoon, five days ago, so he configured the interface to show him the journeys made within that particular time frame.

The journeys reported for the truck showed nothing out of the ordinary. Carter had driven from his house in Setauket to the precinct on Sutter Avenue and then back again, leaving at around three in the afternoon and returning around midnight. There were no deviations, nothing suspicious, no diversions out to the west and into the area that Milton had highlighted.

Nothing that Milton might have considered worthy of further investigation.

One down.

One chance left.

He clicked back to the front page of the site and entered the serial number of the tracker that he had attached to the underside of the Ford Fusion that belonged to James Rhodes. Milton changed the dates to show the previous three days' data and saw, to his disappointment, that it was as mundane as that for Carter. It appeared that Rhodes lived in Rosedale, just to the east of JFK; the car was parked there each night and left for the precinct at three each afternoon.

The pattern was consistent until early this morning.

Normally, Rhodes would have driven to Rosedale from the precinct, but, this time, he did not.

It was odd. The car drove west to Prospect Park. It arrived there at 12.30 a.m. and waited there for ten minutes before turning around and heading back to Rosedale. Rhodes's commute usually took him thirty minutes; he had added an extra forty minutes to his journey home with the diversion. Milton opened another browser window and fired up Google Maps again. The car had stopped on Flatbush Avenue, next to the Brooklyn Botanic Garden. Milton placed the icon in the same spot and scouted the road to the north and south. Flatbush Avenue was wide, with two lanes in both directions and, at least when Google had photographed it, lines of parked traffic on both sides of the road. Rhodes had stopped here for ten minutes at twenty to one on Saturday morning. There would have been nothing there at that time of day.

It was difficult to avoid the obvious conclusion: Rhodes had diverted to Prospect Park to meet someone. It would have been suspicious enough on any normal day—Milton might have suspected a weakness for drugs or prostitutes—but that this had taken place on the same day that Bobby Carter and Landon Shepard had gone missing, when Rhodes would have been one of the last people to see Carter before he disappeared... it set off all manner of alarm bells.

Milton nudged the timeline forward so that he could see where the car went next.

His jaw fell open.

The Fusion had gone to Danforth Street.

It had waited there for eight hours until 9.00 a.m.

And then it had headed east, back to Rosedale. It was there now.

He zoomed in on the location. The car was parked on

Laurelton Parkway, an address immediately to the west of the Belt Parkway. Milton entered the details in Google Maps and scouted the locale. The Parkway was separated by a strip of grass and a wire fence. The properties facing it were a mixture of condos, town houses and row homes. Milton checked on a realtor's site and found that the properties were very reasonably priced; he guessed that the noise from the Parkway and the possibility that the houses were beneath the flightpath for the airport had depressed their value.

There was only so much that Milton could do on his computer.

He would have to pay Rhodes a visit.

100

Mackintosh sat at her desk and stared at the screen. They had lucked out in the investigation into the murder of Alejandro del Cabral. The cameras at Cypress Hills had been serviced two days before the body was found and they were in full working order. Each platform had a camera above the exit to the gates below. She had requested all of the footage for the twenty-four hours prior to the discovery of the body and had got into the precinct at seven so that she could start scrubbing through it.

The coroner had suggested that the body had been in the dumpster for between eighteen and twenty-four hours. She started at the outside edge of that prediction and then rolled forward. Most of the time it was easy. The station was quiet during the day, and the weather had meant that it was even quieter. There were long stretches of time when there were no passengers recorded by the cameras. Trains would arrive and a handful of people would disembark; she would track them from the platform down to the exit and watch them head out onto the street and disappear.

She got to five in the afternoon and saw something to make her immediately lunge forward to stop the recording. It was a Jamaica Avenue train. The doors had opened and a man she recognised had got out.

It was John Smith.

She scrubbed back through the footage and watched again, leaning in closer to the screen.

It was him. She was quite sure of it.

She let the footage run for a moment and was rewarded by a second surprise.

Alejandro del Cabral came out of the car and followed Smith.

She hit pause. There were three ways to leave the station. The main fare control area offered one exit at Hemlock Street and Crescent Street on the southwestern end of the platforms. The other options were the staircases that went down from the tracks to both sides of the street; there were exit-only gates at the foot of each.

The main concourse was the only one with a camera, and she quickly lined up the footage and scrolled through so that the timestamp was five minutes before the time Smith and del Cabral arrived at the station. She reviewed the footage, but didn't see either man. They had left the station by way of the staircase from the platform.

She went back to the feed from the platform. She played the footage again and then again. Smith exited the train and then, five seconds later, del Cabral followed him. Smith paused just beneath the camera and, she thought, took a quick glimpse behind.

Smith had, at his own admission, been inside Euclid station when González was murdered.

And now, here he was, on the same train as a man who

would be dead in a dumpster within the hour. Leaving the station with him.

It couldn't be a coincidence.

It *couldn't*.

101

Milton rode east, taking the Belt Parkway for almost all of the way. The road had been cleared, with huge drifts on either side where the ploughs had sprayed the snow. He turned off at Exit 24B, followed Brookville Boulevard and then the bridge over the Parkway before turning onto Laurelton Parkway. The road was familiar to him from his virtual scouting, and he slowed as he reached the cluster of locations where the Ford Fusion had previously been parked. The car was exactly where it had been marked by the tracker, just outside number 13318. Milton rode on a little farther, parked the bike and came back on foot.

Milton checked the time: it was just after half past eleven.

It was impossible to say which of the properties belonged to James Rhodes. The houses had been built in rows of four, with identical doors set together in pairs, offering access to what Milton assumed were two- or three-bedroom properties. The properties were new and reasonably large and cheap for their size. Milton's assumptions about their competitive pricing were confirmed first by the steady rumble of noise from the Belt Parkway, no more than fifteen metres away, and then, as he made his way along the sidewalk, by the roar as a big 747 lumbered overhead on its final descent into JFK.

Milton made his way to the south, where Laurelton Parkway met Merrick Boulevard. There was a collection of stores there: on the other side of the road was a Dunkin' Donuts, a cocktail bar and restaurant identified as Clippers II from its red awning, and a medical centre; on the side of the road where Milton was standing was Merrick Farm, a large green-painted general store that advertised groceries together with housewares, electronics and toys.

Milton was walking toward the entrance to the store when he saw James Rhodes walking toward him.

There was no question that it was him. Milton saw the shock of blond hair, left long at the back so that it reached down to the collar of the Giants-branded coat that he was wearing to keep warm in the cold. He had an NYPD cap on his head and wore black denim jeans and a pair of walking boots that were scuffed and stained with the wetness of the slush underfoot. He was carrying a large paper bag of groceries clasped to his chest.

Milton was too experienced to betray even the slightest hint of recognition or surprise, and dropped down to tie a shoelace as Rhodes walked right past him. Milton continued and then paused at the crossing at the corner of 234th Street. He looked back and saw that Rhodes had turned left onto Laurelton Parkway. He was going home.

Milton did not want to turn around and follow him. That would be too obvious, and a cop ought to be experienced enough to notice someone changing direction and following, especially on a quiet road early in the morning.

Milton remembered the geography of the area and knew that he would be able to follow 234th Street to the north and then take 133rd so that he came onto Laurelton ahead of Rhodes. He walked quickly, turning right at a beauty supply store and then right again onto 133rd Road. He approached the rear of the row of houses that he had seen before. There was a line of garages, a series of cars parked with their ends poking out into the road, and a dug-out path that led between the houses and the garages back to Laurelton. Milton followed it, his hands thrust deep in his pockets and his head down, cutting as unobtrusive and unthreatening a figure as he could manage.

Rhodes was walking toward him again. There were trees planted alongside the sidewalk and Milton was able to hide behind the trunk of an oak as the cop turned off the road and followed a line of footprints—his own, Milton guessed —across what had been a lawn in the Google photographs to a property that was adjacent to the parking lot and loading area of Merrick Farm. He went to a door, lowered the bag of groceries to the ground, opened the door, collected the groceries, and went inside.

Milton stayed where he was, out of sight of the house, and watched.

102

Milton followed the footprints across the lawn to the front door of Rhodes's house. There was one ground-floor window to the left of the door; Milton looked in and saw the flicker of a TV. He went up to the door. There was no letter slot that he could look through, and the decorative porthole at eye level was fitted with patterned, opaque glass.

He rapped firmly on the door and then thrust his hands back into his pockets again.

He heard footsteps. A key turned in the lock and the door opened.

Rhodes stood in the doorway. "Can I help you?"

"I'm sorry to disturb you," Milton said, affecting an American accent.

"Who are you?"

"My name's Cliff. I wondered if I could talk to you for a moment."

"I'm sorry. I'm a bit—"

"Just a moment? Please—it won't take long."

Milton saw the flicker of annoyance that passed across Rhodes's face. "Okay—quickly."

"Thank you," he said. "I've been thinking about making an offer for the house over the way and I'm just trying to get a feel for the neighbourhood. Been walking around, but I figured the best thing to do would be just to ask someone who lives here."

Milton anticipated that Rhodes would try to close the conversation down as quickly as he could, but he humoured him. "It's a nice place," he said. "You got a lot of workers from the airport here. You can get there in fifteen minutes on the Parkway."

Milton readied himself, waiting for the right moment. "That was what I was worried about. Aircraft noise?"

"That's a problem," Rhodes conceded. "But you get so that it doesn't bother you so much. I hardly notice it these days. Anyway—I got to get to the kitchen."

He started to close the door. Milton took a step forward, blocking it with his right foot while simultaneously taking the pistol from out of his right pocket. He held it close to his body, hiding it from anyone who might have glanced across from the street but obvious enough so that Rhodes couldn't miss it.

"Get inside," Milton said.

Rhodes looked down at the pistol. "I'm a cop," he said, his hand still on the door, still blocking the way ahead.

"No," Milton said. "You're not."

Milton locked eyes with him. Rhodes tried to hold his stare, but he couldn't help glancing down at the pistol that Milton had levelled at him. The tip of Rhodes's tongue dabbed at dry lips and Milton saw his fists clenching and unclenching. He looked back at Milton and took a step back.

Milton came inside and, never taking his eyes off Rhodes, shut the door with his heel.

"Is anyone else here?" he asked.

"No one," Rhodes said.

"Wife? Girlfriend?"

"No. Just me."

Milton flicked the gun to indicate that Rhodes should go into the living room. He did as he was told. Milton followed, assessing quickly: the floor was covered with polished laminate and the walls were decorated with green-and-white striped wallpaper; there was a small dining table with four chairs in the corner, a leather couch and a widescreen TV on a stand was showing *Wheel of Fortune*. The room was extremely tidy; the surfaces had recently been dusted and there was no clutter or junk.

Milton stayed in the archway that connected the living room with the hall. "Close the curtains."

The curtains were the same colour and pattern as the wall. Rhodes pulled them together. "This is a really stupid move."

Milton pointed to the couch. "Sit."

Milton stepped into the room now that he was confident that he couldn't be seen from outside the house. There was a second open doorway and an open serving hatch in the wall that divided the small living room from an equally small galley kitchen. Milton took a step toward it and glanced inside. It, too, was suitably tidy: a gleaming stove, faux-marble countertops that looked clean enough to eat from; a bowl of fresh bananas and apples on the ledge of the serving hatch.

The rooms could have been found inside a show home. It was as if the house had never been lived in.

Milton turned back to Rhodes.

"This doesn't have to be unpleasant," Milton said. "But that's up to you."

"What do you want?"

"I've got some questions for you."

Rhodes looked up at him. "Who are you?"

"That doesn't matter. Where are Manny and Freddy Blanco?"

"Who?"

There were two identical cushions on the couch, one on either side of Rhodes. Milton took one of them and held it against Rhodes's knee. He pressed the muzzle of the pistol into the upholstered softness. "Try again."

Rhodes looked up at Milton; his face was impassive save the spastic tremble of a tic in his cheek. "I don't know who you're talking about."

Milton pulled the trigger. The report was muffled by the cushion, but the bullet punched through the upholstery and blasted into Rhodes's knee. He yelled out, Milton quickly covering his mouth with the cushion. He held it there until the scream had subsided to a muffled moan, and then he removed it.

"Take a moment," Milton said. "I know that's going to hurt."

The colour had drained from Rhodes's face and it looked as if he was going to vomit. "Fuck...you," he managed to say.

Milton looked down at Rhodes's knee. A neat hole had been sliced through the black denim and blood was running out.

Milton held the cushion against Rhodes's left knee and pressed the pistol into it again.

"Let me make something very clear. I think there's more to you than your uniform. In fact, if I had to go out on a limb"—Milton roughly prodded Rhode's injured knee with the Beretta, eliciting a further gasp of pain—"I'd say you're a disgrace to it. Carter and Shepard—I know they're crooked. They worked for Acosta, but I don't think that's news to you. And, suddenly, they've disappeared, and I'm guessing that isn't a surprise, either. Because I think you've been working for Acosta, too—for a long time. Am I right, Jimmy?"

Rhodes looked down, his jaw set in a hard line as he tried to stifle the urge to moan from the pain.

"You don't have to answer that," Milton said. "I don't care. But I *do* care about Manny and Freddy. I know you know who they are. I know you were outside their house this morning. And I think you know where they are, too. So I'm going to ask you again. And, before you answer, think about what's going to happen if I think you're lying to me. Think about whether you want to be in a chair the rest of your life, because I promise that's what'll happen if you lie to me again." He paused. "Where are Manny and Freddy Blanco?"

"Acosta," he muttered between clenched teeth.

"Where?"

"The club."

"Which club?"

"The HoneyPot. Atlantic and Grand. Upstairs."

"What about Shepard and Carter? Did you kill them?"

He nodded.

"When?"

"Yesterday."

"Where are they now?"

"Don't know. Landfill. Cremated. They'll never find the bodies. He's too thorough."

"What does he want?"

Rhodes laughed thinly.

Milton waited for him to speak.

"You."

"Why?"

"You were at their house. When..."

He tailed off, gritting his teeth against a pulse of pain.

"When they came before?" Milton finished for him.

Rhodes nodded. "His brother was there. Savio. You blinded him."

The information meant nothing to Milton. He would have killed the man at the door just as soon as throw the boiling sugar water at him. Savio Acosta and the man whom Milton had shot, they had brought their own fates upon themselves. Milton had no sympathy for either of them.

He had no sympathy for Rhodes, either.

He, too, was the master of his own fate.

Milton had already decided what he would do with him. He had known before he had knocked on the door.

His options were limited.

He couldn't leave him here. Even if he secured him, hog-tied and gagged him, there was too great a risk that he would be discovered before Milton had the chance to find the Blancos. And if that happened, they—and probably Milton, too—were finished.

He couldn't contact Polanski. It had been simple enough for Milton to discern the trail that led from Rhodes back to Acosta, but he had broken the law multiple times to do that: at the very least, there was the use of the illegal tracker, threatening a police officer with a gun, breaking into his house, crippling him. Milton was not restrained by law or protocol. He wasn't interested in whether his evidence would be admissible at trial. And, while Polanski might be able to legitimise all of Milton's conclusions—work back from the answers and provide a route to them that was not illegal—that would take time. Manny and Freddy did not have time. If Rhodes was arrested, then Acosta would find out, and they would have a short future with an unpleasant end.

Milton was not going to let that happen.

He was not constrained by conscience. He was driven by expediency. His morals were black and white. Rhodes had brought himself into Milton's world. He couldn't complain about what that would mean.

He raised the pillow, pressed it against Rhodes's head, and shot him.

103

Milton worked quickly. He located the two casings; they were on the floor, and both of them would be easy enough to find. The cushion was still over Rhodes's face. Milton removed it. The bullet had entered his head just above his right eye. The blowback had been absorbed by the cushion, but, now that it was out of the way, a trickle of ichorous blood rolled down and collected against his brow. He frisked him, the clothes still warm from the dissipating body heat, and removed a wallet from the left jeans pocket and a set of house keys from the right. He opened the wallet and took out three credit cards in the name of James R. Rhodes.

He went through into the kitchen and took a dry dishcloth that had been left hanging over the tap. He used it to open the cupboards, working swiftly and methodically, found nothing of interest and moved back to the living room. He found some correspondence in a neat pile, all of the envelopes addressed to James Rhodes. He opened the cupboards and took down the books on the bookshelves, flipping through them to ensure that they had not been hollowed out. They were all just as they should be.

He went into the hallway, removed his boots, and climbed the stairs to the second floor. There were three bedrooms and a small family bathroom. He searched the bedrooms first. Two were empty, with no furniture or belongings. He disregarded them and went into the room that Rhodes had evidently been using. Once more, the overwhelming impression was one of transience, of a use that was only ever intended to be temporary. Still covering his fingers to ensure that he didn't leave any prints, Milton searched. He found a well-thumbed copy of *Guns and Ammo*, and a collection of loose change. He opened the wardrobe and found two NYPD uniforms still wrapped in the protective sheath from the dry-cleaner's.

There was just the bathroom left to search. There was a bottle of Xanax in the wall-mounted cabinet, the prescription denoting them as for the personal use of Rhodes, James. Milton was about to call it quits when he saw something that made him pause: one of the panels on the side of the bath was not quite flush with the frame. He knelt down and examined it. It was recessed a millimetre or two, providing an exposed surface that, when Milton leaned in close to examine it, betrayed an almost imperceptible scuff. Milton rested his covered fingertips against the corner of the panel and pushed. The panel moved, there was the click of a latch being released, and then it swung back on a hinge mounted near the floor. Milton lowered it gently to the tiles and looked into the storage space that had been revealed in the space around and beneath the tub.

He took out a case with a resin plastic body. He flipped both clasps and opened it, revealing a moulded foam interior that held a Heckler & Koch submachine gun. It was the

UMP9, the 9x19mm variant of the UMP. It had the folding buttstock, the aperture rear sight and the front ring with the small vertical post, and a Picatinny rail on top of the receiver. The UMP9 had only been available for a few months, and this one looked brand new. Milton reached beneath the tub again and brought out ten boxes of ammunition, each box marked as holding fifty cartridges.

Milton put the ammo and the submachine gun to the side and reached into the hiding space again. He pulled out a cellphone and a bunch of keys in a clear plastic bag and then a second clear plastic bag that was heavy with banknotes. The final bag contained the key constituents of a bug-out kit: a small GPS reader, eight quarters, two fake passports in the name of Thomas Jessop and Dan Best, a wallet that contained a series of credit cards in the name of Thomas Jessop, and supplementary cards—a library card, health insurance cards—all of which would help Rhodes to establish a new identity.

Milton put everything back beneath the tub except for the cash, the case with the UMP9 and four boxes of the ammunition. There was a sports bag in the cupboard beneath the stairs. He unzipped it and loaded up with the things that he was taking.

He was nearly done.

He took a mop and bucket that he found in the hall cupboard, filled the bucket with water and mopped down the laminate floor in the kitchen, living room and hall.

He stood on the mat just inside the door to put on his boots, stooped to pick up the sports bag, and went outside, closing the door behind him with his sleeve over his fingers. He crossed the lawn to the street and walked over to the Fusion. He went to the back, checked that the street was clear in both directions, knelt down and reached up behind the fender. He tugged on the tracker, removed it and stood once more. He dropped the device into his pocket and walked to his bike. He put his arms through the handles of the sports bag so that he could carry it on his back, straddled the seat and started the engine.

He glanced back at the house then turned to the road. It was midday. He had things to do.

104

Milton stopped at home to deposit the bag with the things that he had taken from Rhodes's house, but didn't stay. He rode north to Prospect Heights, parked his bike on Classon Avenue and walked back to Atlantic. It was one of the main east–west routes through Brooklyn, a four-lane road separated by a median that was equipped with tall street lamps and cluttered with advertisements for new tyres and mufflers from the auto shop on the other side of the road. This section of the avenue led through a run-down area of town that recalled the pictures that Milton had seen of Brooklyn in the eighties. It had escaped the tide of gentrification that was slowly washing down from Manhattan, and its building stock was in poor condition. There were wide-open spaces where buildings had been pulled down without being replaced, and other buildings that were derelict to the point that demolition would have been doing them a favour.

Milton walked the block. He saw the big ugly box that accommodated AutoZone and, opposite, a confused collection of buildings that comprised the competing Mario's

Auto Repair. Milton kept going, walking by a business that supplied restaurants and a CrossFit studio. An old gas station had been abandoned partway through refurbishment, with the structure clad in heavy-duty sheeting, although the temporary fencing had been moved aside so that a pop-up car-washing business could use the space. The walls were marked with graffitied murals and gang tags, and trash blew along the snow-covered sidewalk.

Milton reached the address that he wanted. The HoneyPot Lounge was on the first floor of a three-storey building on the corner of Atlantic and Grand. Falafel Hut was to the left and a store selling wine and spirits was to the right. Milton stopped so that he could pretend to tie his laces. It was one in the afternoon, and the club was open. The windows were glazed with tinted glass, and it limited his view inside so that all he could see were the dim outlines of furniture and streaks of neon that pulsed in time with the music. The club was accessed through a barred door to the right of the windows. The snow had been cleared away, dumped into a big drift that had gathered at the side of the road.

Milton continued. The Best Burger Palace was the last business on the block, and Milton turned as he went by it and walked down Grand. There were two young men on the corner, both wearing hooded tops and dirty jeans, and they eyed him with baleful intent as he navigated around them and continued to the south. The area was even more dilapidated away from the main drag. The building on the other side was wreathed in scaffold and mesh, but it didn't look as if any work had been carried out there for weeks. There was a big oak tree that had ruptured the paving slabs, a low iron fence around the tree against which two BMXs were locked, and an old Snapple-branded drinks cabinet that had been abandoned half on the sidewalk and half in the gutter. The snow was heavier here, and the road had not been ploughed.

Milton dawdled outside 501 Grand. It was a one-storey addition that had been constructed behind the Burger Palace. An awning extended out to cover the stoop and the steps that led down to the sidewalk. The door was protected by a heavy iron cage. There was an open doorway to the right that offered access to a workshop that was jammed full of catering equipment; the Snapple cabinet had been pushed out of the workshop and dumped in the road. There had been a second opening to the right of the workshop, but it had been bricked over save for a line of windows at the top.

Milton looked back at the young men he had passed; they were talking to a third man, whom they sent down the street to 501. Milton crossed the road and paused behind the trailer of an eighteen-wheeler that had been parked flush with the scaffold. The man climbed the steps, pressed a buzzer and waited beneath the awning. A slot was opened and the man reached through the bars to collect something that was proffered to him. He turned and walked away, stomping through the snow back up Grand to Atlantic. The slot shut again. The purpose of the premises was obvious now: it was being used to deal drugs. The two young men took the money and called ahead to whoever was inside number 501 to confirm that the customers were good to be served. The customers would then be directed over to the slot, where they were given the merchandise. It was a neat system. Keeping the money and the merchandise apart made it more difficult for rivals to rip off the business. And by making sure that the two parts of the transaction—payment and delivery—were separate, too, it was more difficult for law enforcement to make an effective bust.

Milton continued. The rest of Grand Avenue on the same side as the drug business was a single lot. A mesh fence secured it from the street and offered a clear view inside. Milton saw tractor units, boats, construction vehicles and cars. He continued to Pacific Street and looked into the lot. It backed all the way up to the rear of the buildings that faced onto Atlantic. Milton suspected that he might have struck it lucky; the lot would be easy to get into, and the abandoned vehicles would give him more than enough cover to get to the back of the building without fear of detection.

He would check that out later.

105

M ilton walked onto Pacific Street and stopped. It was quiet, everything muffled by the snow.

He could see the rear of the club from here. There was a wide-open space that had been used to accommodate two dozen vehicles. There were cars, buses, an old boat and a truck, most of them wrecks that were no good for anything but scrap and all of them covered by inches of snow. Milton looked up and down the street and, satisfied that there was no one watching, he approached the first mesh gate that prevented access to the lot. It was secured by a chain and padlock; it would be an easy enough thing to snap through the chain with a pair of bolt cutters, but he didn't want to alert anyone that the lot's security had been breached. He went to the second gate. It was secured in the same fashion, but the chain was longer and, when Milton pushed the gate back, he was able to open up a wide enough gap that he could slip inside.

There were five distinct lines of vehicles arranged ahead of him. The densest concentration was to the left and he headed there, slipping into the space between a Volvo that had been totalled in a head-on collision and a red Chevy flatbed truck. He was leaving tracks behind him, but there was nothing that he could do about that. He crouched beneath the roof of the Volvo so that he was not visible from the adjacent Grand Avenue and moved forward. He passed around a tree and then into the narrow space between a boat on a trailer and a black pickup. He stopped again when he reached the stern of the boat. There was a low-loader truck parked in the space between him and the wall that marked the start of the single-storey rear extensions. Milton recalled the geography: the addition to the immediate left was where the drugs were kept; the one directly ahead of him led into the club and, above that, the second and third floors of the building; the addition to the right must have been connected to the Falafel Hut.

There was one final car ahead of him: a new Audi with tinted windows. The tracks that led to its wheels were fresh. Milton took out his phone and took a picture of the plate.

There was no sign of activity ahead of him, and Milton decided to take the opportunity to scout a little closer to his target. He ran forward and reached the wall. There were doors out into the yard from all three properties. They were all solid wood, with no windows, and they were all closed. There was a dumpster next to the first door and Milton clambered onto it, flinching a little at the clash of his boots against the metal lid. The dumpster was tall enough for him to be able to reach up and pull himself onto the snowy roof.

Milton took out his phone and started to take pictures. The roof had been turned into an outside space with a table and chairs. The table was equipped with a patio umbrella and there was a barbecue next to it. Milton crept to his left and hid behind a raised flower bed. The space was narrow, perhaps five metres wide by ten metres in length. It was separated from the roofs on either side by two-metre-tall brick walls.

Milton kept snapping pictures. There were two windows ahead of him, but they had been bricked in. Milton looked up: there were three windows on the floor above. The roof was accessed through a door where the third window on this level would once have been.

He crept forward until he was pressed against the wall. He looked at the door. It was made of wood and looked solid. There was half an inch between the bottom of the door and the floor, but, as Milton lay down flat, he couldn't get down low enough to see through it. It would offer a serious obstacle to anyone who wanted to get inside without an invitation. He took photographs of the door, including the hinges and the handle, checked that the yard was clear, and made his way back to the edge of the roof. He lowered himself down to the dumpster and then down to the snowy ground.

It was going to be difficult to get inside.

Difficult, but not impossible.

106

Milton went back to the entrance. A short line of customers had formed while he had been around the back, and he joined at the end and waited as they all slowly shuffled forward. The two corner boys were still there, but they paid him no attention; if they had seen him return, they would probably have thought that his walk around the block was to summon up the courage to go into the club.

Milton reached the front of the line. There was a booth just inside the entrance with a Plexiglas window and a slot above a narrow counter. There was a woman in the booth, and she stared out at Milton with barely disguised boredom.

"Twenty bucks."

Milton pushed two tens through the slot.

"You been here before?"

"No," he said.

"You gotta buy a drink. You want a private dance, you speak to the girl you like and arrange it directly with her. No touching under no circumstances. You put your hands on, they'll take you out back and make you wish you hadn't. You got it?"

"I do."

The woman snorted disdainfully and indicated with a jerk of her head that he should go inside.

The club was small, with mirrors on all of the walls to try to make it seem larger than it was. There was a bar, where two topless bartenders served the clientele. There was a circular dais in the centre of the room with a pole and narrow catwalks that extended out from the twelve and six o'clock positions. Seats were arranged along the catwalks and around the dais, and the club's early afternoon patrons sat there and watched the show. They left their beers and glasses of spirits on the stage, reaching up to slip dollar bills into the garter belts of the dancers once they had finished their shows and solicited for tips. Milton looked at the men: they were glassy-eyed, ogling the dancers and reflexively putting their drinks to their lips. They were joined by an almost equal number of dancers dressed in very little as they worked the crowd, offering private shows. The girls on the stage watched themselves, too, glancing into the mirrors as their reflections whirled and spun. It was soulless and depressing.

Milton bought an eight-dollar beer and took an empty seat at the runway with the fewest patrons on either side of it. He put the bottle on the catwalk and looked around. There was a door at the back of the room; light spilled out of it as a man opened and closed it. Milton watched the man as he went to the bar. It was obvious that the newcomer wasn't a patron; he didn't spare a glance at the half-naked women and, as he reached the bar, he exchanged words with one of the girls with a bored ease that suggested that he knew her. He took four unopened bottles of beer—another discrepancy as compared to the patrons, since they all had their bottles opened at the bar—and returned to the back of the room. He opened the door and went back inside.

The MC introduced the next dancer up—a black girl with the stage name Pantera—and the routine began again. The women were as diverse as the patrons: they were black, white and Latino; tall and short. They shared a similar body type: small breasts, hard bodies covered in tattoos, and generous behinds. It seemed that the club's focus was on that latter characteristic, with each thrust and jiggle and squat set to the pounding hip-hop soundtrack. Milton watched as the dancer on the stage eased herself up the pole, suspending herself just with her legs as she turned upside down and slid down to rest on her shoulders. She lowered herself all the way down and Milton pretended to watch as she simulated sex, first on her hands and knees and then flipping over onto her back with her high-heeled feet on either side of his bottle.

The track faded out. The MC came over the PA, encouraged the audience to show their appreciation, and introduced the next dancer as Sparkle. Pantera grabbed her discarded underwear and put it back on without a shred of self-consciousness. She teetered down the steps on her vertiginous heels and came over to him.

"You like the show, baby?" she asked.

"I did."

"You want a private show? I'll dance just for you."

"Where do you do that?"

She turned and gestured to the doorway that Milton had seen at the back of the room. "Through there. We got our own booth, just me and you."

"Sure," Milton said.

107

Pantera led the way. The door was ajar, and she opened it and went through. Milton followed. There was a corridor beyond with five doors: four to the left and one at the end. Milton recalled the geography of the buildings from his tour of the exterior of the block. The door at the end of the corridor would open into the rear addition that was the twin of number 501, the premises that were being used to distribute the drugs. The three doors nearest to them were the same: plain, not particularly sturdy, and ajar. The final door was a much more serious affair. It was metal, with a peephole at eye level.

Pantera continued down the corridor. Milton glanced through a crack between the first door and the frame and saw a small booth. A man was sitting on a wooden chair, and a woman was dancing between his spread legs. She ground her backside into his crotch and, as she looked up at the sound of their passing, Milton saw the almost comical boredom on her face.

"In here, baby," Pantera said, opening the second door.

"What's through the door?" Milton asked.

"What?"

"The door at the end of the corridor. Where does it go?"

"You don't want to worry about that," she said.

"Does the club continue upstairs?"

"No," she said. "That's management. Come on."

She opened the door to a vacant booth and waited next to it with her hand on her hip. Milton looked inside: it wasn't much more than a cubicle, with a single chair and just enough space for the girl to stand between him and the door.

"How you want me to dance?" she asked.

"It's all right," he said. "I don't."

"What do you mean?"

"I'm Detective Polanski," he said.

"You gotta be kidding me."

"Afraid not," he said. "I have a few questions for you."

She shook her head vigorously. "I ain't answering shit from you."

"Really?" Milton said. "We can take this to the precinct if you like. I can arrest you now and drag you out there. Makes no difference to me. Might not look so good for you, though."

"You ain't got nothing on me, so don't pretend like you do."

"I've got reasonable cause to believe that you're working as a prostitute. That's enough for me to arrest you. I can be more creative if I have to be."

Her eyes went wide. "I ain't no prostitute!" she said, her voice throbbing with indignation.

Milton shrugged. "But you just offered to give me extras after the dance."

"You motherfucker!" she said, quietening her voice.

"It doesn't have to go that way," Milton said. "I'm not interested in you."

"So what do you want?"

"Information. That's all."

She looked at him, the fight draining out of her. "I fucking hate cops," she said, defeated.

He could smell her: a mixture of perspiration and cheap perfume.

"What's your name?" he said. "Your real name."

"Sarah," she said. "Look, the longer we in here, the more likely it is they gonna send someone back to make sure I'm okay. What you wanna know?"

"The club," he said. "How long have you been here?"

"Six months? Eight... I don't know."

"Who owns it?"

She shrugged.

"Is it Carlos Acosta?"

She held his eye. "If you already know, you don't gotta ask."

"Is he in the club often?"

"Not usually," she said. "But the last week or so, all the time."

"You know why that is?"

"I heard one of the girls who spoke to one of his guys, she said that she heard it ain't safe for him to be out on the street too much right now. This place, they say he thinks it's safe. Can't get to him once he's in here."

"When was the last time you saw him?"

"Today," she said.

"Really?"

"I was here at eleven thirty. I parked my car out on Bergen Street out back and walked the rest of the way.

Carlos has an Audi, parks it in the lot behind the building. It was there when I went by."

"So you saw his car—but you didn't see him?"

She shrugged. "Sure. But he always uses the Audi. He don't go nowhere unless he's in it."

"What about upstairs? Do the girls go up there?"

She shrugged. "Sometimes. They have parties." She left the implicit suggestion of what that might entail.

"How often do you go upstairs?"

"Not often."

"But you have been up?"

Her weary frown was replaced by anxiety. "This about Carlos?"

"Yes," Milton said.

"Then no way, man. No fucking way. There ain't nothing you could do to me that he wouldn't do a thousand times worse."

"It's just information, Sarah. I'm not asking for anything that could ever come back to you. No one knows who I am. You get to walk out of here with no one the wiser if you help me out. How often do you go upstairs?"

She glowered at him resentfully. "Once or twice a week."

Milton tried to be discreet. "So Carlos likes you?"

"Not him," she said, shaking her head. "His brother —Savio."

"Tell me what it's like up there. Just imagine you're out in the corridor, out there." He nodded to the door. "There's a door at the end, on the left. A big metal door. What's inside?"

"You got a flight of stairs."

"Describe them, please."

She shook her head with a mixture of impatience and reluctance. "They go up to a landing. There's another door there, halfway up; they usually leave that open. You step through that and then there's a door that opens out onto the roof. They got a garden up there—they go out and smoke weed in the summer."

"They keep it locked?"

She nodded. "It's like the door downstairs. I tried to open it one time—it's fucking heavy."

Milton indicated that she should continue.

"So you go through the cage door, you turn left, then you go up the stairs again and then you get to the second floor. The whole floor is one big room."

"Describe it."

"It's big. They knocked the walls through. They got couches, a big flat-screen TV, pool table."

"Is it where Acosta lives?"

"No," she said. "He's on the next floor up, on the third floor."

"Tell me about it."

"It's bedrooms," she said. "I only been in the one Savio uses, so don't ask me about the others because I can't help you."

"How many rooms?"

"Don't know. Four?"

Milton concentrated hard, building a picture of the interior that he would be able to rely upon later. "That's good, Sarah," he said. "Nearly done. Last question. Did you hear anything about two people who might have been taken up there? A man and his son?"

She looked at him and gave a slow nod. "Sure. I heard about that. You know who they are?"

"Tell me about them."

"I know a girl who cleans up in the club—used to go to school with her. She says she was here early, like nine o'clock, and they were bringing a young kid and this guy in through the door that goes out to the yard. I asked why; she said she didn't know, just that they took them upstairs."

"Where would Carlos keep them?"

"One of the bedrooms, I guess. Who are they?"

"Doesn't matter," Milton said. "Almost done. You help me a little more and all this worry goes away."

She stared at him. "What do I gotta do?"

"Two things. First of all, I need to know what Acosta looks like."

"Skinny. Got a gold cap in his front tooth; his hair's bleached blond. He thinks he looks like Bruno Mars."

"The second thing," Milton said, "you go outside now like nothing has happened. We didn't have this conversation. Find out whether the two of them are still there and, if they are, which room they're in."

"How am I gonna do that?"

"I don't know. Ask around. Ask the other girls. You'll figure it out." He took a piece of paper and wrote down his number. "Call me when you know."

108

M ilton's phone rang as he walked back to his motorbike.

"Hello? John?"

It was Fedorov. "Hello," Milton said.

"I am calling about your friends. They have left the apartment. They have been away all morning."

"Could I come and see you?" Milton said. "I might need another favour."

"Of course. Have you been to Russian bath before?"

"Not for a long time," Milton said.

"I have one every day, straight after lunch. You come—we can talk."

Milton drove to Sheepshead Bay. He parked his bike on Neck Road and walked to the address he had memorised. He passed market stalls, where old women wrapped up in fur lined to buy *salo*—smoked and salted fat—and then a closed-down matzoh bakery and a vodka joint, authentic and real, the antithesis to the fake places that were popping up in hipster Manhattan.

Milton found the building and went inside. He bought a ticket and was given a towel, robe and slippers and directions to the changing room.

He passed through the bath's main hall. The space was dominated by a full-sized swimming pool. The ceilings were low, and the effect was to imbue the place with a cosy, secluded feel. Milton looked in the pool, but could not find Fedorov. There were two mixed saunas on either side of the pool, and Milton tried both. The rooms were equipped with faucets for cold water buckets. Adults lounged on the hottest benches while children played with the cold water.

There was one more sauna around the back of the changing rooms. Milton pushed open the doors and went inside. It was hotter than the others, and men were allowed to be naked inside it. Milton saw elderly men, their flesh drooping in pendulous folds, drinking beers and engaging in long conversations just as they might have done if they were in St Petersburg or Moscow.

Fedorov was sitting on one of the benches, his legs apart, a towel around his waist.

He saw Milton and waved a hand.

"John," he said.

"Do you mind?"

"No, not at all. Come. Sit."

Milton lowered himself to the bench next to Fedorov. The wood was hot, and it took a moment to get used to it.

"You like?"

"It's warm," Milton admitted.

"Good for the digestion," Fedorov said.

Milton looked over at the Crimean. He was older than Milton, but his body was taut with muscle. He had a tattoo running from his shoulder down to his elbow. It was in Latin: *Si vis pacem, para bellum.*

Fedorov noticed that Milton was looking at it. "You understand?"

"'If you want peace, prepare for war.'"

"Plato wrote about it," Fedorov said. "Have you read the classics?"

"I'm afraid not."

"You should. There is much to learn."

Fedorov got up and poured cold water onto the hot coals. They fizzed and spat, and Milton felt the dizzying wave of heat that was thrown out.

"So," Fedorov said. "Your friends. They were gone when my brother visited this morning. He had food for them. He stayed for thirty minutes, but they did not come back. I thought I should tell you."

"They're in trouble," Milton said.

Fedorov leaned forward. "How?"

"They went back to their house. Someone was waiting for them there, and they were put in the back of a van and driven away. I got there too late to stop it."

"By who?"

"Freddy's evidence could cause a lot of trouble to a man called Acosta."

Fedorov's brows lowered. "Carlos Acosta?"

"You know him?"

"He deals drugs," Fedorov said, his words leaden and heavy with antipathy. "His drugs killed Dmitri. I found out where they came from, but there was nothing that the police would do."

"He's a powerful man. And I'm worried what he might do to my friends."

"Then what can I do to help?"

"I know where Acosta is holding them. There's a strip club on Atlantic Avenue."

"It is where he does his business?"

"One of the places. He took them there this morning. I'm going to go and get them out, but I need help."

"So call the police."

"Acosta owns the police. I can't take the chance."

"So you will do it alone?"

"I told you at dinner—I have experience. If I can get in, I can get them out. But it's getting in that's going to be difficult. I scouted before I came here. I need to get upstairs, but I'll need someone to make some noise so I can do it."

"And this is what you need from me—a distraction?"

"Yes. Nothing difficult or dangerous. I'm thinking of a little stunt in the bar that will divert their attention for long enough so that I can do what I need to do."

Fedorov shrugged. "Whatever you need," he said. "Tell me where I need to be and what you want me to do and I will do it."

"I have some preparations that I need to make," Milton said. "If I come by the restaurant this evening, would that be okay? Ten?"

Fedorov nodded. "And Acosta," he said. "What will you do with him?"

"I haven't decided yet."

Fedorov put out a hand.

Milton took it. "I'll see you tonight."

"I will see you then, John."

109

M ilton rode to the Kings Plaza Shopping Center in Marine Park. It seemed a long time ago that he had visited the branch of Foot Locker there so that he could replace Freddy's stolen sneakers, but it hadn't even been a week.

He remembered the roster of stores and knew that he could get everything that he would need.

His first stop was an outdoor sports store, where he bought two one-pound tubs of Tannerite, a black powder usually used to make explosive targets for rifle shooting. He selected a hunting knife with a serrated edge and a scabbard to put it in. He added a pair of black combat trousers and a black jacket, telling the clerk that he was going to go to Coyne Park range and do some target shooting. Then, he went into Duane Reade and bought a box of latex gloves. He visited Home Depot and purchased two dozen cable ties, a DeWalt cordless drill, a large pack of stump remover, a dozen clear plastic Ziploc bags, a can of spray adhesive, a roll of duct tape, a length of stiff cardboard, a roll of wax paper and a ball of string. Finally, he added a Ryobi inspection scope with a camera on the end of a thin, articulated stalk that a plumber might use to examine the insides of a pipe.

His phone rang as he was making his way back to the parking lot. Milton looked at the display: he didn't recognise the number.

"Hello?"

"Mr. Smith."

He stopped.

"Mr. Acosta."

"Would you still like to see the boy and his father again?"

Milton turned into a doorway and stopped. "I would."

"Then you need to come to Red Hook tonight."

"Where?"

"The grain terminal. At the mouth of the Gowanus Canal."

"I know it. What time?"

"Two o'clock."

"And then?"

"The boy walks."

"What about his father?"

"You and he will stay. I'm going to give you both a chance to persuade me that you won't cause me any more trouble."

"Really? You wouldn't just shoot the three of us?"

He chuckled. "You'll have to trust me, Mr. Smith."

"That's not a very attractive offer."

"It's the only offer you're going to get."

"Can I make a counter?"

Milton heard laughter. "You'd be wasting your breath."

"Here's what I propose, Carlos. It is Carlos I'm speaking to, isn't it?"

There was no reply.

Milton had been thinking very carefully about what he would say when Acosta called him back. He had to give him something to think about.

"This is what I would do if I were you. I would let them both go. Right now. If you do that, maybe you get to walk away with your pretty face in one piece. How's Savio? Or the man I shot? They doing okay?"

The laughter returned, but Milton couldn't mistake the angry, bitter foundation to it. "Two o'clock. If you're not there, they're both dead."

The line went dead.

Milton took a moment to breathe. He was sweating despite the cold.

He put his purchases into the sports bag that he had taken from Rhodes's house, slung it over his shoulders, and set off back to Coney Island.

Milton returned to his apartment and locked the door behind him.

He went into the kitchen, took out the things that he had purchased, took down a bag of sugar from a cupboard, pulled on a pair of the latex gloves and set to work.

He mixed the stump remover and sugar and then poured the mixture into a frying pan of boiling water that he had on the stove. He stirred it in until it dissolved and then let the water boil out, leaving a slurry that was saturated with the flammable chemical solution. He took around twelve feet of the string and placed it in the pan to absorb the mixture; then, when that was done, he arranged it on a cookie sheet and baked it for twenty minutes. He removed the sheet, allowed the cord to cool, and then used the scissors to cut the stiff string into four-inch fuse cords.

He set them to one side and attended to the rest of the preparation that needed to be done.

He took the battery from the DeWalt drill and removed the screws so that the top assembly slid out. There were fifteen NiCad cells that comprised the battery pack, a collection of identical cylinders held together in a neat honeycomb pattern. He removed the tape that held them together and then snipped each connector band so that he was left with the component cells. He pushed the batteries out of the casings and threw them away; he just wanted the casings. He took the first casing, added a bead of hot glue to the flat sleeve on the bottom, and stuck a circle of cardboard to it.

He poured more of the stump remover and sugar into a hot pan and folded it into itself until the sugar began to caramelise. He made half a kilogram of the explosive mixture, heating it until it passed from white to golden brown and then filling each casing with it. He added a length of fuse, pushing it into the mixture all the way to the bottom of the casing, and left it to harden. He repeated the procedure for the other casings until he had ten of them lined up on the counter.

The room was filled with a harsh, acidic smell. Milton opened the windows and carried on.

He took the Ziploc bags, one of the tubs of Tannerite, the spray adhesive, the stiff piece of cardboard, the wax paper and a roll of tape. He took one of the bags, went to the tap and filled it with cold water. He sealed the top and then reinforced the seal with a folded-over length of duct tape. Next, he took the Tannerite, held the water-filled Ziploc bag on the side of the tub that was facing him, then lashed it in place with tape until it was secure. He took the length of cardboard, the same length as his forearm, placed the tub on top of it and then wrapped it around with tape. He took the spray adhesive and emptied it over the surface of the cardboard sheet. Finally, he carefully unrolled the wax paper over the freshly sticky cardboard, cut the paper with a pair of scissors, and then gently lowered his handiwork into the sports bag.

He was done. He filled a glass with tap water and drank it in one go, trying to rid his mouth of the taste of the chemicals that still pervaded the apartment.

He needed a walk to clear his head. He closed the windows, locked the door and made his way down to the street.

———

Milton's phone rang as he made his way down the stairs to his bike.

"Hello?"

"This is Sarah—from the club."

Milton stopped. "What did you find?"

"There's a man and his kid upstairs on the third floor. They're still there."

"Which room?"

"I don't know. Just that they're still there."

"Thank you," Milton said. "You won't hear from me again."

"Fuck you, asshole."

Milton put the phone in his pocket and opened the door to the street.

Milton was next to his bike when he noticed Detective Mackintosh behind him. She was with two uniformed officers.

"Mr. Smith?"

"Yes?"

"I'm arresting you as an accessory to murder."

"What?"

"You have the right to remain silent. Anything you say can and will be used against you in a court of law. You have the right to an attorney. If you cannot afford an attorney, one will be provided for you."

"This is crazy," Milton said.

The uniformed officers stepped forward.

"Put your hands behind your back, please, sir."

"You want to talk to me, we can do it tomorrow. I can't do it now. I've got to—"

"You've got to what, Mr. Smith?" Mackintosh said. "Where were you going?"

Milton bit his tongue.

One of the uniformed officers put his hand on Milton's shoulder. "Put your hands on the hood of the car, please."

Milton recognised the Hyundai Sonata facing his bike. He cursed himself for allowing himself to be distracted enough not to see it. He did as the officer told him and concentrated on maintaining his composure as he frisked him. The man was quick and expert, patting him down for weapons or evidence. He pulled out his cigarettes and lighter and dumped them in the street. He took out his wallet, flipped through it, and dropped it on the hood. His cellphone was next, ending up on the hood next to his wallet. The officer found nothing because there was nothing to find. Milton was grateful that he had left everything in his apartment, but then, remembering what he had left there, he became anxious. He would have a difficult time explaining why he had smoke grenades and homemade explosives laid out in his kitchen.

"Hands, please. Behind your back. I'm arresting you as accessory to murder."

Milton had been cuffed before, and he crossed his hands one over the other; they could rest one against the other that way, and it would be more comfortable. The officer cuffed him as efficiently as he had searched him.

"Where are we going?" he asked Mackintosh as he allowed the officer to nudge him into motion.

"The Seven Five," she said. "I've got some questions I need you to answer."

110

M ackintosh drove into the yard at the back of the station house, and Milton was led in through the same door as he had used a week ago, when he had been brought in with Freddy Blanco to give his evidence about his discovery of González's body. He was booked and then taken down to be searched. His phone and wallet were confiscated, and he signed a voucher to acknowledge that those two items were the extent of the property that had been taken from him. An officer took his name and address. Milton cooperated, hoping that compliance might speed the process and expedite his release. He was fingerprinted, placing his hands on a digital scanner and waiting as pictures were taken and checked.

And then, once that was done, he was led to the precinct's holding cell. The cell accommodated two other prisoners: one drunk, asleep on the bench, and a second man who glared with evil intent until Milton stared back at him and the man decided that he would wait for another patsy.

Milton had no watch, but he had a good sense of the

passing of time. He guessed that it was somewhere between four-thirty and five. He still had plenty of time to complete his preparations for the evening, but the fact that he relied upon someone else's permission for that to happen made him feel anxious. The uncertainty of his situation didn't help, either; he had been arrested for being an accessory to murder, and not for murder. What did that mean? Perhaps that Mackintosh was fishing, that she didn't have enough on him for the full charge, and was going to bring him in to see what she could get out of him at interview. But he was guessing. Was it possible that he had been sloppy with the thug that he had killed in the cemetery? Or, worse, with Rhodes this morning? He couldn't think of how that would be possible, but he couldn't be certain.

Milton sat quietly and tried to keep track of the time. He started to doubt himself. Had he been there an hour? Two? How long did he have? And what would happen to Manny and Freddy if Acosta took them out to the meet and he didn't show?

Milton was led into the same room that Mackintosh had taken him to before. The detective was waiting for him and indicated that he should sit. He did. The officer unlocked the cuff on Milton's left wrist and clipped it around the metal bar that had been set into the wall. Mackintosh thanked him and waved him out of the room.

She pressed a button on the table and turned to look up at the camera in the corner of the ceiling. "This is Detective Rebecca Mackintosh," she said. "Interview with John Smith, commencing at 8.00 p.m. Have you been asked whether you want a lawyer, Mr. Smith?"

"No," he said. "But I don't. Get on with it."

"Mr. Smith confirms that he doesn't want a lawyer." There was a file of notes on the table; she flicked through them, ignoring Milton in an attempt, he suspected, to increase the pressure on him. "I'm gonna lay it all out for you," she said at last. "Feel free to jump in and correct me if I've got anything wrong." She stared at him, but he didn't reply. She continued. "So, you first came to my attention because you say that you found the body of a murder victim in the restroom at Euclid station on Sunday night. José Luis González. You were just passing through, you stopped off to use the facilities, and there he was. Dead. You find the kid in the restroom and you call the police. We bring you here and you give me a statement. How am I doing?"

Milton nodded, but didn't speak.

"Okay. So, just four days later, yesterday, a member of the public finds the body of a man in a dumpster in Cypress Hills Cemetery. The coroner says this guy was strangled, and that he'd been in the dumpster since the previous afternoon. So, that's Wednesday. So, that's three days after you and I met for the first time. We investigated the murder, but it's not the sort of place where people hang out and the weather was shitty that day. We got nothing, and it looks like we're gonna strike out, at least until I took a look at the footage from the cameras at the station. I got to tell you, John, it was a hell of a surprise. There you are, getting off the train, and then, getting off the same train, here comes the guy who was about to wind up dead in the dumpster. Can you see why I had to speak to you again? What a coincidence, right? What are the odds that a guy would find one body and then, just three days later, the same guy is seen with another guy who we later find dead in a dumpster? Got to be impossible, right?"

"Is that a question?"

"Don't you think that's strange?"

"Yes," he said. "It is."

"You're a dangerous man to know."

"It's strange, but it's just a coincidence."

She shook her head. "I'm not buying that."

"I don't care whether you're buying it or not," he said. "The fact that I was on the same train as some guy doesn't mean I killed him. And if you're doubting what I told you about González, then you're saying that you don't believe what Freddy Blanco told you. Was he lying, too?"

"No," she said. "I just don't believe you've told me the whole truth."

"We'll have to agree to disagree on that. You've held me here all afternoon, Detective. Unless you've got anything else, I think it's time you let me out."

She flashed with anger. "Oh, I've got more," she said. "I've been looking into you a little bit more. You've been working here, but it seems like you don't have a visa. So that's a black mark against you right away. I go back a little more, run some searches, and what do I find but a police report from Victoria, Texas. This is from two years ago. Seems you have a track record for violence. You remember that?"

Milton clenched his fists beneath the table. "It was a brawl in a bar," he said, making sure to keep the frustration out of his voice. "Two guys attacked me."

"And you put them both in the hospital."

"That's right."

"You're a violent man, then?"

"No," Milton said. "Not at all. And none of this has anything to do with either of those murders. Do you have anything else?"

"You want to think about that attitude, John. It's not doing you any favours. I've got enough to hold you. I could decide to get you arraigned, but it's a Saturday and the courts are shut. So I can hold you all night. Maybe I send you to the Tombs so you can think about why it'd make more sense for you to cooperate with me instead of giving me attitude. You know what the Tombs are like, John? You ever been there? Seen them on TV? It's worse. Nowhere to sleep. Nowhere to wash. You want to use the toilet, you got to do it in front of everyone. You're making me very tempted to do that."

"Fine. Do what you have to do. But I want my phone call now."

111

Polanski had been thinking about driving north to see his wife and kids when he got Smith's call. He listened, absorbed the news, and drove down from the island to the Seven Five as quickly as he could.

Mackintosh was prowling around outside the interrogation rooms when he arrived.

"You arrested Smith?" he asked her.

"You?" she said without answering his question. "He called you?"

"Why do you have him in here?"

"Because I don't believe a word he's been telling us."

"Go on."

She moved him away from the desk and out of the earshot of the three men who were waiting to be attended to by the sergeant.

"We found the body of a man connected to Carlos Acosta on Thursday," she said. "He was inside a dumpster in the cemetery north of Cypress Hills station. Time of death was estimated sometime on Wednesday afternoon. Strangled. No witnesses. No leads. Looked like we were going to have to eat it until I checked the video from the station. Right about the time we think this guy's ticket was punched, lo and behold, we've got John Smith getting off a train. And then, just after that, we have the victim getting off the same train, too."

"They were on the same train?" Polanski said sceptically. "That's it?"

"You don't think that's weird? That they both got off at the same station, right next to where the body was found?"

"It's a coincidence."

"That's what he said. Just like the fact that he found the body of González. Two deaths that he's at least *connected* with in three days. You don't think that needs digging into?"

"You can't hold him on that."

"That's what he's been telling me."

"And he's right."

"Maybe."

"You got anything else?"

"Some," she said. "He's been working without a visa." She saw him roll his eyes and forestalled his protest with an upheld palm. "The other thing's more interesting. Two and a half years ago, Smith was arrested in Texas. There was a bar brawl and he beat up two men, including the son of the local sheriff. They were ready to arraign him when they got a visit from a woman who said she was with the FBI. She told them they had to let him go, and they did."

"The FBI?"

"That's right," she said.

"Where was this?"

"Little town called Victoria."

"Have you spoken to them?"

"I've emailed. Waiting to hear."

Polanski shook his head. "So he's more complicated than

he told us. Fair enough. But I still don't see how that has anything to do with this."

"He's an illegal alien, working without a visa, and he has a history of violent behaviour. He told us he was a *cook* working in Coney Island. And you think he's just *'more complicated'*? We can't trust a word he's told us."

"But you still don't have enough to hold him for anything here."

"I don't know about that," she said. "I can hold him until the court opens. And, the attitude he's giving me, I'm tempted to do that."

"I'll talk to him," Polanski said. "If I can get anything out of him, I'll let you know. All right?"

She shrugged. "Knock yourself out." She gave him a small key. "For his cuffs," she said, turning away and making her way to the stairs that led up to her office.

Polanski took a moment outside the door to the interrogation room, then reached for the handle and went inside.

112

Polanski went into the interrogation room. Smith was sitting at the table, his left wrist cuffed. The other bracelet was attached to a metal pole that was fixed to the wall.

"Hey."

Smith looked up. "Thanks for coming."

"You want to tell me what's going on?"

Smith looked down at his cuffed wrist. "Bit of a misunderstanding."

"This is a mess."

"You need to get me out."

Polanski rested his hands on the back of the second chair. "Not gonna be easy. I just spoke to Mackintosh. You've got some questions to answer."

"And I answered them."

"She doesn't think so."

"What do you think?"

"I'm still trying to figure that out. But you've really riled her up."

Smith was silent.

"Come on," Polanski pressed. "You're gonna have to work with me if you want to get out. She's trying very hard to pin the dumpster body on you. What happened? You said you were followed after we met. Right?"

"Yes," Smith said. "I was."

"And then what? This guy followed you to Cypress Hills and jumped you?"

"No," Smith said. "I told you—I lost him."

"So the guy in the dumpster is who, exactly?"

"I have no idea."

"It's just a coincidence?"

"That's it."

"Two dead bodies turn up within a week of each other and you're in the vicinity for both of them?"

"It's a big city. A lot of murders."

"Not as many as you'd think," Polanski said.

"I don't know what else you want me to say," Smith said. "I can answer these questions all night, but, if you keep me here, you'll have another two murders to deal with. Freddy and Manny need help."

Polanski paced. He agreed with Mackintosh up to a point: there were plenty of questions that Smith needed to answer, but now wasn't the time.

"We struck out on the van," he said. "I put it out all over Brooklyn, but we got nothing."

Smith stared straight at him, his blue eyes cold and piercing. "The van doesn't matter now. Acosta called me this afternoon. He wants to set up a meet."

"Why?"

"He says he doesn't want the Blancos. He wants me."

Polanski sat down. "Why?"

"Because he's the sort of man to bear a grudge."

Polanski shook his head. "Because of what—"

Smith interrupted him. "On Wednesday, after I met you, I went to the Blancos' house."

"And it was attacked. I know—you said. You fought back and they bailed."

"There were three guys. Acosta's brother was one of them."

"And what did you do to him?"

"Turns out I blinded him."

The feeling of nausea grew stronger. Polanski was confused. He had trusted Smith and had found his steely resolve reassuring in the midst of an investigation that had already turned to shit. But now he wondered just how much of what Smith had told him was true. The revelation that he had been arrested for a violent crime had dented his confidence even more. He found, as he tried and failed to hold Milton's implacable gaze, that it was all too easy to credit Mackintosh's notion that Smith was a killer.

"Blinded? How?"

"Does it matter?"

Polanski felt dizzy. "How did you—"

"I grabbed a mug of boiling water," Smith cut in. "I added sugar and threw it into his face. The sugar helps the water stick. It's not pleasant, but he came at me with a gun. He had it coming." Smith massaged his wrist. "That's why Acosta wants me. It's part revenge, part expediency. I'm a loose end from what happened to González. He doesn't know what I saw or didn't see. And he knows I want Freddy and Manny. There's his leverage. He says he'll swap me for them."

"And you believe that?"

"No, of course not. Freddy's too dangerous. He's using him as bait."

"When does he want to meet?"

"He says he'll call. That's why I need to get out of here. I don't have my phone. He might have already called. Do you think he's going to patiently wait for me to pick up?"

"Okay," he said. "I'll speak to Mackintosh."

Smith held his eye again. "There's something else you need to do."

Polanski exhaled. He felt hollowed out. "Do I want to hear it?"

"James Rhodes."

"What about him?"

"He's been working for Acosta, too. I think he killed Carter and Shepard once Acosta decided that he couldn't trust them."

"How could you *possibly* know that?"

"Because I've been looking into him. I was watching outside the station house on Thursday—the night Carter went missing. Rhodes didn't go straight home. I followed him. He went to Prospect Park and met someone there."

"You know who?" Polanski asked.

"No, but I can guess. He got into a blue Audi. I got the registration."

Smith recited the details of the plate attached to Acosta's Audi.

Polanski took it down. "I can run it."

"I think the car belongs to Acosta. I think Rhodes met him to report on what he'd done. Maybe he was getting paid. But I think Acosta is being very thorough now. Your investigation has rattled him. González was first. Then Carter and Shepard. Now I think he killed Rhodes, too."

"Speculation isn't going to be enough. I'll need a whole lot more than that."

Smith nodded. "Rhodes has been on the four-to-midnight shift. Did he report today?"

Polanski shrugged. "Don't know. I can check."

Smith leaned back. "I'm not going anywhere."

Polanski left the room. He went to the counter and asked the sergeant for the duty roster. He took it and ran his finger down the line of officers who were out on tour. Officer James Rhodes was marked as absent.

Polanski went back to Smith. "You're right. He didn't report."

"Send someone to his house. I went this morning. His car was outside and the curtains were closed. I knocked on the door, but there was no answer."

"Jesus," Polanski said again. "Why do I get the feeling you're holding out on me?"

"I'm not," Smith said. "I'm just thorough. A cop and an ex-cop go missing, I'd want to check that the new partner doesn't know anything."

"You think we haven't checked him out?"

"I'm not saying that. Just see if you can find him."

Polanski felt foreboding adding to his sense of frustration and helplessness. He had been so focused on Carter and Shepard ever since Freddy Blanco had identified Shepard as one of González's murderers that he hadn't had the opportunity to spend any time looking at Rhodes. He felt as if events were running out of control.

"Polanski?"

He pulled himself out of his detachment.

"Can you get me out?" Smith said.

Polanski nodded. "I'll have to speak to my boss and then I'll need to smooth it out with Mackintosh. But probably. If I do and Acosta calls you, I want you to let me know. You can't do this on your own. Do we have a deal?"

"You think I want to take on someone like that?" Smith said. "You'll be the first person I call."

"Good," Polanski said. He took the key, went around the table and unfastened the cuff.

Smith rubbed his wrist again. "Thanks."

"Wait here. I'll take care of the paperwork and then you can go."

113

Sergeant Richard Haynes parked his car around the back of the club and, after making sure that there was no one around, he went in through the side entrance. He knocked on the first door at the foot of the stairs and waited until it was opened; then, he climbed up to the landing, went through the open second door, and continued into the lounge area, where Acosta and two of his heavies were watching football on the big TV.

"Hey," he said.

Acosta turned. "Look who it is," he said. "My favourite policeman. How you doing, Dickie?"

"Doing okay, Carlos. Be even better if one of you went and got me a scotch."

Acosta turned to one of the men, flicking his fingers toward the bar. The man levered himself off the couch with a grunt of resentment and slouched across to the bar.

"What's the score?" Haynes said, nodding to the screen.

"Eagles just lost. Giants going to the playoffs."

Haynes was more of a Knicks fan and had no interest in football; he doubted that Carlos did, either, except insofar as he was making money out of the illegal books he ran.

"I'm sorry about Shepard," Acosta said. "I know you two went back."

"Yeah," Haynes said. "We did. But he got sloppy. I don't see there was another way."

"And thanks for keeping him in the loop about your boy's investigation."

"You paid for it," Haynes said. "You still want me to keep you in the picture?"

"Sure. You come straight to me now."

"That works."

Acosta sat up straight. "What you doing here, Dickie? This ain't no social call."

"No," he replied. "It's not. Your friend John Smith was arrested this afternoon."

"Shit," Acosta said. "What for?"

"They've been questioning him about the guy you had on him. The one who ended up in the dumpster up at Cypress Hills. They've got footage of them both coming out of the subway together."

"And they arrested him for that?"

"Second dead body he's been associated with in less than a week. Enough to pull his ass off the street for ques tioning, sure."

Acosta closed his eyes and exhaled impatiently. "I set the meet-up with him for two—"

"It's okay." Haynes spoke over him. "Polanski called me. Smith told him he had to get out. He said you've got the kid and his dad and that you were going to call him back about a meet."

"Going to call him back? I already called. It's tonight."

"So it's all good."

"You lost me."

"Think about it, Carlos. He could've told Polanski that the meet has been arranged, but he didn't. You told him to come on his own?"

"What do you think?"

"So that's what he's going to do. He has to get out, so he says to Polanski that he needs to be around when you call. He swears to Polanski that the moment he hears from you, he's going to tell him. But if he had said that you've *already* called, and the meet is *already* set up, there's no way Polanski lets him go back out on his own. Smith is smart. He's thinking."

"So is he out or isn't he?"

"Polanski called me and asked me what I'd do. I said it was his call, but I said they got nothing on him, and that, if he lets him out, he can make him promise to call once he hears about the meet. I said that's what I'd do if it were me. He agreed. They let him out twenty minutes ago."

Acosta nodded his satisfaction. "You think he's gonna show?"

"Yes. I do. But you want to be careful with him. Real careful. He's dangerous. He's already killed one guy you sent after him. Shot another and..."

"Yeah," he finished. "And he maimed my baby brother. I know what he did. Yeah, he's dangerous. But I'm dangerous, too."

Haynes's scotch was delivered. He took a sip, the warmth banishing some of the cold from outside. "Where's the meet?"

"Red Hook," Acosta said.

"You want me to sit in? Might be able to help."

Acosta laughed. "Shit, Dickie, I ain't being funny, but how old are you? Sixty? Sixty-five?"

"That's it," Haynes said, returning the younger man's grin. "You just laugh it up. But I've got more experience in my little finger than you got in your whole body. I'd want me around if I was figuring this mess out."

"How much is it gonna cost me?"

"I'll give you this one for free," Haynes said. "I need a favour later, I'll call you."

Acosta made a show of thinking about the offer.

"You're on. We're leaving in ninety minutes. You want to go and get a dance downstairs? Tell them I said it's on the house."

PART VII

SATURDAY

114

M ilton collected the bag with the items that had been confiscated, signed the voucher, and hurried out into the street. It was midnight; he was already two hours late for his meeting with Fedorov and, if the Crimean wasn't able to help, Milton knew that his carefully considered plan would fail. He took out his phone and dialled the number for the restaurant.

Fedorov picked up. "Hello?"

"It's John Smith," Milton said as he started to walk north toward Pitkin Avenue.

"John—is everything okay?"

"I'm sorry I'm so late. I had something unexpected come up—it's sorted now. Can you still help me?"

"Yes," Fedorov said. "Of course. What do you need me to do?"

"I need you to go to Atlantic Avenue. There's a car wash on Washington Avenue. Do you know it?"

"No," he said. "But I will find it. When?"

Milton reached Pitkin and saw a yellow cab approaching him. He stepped out into the road and waved it down.

"Can you be there in an hour?" he said as the cab pulled over. "One o'clock?"

"Yes," he said. "I will see you there."

Milton ended the call and opened the door of the cab.

"Coney Island," he said. "As fast as you can."

The roads were quiet and, even with the treacherous conditions, the cabbie was able to make good progress. They reached West 24th Street just before 12.25 a.m. Milton paid the driver and ran to his block, taking the steps two at a time so that he was gasping by the time he reached his floor. He went inside. He took a small satchel and put three of the homemade smoke grenades inside. He put the satchel into the larger sports bag that he had taken from Rhodes's house, adding the rest of the grenades, the Tannerite charge, the inspection camera, the UMP9 and two spare magazines. He picked up the Beretta he had used to shoot Rhodes, took a cloth and wiped away his prints. He used the cloth to pick up the gun by the edge of the grip and sealed it in a Ziploc bag. He put the pistol in the sports bag, too.

He changed into the black clothes that he had purchased, took the sports bag, stuffed his balaclava into his pocket and grabbed his helmet. He paused, took out his phone and set it on the table. Then, finally, he ran back down to the street again. He put on his leather gloves, got onto his bike and rode north, opening the throttle as he crossed Coney Island Creek and merged onto the empty Belt Parkway. The wind rushed around him as he pushed the bike up to fifty, aware that, if he was stopped, police would find that he was carrying a bag full of explosives, a submachine gun and a pistol that could be tied back to the murder of a serving police officer.

He had no choice: he had to be quick.

He reached Red Hook and saw the huge grain terminal at the mouth of the Gowanus Canal. That was the rendezvous that Acosta had chosen. It was a twenty-minute drive from the club. Milton guessed that Acosta would leave no later than one thirty in order to be there to make the meet. But he might feasibly leave much earlier than that. Milton had to have put his plan into action before that happened or it would all be for nothing.

Alexei Fedorov was standing next to the car wash at the junction of Atlantic and Washington, just as Milton had requested. He was stamping his feet against the cold, his head covered by a military-style *ushanka*, the flaps fastened around his chin to protect his ears, jaw and chin from the chill.

Milton rolled the bike to the side and checked his watch: it was two minutes before one. He dismounted, removed his arms from the straps of the bag and wheeled the bike across the sidewalk to the car wash. There was a forecourt to the left of the car wash, and Milton locked the bike there. It was out of the way, and he would be able to pick it up again before the business reopened on Monday.

Fedorov walked over to him.

"Thank you for coming," Milton said, putting out his hand.

Fedorov took it. "You are welcome, John."

"We need to be quick," Milton said. "Can you walk with me?"

"Of course."

They set off. The club was one block to the east.

"What do you need me to do?" Fedorov asked.

Milton unzipped the bag as they walked. He reached inside and, making sure that the road was empty, took out one of the grenades. "You know what this is?"

Fedorov took it. "Explosives?"

"No," he said. "You light the fuse and they'll make a lot of smoke. They're not dangerous." Milton removed the two remaining grenades from the satchel and handed them to Fedorov.

"What do you want me to do with them?"

"There's a strip club on Atlantic Avenue, just up ahead on the right. The HoneyPot."

"Okay."

"The boy and his father are being held there. There are rooms upstairs. That's where they are."

"And you will break in?"

"That's the plan. But I need a distraction."

"I see," Fedorov said. He held up the grenades. "And this is it?"

"Yes," Milton said. "Get into the club and go to the back, somewhere you won't be seen. Light the fuses and drop them under a table. They'll put out a lot of smoke—it'll look like a fire."

"And you?"

"I'll be in and out. It won't take long."

Fedorov nodded. "I can do that."

"Thank you," Milton said. "I appreciate it."

They approached the corner of Grand Avenue, passing beneath the scaffold that clung to the large building on the corner.

Milton looked at his watch. "I've got ten past one," he said.

Fedorov checked his own watch, then adjusted it a little. "And me," he said. "When do you want me to do it?"

"In ten minutes."

Fedorov nodded. "I understand. Shall we meet at the restaurant afterwards?"

"Yes," he said. "Thank you. And be careful."

"And you," the Crimean said. "Good luck."

He gave Milton a nod, waited for a sedan to turn off Atlantic onto Grand, and then crossed the road. Milton turned off and hurried to the yard at the back of the building. He would have to move fast.

115

Milton reached the rear of the block and looked through the fence. The Audi was there, parked in the same space as it had been before. Tracks from the wheels led to the gate and then out into the road. The snow was coming down more heavily now, and the tracks were slowly being erased. Milton could see the light from the windows of the building. It was too far away to make out much more than that, but he was confident that Acosta was present.

Milton looked at his watch.

1.13 a.m.

Seven minutes to go.

Milton trusted that Fedorov would do what he had promised to do; he just had to concentrate on executing his own part of the plan.

He opened the bag and took out the balaclava and a pair of latex gloves. He put the balaclava on, tugging it down until it was snug, and then replaced his leather gloves with the latex ones. He went to the gate and pushed it open enough to pass his bag through. He wriggled inside, collected the bag again, and then hurried to hide behind the hood of the flatbed truck.

He checked his watch again.

1.15 a.m.

He slung the bag over his shoulder, looked around the side of the truck, and ran to the boat. He paused there, listening for anything that might suggest there was someone else in the yard with him and, when he could hear nothing, he took another breath and then ran for the wall.

He checked his watch once more.

1.17 a.m.

He clambered onto the dumpster, hefted the bag up and shoved it until it was on the roof. He reached up, grabbed with both hands, and hauled himself up after the bag. He took the bag and made his way up the roof garden until he was behind the tree that he had used for shelter when he'd scouted the set-up before. He opened the bag and worked quickly. He removed the UMP9 and one of the box magazines containing an additional thirty rounds of ammunition. He had sixty rounds with the magazine in the weapon and the spare. That ought to be more than enough.

He took the hunting knife and attached the scabbard to his belt.

1.19 a.m.

Milton kept low and scuttled forward to the wall of the main building and the heavy wooden door that led inside. He lay flat on the roof. He took the inspection scope from its pouch and slid the camera beneath the door. He studied the display and saw the landing just inside the door, a metal door to the left and a flight of stairs up to the top floor directly ahead. The top floor was lit, with illumination spilling out of an open door onto the top landing.

He opened the bag and took out the improvised

breaching charge. He peeled away the wax paper, stuffing it back into the bag, and then pressed the sticky board against the metal door over the latch.

1.21 a.m.

It should be happening right about now. He watched the feed from the camera and waited.

Fedorov checked his watch.

1.15 a.m.

There was no queue and he was able to walk straight inside. There was a booth with a Plexiglas screen and a slot at the bottom.

"One, please," he said to the woman behind the screen.

She looked at him with lazy suspicion. "I ain't seen you before. You from Brooklyn?"

"Little Odessa," he said.

"What you doing up here?"

"Business. I want somewhere to get a beer. Is that okay?"

"Twenty," she said, putting a piece of gum in her mouth and starting to chew.

Fedorov took out his wallet, opened it, and pulled out a twenty. He pushed it into the little tray beneath the slot in the glass.

The woman took the bill and put it into a cash drawer. "No touching the girls. You do that, there'll be trouble. You understand?"

"Of course," Fedorov said.

He looked at his watch.

1.17 a.m.

He went into the main room and looked around. The room was small. There were three men at the bar, a topless bartender looking at messages on her phone, and a dozen customers spread out around the central dais and the catwalks that reached away from it. A girl was upside down on the pole, her legs spread as she slowly lowered herself to rest on her shoulders.

Fedorov made his way to the tables at the back of the room. He took out his phone and pressed SEND on a text message that he had already prepared.

The reply came at once: "*OK.*"

He checked his watch again.

1.19 a.m.

He sat down with his back to the wall. It was comfortably dark here, and he was able to take out the homemade grenades and obscure them beneath the lip of the table. He took his lighter, thumbed flame, and touched it to the three fuses. He reached down and rolled the grenades so that they skidded across the floor into the corner of the room, away from him.

Smoke almost immediately started to billow up from the floor, a grey cloud that gushed up toward the ceiling.

The dancer saw it first. "Fire!" she yelled, pointing at the expanding cloud of smoke. "Fire!"

116

Milton watched the feed from the inspection camera. He saw movement. A man emerged at the top of the stairs, calling back into the room as he started to hurry down to the landing and the door. The camera was small, and Milton had it pressed up tight against the frame of the door and a millimetre or two beneath it; it would be difficult to see, especially if attention was being drawn somewhere else. The man reached the landing and paused there. His white Nikes were just inches away from the scope, so close that Milton could see the stitching and the smudges of dirt on the sole. Milton couldn't see what he was doing, but he heard the sound of a heavy lock being opened and the bottom of the door scraping against the floorboards as it was pulled back.

Milton was about to withdraw the camera when he saw a second man come out of the room at the top of the stairs and hurry down to the landing. He heard the man shout—it might have been an instruction to wait—and saw his feet pass by the camera as he went through the open door and started down the stairs to the ground floor.

Now.

Milton removed the camera, stuffing it back into the bag as he moved back. He made his way back to the raised brick planter, which was tall enough to offer him protection from what he planned. He aimed the UMP and fired a single round into the tub of Tannerite.

His aim was true and the tub exploded. Using an impulse charge to breach a door was a simple enough principle that Milton had learned first-hand while he had been learning to jet-ski at the Special Boat Service's facility down at RM Poole: the faster you hit a body of water, the harder that water would feel. The water spread the force of the blast into a channelled area, punching into the door with enough force to blow out the lock. Milton got up, kicked the door open and hurried inside.

Milton knew exactly what to do and what order to do it in. He lit two smoke grenades, rolled the first down the stairs to the ground floor and then tossed the second up the stairs and into the room beyond.

Smoke started to trickle from them both as the fuses burned, and then, as the flame reached the mixture of potassium nitrate and sugar, a thick gush of smoke billowed out of each.

The door was on Milton's left. It was composed of thick metal, hung on three hinges and with a reinforced latch. He pulled it shut and turned the key in the lock. The only way that the two men he had seen could get back to the top floor would be for them to go into the yard and then climb up to the roof and enter through the door Milton had just blown up. It would take time to realise what he had done, and more time to react to it.

Milton did not intend to give them long enough to do that. He raised the UMP and hurried up the stairs.

Smoke billowed out of the open doorway.

He reached the top landing. He stayed low and recce'd the way ahead. It was as the girl had described it to him: the entire top floor had been made into one large room. There were several couches, a safe standing on the floor in one corner, a thick rug on the floor and a sixty-inch flat-screen TV mounted on the opposite wall.

There were two men in the room.

The man nearest to Milton was in his sixties. His skin was the rich colour of chocolate, and his face was framed by white hair and a beard. He wore a pair of glasses with oval lenses and was dressed in a suit.

The second man was younger. He was on the sofa, just arranging his legs beneath him so that he could stand. His skin was brown, lighter than the older man's, and his hair had been bleached blond. He was wearing a purple suit that, while garish, had probably been expensive.

Milton recognised Acosta from the description that the stripper had provided.

Milton aimed the gun into the room.

"On your knees," he said.

The older man took a step toward him. "I'm a police officer."

"On your knees."

Neither man did as he was told.

Milton fired, sending a single round into the floor between the older man's feet, and then swivelled back to cover Acosta, too.

"On your knees now."

The older man did as he was told. Milton glanced across at Acosta.

"And you, Carlos."

"Who are—"

Milton fired again. The round sliced into the upholstery a foot to the right of Acosta.

"All right, man, all right!"

He dropped down to his knees.

"Hands on your head. Lace your fingers."

Milton approached the older man. He turned him around so that he could watch Acosta, told the man to put his hands behind his back and looped a cable tie around both his wrists. He tightened it and then used his foot to push the man flat onto his face.

He turned to Acosta.

"On the floor. Face down."

He did as he was told. Milton pinned him down with a knee in the small of his back, reached for his right hand and yanked it all the way around. He took the cable tie from his pocket, shoved the right wrist and then the left through the loop in the tie, and then closed it until there was no more slack. He frisked him quickly, removing a bag of weed, a wallet, a roll of bills and a key with an Audi fob from his pockets. He dumped everything but the key, putting that into his own pocket.

He grabbed Acosta's shirt and hauled him to his feet.

"You're crazy," Acosta mumbled.

"You won't be the last person to say that. Where's the boy and his father?"

"Upstairs," he said.

"Show me."

Milton let Acosta lead the way to the stairs. They climbed up to the top floor. The girl's description had been accurate: there was a corridor with four doors leading off it, two on each side.

"Which room?" Milton said.

Acosta nodded to the nearest door on the left.

There was a key in the lock; Milton turned it and opened the door.

The room had no furniture. Milton looked around Acosta and saw that Manny and Freddy Blanco were inside. Their wrists had been secured behind their backs with cable ties and then a pair of cuffs attached the ties to a cast-iron radiator. They had been blindfolded, too, but both turned to the door at the sound of it opening.

"It's okay," Milton said. "It's me."

Manny's face showed panic beneath the blindfold. "They took us—"

"It's all over," Milton interrupted. "I'm here to get you out."

He turned to Acosta and kicked him in the back of the knees. The Dominican's legs buckled and he collapsed. "Face down on the floor. If you move, I'll shoot you."

Acosta flattened himself to the boards. Milton unsheathed his hunting knife. He crossed the room to the Blancos and removed their blindfolds. Both father and son were terrified, squinting into the sudden light, dread shining from their eyes. Milton worked quickly, slicing through the plastic ties that bound their wrists.

"Do exactly as I say," Milton said. "Stay with me and don't panic. You're going to be fine."

Manny gaped at him.

"Tell me you understand, Manny."

"I understand. I—"

"Good," Milton cut in firmly. "Now—we're going downstairs and then we're going to leave. Ready?"

Manny nodded.

Milton reached down and helped him to stand. "Let's go."

117

Milton grabbed Acosta by the scruff of his shirt and hauled him back to his feet again. He shoved him out of the door and turned him around to face the stairs. "Down," he ordered.

They gathered in the main first-floor room. The older man hadn't moved.

"Him," Milton said to Manny, gesturing at the old man. "Frisk him for me."

Milton dragged Acosta backwards across the room to the safe.

"What's the combination, Carlos?"

"Fuck y—"

Milton backhanded him across the mouth.

"What's the combination?"

Acosta glared up at him, his face a mask of hatred. "You're a dead man," he said. Milton put the muzzle of the UMP against his head. "6850," Acosta spat.

Milton turned the dial to the right through four turns and then stopped on the six. He turned the dial to the left, passing the eight twice, stopping there on the third time. He turned the dial to the right, passing the five once before stopping on it the next time. Finally, he spun the dial to the left and stopped at the zero.

The lock disengaged and the door opened.

The safe was full of money. Milton did not have the time to guess at how much was there, save that there was a great deal of it. The bills were fastened with rubber bands, and Milton took two thick wads of fifties and pushed them into his pocket.

"What is this?" Acosta said. "You rollin' me? Seriously? Are you crazy?"

"Shut up, Carlos."

Milton reached into his pocket and took out the Beretta. It was still in its plastic bag. He undid the bag, removed the gun and pressed the grip into Acosta's right hand.

Acosta swallowed. "What are you doing?"

"Hold it."

Acosta did as he was told and Milton deposited the weapon in the safe. He shut the door and spun the dial.

Milton crouched down and spoke quietly into Acosta's ear. "Just so you know," Milton said, keeping his voice low enough so that the Blancos wouldn't be able to hear him. "That's the gun I used to kill James Rhodes this morning. The police are at his house now. They're going to find him, and then they're going to find the gun that killed him in your safe with your prints on it. They'll think you did it. You're going to go away for a long time, Carlos. A long, long time."

"Take that off," Acosta said. "I wanna see your face. I wanna see it before—"

Milton silenced him with a second backhanded slap.

"Jesus," Manny exclaimed.

He was crouched over the older man. He had a holstered pistol in one hand and a wallet in the other.

"What is it?" Milton said.

"He's a cop. Look."

The wallet opened to reveal an NYPD detective shield.

"Name?"

Manny looked at a credit card. "Richard Haynes."

Milton remembered the name from a conversation with Polanski. Haynes was Polanski's senior officer.

"You're the leak in Internal Affairs."

The old man was still on his belly. He turned his head so that he could glare up at Milton, but said nothing.

"Can you remember how to handle a weapon?" Milton said to Manny.

"Sure."

"Take his gun and cover Acosta."

Manny took Haynes's pistol out of the holster and held it out in both hands. He nodded that he was comfortable with it.

Milton grabbed Haynes and encouraged him to stand. He marched him up the stairs and tossed him in the room that had been used to imprison the Blancos. He shoved the older man to the wall, pushed him down to his knees and turned him around so that his cuffed wrists were next to the radiator. He took a third cable tie, looped one end around the radiator, fed it through the tie that restrained Haynes, and then yanked it until it was tight.

Haynes slumped against the wall, his head hanging limply. The fight had gone out of him. Perhaps he was wondering how he would be able to explain how he had come to be in the headquarters of one of Brooklyn's most notorious drug dealers. That would be difficult to do, especially when the Blancos could implicate him.

Milton shut the door, locked it and pocketed the key.

He descended the stairs and turned his attention back to Acosta.

"Get up."

He yanked on the tie, wrenching the Dominican back up to his knees. He yanked again and Acosta stood.

"Get behind me," Milton said to Manny and Freddy. "Cover the stairs."

He grabbed Acosta and manhandled him to his feet. "Get moving, shitbird. Time to go."

118

Acosta went first down the stairs. Milton was tight behind him, his left hand on his shoulder with the muzzle of the UMP pressed against the back of the Dominican's head. Freddy came next and his father brought up the rear, covering them with the detective's confiscated gun.

"You know who I am?" Acosta spat back at Milton. "You making a big mistake. I'm telling you, you have no idea the kind of mistake you're making."

Milton ignored him.

They reached the landing.

"I'm gonna fucking kill you," Acosta said.

Milton bunched his fist and punched Acosta in the back of the head. "Shut up, Carlos," he said.

Milton shoved him through the open door onto the roof. He grabbed the bag of gear that he had left there and tossed it over the edge; it landed with a soft thud in the snow below.

"I'll pay you," Acosta said. "How's that? How much do you want?"

Milton pushed Acosta between the shoulder blades, impelling him to the edge of the roof.

The Dominican teetered on the lip, looking down into the yard. "I can't climb down there," he complained.

Milton kicked him in the small of the back. Acosta disappeared over the side, falling through the steep drop and ending up on his back in a shallow drift that cushioned his fall.

Milton hopped down to the dumpster and then down into the snow next to Acosta. Freddy followed, then turned to help his father.

Milton knelt down, grabbed Acosta's jacket, and pulled him to his knees.

The snow was falling heavily. The abandoned vehicles in the yard had already been blanketed with another half an inch. The light from the windows behind him cast out enough illumination for him to be able to see the mess of footprints that led into the yard from the direction of the gate. His own prints had been covered; these prints were new. There was a bunch of footprints that funnelled into the yard between a pickup truck and an old US Postal Service van. The footprints split off into individual tracks that led to the left and the right.

Milton reached with his left hand and grabbed Acosta by the shoulder. He pulled him closer, holding the submachine gun ready.

"Come out," Milton called. "Get out here where I can see you."

Milton saw a man emerge from behind the red truck. He was wearing a plastic Barack Obama mask that covered his face. The mask had large, exaggerated white teeth. The man was toting a shotgun, and it was levelled at Milton.

"Drop the gun!" Obama called out.

Milton snaked his left arm around Acosta's neck and started to move back toward the wall. He put himself and Acosta between the man with the shotgun and the Blancos.

A second man emerged from behind the trailer of the truck. He, too, had a shotgun. He was wearing a plastic mask that bore a passing resemblance to Bill Clinton.

Both men looked as if they knew how to use their weapons.

"Drop the gun."

The third man to come out from behind the truck wore a George Bush mask. He had a pistol in his hand and it, like the two shotguns, was aimed at him.

Milton recognised his voice.

Fedorov.

Milton pulled Acosta tight against his body and aimed the UMP around him at Fedorov. "What are you doing?"

"Drop the gun, John. Please."

"What are you doing?"

"I want him," Fedorov said, gesturing to Acosta.

"Well, you can't have him."

"You are not in a position to argue. Please. I would rather that we could finish this amicably. I do not want to see you get hurt."

"So point those guns somewhere else and let us be on our way."

Milton looked at Clinton and Obama. He guessed that the other two men were Fedorov's brothers.

"You and your friends are free to go," Fedorov said. "Just not with him."

Milton looked from Fedorov to his brothers. He was badly outnumbered and they had him in a crossfire. There was nowhere for him to go: the door in the wall behind him was locked, the fence on either side was too high, and, besides, those shotguns would chew him up the moment he tried to make a move. And more important than that was the fact that he was with the Blancos. He had more to consider than just himself.

Acosta struggled in Milton's grip. "Who the fuck are *you*?" he said to Fedorov.

"Your drugs were responsible for the death of my son."

Acosta squirmed. "What you *talking* about, man?"

"You had a dealer in Little Odessa. A young man. The same age as my son. They became friends. Your dealer gave my boy heroin. A little at first, to tempt him, and then more. He stole from me, Mr. Acosta. The day before he died. My own son stole money from my business to buy the drugs that killed him. Do you know how that made me feel? That I was complicit in his death?"

"I'm sorry about that," Milton said before Acosta could reply. "But he's going to get justice. That's why I'm here."

"Justice? What justice? You will take him to the NYPD?"

"Yes, I—"

"But you said yourself that you could not trust them. You said that they are all corrupt."

"Not all of them," Milton protested.

"A few bad apples?" Fedorov asked scornfully.

"There's one man I trust. A detective. He's been building a case against Acosta for months. He can close it now."

Fedorov shook his head. "And this detective, he is interested in corrupt officers, yes? That is his focus?"

"Not just—"

"Mr. Acosta could choose to cooperate. Perhaps he could give the detective what he really wants. All the corrupt policemen handed to him on a plate. And what would that mean for him? A plea bargain? A little time, then back out to sell his poison again? More children killed so he can make a little more money? Surely you can see how that is not justice. You can see how it is unacceptable."

Milton felt a hand on his back: Manny or Freddy, he couldn't be sure.

"This is not a negotiation," Fedorov said. "Acosta is a dead man. But I do not want to hurt you or your friends. Please. Both of you, drop your guns and step away from him."

Milton was all out of options. "Do what he says, Manny."

Milton dropped the UMP into the snow and released his hold around Acosta's throat. The Dominican dropped down to his knees, the icy crust crunching as he plunged into it.

"This is a mistake," Milton said.

"We can disagree about that. Go. Before I change my mind."

Milton stooped down to collect his bag and trudged through the ankle-deep snow. He put himself between the three men and the Blancos, gesturing that Manny and Freddy should pass on the other side of him. Sergei and the older brother turned to cover him as he went by them. Milton made his way to the Audi and blipped the locks. He told Manny and Freddy to get into the back. He opened the front door, tossed his bag inside, and slid into the seat. The gate to the road had been opened and pushed back. Milton started the engine and edged out into the road.

There was an old panel van parked outside the open gate, the rear doors open and the engine running. Milton ignored it.

He heard the sound of raised voices behind him, but he didn't look back. Milton straightened the wheel, pushed down on the gas, and started away into the blizzard.

119

It was two thirty in the morning. Polanski sat in his office, keeping himself awake with as much strong coffee as he could stomach. He realised that he hadn't had more than a couple of hours' sleep on the office couch since he'd moved the case to Manhattan. His eyes felt red and raw, and he ached in places he had never ached before. It was only the adrenaline and the caffeine that were keeping him upright.

Detective Walker had just called in her report. She had tried to contact Officer Rhodes by phone, but her calls had gone unanswered. She had driven across to Rosedale and had forced the door to his modest house. Rhodes was dead on the couch in his sitting room. He had been shot. Two times and, both, she suggested, from close range: one in his knee and the other in his head. The casings were on the floor. Her search of the premises had revealed the proof of Rhodes's perfidy: a cache that had been cunningly hidden in the space beneath the bath. It contained the fake documents necessary to effect a changed identity in the event that he needed to bug out.

Polanski stared at the screen. The blue dot that indicated the location of John Smith's cellphone had not changed. It was in the same place as it had been since the trace had been activated. Smith was at home and had been for the past three and a half hours. Polanski had listened to Smith's story, but he was no one's fool. What he had said about Acosta and the Blancos was possible, but outlandish. Polanski wasn't prepared to trust him blindly, especially not after Mackintosh had provided a glimpse into his history and, at the same time, shone a light upon a violent streak that he kept well hidden.

He had spoken to Mackintosh before they released Smith and a compromise had been reached. She would accede to his request on the basis that they kept a close eye on him. Polanski had agreed; he might have taken the same steps even without her laying down the requirement. Assistant District Attorney Mantegna had filed an emergency request for a trace to be put on his phone; the request had been granted and the provider had complied within ten minutes of receiving the order.

His phone buzzed on his desk.

He picked it up.

"Smith?"

"Where are you?"

"Manhattan. Where are you?"

"Just leaving my apartment."

He looked at the computer; they should have been able to see whether there had been activity on the phone. "Has Acosta called you?"

"No—Manny Blanco did."

Polanski found it. Smith had just received a call from a landline. The number was unfamiliar.

"Where are they?" he asked.

"They got away," Smith said. "They're on Atlantic Avenue. You need to go pick them up."

Polanski looked at his computer. The location of Smith's phone had moved. It was to the north of the apartment, and, as he stared at the screen, it kept moving.

"*You* need to go," Smith insisted. "Not someone from the precinct."

Polanski heard the sound of an engine turning over. A motorcycle engine. He grabbed his coat and started across the floor. "I'm going now," he said. "Where are they?"

"Outside the Barclays Center. They said they were held in a room above a strip club not far from there. The HoneyPot."

"How did they get out?"

"He didn't say."

Polanski reached the lobby and jammed the button to call an elevator. "I'm on my way."

EPILOGUE

1

M ilton had never been much of a fan of Christmas. His childhood memories were always coloured by the deaths of his parents. There had been eleven holidays before they had been taken from him, and, although he knew that there must have been happy times, he couldn't remember many of the details. And, for those fragments that he could recall, he doubted the veracity of his recollections. It was as if the weight of his subsequent misery rendered the suggestion that he might have enjoyed them preposterous.

Christmas was just another day to him now. He rose early, as usual, packed his belongings into a large bag and put it over his shoulder. He locked the door of the apartment and went down to the street.

The snow had been stubborn. The weather had been frigid for a week, but there had been no fresh falls and, eventually, as Christmas approached, the temperature had started to climb. The covering on the roads and sidewalks had been churned up into dirty slush and the drifts had started to thaw.

Milton put his earbuds into his ears and set off, walking his usual route to the south. There were more people out today than usual: families taking the air before the chaos of opening presents; elderly husbands and wives strolling along the boardwalk, hands clasped tightly together. He passed the tennis and basketball courts of Brighton Playground and the wide space of the parking lots, where patches of asphalt were beginning to show as the snow and ice melted away.

He approached Café Valentin. He saw the familiar figure of Alexei Fedorov sitting on the bench outside the restaurant. He took the earbuds out of his ears and paused his music.

"John," Fedorov said. "Merry Christmas."

Three days had passed since the assault on Carlos Acosta's hideout. The Crimean was not obviously different—although it wasn't as if he had been pretending to be something else during their previous meetings. Milton had seen the hardness that lay beneath his generosity. His brothers had it, too, although they had less motivation to make Milton feel welcome in their company and had done little to soften their rougher edges. Milton had known that there was more to Fedorov's business than his restaurant. There was crime down here, and plenty of it: racketeering and protection and all of the other delinquency and malfeasance that was drawn to closed communities. There would be wolves and sheep, and it was obvious that Fedorov and his brothers were not sheep.

"Thank you for coming," Fedorov said. "I would like to talk to you. I want to make sure there is no bitterness between us."

"What did you do to Acosta?"

"I made sure that he will not spread his poison again."

"Dead?"

"Of course," Fedorov said. "It was justice. A justice that would not have been delivered if I had allowed you to take him to the police."

Milton didn't answer.

"Acosta owed me a debt," Fedorov went on. "He owed me more than he owed you."

Milton was too tired to fight. And it was difficult to disagree with the Crimean: he did have more invested in seeing Acosta brought to justice. Their forms of retribution were not so dissimilar, either. Milton would have preferred to have ended Acosta, just as he had ended Rhodes. He had stayed his hand because Freddy had already seen enough death and because Polanski had deserved the chance to close his case.

"John," Fedorov pressed. "I need to know that there is no trouble between us."

Fedorov stared at him. Milton wondered if there was a threat hidden beneath the surface of that request.

"I don't blame you for what you did," Milton said. "I would have done the same. But I can't pretend it didn't happen."

"I understand," Fedorov said.

Milton shrugged the bag onto his shoulder so that the weight was borne more evenly. He made to leave.

Fedorov placed his hand on Milton's arm. "You got what you wanted?" he continued. "Your friend and his boy are safe?"

"Yes," he said. "They are."

"I am sorry that I misled you. I would have preferred to be honest."

Milton removed Fedorov's hand from his arm.

"Are you leaving?" Fedorov asked, indicating the bag.

"I am."

"If you ever find yourself in need of work, I am always looking for men like you."

Milton shook his head. "Thanks," he said. "But I work best alone."

The Crimean shrugged. "If you change your mind, the offer remains open."

"Goodbye."

Fedorov stepped aside and Milton set off again. He reached for the in-line controls and pressed play, Kasabian's 'Stevie' resuming. He walked on for a hundred yards and then glanced back. Fedorov was gone.

Milton took the Q Train from Coney Island and headed into Manhattan. The car was quiet. Someone had left a copy of yesterday's *Post* on the back of the seat and Milton took it, flipping through the pages as the train rumbled to the north. The story of the corruption in the Seventy-Fifth Precinct had filled the pages of the newspapers ever since it had broken three days earlier. It was being reported as a resurrection of an old problem that the NYPD had hoped had been put to bed. It had everything: an informer stabbed to death in a New York subway station; a crooked police officer and his ex-partner, both missing and presumed dead; a drug dealer who had also gone missing, presumably on the run after a gun found at his property was tied to the murder of a policeman in his Rosedale home; a sergeant in Internal Affairs suspected of being on the payroll of criminals after being found at a property where the dealer had conducted his affairs across East New York. The special prosecutor had been front and centre, leading the daily news conferences that shed more and more light on the corruption that had forced its tentacles deep into the precinct house on Sutter Avenue.

The train rolled into Forty-Ninth Street station. Milton disembarked and made his way to the exit.

2

————

The uniformed officer looked back at Mackintosh. They were standing outside the door to John Smith's apartment. The cop had a battering ram that looked as if it would make very short work of the flimsy wooden panel. There were three other officers between the cop with the ram and Mackintosh. All three of them had their weapons drawn.

Mackintosh was tense with anticipation. The email from the Victoria police department had arrived late yesterday evening. They had apologised for the delay, blaming an administrative snafu, but had requested that the NYPD hold John Smith. Mackintosh had contacted the officer who had sent the memo and had learned that the Texans were very keen to speak to Smith. The FBI agent who had taken him from their custody had not been from the FBI, after all. The agency had reported that there was no woman working for them with the name that she had given or fitting her description. As far as they were concerned, Smith was a wanted felon and the woman was wanted for impersonating a federal agent. She had spoken to Polanski and passed on the news. He had reported that he hadn't spoken to the Englishman since his release.

"Ready?" the officer asked.

Mackintosh nodded. "Do it."

The man drew back the ram and then crashed it into the door, just below the handle. The wood splintered, the lock smashed and the door flew inwards.

"Police!" the first of the three waiting officers yelled as he hurried by the first man and went into the apartment. The others followed, with Mackintosh bringing up the rear.

The apartment was tiny. They cleared the bedroom, living room and bathroom within thirty seconds.

There was no one there.

There was nothing that indicated that anyone lived here. No clothes in the closet. No belongings in the living room. No food in the refrigerator.

"Shit," Mackintosh cursed.

They were too late.

"Shit!"

Smith had gone.

3

There was a crowd of people around the rink at the foot of the Rockefeller Center. The huge tree, decorated with thousands of lights beneath a single star, cast out multicoloured patterns across the ice as skaters swooped around the rink. There was hot chocolate and warm shortbreads, and the atmosphere was festive and friendlier than Milton was used to in the city. People smiled and wished him happy holidays as he politely worked his way through the crowd to the spot next to the statue of Prometheus where they had agreed to meet.

Manny and Freddy were waiting for him there.

"Merry Christmas," Manny said with a wide smile.

"And to you. How are you doing?"

"We're good," Manny said.

"The new place?"

"It's nice. It's bigger than before. I don't know how long they'll let us stay there, but, well... we're good."

They both looked well. Freddy was standing in front of Manny, with both of his father's hands resting on his shoulders. They looked relaxed; more so, Milton realised, than he had ever seen them. That was unsurprising. They had been through an ordeal and only now were they coming out the other side of it.

"Detective Polanski even got us a tree," Freddy said, beaming.

"He did," Manny said. "Brought it over last night." He leaned down and spoke to his son. "You want to go on the ice?"

Freddy said that he did, and Manny took out a ten-dollar bill and gave it to him. There was a short queue of people waiting to get tickets, and the boy went and joined it.

"How's he doing?" Milton asked.

"He's good. Really good. He started the new school this week and says he likes it. And he's really taken to Polanski. They get on well."

Freddy paid, put on his skates and made his way onto the ice.

"Has he skated before?" Milton asked.

"No," Manny said. "But he learns fast."

Freddy jerked a little, his arms windmilling as he fought to maintain his balance, but he quickly became steadier.

"What happened to Acosta?" Manny asked. "I know that's bugging Polanski. Me too. They still don't know where he is. It does make me wonder—"

"You don't need to worry about him," Milton said.

"How can you say that?"

"Because he's not coming back."

"He's dead?"

"You don't need to be concerned about him."

Manny nodded. Milton knew that he trusted him, and he didn't ask for more.

Freddy went by the barrier, his skates scraping against

the ice. He waved and smiled, evidently proud that he could remain upright

"What are you doing later?" Manny said. "Do you want to come and have lunch with us?"

"I'm good," Milton said. "But thanks for asking."

"You have plans?"

"I'm seeing a friend," Milton lied. "But it's good of you for thinking of me." He looked at the time. "Actually, I've got to go. I'm running late."

Manny looked as if he was about to protest, but he did not. Instead, he put out his hand. Milton took it and didn't resist as Manny brought him in closer for an embrace.

"Thank you," Manny said, his voice catching.

Milton gently disentangled himself and saw that Manny's eyes were wet.

Milton started to turn, then remembered. "I have a present for you."

Milton took out the smaller bag that he had brought with him. Manny took it and pulled back on the zipper. The money that Milton had taken from Acosta and Rhodes was inside. Milton had counted it: there was twenty-five thousand dollars there, made up of five hundred fifty-dollar bills.

Manny's expression became wary. "I can't take that."

"You can," Milton said. "Acosta nearly ruined your life. You've had to move. Freddy's had to change schools. You deserve to be compensated for that."

"No." He shook his head. He closed the zipper and held the bag out for Milton to take.

"You'll need it," Milton insisted. "What about college? Does Freddy want to go?"

"Sure."

"So put it somewhere safe until you need it. Spend a

little at a time. Don't be extravagant, and don't try to put it in a bank. If you're careful, you'll be fine."

Manny let his arm, and the bag, fall down to his side. "Thank you."

"And there's this." Milton reached into his pocket and took out an envelope. He gave it to Manny. "It's for both of you."

"What is it?"

"Two tickets for the playoffs."

"I can't accept—"

"A friend of mine has a box," Milton explained. "I told him what happened the last time Freddy went. He wanted to do something. It didn't cost me a cent. You can have them on one condition—"

"No drinking," Manny cut in. "Don't worry. I'm good. I'm not letting him down again."

Manny reached up and wiped his eyes with the back of his hand. He reached into his bag and took out a card of his own. "And for you," he said, his voice breaking a little. "It's just a card. But Freddy went and got it himself."

Milton thanked him and slid the card into his pocket.

"Goodbye, Manny. Good luck."

He made his way into the crowd of onlookers. He glanced out onto the ice and watched, for a moment, as Freddy slid around the rink with growing confidence, seemingly carefree and happy. Milton felt a lump in his throat. He swallowed, his mouth dry, and made his way back to the street.

4

Polanski was waiting for him outside the Applebee's on the corner of 50th and Broadway.

"Merry Christmas," Polanski said.

"You too," Milton replied. "You want to walk with me?"

"Sure."

They set off, joining the scrum of pedestrians waiting to cross Broadway.

"Thanks for the call," Milton said. "I appreciate it."

Polanski nodded to the bag on Milton's shoulder. "Going somewhere?"

"I thought it might be best," Milton said.

"Mackintosh won't stop. She's convinced you killed the guy in the dumpster."

Milton didn't respond.

Polanski glanced over at him. "And I'm convinced you were at the HoneyPot."

"Can you prove that?"

"Probably."

"And?"

Polanski shrugged.

They crossed the road.

"I've been thinking about it," Polanski said. "I don't know if I see the point. It seems like I've got all the answers I need. I got a gun from Acosta's safe with his prints on it. The ballistics evidence says the gun's a match for the one used to kill Rhodes. And I got Freddy's evidence that Carter and Shepard killed González."

"So you've got everything you need."

"Looks that way, doesn't it? And it was all tied up with a pretty little bow. It couldn't have been more convenient."

Milton was relaxed. Why would Polanski want to unravel everything? Discovering the truth—that Milton had killed Rhodes, freed the Blancos, then framed Acosta— would not serve the narrative. Justice had been done, and that was enough. It made more sense to keep the truth of exactly *how* it had been done under wraps.

They walked on in silence.

Polanski spoke first. "You know I don't work Brooklyn any more?"

"I didn't."

"I've been transferred to the special prosecutor's office."

"I'm not surprised. You're good. And you're a straight shooter. You're exactly what the NYPD needs right now."

"The Seven Five and Internal Affairs in Brooklyn are being fumigated. The commissioner's putting together a task force to root out the bad guys. I'm on the team."

"What about your old boss?"

"We found a ton of money in his attic that he can't account for. He was bought and sold like the others. He's looking at jail time."

Milton had wondered whether Polanski might be rewarded with Haynes's old job, but he figured that maybe he had moved beyond that now. After a year or two of seasoning with the special prosecutor, he would be able to go anywhere he wanted.

"Your family?" Milton asked.

"We're good. Moved back home again yesterday. Just in time for Christmas."

They reached the subway entrance.

"This is me," Milton said.

He put out his hand and Polanski took it.

"Look after the Blancos," Milton said.

"I got it. They'll be fine."

"I know."

Milton took his hand away, nodded once, and started down the steps that led to the station. He had a short ride to Penn Station. Amtrak's Palmetto service to Miami was due to leave soon, and he didn't want to miss it.

GET EXCLUSIVE JOHN MILTON MATERIAL

Building a relationship with my readers is the very best thing about writing. I occasionally send newsletters with details on new releases, special offers and other bits of news relating to the John Milton, Beatrix and Isabella Rose and Soho Noir series.

And if you sign up to the mailing list I'll send you this free Milton content:

1. A free copy of the first John Milton novel, The Cleaner.

2. A free copy of 1000 Yards, a dip into Milton's case files that finds him in North Korea with a sniper rifle and bad intentions.

You can get your free books **for free**, by signing up here.

ALSO BY MARK DAWSON

IN THE JOHN MILTON SERIES

One Thousand Yards

In this dip into his case files, John Milton is sent into North Korea. With nothing but a sniper rifle, bad intentions and a very particular target, will Milton be able to take on the secret police of the most dangerous failed state on the planet?

Free Download

The Cleaner

Sharon Warriner is a single mother in the East End of London, fearful that she's lost her young son to a life in the gangs. After John Milton saves her life, he promises to help. But the gang, and the charismatic rapper who leads it, is not about to cooperate with him.

Buy The Cleaner

Saint Death

John Milton has been off the grid for six months. He surfaces in Ciudad Juárez, Mexico, and immediately finds himself drawn into a vicious battle with the narco-gangs that control the borderlands.

Buy Saint Death

The Driver

When a girl he drives to a party goes missing, John Milton is worried. Especially when two dead bodies are discovered and the police start treating him as their prime suspect.

Buy The Driver

Ghosts

John Milton is blackmailed into finding his predecessor as Number One. But she's a ghost, too, and just as dangerous as him. He finds himself in deep trouble, playing the Russians against the British in a desperate attempt to save the life of his oldest friend.

Buy Ghosts

The Sword of God

On the run from his own demons, John Milton treks through the Michigan wilderness into the town of Truth. He's not looking for trouble, but trouble's looking for him. He finds himself up against a small-town cop who has no idea with whom he is dealing, and no idea how dangerous he is.

Buy The Sword of God

Salvation Row

Milton finds himself in New Orleans, returning a favour that saved his life during Katrina. When a lethal adversary from his past takes an interest in his business, there's going to be hell to pay.

Buy Salvation Row

Headhunters

Milton barely escaped from Avi Bachman with his life. But when the Mossad's most dangerous renegade agent breaks out of a maximum security prison, their second fight will be to the finish.

Buy Headhunters

The Ninth Step

Milton's attempted good deed becomes a quest to unveil corruption at the highest levels of government and murder at the dark heart of the criminal underworld. Milton is pulled back into the game, and that's going to have serious consequences for everyone who crosses his path.

Buy The Ninth Step

The Jungle

John Milton is no stranger to the world's seedy underbelly. But when the former British Secret Service agent comes up against a ruthless human trafficking ring, he'll have to fight harder than ever to conquer the evil in his path.

Buy The Jungle

Blackout

A message from Milton's past leads him to Manila and a confrontation with an adversary he thought he would never meet again. Milton finds himself accused of murder and imprisoned inside a brutal Filipino jail - can he escape, uncover the truth and gain vengeance for his friend?

Buy Blackout

IN THE BEATRIX ROSE SERIES

In Cold Blood

Beatrix Rose was the most dangerous assassin in an off-the-books government kill squad until her former boss betrayed her. A decade later, she emerges from the Hong Kong underworld with payback on her mind. They gunned down her husband and kidnapped her daughter, and now the debt needs to be repaid. It's a blood feud she didn't start but she is going to finish.

Buy In Cold Blood

Blood Moon Rising

There were six names on Beatrix's Death List and now there are four. She's going to account for the others, one by one, even if it kills her. She has returned from Somalia with another target in her sights. Bryan Duffy is in Iraq, surrounded by mercenaries, with no easy way to get to him and no easy way to get out. And Beatrix has other issues that need to be addressed. Will Duffy prove to be one kill too far?

Buy Blood Moon Rising

Blood and Roses

Beatrix Rose has worked her way through her Kill List. Four are dead, just two are left. But now her foes know she has them in her sights and the hunter has become the hunted.

Buy Blood and Roses

Hong Kong Stories, Vol. 1

Beatrix Rose flees to Hong Kong after the murder of her husband and the kidnapping of her child. She needs money. The local triads have it. What could possibly go wrong?

Buy Hong Kong Stories

Phoenix

She does Britain's dirty work, but this time she needs help. Beatrix Rose, meet John Milton...

(17,000 word charity novella)

Buy Phoenix

IN THE ISABELLA ROSE SERIES

The Angel

Isabella Rose is recruited by British intelligence after a terrorist attack on Westminster.

<u>Buy The Angel</u>

The Asset

Isabella Rose, the Angel, is used to surprises, but being abducted is an unwelcome novelty. She's relying on Michael Pope, the head of the top-secret Group Fifteen, to get her back.

<u>Buy The Asset</u>

The Agent

Isabella Rose is on the run, hunted by the very people she had been hired to work for. Trained killer Isabella and former handler Michael Pope are forced into hiding in India and, when a mysterious informer passes them clues on the whereabouts of Pope's family, the prey see an opportunity to become the predators.

Buy The Asset

IN THE SOHO NOIR SERIES

Gaslight

When Harry and his brother Frank are blackmailed into paying off a local hood they decide to take care of the problem themselves. But when all of London's underworld is in thrall to the man's boss, was their plan audacious or the most foolish thing that they could possibly have done?

Free Download

The Black Mile

London, 1940: the Luftwaffe blitzes London every night for fifty-seven nights. Houses, shops and entire streets are wiped from the map. The underworld is in flux: the Italian criminals who dominated the West End have been interned and now their rivals are fighting to replace them. Meanwhile, hidden in the shadows, the Black-Out Ripper sharpens his knife and sets to his grisly work.

Get The Black Mile

The Imposter

War hero Edward Fabian finds himself drawn into a criminal family's web of vice and soon he is an accomplice to their scheming. But he's not the man they think he is - he's far more dangerous than they could possibly imagine.

Get The Imposter

ABOUT THE AUTHOR

Mark Dawson is the author of the breakout John Milton, Beatrix Rose and Soho Noir series.

For more information:

www.markjdawson.com

mark@markjdawson.com

Printed in Great Britain
by Amazon